DRAGON HUNTER

MASE EVANS

For my husband, who taught me that love
doesn't always start at first glance. Thank you for being
my favorite person <3

DEOVARIA
RAYFAIT MOUNTAINS
SOBORG
AERICORA
CREVIA
NOZAC
DRURA

Prologue

The castle door burst open, scattering bits of rock and dirt as it scraped against the uneven ground. Caeden's attention snapped from the flower he twisted between his fingers to a disheveled-looking guard. In his haste, the guard tripped over his own feet and stumbled through the doorway. Dread pooled in the pit of Caeden's stomach. His eyes tracked the man's twitchy movements, taking in his wild eyes and heaving chest.

Soldiers arrived at the castle earlier from a station along the border between Aericora, Caeden's home kingdom, and Deovaria. Since they'd arrived, Caeden had a nagging feeling something bad was happening. He hadn't shaken it since the armored coaches pulled into the courtyard.

"Your Highness," the guard said, taking several long strides forward. He stopped in front of the young prince before he knelt to the ground, leveling his gaze with Caeden's before he continued. "The King has requested to see you."

His words were calm, despite the fear etched into every feature of his face.

Caeden's heartbeat sped up. He wiped his sweaty hands on

his pants, the flower slipping from his small fingers before he nodded to the guard.

Generally, his father would send one of Caeden's servants to fetch him. If he'd sent a guard, he hadn't had time to find anyone else. Something wasn't right.

Caeden stood. "What for?" he asked the guard. Confusion muddled with the fear sitting heavy on his chest.

The soldier's eyes flicked to the right, then to the left, as if expecting someone to jump from behind the flowerbeds. Finally, they landed back on the prince's face. "Your father simply asked me to escort you to him, Your Highness."

The answer was a lie, and Caeden's unease intensified as the words washed over him.

The guard stood and gestured for Caeden to follow him back inside. He walked beside the guard as they wound their way through the hallways toward his father's study, his heartbeat matching the pace of their quick footsteps against the white tile floor. The castle halls were dimly lit and gray, adding an eerie feeling to their tense, silent walk.

The door to the king's study was shut, and muffled sobbing from inside drifted out into the hall as they rounded the final corner.

That was his father crying.

His legs felt heavy as panic began to settle over him.

Something was very wrong.

He turned to ask the guard again why his father wanted to speak with him but couldn't force the words out.

He'd never heard his father cry in all his nine years.

"This way, Your Highness," the guard said, urging Caeden forward with a gentle hand against his back. The guard's hand trembled as he reached for the doorknob and guided Caeden inside.

The king's tear-streaked face was all Caeden saw.

His father looked up, his brown eyes meeting Caeden's green ones as grief and fear flashed across his features.

Caeden stayed frozen in place. He didn't want to know what caused the sorrow etched into each inch of his father's face. His father was strong and healthy, the epitome of a king in his prime, but at that moment, he looked so frail. Caeden feared even a light breeze could shatter him into a million pieces.

Caeden took in the room; a woman standing beside his father, one of the many members of his father's court, judging by the way she held herself. He'd met each of them at various events, but their faces all blurred together. He recognized her stance, though. It was the stance of someone who had spent years proving themselves worthy of holding the kingdom's fate in their hands. Every member of the court had it, and this woman gladly accepted the burden placed on her shoulders.

"What—what's going on?" Caeden stammered.

His father wiped frantically at his face with the sleeve of his shirt to hide his tears.

The king opened his mouth to speak, but no words came out. Instead, he shook his head and motioned with a hand for Caeden to come further into the room.

He hesitated, but did as his father asked. His legs shook beneath the weight of his body as he walked across the carpeted floor and around the large desk to stand before the king.

His father wrapped him in a hug before Caeden had time to register what he was doing. Tears pooled in Caeden's eyes and he buried himself in the soft silk of his father's shirt.

"Leave us," the king said, his voice hoarse and muffled through Caeden's wavy hair.

The court members obeyed, their footsteps thumping against the floor, signaling their departure. A moment later, the door closed.

"It's your mother and sister," the king said, his voice strained, as if forcing the words past a lump in his throat. "They—they were attacked at the festival."

Caeden's heart stopped.

The world around him dimmed. The next words from his father's mouth sounded far away through the ringing in his ears.

"They were attacked by dragons, and..." His father trailed off, a loud sob making his words hitch. "They're gone."

Even though the words were dull in Caeden's ears, they still sent a wave of anguish slicing straight through his chest. The words sounded like a lie. They couldn't be gone. They were alive and well. They couldn't be...

"No," Caeden said, shaking his head. He pushed away from his father so forcefully he stumbled back a step.

He was lying. It wasn't possible. The dragons stopped killing people years ago. The war was over.

But as he looked up and met his father's gaze again, the words replayed in his mind.

They're gone. They're gone. They're gone.

And any doubt he'd had shattered.

More tears streaked down his face, hot and wet. They ran from his eyes and dripped onto the collar of his shirt.

"I'm so sorry," Caeden's father whispered, pulling the young prince into another embrace. "They're dead, my son. They were killed by the Deovarians."

The days following the deaths of the queen and princess passed in a blur.

Endless court meetings were held, and Caeden attended all

of them, despite the pushback regarding his age he and his father received from the court.

They were going to war against Deovaria, the kingdom that sent soldiers and dragons into the small town of Silran and killed everyone there. Hundreds, if not thousands, more would die, but the court said it would be worth it when they won the war. Caeden believed every word.

But it wasn't enough for Aericora to win the war against the Deovarians.

The Dragon Lord, Deovaria's king, orchestrated the attack that led to the deaths of his mother and sister. At that age, he kept it to himself like a closely guarded secret, but Caeden promised himself this war would not end until the Dragon Lord met the same fate as his family.

Chapter 1

Caeden massaged his temples as the voices of the members of the King's Court washed over him, overwhelming his senses and causing his head to ache.

He and his father, King Aillin of Aericora, had been in a meeting with the war strategists, military personnel, and other courtiers who made up the king's most trusted group of advisors for over an hour. Deovaria had attacked another town earlier that week and killed over five thousand people. They hadn't overtaken the entire town this time, but over the course of the past eleven years, they'd pushed Aericora's border back nearly fifty miles, and that number was growing.

"We've lost nearly two hundred thousand men and women to this war," Ronan Atkyn, the castle's Head of Security and primary military instructor for the occasional groups of soldiers brought to the castle's training grounds, stated. "Not to mention how thin the castle's guard is spread."

There was an edge to Ronan's voice, and Caeden hoped no one else heard it. For two years, Ronan had been arguing to bring some of the soldiers from the field back to guard the castle, but to no avail.

This was the first time in a while that the man wasn't drunk off his ass, but the only reason Caeden knew as much was because Ronan was his closest friend. He saw Ronan outside of court meetings far more than anyone else. Either because they spent the night drinking together in Ronan's small home, or because Ronan was secretly training him when they could avoid the prying eyes of the court. They'd been training in secret for a while, but their sessions were so sporadic that Caeden's skills hadn't gotten much better, despite the hours they'd spent working to get him field-ready.

Caeden spent most of the war arguing with his father about receiving proper training from the higher-ranking soldiers who had trained groups at the castle. He'd had no luck convincing his father, but when Ronan arrived a couple of years ago, and they'd become friends, he'd offered to train Caeden so long as the king didn't find out. It was the easiest decision Caeden had ever made.

Ronan's words rang in Caeden's ears, and memories of the guard finding him in the garden after his mother and sister were killed flashed through his mind.

Anger and hurt flared through him. Images of his sister, Amelia, her shining blond hair, and his mother, Anna, and her gentle smile resurfaced in his mind.

He'd been nine years old when the war started. Before, Aericora had five neighboring kingdoms: Drura, Crevia, Nozac, Soborg, and Deovaria. Deovaria was the smallest of the six kingdoms, but not long after their current king claimed the throne fifteen years ago, war had broken out.

When Deovaria's king—a man referred to only as the Dragon Lord—took over, he'd brought with him the ability to control the dragons from the Rayfait Mountains that lay primarily behind Soborg. No one knew for sure, but most assumed the Dragon Lord had gained the ability to control the powerful creatures during his sudden disappearance into the mountains nearly ten years before he returned to assume the throne.

Most believed he'd acquired some sort of rare magic during his time away, but the source of the magic remained a mystery.

Not a year after the Dragon Lord took the title of King of Deovaria, he'd declared war on Soborg. With the dragons to aid in their attack, and no form of defense yet uncovered, Deovaria overtook Soborg and claimed their land after a few short months.

The other kingdoms were prepared for attacks. They'd assumed Deovaria claimed Soborg with the intention of expanding their land into the mountains and adding more dragons to their arsenal, but Deovaria went silent after that for almost three years.

When the other kingdoms let their guard down, Deovaria attacked Aericora. They'd attacked the small town of Silran along the border between their two kingdoms. A large festival was held there every year, and multiple members of the court, including Caeden's mother and older sister, had attended. They were all slaughtered at the hands of the Dragon Lord and his armies.

Aericora had been at war with Deovaria ever since.

So far, Aericora had held their own against their attackers, but only because a soldier had managed to accidentally discover that the scent of lavender somehow inhibited a dragon's ability to call on its magical capabilities after his wife had brought a bouquet of the flowers with her during a visit to the front lines. They were attacked while she was still there, and the soldiers discovered that their abilities were rendered useless whenever a dragon went near the tent she was hiding in.

It was a small win for Aericora, but it wasn't enough to prevent the Dragon Lord from taking over their land.

When the war started, Caeden wanted nothing more than to join the military. He'd felt it was the only way to help his kingdom win, but that changed as the years passed. His end goal was still to fight alongside his people, but for the time being, he'd resigned himself to attending court meetings and doing all he could within the confines of the castle's walls.

He'd asked his father a handful of times about receiving proper training, but each time he was met with a stern no from his father. He wasn't angry with his father for refusing to send his only heir to the battlefield, but it wouldn't prevent Caeden from learning all he could from Ronan in the meantime. Even if it took another ten years, he would be alongside the soldiers of his kingdom when they finally won this war.

"Have we considered reaching out to our neighbors again, Aillin?" a slim, older woman named Muire Breac, who had been on the king's council for as long as Caeden could remember, asked his father. She'd been the one to bring the knowledge of the queen and princess's murder to his father all those years ago.

Hearing his father's name slip through her lips was nothing new, but it always took him by surprise, and he had to keep the surprise from showing in his expression.

"They'll want money," a man who Caeden only recognized from their brief meeting a few weeks ago when he was instated into the King's Court, pointed out. He had striking green eyes that were eerily similar to a snake, and it was the only feature Caeden recalled from their brief conversation.

"We have it," Muire replied. "Even with the war, we have more than enough funds to buy their soldiers."

She'd said the same thing five years ago. She hadn't been right then, and she likely wasn't now.

"They refused to send aid last time, even with the offer of payment," a large man with broad shoulders and a beard down to his stomach named Fionn, countered.

"That was years ago," Muire argued. "If we lose this war, who knows which kingdom Deovaria will go after next? Perhaps they've realized this since we last requested aid."

"They've had plenty of time to do so," Caeden agreed, though he wasn't sure whether he wanted his kingdom to use its resources for something that had failed them once before.

The most it would cost was travel expenses for a few messengers. But finding a messenger would be difficult; few were willing to transport messages after so many messengers had died.

"We don't have many other options if we intend to get our hands on more soldiers," Caeden's father stated. He sounded as resigned to the idea as everyone else. The king turned to a young boy with an eager, yet equally anxious, expression. He held a pad of paper in his hand and was scribbling meeting notes until the king turned his gaze on him. With the king's eyes on him, he stood paralyzed. "See that letters are prepared to send to Crevia, Drura, and Nozac asking for soldiers. Tell them we can offer gold and will discuss other forms of payment if necessary. Have them on my desk to be signed by this evening."

The boy nodded too quickly and made a note on the pad of paper he held.

The meeting ended soon after, and the king dismissed everyone in the room with a weak wave of his hand.

Chairs scraped against the floor as the advisors stood and took their leave, but Caeden remained behind.

Ronan was the last court member to leave. His steps were slow since he leaned heavily on his cane; he couldn't place too much weight on his injured leg after it was shot clean through with an arrow during a mission a few years prior. He gave Caeden a backward glance over his shoulder, a question in his hazel eyes, but said nothing before he left.

Caeden stayed quiet until the door was firmly shut behind his friend.

His father met his gaze from across the table and raised an eyebrow. It wasn't unusual for Caeden to stay late after a meeting, but it was usually because Caeden had questions if he did.

The questions he had today had nothing to do with the meeting. It had been a while since he'd last prodded his father with the prospect of receiving training, and he'd spent the past couple of hours working up the nerve to do so.

"I want to be out there with them," Caeden stated, knowing exactly how childish the words would sound, even before they passed through his lips. It couldn't hurt to bring it up again, even if he already expected his father's response.

The king sighed and sat back further in his chair. "You need to be here. You know that, Caeden," his father said. Disappointment clung to his voice, and Caeden did his best to ignore the sting he felt from it.

Caeden reminded himself again that there were reasons he needed to remain in the castle. Even if he wished he could disregard his position as the heir to the throne and run off to kill those responsible for the deaths of his loved ones, he couldn't do that. One day, he would fight alongside his people, but it wouldn't come at the expense of his responsibilities. It was his job to learn his future role as king.

"I know," Caeden sighed.

The king's face softened. "I know this is about your mother and sister." His voice was gentle, reminding Caeden of the tone his mother used to use with him.

"It's more than that," Caeden told him. "It's not just about Mom and Amelia. Our people's mothers and sisters, and their fathers and brothers, are dying, too." He gestured in the general direction of the nearest town to the castle, Puroux. "I know I'm needed here, but I want to fight with our soldiers to protect those they love from experiencing what we did."

The king sighed again. "I know you want to help them," he said. "But I can't see that you receive training when it's so likely you would die on the battlefield. You're my only heir. Our kingdom would fall apart if you were killed. We have plenty of soldiers fighting for us. It's not worth the risk."

"They're dying faster than they can be replaced," Caeden reminded him. His words came out weak. "What use is an heir without a kingdom to rule?" The thought had circled through his mind repeatedly for months. He hadn't intended to say the words aloud. They slipped out before he could stop them.

The king clenched his jaw, and Caeden watched multiple emotions play across his father's face as he mulled over Caeden's words. When he spoke, he sounded as defeated as Caeden felt. "We'll wait to hear from our neighbors," he said. "If we only receive a no, I will consider discussing you being trained with the advisors. However, even if you receive full training, you will not be sent to the field as a soldier. It is too dangerous, and there are plenty of safer options where you could still be useful."

Caeden nodded his understanding.

It was a far better answer than he'd been expecting.

It was long past dark when Caeden snuck out of his room. The castle's halls were dark, lit only by candles placed every twenty or thirty feet along the walls, casting ghostly shadows along the gray brick and white tile floors. The lack of light made it impossible to piece together the images portrayed in the paintings and tapestries hanging on the walls. He knew this route better than the back of his hand, which extended to the images his mom had hung throughout the halls.

Caeden kept his footsteps light as he meandered through the hallways toward the back of the castle. Two separate doors led outside at the very back of the castle: one leading out to the unused training field and one leading into the extensive garden. They were so close that one could easily mistake which led to the garden and which led to the training field if not for the way the path to the garden was so lavishly decorated since it was often taken by nobles when they held outdoor parties, unlike the other hall.

Caeden veered down the opposite path when the hall split. The door he needed was small and wooden and rested on severely rusted hinges that produced a similar sound to the one that led into the armory. He was far enough away from the highly occupied areas of the castle that no one would hear him leaving unless they'd gotten themselves lost in the darkness. That didn't ease his nerves as much as he wished.

The cool breeze from outside hit him hard as he pulled the door open and stepped into the night. A shiver ran through him as the cold swept over his body.

Given the late hour, it was too dark to see, but he could picture the training field to his left. During the day, fifteen archery targets and twenty patches of dirt where the castle staff prevented the grass from growing sat in the distance. Aside from Caeden's occasional secret training sessions with Ronan, they hadn't been used in nearly two years.

On the other end of the field, to Caeden's right, was a small wooden shack with orange candlelight spilling out from its ajar windows. The shack sat alone near the edge of the forest skirting the castle, which was exactly the kind of privacy Ronan enjoyed. His shack was close enough to the castle for Ronan to perform his duties as the castle's Head of Security. Still, it was secluded enough that he rarely drew the attention of the court or Caeden's father without intending to.

Caeden approached the shack and gently rapped his knuckles against the door.

The quiet thump of bare feet padding against the wooden floors inside reached his ears before the door creaked open.

"Whatcha needin', princy?" a very drunk Ronan asked as he pushed the door open wide enough for Caeden to enter. Ronan leaned heavily against his cane and his cheeks were flushed pink.

Inside was a small sitting room with a couch, a coffee table, and a nearly empty bookshelf. The kitchen was to the right of the sitting room, and a hallway ran between the two, leading to Ronan's bedroom at the back of the shack.

Caeden shrugged. "What do you have to drink?"

Ronan's grin was a hair too wide, and his cheeks deepened in color. Moon and candlelight gleamed off his sweat-soaked skin, despite the cool night air, making his curly honey-blond hair stick to his forehead.

"It's a whiskey night," Ronan responded as he shut the door. Mischief sparkled in his eyes, and the corners of his mouth quirked upward in a grin before he hobbled across the shack toward the kitchen. He hardly kept any food stocked in the kitchen, but bottles of every kind of alcohol imaginable lined the counters, and more hid in the cabinets.

After Ronan was injured, he was offered the job as the castle's Head of Security, since the man who had held the position previously was trying to retire. Ronan was an amazing soldier a few short years ago, and he was younger than most other soldiers with his skill level. When Caeden's father heard of Ronan's injury, which had made him unqualified for field work, he sent the job offer almost immediately. Not one advisor argued against Ronan assuming the position; despite him being in his early twenties, he had more skill than most of those they'd been considering hiring.

The shack Ronan got was arguably too little space, but he'd said he only needed enough space to store his drinks and, occasionally, invite an attractive woman into his bed, though occasionally tended to be an extreme under-exaggeration.

Caeden met Ronan only a few weeks after he'd first arrived at the castle. He'd attended his arrival and official welcome into the King's Court but hadn't spoken to him much until after Ronan had caught him attempting to train on his own late one night.

Before they'd started training together, Caeden had been trying to teach himself how to wield weapons. When the previous Head of Security was in charge, the armory was typically unlocked, but Ronan remedied that immediately.

At first, Caeden thought the hinges had finally rusted so much that the door would forever remain shut, but before he'd been able to give it a second, more forceful try, Ronan's laugh startled him and pulled his attention away from the door.

"Thought I heard someone sneakin' 'round out here," Ronan had teased, the same smirk Caeden had grown accustomed to on his face. "Didn't think it'd be you."

Caeden confessed that he'd been trying to teach himself how to use the weapons in the armory. They'd talked and drank for hours that night, and in time, Caeden gained a best friend and a teacher.

Ronan grabbed a bottle of amber liquid off the countertop

and unscrewed the cap before pressing the bottle to his lips and downing multiple mouthfuls of whiskey. He pulled it away and wiped his mouth with the back of his hand before offering the bottle to Caeden.

Caeden accepted the bottle but went to the couch to sit before he drank, mostly hoping Ronan would join him before he got too drunk to walk. The liquid burned when he swallowed, and tears welled in the corners of his eyes. A shudder ran through him, but he got down a few mouthfuls before he pulled it away.

"Easy, princy," Ronan said, laughing lightly. "It ain't goin' nowhere."

A second shudder ran through Caeden's body at the idea of taking another drink from the bottle. Instead, he set it down on the glass coffee table in front of the couch.

Caeden didn't drink often—at least, not compared to his friend—but after spending the day working himself up to ask his father again about training, the prospect of his thoughts being dulled sounded far more pleasant than usual.

"How'd the conversation with the old man go?" Ronan asked. He was distracted as he eyed the bottle of whiskey, contemplating whether to drink more. The distracted look lasted barely a second before his hands wrapped greedily around the stout neck of the bottle and he pressed it back to his mouth.

A smile tugged at Caeden's lips at the way his friend spoke of his father. Very few dared to refer to the king in the relaxed manner Ronan did. It had taken him a while to grow used to it when he and Ronan first became friends, but now he liked the normalcy of it.

Caeden shrugged in response, the smile not leaving his face. He told Ronan the details of his earlier conversation with his father.

It may not be his place to fight in the war, but it didn't feel right that his people were losing their lives when he sat safely inside the lavish halls of the castle. It didn't feel right that he wasn't doing more to help slaughter those responsible for the deaths of his mother and sister – and the thousands of others who were killed.

Ronan raised an eyebrow at him when he finished speaking. "Wow," he breathed. He let out a low whistle. "Didn't expect it to go that well. He 'bout ripped your head off last time."

"It wasn't a yes," Caeden pointed out, though he knew how ridiculous it sounded.

"Slow yourself, princy," Ronan told him, amusement pulling at the corners of his still damp lips. "He already lost two of ya. Chances are he'd do 'bout anythin' to avoid losin' the only one he's got left. Not to mention the whole, ya know, prince thing." He waved a hand in Caeden's direction to emphasize his point, an amused smile clinging to his face.

"I know. I shouldn't want to do this as much as I do, I just…" Caeden trailed off, but Ronan nodded, ensuring Caeden he understood his words.

He had no good reason for wanting to fight, though that hadn't stopped him from wanting to over the years. He wanted revenge for his mother and sister's deaths, and he would get it. He just needed to do so without sacrificing his other responsibilities.

Ronan held out the bottle. "More whiskey to drown your sorrows?"

Caeden smiled and took the bottle from his friend before taking another long swig. The edges of his thoughts were hazier, but it wasn't enough to dull the stress surrounding the war and his place in it.

He was angry, and pushing the anger aside wasn't always easy.

His kingdom was losing a war to a power-hungry man who had acquired ancient magic that could control dragons. His people had done nothing to instigate the Dragon Lord's wrath. His *family* hadn't. And yet, they were still being slaughtered. They were losing a war that never should have started.

Ronan leaned back into the corner of the couch and rested one arm along the back of the couch and the other on the armrest. "Listen, princy," he said, his words slurring together around the edges in a way that made Caeden want to laugh. His head lolled on his shoulders, and his smile was wide with an air of mischief that Caeden had grown fond of. "All matters of your heritage and whatnot aside, ya got a good life. The war is…" He paused, and something flickered across his face that Caeden couldn't quite place before it disappeared. Ronan cleared his throat and continued. "Brutal. Hundreds of soldiers die each week. They're stabbed, burned, frozen, poisoned, shot, and otherwise beaten to death. Ya sure that's what ya wanna be gettin' yourself into?"

He'd been asked that question before. His father had posed a similar one the first time Caeden had asked to receive military training.

The truth was, he didn't know. He didn't know how he would handle that much death. But he hadn't given himself time to think over that detail. It felt wrong to stay hidden in the castle while a war raged outside. He needed to do something more. He needed to stand alongside the soldiers who weren't given the same choice he was.

So, he gave his friend the same answer he'd given his father, despite not knowing whether it was the entire truth. "I'm sure."

Ronan sighed. "If you die, I ain't attendin' your funeral," he told him as seriously as he could manage. The grin on his face gave away the joke immediately.

Caeden laughed. "It's a good thing I'm not planning on dying anytime soon."

Chapter 2

Caeden waited impatiently as the days passed with no word from his father or the court regarding whether they'd received a response from any of their three neighboring kingdoms. It had been two weeks, plenty of time for their neighbors to respond, but he hadn't received a summons from the court.

Part of him wondered if the court had met without him present, but he was the heir, and that seemed unlikely.

No matter what the responses they received said, his chances of getting proper training were unbearably low. Still, he hoped that even if their neighbors all declined, his father would be true to his word and speak with the other court members.

Caeden stared at the ceiling above as the chirping of cicadas outside echoed around his room through the open window beside the head of his bed. Worries circled through his mind as he lay there, contemplating what could have caused the delay. Their neighbors might not be responding, but that was hardly a wise political decision. It was also possible that the messengers were killed by Deovarian soldiers, but Deovaria seemed to stop killing messengers a while ago.

He sighed and threw his legs over the edge of his bed.

Wasting his energy on this would get him nowhere. He could be out training with Ronan rather than lying here. He could read up on the dragons like he'd been trying to convince himself to continue with for months.

It was already late, and the sun would rise in a few hours. There wasn't any point in trying to sleep, anyway. Ronan would be long past asleep, or busy entertaining another woman who worked in the castle. He had no good excuse for avoiding the library, other than his head being too cloudy from his lack of sleep. He likely wouldn't retain any information if he went there.

Instead, he climbed out of bed and changed into an old pair of pants and a loose-fitting cotton shirt he kept hidden for specific occasions. After he dressed, he slipped out into the hallway. His feet were bare, and the cold from the tile bit into his skin as he walked through the deserted corridors. He hissed between his teeth, but putting on shoes would have made too much noise, and he didn't want to wake his father if he could avoid it.

He snuck down the hallway, past the double doors leading into his father's bedchambers, and stopped in front of an equally exquisite pair. The bright yellow doors hung on gold hinges and intricate flowers that matched the hinges were painted across the front.

Caeden pushed the doors open and crept inside, careful to shut them silently behind himself. The harsh scent of fresh paint from his most recent trip here hit him like a brick wall as he stepped into the room.

His hands shook at his sides as he turned to face the inside of Amelia's old bedroom.

His sister's room was barren inside except for her old canopy bed, a desk sitting against the wall by the large, floor-to-ceiling window overlooking the training field outside, and a few boxes of things that had been packed up for her when the painting project had begun nearly eleven years ago.

After Amelia and their mother died, Caeden's father demanded that all his wife's belongings be cleared out of their shared room. The king claimed seeing her things was too painful for him, which Caeden understood, even if he hadn't shared the sentiment. But when his father tried to have Amelia's room cleared out, Caeden stood his ground and convinced him to let it stay the way she left it. Or as close to how she'd left it as possible. At first, his father hadn't wanted to, but he'd given in.

When Amelia was born, the room was a pale pink, which Caeden's big sister spent most of her later years complaining about. It wasn't until shortly before she and their mother left for the festival that their parents agreed to have the color redone. The painters arrived a day after they'd left, intending to paint the walls to match the shade of yellow covering her doors.

The painters only finished one wall before word of the deaths of the queen and princess had reached the castle. The king paid the painters in full but requested they abandon the project since that, too, was too much for him to bear after losing them.

The leftover paints and brushes sat in a corner, along with a large ladder, which laid flat on the ground next to Amelia's boxed-up things.

Originally, Caeden only started coming to his sister's room to watch the soldiers train out in the training field when he'd been younger. A few years ago, he'd slowly finished painting the walls when those groups had become fewer and far between. He'd finished all but one of them, since he had little time to dedicate to the project. He hoped this would be the year he'd finish it for his sister. It would be his secret gift to her on the anniversary of her death, if he could have it done in time.

Memories of his sister flashed through his mind as he painted the walls.

A few days before they'd left for the festival, she'd dragged him through the halls to her room before announcing that their father had hired painters to redo the color. The smile that lit up her face had made one of equal size spread across his lips despite the irritation he'd felt from being pulled around by his older sister.

Caeden spent the rest of the night in his sister's room. He only stopped when the sun rose from behind the horizon outside.

He poured the leftover paint back into the can before he resealed it and rinsed the remaining paint from the brush. He left the damp brush resting on the closed can before exiting the room. His head was foggy when he returned to his room, and he wasn't sure how much of it was due to his lack of sleep or the paint fumes he'd subjected himself to.

When he returned, Teafa, the head maid and the woman who used to supervise Caeden and his sister when they were children, was waiting for him.

Someone often came to assist him in the mornings, but it had been a long time since that person was Teafa. She had far better things to do than assist the crown prince in picking out his clothing, which likely meant she'd brought news from the court.

Teafa had her arms crossed tightly over her chest when he spotted her, and she had a look on her face that he and his sister were afraid of years ago. She used to scare him with only a glance, but he'd grown since then.

She eyed the paint stains on his hands before her eyes traveled to his face.

It didn't matter whether anyone knew he was painting his sister's room, but Teafa's obvious displeasure over the fact irritated him. She and his parents had both instilled the importance of his role in him since he was young, and even though she was no longer responsible for him, she still took him doing anything she disapproved of as a personal offense.

"Your father's requested your presence in a meeting this morning," she said, bypassing any formal greeting. She was like family and hadn't bothered with formalities since before Caeden had been born.

Caeden's heart skipped a beat at her words. A combination of excitement and nervousness mingled in his chest.

This meeting had to be about their neighbors' responses. Teafa wouldn't have come to find him for a normal meeting.

"When are they starting?" he asked as he walked past her and to the clothes she'd laid on the edge of the bed for him.

Teafa let out a puff of air between her lips. "As soon as you finish moonlighting as a painter and start taking your princely duties seriously," she told him with a more irritated huff.

She'd never been one to keep her opinions to herself, and it never failed to get under Caeden's skin when her disapproval was directed at him.

"I take them seriously," he argued as he pulled off his paint-covered shirt.

Teafa rolled her eyes. "Attempting to get yourself shipped off to war is not your responsibility."

Caeden opened his mouth to retort, to argue that his desire to fight wasn't keeping him from upholding any of his responsibilities, but she held up a hand to silence him before he could speak.

"Word gets around. Don't pretend you haven't been dying to leave all of this behind and be some crazy war hero." Her eyes shifted to the shirt on the edge of the bed and her expression softened. "I know you miss them, Your Highness."

Caeden ignored the way her comment made his heart ache. "It's not about them," he lied, trying to avoid sounding defensive.

She would see through the lie, but he didn't want to discuss it. He didn't enjoy talking about the endless pit of pain and rage that grew deeper and darker every day.

Teafa sighed and he could hear her steps retreat toward the door. "It's always about them," she whispered as she slipped through the door and shut it behind herself.

He wasn't sure if she'd intended for him to hear her words, but they lodged themselves straight into his heart, regardless.

Caeden shook his head, clearing her words from his mind, and finished getting dressed. He buttoned up the front of his shirt and slipped the belt around his waist through the loops of his pants before he left the room.

The halls were still quiet around him when he exited his room. The castle's staff were busy preparing breakfast and ensuring everything was in order for the day ahead. The candles in the hall nearest his room were all lit in the time it took him to get changed, but the corridors leading in the training field's direction and toward the Grand Hall remained dark.

The door to his father's meeting room was propped open when he arrived, and the voices from inside spilled into the hallway. Their chatter didn't quiet in the time it took him to enter the room; they'd likely started long before he arrived.

"Ah, Prince Caeden," a man's voice said as Caeden entered the room.

He turned to the man with the green eyes who had attended their last meeting. He still hadn't learned the man's name, but today he was dressed in full military attire with a sash draped over his shoulder displaying fifteen different metals he'd been awarded. It was strange that Caeden couldn't recall the man's name, considering the number of times he must have been present in the castle before he became a member of the court to receive those metals.

He pushed the strange feeling away when he realized he was in his mid-forties, and that he'd likely received those metals before the war with Deovaria began.

The king sat at the head of the table with his hands clasped in front of him, his eyes roving over a large paper map set in the table's center. He had a distant look in his eyes, as if something troubled him. His attention darted to Caeden when the green-eyed man spoke, and whatever was on his mind seemed to disappear.

Caeden walked in and took a seat at his father's right side. Whatever discussion they'd been in the middle of ceased.

The king cleared his throat, and everyone's attention turned to him. "As you're all well aware, Aericora's soldiers are falling faster than they can be replaced," he started, his voice strong throughout the room. He turned his attention to Caeden before continuing. "It seems we've reached an agreement with our neighbors to get us the soldiers we need. We've been in contact with the kings and queens of Drura, Crevia, and Nozac for the past few days. All of them asked for more than just a payment in exchange for soldiers. Drura asked for a more permanent arrangement that would allow them to have a hand in our political affairs and grant them a yearly pension."

"They're afraid of us," Muire continued. "We have the largest kingdom, and if we win against Deovaria, we could learn their secrets and gain the power to control their dragons. They want to have a hold on us that would keep them safe. All three kingdoms do. And they know we are desperate for soldiers."

Caeden's father nodded in agreement.

Fionn spoke next. "The court met a few days back to discuss

how to proceed. Under normal circumstances, we would never consider allowing another kingdom into our court. However, as Muire stated, we are growing more desperate as the situation grows more dire by the week."

Caeden's eyes shifted between the advisors in the room and his father. What were they getting at?

"As much as I would love not to have to worry about such things, we must ensure none of them will overthrow us in the future, if that is their endgame," the king said. "And we have agreed that it would be best if only one kingdom is given that kind of power in our court." He turned a pointed look to Caeden. "Drura, Crevia, and Nozac have agreed to send us their soldiers should we agree that our prince will wed one of their daughters."

Caeden's heart stopped, and his jaw fell slack.

His father couldn't be serious.

Marriage?

Caeden opened his mouth to protest, but the king continued before Caeden had enough time to put together a reasonable response. "Only the kingdom from which you choose your future bride will send us aid. In exchange, she will attend our court meetings and be free to express her concerns about future decisions as everyone else here is. She can also send a pension to her kingdom yearly, but the amount will be limited. The financial aid will stop at the end of her life. Since she would be your wife, her loyalty will lie with Aericora, and she will be watched closely as part of the Royal family to ensure she is not sending confidential information back to her kingdom."

Caeden's head spun as he listened to his father speak.

It was a suitable arrangement. She would be watched closely by the castle's guards for her safety, and Caeden would have to spend his time with her as well. They'd certainly thought it through.

The arrangement of the funds wouldn't be permanent, since they would end when she died, but it was beyond fair enough for the other three kingdoms to agree. She wouldn't easily be able to report back to her kingdom since, as his father had said, her loyalty would need to lie with Aericora since she would be their queen. And any suspicious conversations would be easy to catch.

It seemed as flawless as they could manage.

"In exchange for your cooperation in this endeavor," Caeden's father continued, "we've arranged for Eryn Gedding to be brought to the castle to ensure you receive the same level of training as the soldiers who are currently fighting on the battlefield."

Caeden's mind raced with the information.

Marriage. In exchange for training?

He could be trained.

He could learn to fight and help his people kill those responsible for the war and the deaths of his loved ones.

And by Eryn Gedding.

He'd heard that name countless times. She was a young soldier who had climbed the ranks faster than any other soldier in their history. She was only twenty, but was already a First Rank Dragon Hunter, a title that usually took soldiers ten to twenty years to achieve.

The marriage aspect was far less appealing. An arranged marriage hadn't occurred in his kingdom for hundreds of years. He'd never imagined the possibility of marrying a woman he didn't love.

But there would be no point in marrying a woman he loved if they all died in a useless war. And it wasn't as if he couldn't grow to love whoever he married.

Ronan caught Caeden's eye from across the table, and he raised a curious eyebrow at him, questioning how he planned to respond to the offer.

Caeden refocused his attention on the table of advisors in front of him.

"I'll do it," he said before giving himself enough time to think over his decision.

He'd been after this for years. He would not let the cost stop him from getting the training he needed, even if it were marriage.

The king nodded, and Caeden noticed a flicker of sadness cross over his features for a split second before it disappeared. "Very well. We'll send word to our neighbors and have the princesses here within the next few weeks. And we will send for Miss Gedding. We'll arrange for you to have time with the princesses before deciding which to marry, but we are very limited, given our current outlook on the war."

Caeden heard the words, but they didn't register in his mind. He was going to be trained. The words circled through his head repeatedly. It had always felt out of his reach, but it wasn't anymore.

Muire cleared her throat from the other end of the table. "If I may, I'd like to discuss with our prince which of the women would be the most suitable choice, given our current needs."

The king waved a hand in her direction, signaling her to continue as Caeden pulled himself from his thoughts and focused on the advisor.

"To start, Crevia has the largest army. They are also asking for a low dowry in exchange for their daughter. However, Crevia is in the most debt. Once the marriage is official, they will require most, if not all, of the limited yearly penchant, whereas Drura and Nozac are less likely to require any.

"Nozac is asking for the highest dowry, while also having the smallest military. They are a fine option, but Crevia or Drura would be far better.

"Drura is military based. They have the smallest population, but a fairly large army, and they will be highly trained soldiers. They are asking for the lowest dowry and have only half the debt that Crevia has. In my opinion, Your Highness, I believe your best choice for a wife and for the future of our kingdom, would be to marry the princess of Drura."

"The yearly funds will be limited to an amount we can handle," Fionn reminded them. "And, in that case, I disagree. I believe Crevia would be a far better option. They are asking for a midrange dowry. However, they have far more soldiers than Drura does. I understand that Drura's soldiers are better trained, but Drura's population is still less than a third of Crevia's."

"We have a longer history with Drura," Muire argued. "We've been allies before, on multiple accounts. It may benefit us in other ways to keep our allies as happy as possible. If we anger them with our decision, we could end up with another kingdom attempting to war with us."

Caeden swallowed hard as he listened to the two advisors argue. They both made valid and important points that he would take into consideration. Having all the information would serve him well, but their argument made his stomach twist into knots. The chances of him falling for any of these women were incredibly slim, but on the off chance he did, it would spur arguments between the court members.

Caeden's mind raced, drowning them out. From what he'd gathered so far, his time with the princesses and his training with Eryn Gedding would happen simultaneously. Outside of court, his responsibilities only consisted of his father's few requests, but combining them with choosing a wife and his training would pose a challenge.

The two advisors argued back and forth before the king silenced them with a hand in the air. "That's enough," he said, his voice stern.

Caeden cleared his throat, catching the attention of the others in the room. "I have an amendment that needs to be made before we move forward with this agreement," he stated, keeping his voice as commanding as he could, even as a pang of worry seeped into his chest at what they might say in response to his terms.

Curiosity and worry etched themselves into the features of his father's and a few of the others' faces.

Caeden forged ahead before giving any of them time to speak.

"While these women are here, and while I am training with Miss Gedding, I would like to be exempt from all court meetings. I ask to be sent meeting notes, and I will review them when I can spare the time. However, attending in person wouldn't allow me enough time to make a proper decision for a wife, or to retain the training from Miss Gedding. I will consider your suggestions, and apply them when making my decision for a wife, but I'd very much appreciate having adequate time in my days to prioritize these new responsibilities."

Murmurs rose in the room, but with so many people in such a small space, he couldn't discern what any of them were saying.

Only Ronan remained silent, a half grin on his face that only Caeden was meant to see.

"You'll continue to attend meetings after your engagement ceremony, then?" the man with the snakelike eyes asked. He sounded suspicious, as if he was trying to determine whether Caeden's true intentions were to get out of court meetings permanently.

"Yes." Caeden nodded, ignoring the man's strangeness.

Muire cleared her throat. "I think it is unwise to make such a large decision on your own, Your Highness."

"I wouldn't be deciding alone," he told her, with far more confidence than he felt. "I would appreciate your suggestions and advice, and I would be happy to discuss more once the princesses arrive, so long as I have the time. I simply want to ensure I have enough time to tend to my responsibilities while these women are here."

"He'll also be the one married to whoever he chooses," Ronan offered, the grin he'd had before replaced with a far more serious look than Caeden had seen from him in quite a while.

Fionn grunted in agreement, though he didn't look pleased with the idea, either.

"He is capable of making this choice without coming to us with every minuscule thing that will arise," the king stated.

All eyes turned to the king, and Caeden's nearly bulged out of his head.

An amused snort came from Ronan beside him, and Caeden kicked him in the calf beneath the table.

He'd never heard his father address the court in such a manner before, and he wondered if the reason was related to the flicker of sadness he'd caught on his face a moment ago.

The king cleared his throat, and the tension ebbed from his body. "He will be king soon enough, and he has attended all court meetings since he was nine. I believe he has gained the proper skills to make an informed decision that will benefit our kingdom."

Another whispered debate filled the room, but it died quickly this time.

"Very well," Muire agreed, speaking on behalf of the rest of the court members. "You are exempt from all meetings of the court beginning as soon as the princesses arrive. We will ensure meeting notes are sent to you immediately after court proceedings are executed. Should any issues arise from this on either the court's end or yours, Your Highness, we will make swift arrangements to remedy them."

Chapter 3
Eryn

Eryn's fingers stung from when she'd scrubbed them raw barely half an hour ago, attempting to get the blood off her hands. Crescents of red still hid beneath her fingernails, but she'd learned long ago there was nothing she could do to wash it away entirely. Maybe eventually, she wouldn't have to.

She sat near the edge of the forest that backed their small camp, her bow cradled in her lap as she scraped a new design into its wooden lower limb with her dagger. She sat with her back facing the camp, not wanting to dwell on the things within the camp's four borders that hinted at the carnage from the fight earlier that day.

Cuts and scratches lined her arms and legs, but she'd suffered nothing compared to the enemies who had met the end of her blade. She'd lost count of how many Deovarian soldiers she'd killed that morning, but the three dragons she'd put to death were still clear in her mind. Two Royal Talons and one drake.

The fight hadn't lasted long, but her body ached. She'd fought hundreds of times, but a week without a proper fight left her feeling as tired as she'd been after her first.

Pathetic.

Footsteps approached her from behind, but her eyes remained glued to her bow as she continued to chip away at the start of her new design. Her bow was nearly out of space by now, each small pattern marking a new battle she and her comrades had won.

"The others want a report," Isbeil, one of the few other Dragon Hunters who made it up to a First Rank, said.

They'd been in the same unit when Eryn had picked her specialty years ago, despite their age difference.

Eryn still didn't look up. "I'll be there soon."

She could picture the frown Isbeil likely wore on her face. Instead of leaving her alone to finish her work, the older woman sat beside her in the grass.

"I'm fine," Eryn told her before Isbeil had time to say anything else.

"You always are," Isbeil responded.

The corner of Eryn's mouth quirked upward. She liked Isbeil more than she liked most people. She wasn't close with any of her fellow soldiers anymore, not since they'd started losing more and more fights, and those she'd once called friends were killed off one at a time, but she liked her all the same. She'd known since the beginning to keep her distance. Getting attached meant losing those you loved.

She refused to get too close to anyone since the brutal reality hit her a couple of years ago.

She hadn't lost him entirely. He wasn't dead. But he had been close to it.

The dagger she held only served as a reminder. He'd given it to her years ago, and though it was one of her favorites, the memories always came back when she looked at it if she forgot to keep them at bay.

Her smile fell away at the thought.

"How many casualties?" Eryn asked, glancing at Isbeil before tucking the dagger into the holster she wore on her calf.

"A little over a hundred," Isbeil answered, regret lacing every word as if that number was her fault. "We don't have an exact count yet. Silis is working on it, but it's taking a while."

Eryn nodded. She slung her bow with its unfinished design over her shoulder before climbing to her feet. "Let's get this over with."

Soldiers were running around the camp, most working to help ensure anyone injured was taken care of while others worked to ensure the jobs of the injured soldiers didn't fall to the wayside. Food still needed to be served, scouts still needed to be sent out, a report needed to be sent to the castle, and a final count of their remaining weapons needed to be done.

Eryn and Isbeil dodged soldiers as they wound their way through the camp to the large tent set in the very center. It housed their strategies, best weapons, and, most importantly, the maps of their camps along the Deovarian border.

The other camp leaders were already inside, all ready to give their own version of a report.

Samuel, a stocky man with a temper shorter than his height, stood in the center of the space. He oversaw their camp and communicated with the castle and other nearby camps. He arranged for soldiers to be moved around and kept track of the official number of soldiers within their grounds. He was also responsible for informing families of the deaths of their loved ones after a fight.

"How'd we do?" he asked the gathered group of six, not bothering to start their meeting formally.

"A hundred and seven were confirmed dead," Silis, a top-ranking fighter who was one of the coldest women Eryn had ever met, said.

Eryn gritted her teeth before remembering she needed to speak next. "Nothing unusual to report from the fight," she stated evenly, despite the anger she felt after hearing the number of her fellow soldiers who were now dead. "Deovaria brought in fifteen dragons with them: ten Royal Talons and five drakes. They only left with two Royal Talons still alive. They bring far fewer with them each fight. Either we are killing them off faster than they can gain more, or they are attempting to hit our camps just hard enough that we're unable to fend them off in a larger-scale attack."

Samuel nodded. "We don't have any solid evidence to support either, but the other camps also report minor attacks like this. We've been suspicious that Deovaria's planning something, but we don't know what, and we've heard nothing from the castle in weeks that could support that theory."

Well, that wasn't surprising. They hadn't heard from the castle in months. Not that they provided much helpful information, anyway.

The castle requested visits from certain soldiers often enough, Eryn included, not that she'd been able to make the requested date, but it seemed like the only time they could offer them helpful support was when soldiers were sent there to gather information in person. They could hardly ever gather enough information from the letters the castle sent. However, it was probably because of the Deovarians interrupting their correspondence. Either that, or their leaders at the castle didn't know their heads from their asses. Either was a possibility at this point.

Eryn hadn't been to the castle in years. She'd spent a single summer there when she'd been a teen to take a training course, and all she'd seen was a lavishly decorated castle filled to the brim with servants tending to every need of the King and his son. There were parties held while she was there. The fact that they were at war hadn't stopped them from taking place, never mind the wasted hours they spent in the dining hall feasting on finely crafted meals and endless amounts of wine.

She'd caught the prince watching their training sessions every day from a window overlooking the training field, but that likely wasn't to help them better understand what their soldiers were capable of. He wouldn't have been sneaking around if he'd been doing it for the kingdom's benefit.

Eryn and the other camp leaders discussed all matters related to the attack, including how much more supplies they would need from the castle, plans to dispose of the bodies of their dead compatriots, strategies to best help them avoid losing so many soldiers in similar attacks, and plans to move their camp forward a few miles to push Deovaria back.

Those miles were hardly a fraction of what Deovaria had taken throughout the war, but at least they'd gained something back.

Samuel nodded, jotting down all the things they discussed on a pad of paper. "That'll be all for now," he told the assembled group. "Please get back to your stations. Eryn, would you stay behind a moment?"

Eryn raised an eyebrow at him as the others filed out of the tent. "Is something wrong?"

Samuel finished whatever he was still writing on the pad of paper and glanced back up at her. "Not as far as I'm aware," he said cryptically as he removed an envelope from a drawer in the table that the large map of Aericora's border with Deovaria sat on.

Eryn's eyes stayed trained on the King's crest stamped to the letter. Her name scrawled in black ink across the front.

"What is this?" she asked, taking it from him before turning it over to examine it. It had to be a summons to the castle. She'd only received one other, though, and it wasn't stamped like this. It wasn't directly addressed to her, either. This came from the King himself, not from the court like those they received most often.

Samuel gave her a look before rolling his eyes and turning back to his pad on the table. "Is the seal broken or not?" he asked, irritation lacing his words. "I don't know."

"Your glowing personality is always what I liked about you, you know," Eryn responded sarcastically, returning his eye roll.

She ran her nail beneath the edge of the envelope, cracking the seal to remove the parchment folded inside. She read it over once, trying to discern what she was reading. She read it again, only to find the words held the same meaning the second time.

Irritation like she'd never felt before flared through her. This had to be some sick joke.

Samuel chuckled. "That bad, eh?"

She glared up at him over the edge of the parchment. "You're going to have to find yourself another Dragon Hunter," she snapped, unable to keep her anger at bay. "I've been summoned to the castle indefinitely."

That caught his full attention. He set his pen down. "Oh? What for?"

"To train the prince, apparently."

Chapter 4

Caeden eyed the target a hundred yards away from where he stood in the center of the grass training field. He drew back the bowstring and readied himself to make the shot.

It had been two weeks since he'd met with the court and agreed to marry princess in exchange for his training with Eryn Gedding, and they'd told him earlier that the princesses would arrive in two days. Eryn Gedding would arrive in the morning.

Caeden took a deep breath through his nose and let it out through his mouth, attempting to keep his hands steady as he aimed the arrowhead for the center of the target.

"Fix your feet, princy," Ronan said from over Caeden's shoulder. He sounded amused.

Caeden widened his stance, his eyes remaining on the center of the target ahead. Once his feet were firmly on the ground again, he loosed the arrow. It cut through the air before disappearing over the top of the target and into the dense forest.

He cursed beneath his breath as he lowered the bow to his side. He hadn't had high hopes for the shot, but the disappointment still stung.

Caeden turned around, his gaze landing on Ronan standing ten feet away from him, his hand wrapped around the top of his cane so tightly that his knuckles had turned white in the darkness. He had a sword strapped around his waist, and a quiver of arrows and a bow thrown over his shoulder. A flask of something that definitely wasn't water hung from his wrist. Strands of his honey-blond hair stuck to his damp forehead and a thin sheen of sweat across his face made his skin glisten in the moonlight. His cheeks were rosy and the smile on his face was crooked. He wasn't outright drunk yet, but he was getting close.

"One more hour?" Caeden asked. A teasing smile pulled at the corners of his mouth before he could stop it. "Or am I keeping you from someone?"

Ronan grinned mischievously. "I've got a date of sorts to get to later this evenin'," he said cryptically, as if Caeden wasn't aware of his nightly endeavors.

Caeden's smile widened. "I'll do my best to make sure you're back in time," he told him.

"Much appreciated." The mischief still clung to his features, turning the corners of his mouth upward.

Caeden turned to the target and pulled a second arrow from the quiver slung over his shoulder. He readied the bow again, but Ronan's words from a moment earlier rang through his mind. He shifted his stance wider before releasing the arrow. The arrow struck the wooden board, but missed the bright stripes of the target by a good five or six inches.

"Better," Ronan offered.

Caeden gritted his teeth. "Still not good enough," he muttered. He sighed and pulled yet another arrow from the quiver. From where he stood, the feathered ends of twenty arrows stuck into the target were visible, only one of which had struck the center.

Behind him, Ronan readjusted his cane in the uneven grass. He cleared his throat. "She's comin' tomorrow, ain't she?" he asked.

Caeden frowned, but didn't turn away from the target. "Gedding?" he asked, then released the arrow. It sliced through the air, and Caeden held his breath.

For a split second, it looked like it would strike true and embed itself into the center circle of red paint, but that second ended, and it sailed past the wooden frame and into the woods along with the many others he'd shot over the months. A loud thwack echoed through the air as it hit a tree somewhere behind the target, and Caeden cringed.

He'd practiced with Ronan for over a year, yet his skills hadn't improved. But their training sessions weren't consistent. Hopefully, the consistency he would get with Eryn Gedding would make all the difference.

"Eryn," Ronan corrected, bringing Caeden's attention back to their conversation. "She doesn't like bein' referred to by her last name. Not by me, at least. She 'bout stabbed me clean through the last time I used it in front of her."

Caeden could hear the smile on his friend's face when he spoke, despite the darkness preventing him from seeing it.

He shouldered the bow and turned around. He raised a curious eyebrow. "You know her? Why didn't you mention that?"

It wasn't surprising that they knew each other. Only a fraction of their military was as highly ranked as Ronan and Eryn, and most who were tended to know one another. Given that both Ronan and Eryn would've been close in age when they'd started their training, the chances of them crossing paths were higher. It was odd that Ronan hadn't mentioned knowing Eryn in the last two weeks.

"It's been years," Ronan explained, an almost wistful look settling over his features. "We trained together, but we didn't see each other much when we joined the ranks. We were stationed together, but she started trainin' to be a Dragon Hunter, and I started learnin' stuff to work with the spies they were stationing in Deovaria. I was a fighter, but havin' the trainin' meant I'd have more opportunities. Also meant I didn't get to see her as much." He shrugged, then glowered down at his injured leg. "After my *injury*," he said the word like it left a bitter taste on the tip of his tongue, "I was brought here, and I haven't seen or heard from her since. She's done good for herself, from what I've heard."

There was a sadness in Ronan's eyes, but he covered it with a smile so quickly Caeden figured it was best not to mention it.

Instead, he nodded in response.

He didn't know many specifics about Eryn Gedding, aside from knowing that she'd risen in the ranks quickly after leading a successful mission into Deovaria's borders. He'd heard her name a lot after that mission, and from what others said, she was one of the best soldiers Aericora had.

Maybe that was why his father had chosen her to train him. Being as skilled as she was, she could teach Caeden enough that he wouldn't get himself killed if he was sent to the front lines.

"What's she like?" Caeden asked, shouldering his bow. He'd wondered for days what his soon-to-be mentor was like, and Ronan was the only person who knew anything about her that he couldn't find in a field report.

Ronan raised an eyebrow at him, and the corner of his mouth twitched before a wide grin spread across his face. He chuckled. "Eryn Gedding is gonna train your royal ass so hard you're gonna wish your father hadn't ever agreed to bring her here at all." He shook his head, the smile not leaving his face. "That woman acts as if the concept of bodily harm is foreign to her. Sore muscles? Covered in bruises? Get over it. Not to mention how she's gonna be fillin' that pea-sized brain of yours with all those endless dragon facts she's got. You're gonna be readin' so many books, your heads gonna wanna explode. Trust me too, 'cause she's already put me through it more than once."

Ronan paused, and Caeden used the opportunity to let his words sink in.

Either Ronan was doing his best to convince him that Eryn would be one of the best teachers he could get, or he was trying to scare Caeden out of training with her at all. But from what he'd said, Eryn would ensure he learned everything she had to teach, which was exactly what he needed. He could handle the abuse if it meant he was one step closer to fighting against Deovaria.

Ronan's expression shifted from amused to the same wistful look he'd had a few moments before. He shook his head again before he spoke. "She's a good woman, princy. She'll be hard on you, but so long as you show her some respect and give her time, you'll see she's not as mean and tough as she pretends to be." The corner of his mouth quirked upward again. "Just don't tell her I told you so."

"She's as good as they say?" Caeden asked. He was sure he knew the answer to the question already, but he wanted to hear Ronan confirm it. If there was one person he trusted to tell him the truth, it was him.

Ronan thought it over, his brow furrowing while he tapped the tip of his cane against the ground. He grabbed his flask and took a long drink, still seeming to mull over the question.

"She's better," he answered finally. "And I ain't just sayin' that 'cause I know her."

Caeden cracked a teasing smile, despite his relief at hearing those words. "I know," he said. "You aren't always a conniving ass. Only most of the time."

Ronan took another long swig. "Well, now you're just makin' me seem like a good person. That ain't cool, princy. I've got a reputation to uphold. Good soldier, yes. Good person, not so much."

Despite how Ronan attempted to display himself to most of the castle's residents, Caeden had learned long ago that he was, in fact, a good person. Few knew him well enough to see through the image Ronan portrayed of himself. He was reserved mostly when around members of the court, only offering his opinion on matters where he knew his input would be helpful. He spent the rest of the time flirting with every woman he passed. He'd seen less of the latter side, but only because he preferred to avoid being involved in those encounters.

The sound of bare feet rustling in the grass caught Caeden's attention, and his head snapped to the right.

A figure draped in a long, black cloak obscured the light from the castle before they disappeared into the shadows again. It didn't even take Caeden a second thought to realize it was Ronan's guest making her way somewhat stealthily toward the small shack at the edge of the clearing.

"Speaking of impressions," Caeden teased, doing his best to avoid his voice catching the woman's attention on the other end of the field.

Ronan grinned, and Caeden snorted a laugh.

"Well," Ronan said, his eyes lingering on the shadows surrounding his small home where the woman had disappeared. "That's my queue. Don't forget to lock up. I don't need to be gettin' in trouble 'cause you've got a terrible memory."

Ronan leaned on his cane while he rummaged around in one of his pockets. He pulled out a large ring of keys from it before he tossed them haphazardly in Caeden's general direction.

"G'night, princy!" Ronan called quietly over his shoulder before he hobbled across the clearing while Caeden fumbled as he attempted—and failed—to catch the ring of keys.

Caeden smiled as he watched his friend disappear into the night before bending to retrieve the keyring.

Once Ronan disappeared into the darkness, Caeden approached the target. He retrieved the arrows from the wooden target and gathered the ones littering the ground or the trunks of trees along the edge of the forest. He only recovered thirty of the fifty he'd started with earlier that night, and he replaced them into the quiver over his shoulder before heading back toward the armory.

The armory was built into the side of the castle. The only entrance was a small wooden door on the opposite side of the training field from where he and Ronan had been practicing.

Caeden pushed open the door, and it squeaked on its rusted hinges. He replaced his bow and quiver, the two throwing knives he'd strapped to his thighs and the long sword he'd hung from his waist.

Now that he'd been training with Ronan for some time, he'd suggested Caeden train while wearing other weapons. The method made sense, especially since he'd be required to do the same thing when he convinced his father to send him to join their kingdom's soldiers, but it did inhibit his movement. That was the whole point, but he couldn't even hit the target without the added discomfort.

He wondered what Eryn would suggest he do once she arrived the following day. She had no way of knowing he'd spent any time practicing before her arrival, and he wasn't so sure he wanted to tell her when she arrived and risk that information getting back to his father or the court.

He gripped the hilt of the sword tightly as he replaced it on the rack inside of the dark room. He needed his training with Eryn to go well or he'd never be able to convince the court to let him fight.

He almost wanted to tell her about his minimal training so she could pick up where Ronan would leave off. As long as the court didn't find out about his training with Ronan, it would look like Caeden's abilities would be coming along quickly. It may not help him get to the field faster, but he didn't see how it could do anything but benefit him if they were convinced he was a faster learner.

"Your Highness," a quiet voice whispered from somewhere near the still-open entrance to the armory.

Caeden jumped, adrenaline coursing through every inch of his body. He spun to face a girl no older than fifteen or sixteen.

He let out a breath in relief as he took in her black cloak and the silver patterns embroidered into the sleeves and the edge of the hood, marking her as one of the castle's servants.

Frantic nervousness clung to the girl's features. Her amber eyes darted around like she expected something to jump out of the darkness. She kept her lips pressed together in a thin line, and her cheeks had a childlike roundness.

"Yes?" Caeden asked, unable to form any other words with the adrenaline rushing through him.

After the court meeting earlier, everything important should've already been discussed. Unless something urgent happened with the war, there shouldn't be any reason for anyone to send for him. But if something urgent arose, someone other than the teenaged girl who stood before him would've found him.

The girl stopped scanning the edges of the room and refocused on him. She bowed forward at the waist before she spoke again. "The King, uh, your-your father," she stammered, her cheeks reddening so much he could see it in the darkness, "has requested an-an audience with-with you… Your Highness."

Caeden frowned. "At this hour?"

If this was related to the war, the princesses, or Eryn Gedding, it was strange that his father wanted to meet with him alone. Over the past couple of weeks, the king avoided speaking privately about any of it—especially the princesses and Eryn Gedding—to avoid any strife it could cause with the court.

He and his father knew by now that it never boded well for them if his father appeared to be putting his son's feelings over the kingdom's safety. Even if the advisors set most of the stipulations before Caeden was aware of it.

The girl nodded vigorously. "Yes," she squeaked too quickly, her voice almost ear-piercingly high. "He-he has asked for you-you to be brought to-to him." She stood a little straighter, but her eyes remained downcast, and her head stayed bowed as she motioned in the direction of the doorway. "If-if you would please come with-with me, Your Highness."

"Very well," Caeden replied before double-checking that he'd replaced all the weapons he'd borrowed. He followed the young girl and stepped outside of the armory after her.

He locked the door before they continued through the extensive field toward the door leading back inside the castle. He would return the keys to Ronan first thing in the morning.

The girl walked ahead of him. She glanced around anxiously as they walked through the darkness. Her nervousness seemed contagious because before they'd made it halfway across the field, Caeden could've sworn he felt someone's eyes on the back of his head. It was a ridiculous thought, but he couldn't shake the feeling.

Caeden glanced behind himself as they walked but found no one anywhere in sight. He shook his head, chiding himself for being so childish as they passed through the doorway. The girl shut the door behind them.

The girl led Caeden through the castle's halls until they reached his father's study. She rapped her knuckles gently against the door three times before the king's deep, rather tired, voice called for them to come in. She pushed the door open for Caeden, and he stepped past her before closing it behind him.

The king sat in his usual chair behind his large wooden desk. He sat slumped over a pile of papers, the flickering orange light from the fire in the hearth to Caeden's right making the dark circles beneath his father's eyes even more apparent than they usually were.

"You asked to speak with me?" Caeden asked, his voice echoing through the room. The barren bookcases in his father's study weren't enough to pad the space, and he always forgot about the echo.

The king nodded, but the movement looked like it cost him far more energy than it should've.

"Please sit," the king said, gesturing to the two chairs on the other end of his desk.

Caeden's heart ached in his chest for his father as he watched him blink the ever-present sleepiness from his eyes.

He hadn't been this stressed and tired when Caeden was younger. He'd been happier. He hadn't had to spend every waking moment of every day buried in endless papers and war strategy meetings.

Maybe if Caeden's mother were still alive, he would've taken an hour to himself each day to rest. No one could get his father to take care of himself like his mother used to. But a war wasn't raging when his mother was alive, and his father's responsibility to their people hadn't been nearly as great.

Caeden stepped inside and sat in one of the two open chairs.

Almost absentmindedly, his eyes drifted to the bookshelf behind his father's seat, where a sheet of yellowing paper with a sloppily painted sunflower sat behind a small, black box holding a warped ring with an almost glowing sapphire stone set into its center.

His sister did the painting only days before she and their mother left the castle for the last festival they would attend. She'd been upset when she'd messed up the flower's petals, and Caeden could still picture her tear-streaked face when their father promised her it was the most beautiful painting he'd ever seen. The ring had been his mother's wedding band and was one of very few things to survive the flames of the first attack. The gem in the center of her ring was the only one in the kingdom that glowed, and the only answer Caeden got from his mother when he'd questioned why was a smile and wink before she would whisper that it was magic, like it was a secret between just the two of them.

He hadn't believed her; instead, he only wrinkled his small nose at her, which would make her smile, before she'd wrap him up in a hug.

"Did I do something?" Caeden asked as he turned his attention to his father and shoved away the thoughts of his mother and sister.

The king shook his head, but Caeden wasn't sure whether it was the answer to his question or not. "It appears Miss Gedding has arrived early to avoid the crowds of the welcoming ceremony that we are no longer holding." A hint of amusement was hiding in the edges of his father's small smile, but it faded. "I suppose word of the cancellation didn't reach her during her travels. She was shown her room and has turned in for the night, but she'll join us for breakfast in the morning. Your training with her will begin tomorrow afternoon. I have already spoken with her and arranged for her to have full access to all the training equipment you will require."

Caeden fought to suppress the smile threatening to pull the sides of his mouth upward. He'd be starting a day early due to her early arrival. Along with simply having an extra day to train, it would give him enough time to understand how their training sessions would be carried out before the princesses arrived.

Caeden nodded in response to his father.

"Additionally," his father continued, his voice softer, "I have been in contact with the royal families from Drura, Crevia, and Nozac. I've arranged for the princesses to stay in the castle for a few extra weeks to give you more time to get to know one another." The king gave him a sympathetic look. The king cleared his throat and continued, "I would prefer you find a bride who will be someone you can become friends with."

Caeden's stomach tightened at the idea of spending multiple extra weeks attempting to court three separate women at once.

Over the past weeks, Caeden wrote off the idea of loving whoever he chose for a wife. He would make his decision based on whether he felt she would make a good queen for his kingdom and on what her kingdom could provide his in relation to soldiers. He needed a wife he could communicate with and who would be on the same page with court matters. It likely wouldn't be easy to gauge such things in casual conversation, but that was his goal.

He didn't enjoy the idea of analyzing each of the princesses so thoroughly, but he already agreed to the terms set out by the court, and the extra time his father had arranged for them to stay would allow him more time to ensure he made the right choice, even if it made his stomach twist into knots.

"Thank you," Caeden told the king. He could pretend for his father's sake that he was happy with the changes.

Chapter 5

The early morning sun shone brightly into the large dining hall, lighting the space with a bright pink glow. An array of flowers and candles crowded the center of the table, but the remaining space was just as empty as it always was.

The room was empty, aside from Caeden and his father, who had already taken their seats. The king sat at the head of the table, and Caeden sat to his immediate right. Both Eryn Gedding and Ronan were supposed to join them for breakfast, but neither had arrived yet, though they weren't late.

Caeden expected Ronan to be late regardless, considering the man hardly bothered to show up on time to anything, unless it would cost him his job. He blamed his tardiness on his inability to walk without leaning on his cane, which he claimed greatly slowed the process. It wasn't a lie, but Ronan could walk just as fast as anyone else when he wanted to. The reason he was always late had nothing to do with his leg, and everything to do with his drinking problem and his love of spending late nights with women.

When Ronan was hired at the castle, he'd gotten strict

instructions to fix his drinking problem. He'd made a good show of sobering up, but Caeden and the multiple women who shared Ronan's company knew the truth.

His drinking stemmed from his injury in the field, though he'd admitted to being a drunk beforehand. He'd been shot in the field during a mission into Deovarian territory, but Ronan refused to talk about it any more than to say he'd been unconscious when it happened and that he was thankful he hadn't had to feel the full extent of the pain.

The king cleared his throat, making Caeden jump and his attention snap to where his father was sitting. His father pulled a glass of deep red wine to his lips and took a long drink.

The door to the dining hall opened slowly. Two guards were needed on each side to open the heavy wooden doors. Even with four guards in total, it took them some time to open them.

When the crack between the two doors was barely two feet wide, a woman with raven black hair and the most stunning blue eyes he'd ever seen shoved her way through and strode inside. Two guards flanked her, rushing through the small opening behind her.

The woman glanced at the two guards following her with an irritable expression, but it disappeared when she faced forward again, replaced with a bored one instead.

"Miss Gedding," the king said, his voice echoing throughout the room. "Thank you for joining us this morning. I trust your room and service have been to your liking, and you were well taken care of?"

Eryn glanced up at him. Her eyes passed over his face quickly, before they shifted to Caeden. Curiosity lighting her features, she eyed him up and down before she turned to the king again. "Yes, the room and your staff are lovely," she replied.

The way she stood reflected confidence, but her voice

sounded stiff, and her hands fidgeted near the hilts of her daggers strapped to her thighs. She looked both uncomfortable and angry but it was impossible to discern the genuine emotion from the coverup.

Eryn took a seat at the table on the side opposite Caeden. One guard moved to pull out her chair for her, but she smacked his hand away before she did it herself and sat down.

Caeden eyed the guard behind her as he massaged his hand where the Dragon Hunter had hit him.

"Excellent," the king said, ignoring the strange display.

"I take it this is my new student?" Eryn asked, nodding in Caeden's direction. Her eyes locked on the king's face, not bothering to acknowledge Caeden's presence.

Caeden cleared his throat. "Yes," he responded, before his father could. He didn't like the dismissive way she was treating him already. "Prince Caeden of Aericora. A pleasure to meet you."

Eryn's attention shifted to him, and the corner of her mouth twitched up in what Caeden could only assume was amusement. "Eryn Gedding," she replied. "First Rank Dragon Hunter of the Aericora military. I look forward to—"

Before she could finish the sentence, the doors to the dining hall creaked open again, and Ronan stumbled his way through. He glanced at each of them and a smile formed on his face. "Don't wait to eat on account of me bein' late," he announced, the amusement he felt at his joke playing across his features as he made his way further into the room and sat beside Caeden.

Caeden caught a flash of irritation across his father's face, but the king said nothing but his usual line to welcome the man.

"Miss Gedding, this is Ronan Atkyn, our castle's Head of Security and our primary military instructor," the king said before he turned his attention to Ronan. The annoyance he'd felt toward him a moment before was gone from his expression. "Ronan, this is Eryn Gedding. She'll ensure Caeden is trained to the same extent as our soldiers fighting in the field, and I trust you will aid her in any way she may need."

Ronan's gaze fell on Eryn, and a smile pulled at the corners of his mouth. It was one of the kindest smiles Caeden had ever seen on Ronan's face. A glance at Eryn confirmed Ronan wasn't the only one happy about their reunion. Whatever they'd meant to each other before they'd parted ways hadn't just been friendly. The look they shared was enough to confirm it.

It was odd that Ronan hadn't mentioned that earlier. He talked about every woman he'd been with, so long as it wasn't a member of the castle's staff Caeden knew.

"Of course," Ronan said to the king. He turned his attention back to Eryn. "Good to see you again." His words came out stiff, but it was clear it was only because he was trying to suppress a wide grin.

Eryn dipped her head in return. "You as well."

"Very good," Caeden's father said, bringing everyone's attention back to him.

Before anyone said anything to continue the conversation, four servants emerged through the wooden door directly behind Eryn. Each one carried a silver platter of food for a person seated at the table. They brought the trays to each person at the table and set them down silently before leaving just as quietly.

They dug into the food, and the room filled with a borderline uncomfortable silence before Caeden's father broke it between mouthfuls. "What made you decide to join the military?" he asked Eryn, who looked surprised that anyone had spoken to her.

Eryn swallowed the food in her mouth before she spoke. "I've spent my life surrounded by soldiers," she explained. "I first learned to fight when I was young from a family friend, and it was never really a choice after. I've always wanted to help defend my kingdom."

The king nodded. "Was there any reason you opted to be a Dragon Hunter?"

Eryn's eyes flicked to Ronan with something like fear hiding in the edges of her expression before she cleared her throat and turned back to the king. Any nervousness she'd had was gone, replaced with an expression that was nothing short of cool and collected. "I've been fascinated with dragons for as long as I can remember," she said. Her voice was higher pitched than before. "My interest peaked after seeing how powerful they were with my own eyes."

The answer was as cryptic as possible, effectively ending the king's ability to press the subject more without interrogating her.

Ronan made a noise in the back of his throat that wasn't loud enough for anyone but Caeden to hear. Ronan fixed his eyes on his food as he brought a forkful to his lips. He'd been silent so far, and Caeden wondered if he and Eryn's relationship was more strained than he'd implied.

He raised a confused eyebrow at the man sitting next to him. Caeden couldn't decipher the look on Ronan's face when he glanced at Eryn sitting in front of him. It resembled warmth, which wasn't a way he'd ever seen Ronan look at a woman before.

Caeden shook his head to clear the confusion away before he let himself run too far away with the thought.

The king stopped to sip his wine, leaving the room with an awkward silence once again.

"Your name is attached to some very successful missions over the past few years," Caeden stated. It wasn't a question, and he wasn't sure what he expected Eryn to say in response, but he would rather end the silence, even if it meant starting an awkward conversation instead.

Eryn cracked a half smile, but didn't look up at him. "I would hope so. I led most of those missions." She picked up her glass of wine but made no move to bring it to her lips. Instead, she only swirled the liquid around the glass, her eyes locked on it. "I've led sixteen missions in the past three years. Lately, I have specialized in getting us into Deovarian territory on missions since I've taught my soldiers how to fight off dragons, even without the help of lavender flowers to inhibit their abilities. Thirteen of those missions have been successful, ranging from rescue missions to claiming multiple square miles of Deovarian territory. I also analyze Deovaria's tactics during attacks, primarily their uses for their dragons."

Caeden raised an eyebrow. He only knew of a handful of the missions she talked about. Her first had been a rescue mission to save soldiers who were being held in Deovaria's capital, the second had been a mission to destroy a large portion of Deovaria's weapons, and the third he could recall had been when she led soldiers into a town and overtook it within a day.

Those were the only ones big enough to earn the attention of the court, but he hadn't known of the others she'd successfully overseen.

"She was young when she joined, too," Ronan said, drawing everyone's attention. "She's only been in the military for six years."

"Oh?" The king turned his attention to Eryn.

Eryn nodded. "I started training when I was fourteen," she explained. "I got stationed in the field at sixteen and earned the title of a First Rank Dragon Hunter after I turned eighteen."

Caeden knew she was young and had advanced quickly, but that kind of advancement in only four years was extremely impressive.

The rest of the meal passed with the king and Eryn exchanging words between bites of food.

He asked her for more specifics on the missions, and she gave him the same details they'd already heard from the reports. It kept the room from falling silent again, and despite knowing the information already, it was far more pleasant than the silence.

Caeden watched Eryn as she spoke to his father. She seemed on edge still, but she'd relaxed since she'd first arrived. She was cryptic with her answers to most of the questions she was asked, which made a strange feeling settle into the pit of his stomach. He knew the answers to all the questions, but he couldn't shake the feeling that she was leaving things out, though he couldn't find any missing pieces in the information she reiterated.

Once they finished with their meal, the servants returned and cleared away the plates and glasses.

The king explained to Eryn that the princesses would arrive the following day and Caeden would split his time between his training and spending time with each of them during their stay. He emphasized the importance of their comfort in the castle and how Caeden would be responsible for it.

His father worded it in a way that made it sound like Caeden would not be spending half of his days attempting to court three separate women, and the sick feeling in his stomach only grew as he listened. He didn't think it sounded becoming of a prince either, but he doubted anyone was oblivious enough not to put the pieces together.

Eryn clenched her jaw as his father spoke, revealing her irritation at hearing what he had to say. Her expression lasted a moment before it vanished, and she plastered on a bright smile that was clearly forced. "Of course, Your Majesty."

She bowed, then turned her attention to Caeden. He caught the disdain in her eyes and the annoyed twitch of the corner of her mouth when she looked him over. She hid that, too, after only a second. That split-second expression was enough to invoke a flash of his own irritation. He hadn't yet had enough time with her to give her a reason to dislike him.

"Be at the training field in an hour," she instructed him, her tone as cold as ice. "I'll find you when I get there."

She left the room before Caeden had time to form a response that wouldn't match the tone she'd used.

♥ ♥ ♥

Caeden returned with Ronan to his shack to wait until his training with Eryn started. He fidgeted while he waited, bouncing his leg up and down against the edge of the couch.

Ronan only gave him an amused smirk when he bothered to look over the edge of his flask.

Eryn knocked on the door fifteen minutes earlier than Caeden was expecting her.

He'd expected the knock, but he jumped at the sound regardless, and Ronan's smirk widened from where he stood in the kitchen in a way that implied he'd been expecting her to arrive ahead of schedule.

Without waiting for an answer from either of them, Eryn pushed open the door with an agitated huff. Her eyes landed on Ronan first, then continued to search the room until she spotted Caeden sitting on the couch.

She pressed her lips together, her eyes blazing, and placed her hands on her hips. She took in a long breath. "Training is in the field," she said. She was fighting the urge to yell at him. "Not in the shack."

Caeden reminded himself he didn't know her, and Ronan said she would be like this until she warmed up.

He bit the inside of his cheek hard enough that the copper taste of blood filled his mouth, but it kept him from saying anything he might regret. He didn't like how she treated him, but she was attempting to be polite, and he didn't need to give her an actual reason to be rude.

Caeden kept his tone even when he responded. "You told me to meet you in an hour. I was under the assumption I had fifteen more minutes."

Eryn clenched her jaw, still trying her hardest to hide her anger. "Soldiers are always early to training," she said tightly.

Caeden nodded in acknowledgment before he climbed to his feet and walked past her and out the door. Eryn remained behind him, and he used his moment alone to take in a slow breath as the faint sound of Ronan's light chuckle and Eryn's exasperated sigh drifted out from the still-open doorway. He couldn't afford to let her anger get to him. He needed this training and would not get it if his teacher wasn't willing to work with him, which she wouldn't be if he lost his temper with her for no reason.

He waited thirty yards away from the shack for Eryn to emerge. He could hear their muffled voices as she and Ronan exchanged a few words before she exited the shack a moment later.

"What are we starting with?" Caeden asked once she was close enough to hear him without him having to yell.

She was dressed in a simple tank top and leggings, and Ronan's ring of keys was now in her hand. He'd expected she'd choose to focus on teaching him about dragons at first, but judging by her attire and that she was holding the keys to the armory, he realized he shouldn't have been so quick to make that assumption.

"Rule number one: always be early," Eryn said through gritted teeth. She tossed the keys into the air before catching them in her opposite hand. She walked past him in the armory's direction and spoke without looking back at him. "I need to establish how much that moron has taught you, apparently." Caeden wasn't sure if he was hearing affection or annoyance in her tone when she spoke about Ronan. "He chooses right now to mention you two already started some training of your own."

Caeden felt his face heat and was glad she couldn't see it. It surprised him that Ronan mentioned the training with the trouble they could end up in.

Eryn held out a hand and began listing things off on her fingertips. "We're going to go over archery, sword fighting, hand-to-hand, explosives, poisons, and, my favorite, knife-throwing so that I can get a baseline of your physical capabilities, and we'll work from there. And since very few people know anything about dragons, that man included," she tossed an irritated look in the direction of Ronan's shack, "I'm going to start from the very beginning to ensure you're versed before they throw you to the wolves or whatever their plan for you is."

He chose not to mention that, of her list, he'd only ever practiced sword fighting as a child and some mild archery and hand-to-hand tactics with Ronan.

Eryn led him to the opposite end of the field and the armory. She said nothing as they walked, and Caeden contemplated whether breaking the silence would be a good idea. From what he'd seen so far, keeping his mouth shut seemed like his best option if he wanted any chance of getting on her good side.

Eryn unlocked the large wooden door and disappeared into the darkness inside without bothering to light one of the small candles on the table just inside the doorway.

Caeden waited in the entryway for her. He could hear metal clanking against metal inside as she picked out various weapons in the darkness.

She must have been here for a while during her years of training with how she could weave her way through the mess inside without knocking into the supplies.

He'd never paid attention to the faces of the soldiers brought to the castle, and those he had noticed blurred together. He'd snuck into his sister's room hundreds of times as a teen to watch their training through the window in a vain attempt to learn any techniques he could. The faces of the people performing those techniques hadn't mattered.

The soft rustle of Eryn's light footsteps against the dirt floor reached him before she came back into view. She held a bow and quiver of arrows over her left shoulder, two sheathed swords over her right, a small pouch of what he assumed were poisons and explosive materials strapped to her waist, and two daggers in either hand. She had a smile on her face and a mischievous glimmer in her bright blue eyes that made his stomach twist into nervous knots.

The look in her eyes confirmed she wouldn't go easy on him.

Chapter 6

Eryn led Caeden into the field and to the archery range where he and Ronan had practiced the previous night. She stopped fifty feet from the target and pulled the bow and arrows off her shoulder before passing them to him, along with instructions to hit the target. She waited with a curious expression while he fumbled with the bow.

Caeden turned to the target and eyed the painted stripes on the board ahead of him. He pulled an arrow from the quiver and readied himself for the shot, his hands shaking as he remembered how badly he'd done the night before.

Ronan's suggestions rang through his mind, and he widened his stance. He pulled back the bowstring and let the arrow fly. It sailed just over the top edge of the target and disappeared. Eryn snorted a quiet laugh behind him, and a wave of irritation hit him. He pushed down his frustration before he turned back to face her.

"Are you aiming?" she asked, raising a curious eyebrow at him as she crossed her arms over her chest.

He wasn't sure if she was making fun of him or genuinely

asking. He wanted to respond to her assuming that the former was true, but he bit back the unsavory remarks forming on the tip of his tongue.

"Yes," he answered.

Eryn's eyes shifted from the bow Caeden held to the target ahead of them, then back. "Okay," she said, drawing out the word as if trying to convince him and herself that she believed him. She waved a hand between them, motioning for him to continue. "Do it again."

He did as she instructed and grabbed a second arrow from the quiver. He pulled the string and lined the tip of the arrow with the bullseye mark on the target.

He let out a breath before he released it.

"Don't do that," Eryn said, before the arrow flew even halfway to the target across the field. "Don't shift before you make the shot. When it's lined up, let it go. Don't spend too much time preparing yourself for it. Try again."

"Okay." Caeden repeated the motion; this time the arrow struck the target only six inches from the center.

It was one of the best shots he'd made since he'd first picked up a bow, and his mouth nearly dropped open as he stared at it. That couldn't be the only reason he'd been unable to use a bow and arrow.

"That's a first," he whispered, unable to take his eyes off the target.

"Good," Eryn said. "Again."

He did as she told him, but a breeze blew past them this time right as he released the arrow, and he missed the target again.

Eryn waved a dismissive hand in the direction the arrow had flown off in, but Caeden couldn't quite suppress his disappointment at another failed attempt.

"That was the wind," she assured him.

Her words helped to ease his disappointment more than he expected.

Eryn stepped up beside him, close enough that the scent of lavender from her clothes and hair filled his senses.

He'd always liked that scent, even before he'd learned how helpful it was in keeping his kingdom's soldiers alive against the dragons under Deovaria's control.

"Hold the bow out again," Eryn instructed, bringing his attention back. He did as she told him, and she moved his elbow up higher when he pulled back on the string. "You want to pull it past your cheek. Keep your arm as even as you can with the arrow. Think of it as an extension of your arm. It's ridiculous, but it works."

Ronan had taught him the same trick long ago. All the tricks he'd offered him had proved useless thus far. But after getting so close to the bullseye, he was willing to try again.

The arrow embedded itself into the target again that time, but barely hit the outermost ring. He'd been closer with his previous shot, but this was better than he did most other times he'd practiced.

"That one was you," Eryn said, bursting his momentary bubble of pride. The complete annoyance in her tone didn't help either, and he gripped his bow tighter.

She had a right to be annoyed, but he doubted she would've been as frustrated if she'd seen how badly he'd done the last time he'd practiced.

They continued with the bow and arrow for another hour. After those two shots, Caeden missed the target every time. He struck the wooden board, but the rings at its center could've been magically enhanced to move independently with how many times he missed.

For the first while, Eryn was calm with him, despite the

apparent frustration written into her expression, but after a while, she lost her patience.

"It's not that hard," she snapped as she snatched the bow from him and pulled an arrow from the quiver still slung over Caeden's shoulder. She taught him how to stand, knock the arrow, aim, and where to look. She explained it as if she were teaching a frog how to accomplish the task. But Caeden already knew all these things—if not from learning them from Ronan, then from her going over each of them with him already.

She loosed the arrow, and it struck the bullseye on the target.

Caeden's frustration hit a boiling point as she spun back around to face him with a fire so intense in her eyes it could've made a dragon cower.

"I know it's not," he said through clenched teeth, trying to keep from directing his frustration at her. "You yelling at me doesn't help me do any better."

She laughed, but there was no amusement in it, only bitterness. "Trust me," she said, a warning in her voice. "You'll know when I'm yelling."

After they finished archery, Eryn tested his knowledge of poisons, which lasted only a few moments since it was practically nothing.

Caeden knew a few things about poisons, but his knowledge was limited to what signs to look for when attempting to tell if someone's food was laced with a lethal substance. He'd learned most of those tidbits of information from his father when he'd been far younger than any child should ever have to be, since a Deovarian spy had attempted to poison the king's meal. Luckily, his father tasted the difference in the wine before he swallowed it, and the poison only made him ill for the rest of the day.

Before they had spent ten minutes discussing the topic, Eryn closed the small pouch that contained multiple vials of poisons and a small booklet with an irritated eye roll, before proclaiming she'd be teaching him from square one.

After that, they focused on hand-to-hand combat.

Hand-to-hand was another skill Caeden had spent little time learning, mostly because it was difficult for Ronan to teach.

Eryn stood across from him, her arms lifted to protect her face. She kept her hands bent into crescent shapes, rather than in fists like he'd seen other fighters do.

It was odd, and his mind raced with plausible reasons she could have for holding them like that. He opened his mouth to ask her about it but thought better of it and mimicked her stance instead. He would not start by questioning her methods.

Eryn looked him over once before she threw a punch toward his stomach without any forewarning.

He barely stepped out of the way before her fist connected with his abdomen. Despite his dodge, her knuckles grazed against his side, and he clenched his jaw from the pain as it flared across his lower ribs and spread out over his stomach.

"What was that?" Caeden snapped as he turned to face her. All his frustration from her attitude toward him bubbled up enough that he couldn't suppress it before it seeped into his voice.

He'd expected her to look over his stance like she'd done when they'd practiced with the bow and arrow, adjusting small things here and there with the same pursed lips and crinkle between her brows she had earlier. Not start with a punch straight to the gut.

Eryn rolled her eyes and lifted her hands again. "You aren't going to be ready when an enemy attacks you."

He'd heard that exact sentence from Ronan, but he didn't see how he was supposed to fend her off if he hadn't learned the basics yet.

Eryn took one large step closer to him and aimed an elbow at the side of his face. He ducked away, but her other hand was balled into a tight fist and waiting for him. She hit him square in the ribs again. It wasn't as painful as the last hit. He appreciated that she'd attempted to be gentler, but that didn't stop his annoyance from flaring even more.

They continued like that for another hour, and by the time they were done, every muscle in Caeden's body ached from the repeated hits and kicks she'd landed on him. He supposed he was lucky she'd pulled her punches as much as she had, especially after what Ronan told him about her.

Sword fighting came next. Despite his frustration from their hand-to-hand fighting, his mood lifted with the anticipation of the familiar weight of a sword in his hand.

This portion of their training went far better than anything else since he'd spent considerable time practicing it.

In addition to Ronan's occasional training with a sword, he and his father had spent afternoons practicing with dulled wooden swords when he was five or six years old. His father turned it into a game, since there hadn't been a reason for him to need the skill. Amelia had joined them when they'd practiced, and they'd learned how to wield the weapon together. He'd never been as good as his sister was before she'd died.

Back then, his father used to push him to learn it, saying it was a good skill to have, but after the deaths of the queen and princess and the war began, his father stopped making the time to practice with Caeden. At first, it was because of the war and his father's responsibilities that arose from it. But since then, his father had avoided ever starting up again—likely to avoid Caeden getting too many ideas about the front lines.

Eryn cleared her throat from a few yards away, and Caeden turned his attention to her. She tossed him a dulled blade, and he fumbled with it, only barely catching it before it hit the ground at his feet.

The sword was small, and it was weighted for someone who was at least a few inches shorter than him. He tossed it from hand to hand, getting a feel for the blade before Eryn attacked him again.

"Mine isn't weighted properly either," she told him once she noticed what he was doing. She was standing across from him with her sword in her hands. She held it loosely at her side and swung the tip back and forth an inch or two above the ground. "It'll work just fine once you get used to it. And it's helpful to learn to wield a blade that isn't made to your specifications."

Caeden nodded in response, his eyes not leaving the blade in her hand.

Both Ronan and his father taught him the same thing. He could imagine hundreds of instances where that kind of skill would be useful, even something as simple as grabbing the wrong sword by mistake in the heat of a battle.

Eryn lifted her sword, and the two of them circled one another around the edges of the small ring of dirt they stood in.

She lunged for him, the tip of her sword glinting in the sunlight, and he pivoted just out of her reach while slamming the flat edge of his blade against hers, attempting to make her lose her balance.

Their eyes met briefly, and she raised a curious eyebrow at him, surprise etched into the features of her face. "Not bad, little prince," she said as she rightened her feet against the ground.

Eryn slid her sword along his until the tip of her blade almost reached the hilt of his. She pushed off him, the momentum making him trip, and she aimed a blow for his left side while he regained his footing.

Caeden blocked her before the blade connected with his

throbbing side, but it was far closer than he liked. He leaned into his sword, pressing her backward toward the edge of the circle.

A half smile pulled at the corners of her mouth, and her bright blue eyes lit up at the challenge. "Nice try."

He didn't have time to register her words before Eryn angled her body away from him and sidestepped. She released the pressure against his blade so suddenly that he stumbled forward and fell face-first into the dirt.

Pain erupted across Caeden's chest and jaw where his body connected with the hard earth, and he groaned. His sword landed a few feet away from him, but he lost track of it during his fall. A fatal mistake, if she were an enemy attempting to kill him.

In an actual fight, he would've been dead before his body hit the ground.

"Not bad," Eryn mused, more to herself than to him. He expected to hear sarcasm in her voice, but her words came out genuine.

Caeden turned himself onto his back, every muscle in his body begging him to do anything but move. If this was any indication of his daily routine, training with her would be painful. He likely wouldn't be able to walk by the time the sun crested the horizon in the morning.

Eryn offered him a hand up, which he stubbornly refused before he climbed up to his feet. He caught an amused smile playing across her lips, but it was gone before he could register that it was there at all.

They followed up sword fighting with knife-throwing, which he was just as bad at as he was at archery.

By the time they finished with the knives, Eryn's mood had soured back to the same gloomy irritation it was when they'd started.

Explosives were next, and she got through opening the large textbook before he finished explaining that he'd never studied the subject before. He'd only heard of explosives being used a few times over the entire course of the war, and it was easier to push to the side when he'd considered what would get him closer to the battlefield. His explanation resulted in Eryn slamming the book shut with an angry huff. Eryn let out a long sigh, her shoulders sagging as if Caeden had dropped the weight of the world onto them.

They were finished for the day, and she looked like she would give anything to get back to the battlefield rather than stay to finish training him.

"Explosives are the least important, anyway," she stated in a way that suggested she was grasping for anything to keep her calm. "They're a last resort in the field. It's too likely that when one goes off, it'll send shrapnel at some of our men, or blow them up altogether."

He'd heard stories of explosives going off, and they ended in precisely the sort of scenarios she described. None of them were pleasant to hear, but even as his stomach twisted into knots while he'd listened to the advisors go over the details of the carnage, each time the explosives were essential.

"Knife-throwing is vital," she continued, rubbing her temples with her fingers as she stared at the ground between her crossed legs. "It's essential in Dragon Hunting, especially. The beasts are hard enough to kill; if you can land a well-aimed blade, it could be the difference between life and death. You'll need to understand more of the basics surrounding poisons, but they aren't nearly as important. Spies are generally the ones who use them, along with the occasional explosives as well, and I'm assuming you aren't trying to be a spy since I'm the one teaching you and not that moron." She nodded toward Ronan's shack.

Caeden had never specified to anyone what he wanted when it came to training, and it didn't matter, so long as he learned the skills he needed to win a fight against his kingdom's enemies. Dragon Hunting seemed like a useful skill when he considered his end goal.

"Your swordsmanship needs work, but you're better at that than anything else. Hand-to-hand will be our primary focus, and I'll assign you some light reading to brush you up on dragon basics before we dive into that. To kill them, you have to understand what they can do. It will take some time to get you trained, even if I didn't have to work around your 'princely duties.'" She rolled her eyes to exaggerate her already apparent annoyance.

Caeden grimaced at how she said her last words, another spark of irritation bubbling up inside him.

It hadn't been his idea to invite the princesses into the castle, much less to make him the one solely responsible for making sure they were comfortable during their stay, but Aericora needed an army, and he needed to marry one of them to get it. He wasn't as comfortable with the idea as she seemed to imply. He kept his feelings on the topic to himself rather than explain any of it to her. She was here to train him, not get involved in court matters.

It was long past dark out, and the surrounding air held a chill to it that settled itself deep into Caeden's bones. They were heading into winter, but it was the first time since spring that the night air made him shiver and goosebumps rose along his arms and legs.

His entire body ached from the beating he'd taken from Eryn's training, and his head felt heavy from the sudden wave of exhaustion beginning to settle over him. The cicadas chirping would've lulled him to sleep a long time ago, if not for Eryn's intent to push him to the breaking point.

It was good, though. Her pushing him, as much as he disliked her attitude when he didn't do well, meant he would get through his training faster and be a better soldier because of it.

Eryn pulled the ring of keys from where she'd kept them tied to her hip all day, and climbed to her feet in such a swift motion it made Caeden's head spin. He stood after her and followed her to the armory with the weapons he'd used throughout the day in hand. They replaced the weapons in the armory, and Eryn locked the door behind them.

"What time are we starting tomorrow?" Caeden asked as he tried—and failed—to suppress a yawn.

Eryn gave him a look that could kill over her shoulder before she rolled her eyes and turned away. She started back toward the opposite end of the field to return Ronan's keys without looking back to see if he was following.

"Early afternoon," she responded, her voice as cold as the night air around them. "I spoke with the king this morning and convinced him that if he ever wants to see you trained, I'll need at least a few extra hours with you for training each day. I get you have women to entertain or whatever, but I can only afford to waste so much time here. I need to spend as much of that time training you as possible, or you'll never live through your first day on the battlefield."

Chapter 7

Margaid

The castle was bigger than the princess expected. It stood a few stories taller than her own back home, with shining golden tiles lining its pointed towers, and strong gray brick supporting its walls.

The gates depicted a blue and gold shield, a dragon head at its center with golden flames flaring from its open mouth and an overly embellished crown sitting atop its head: Aericora's royal crest. It was worn on the sleeves of the castle guards standing just outside the gates, ready to open them as soon as her coach approached.

Margaid's coachman stopped the horses just outside the gates, the sound of the horses' hooves coming to a sudden stop. Muffled voices filtered into the cabin where she sat as the coachman exchanged words with the castle guards.

She couldn't make out the words, but the coachman needed to provide a parchment stating the purpose for her arrival before they would be allowed entry into the castle. Aericora's King had sent them out recently, but she had yet to see the letter herself.

She twisted her ruby necklace between her fingers as she waited in the coach, butterflies fluttering inside her stomach. Her necklace was her only comfort in this strange place—the only thing she'd brought from home. Everything else, including the clothes she wore, were new.

More words were exchanged outside, and she watched through the small window as the guard stepped aside to allow the coach to pass through the gates. They creaked as they opened, and the carriage suddenly started again, the thumping of the horses' hooves loud in her ears.

The coachman pulled the carriage to a stop in the large courtyard outside the castle's main entrance. A ceremony was planned for her and the other princesses' arrival, but because of the risk Deovaria posed to the kingdom, Aericora canceled it. Instead, they'd decided it was safer for a maid and a few guards to meet them outside and escort them to their rooms before meeting with the king and prince.

The coachman remained seated as two guards and a young maid approached the carriage. One guard knocked on the door before the other pulled it open. Warm sunlight flooded in, and the open door allowed Margaid a full view of the front of the castle.

The second guard, the one who knocked, offered her a hand, which she took, allowing him to help her down the front steps of the carriage. She curtsied before him, unsure what the customs in Aericora were for this sort of encounter. In her home kingdom, it was customary to curtsy to a guard or soldier offering a hand, regardless of rank or station. It was a way they showed politeness, but she knew other kingdoms rarely viewed it in that light.

The guard bowed his head in return, and a smile touched the corners of her lips. She'd done the right thing.

Margaid turned to the young maid standing before her. She looked between eighteen and twenty, with long golden hair that spilled down her back in thick curls. Her bright smile showed off her stark white teeth and made her eyes crinkle at the corners. The girl bowed down in front of her, and Margaid returned the gesture.

"Welcome, Princess Margaid of Crevia," the girl said, her smile widening, if possible. "My name is Grian. I'll be tending to you during your stay in the castle. I trust your travels were quick and enjoyable?"

Margaid returned the girl's easy smile, though it didn't come as easily on her own face as it appeared on the maid's. "Aside from a brief run-in with the Deovarian army, yes," she told Grian. "Your kingdom is lovely. I haven't traveled to see so much forest and greenery before."

Grian's face paled at the mention of the Deovarian's and her cheery exterior faltered for a split second before she pulled it back into place. "Well, I'm glad to hear it wasn't too much trouble," she said. "I'll have the guards fetch your bags and bring them to your room." She gestured past herself toward the castle doors looming ahead of them, their intricate gold detailing catching the morning sun and sending rays of light dancing in every direction. "If you'd please walk with me, I would love to show you around the castle and familiarize you with the main halls before we take you to your room. I apologize for how quickly we will need to get you situated. Breakfast is an hour from now, which doesn't leave us much time to show you around. And I'm sure you would enjoy a warm bath after your travels here."

The words fell from Grian's mouth, and Margaid struggled to keep up with her. She was in much more of a rush than her otherwise relaxed demeanor suggested. "All of that sounds lovely," she assured her. "My apologies for arriving so late. We got held up, as I mentioned. I'd be happy to save bathing until after our meal, if that would allow us enough time to tour the castle?"

Grian shook her head vigorously, her eyes widening. "No, Your Highness! There's no need for that! We'll have plenty of time."

Bathing was necessary then, Margaid noted, putting on another smile. She needed to know her way around more than she needed to bathe before breakfast, but she didn't push that fact any further. She hadn't traveled before leaving for her journey to Aericora, but she wasn't a stranger to being out in the wilderness for extended periods, either. She'd bathed multiple times in streams and rivers they passed on the way here, but that hadn't gotten her anywhere near as clean as a bath inside the castle would. She didn't yet smell enough that she felt uncomfortable dining with the royal family, though.

Grian led her inside the castle. She noticed the vastness first. The hallways were long and wide enough for ten people to fit shoulder to shoulder. Tapestries and paintings hung on the walls, and crystal chandeliers hung from the ceiling above her head. Sconces lined the walls to her left and right, but they were currently unlit and empty, and she assumed their use was reserved for the middle of the night.

She was taken first to the kitchen. Hundreds of servants bustled around her, running to and from in a hurry to complete their tasks before breakfast was served in an hour. Some glanced her way and offered smiles, but they quickly returned to their work. Grian told her she was welcome in the kitchens any time for a snack and that servants worked around the clock to ensure no one went hungry.

Next, they visited the Grand Hall, which was almost empty

aside from two large chandeliers hanging near the center of the room. The room was dark and lacked any real personality, likely because it was rarely used with the war raging.

After was the dining hall, though Grian didn't bother to show her the inside, since they would dine in there soon. The dining hall was followed by the library, which looked the same as every other library she'd ever seen.

"Last, I was going to take you down to the garden and the training field, but I don't think we have enough time for that this morning," Grian said, her cheeks reddening. "The doors are at the back of the castle, so it's a bit of a walk. Though you can see the garden from your room. I will have to show you in person some other time."

Margaid offered her a smile. "That's perfectly fine," she told her, hoping her disappointment didn't show. The view wouldn't do her any good if she couldn't see it in person until someone found the time to give her a second tour. She doubted they would want her snooping around to find it herself.

"They should have your things all set up in your room by now," Grian said, holding the door for Margaid to pass through. "And I will be quick to draw you a bath as soon as we are upstairs."

"Thank you," Margaid told her as she passed through the door, nearly running into a man ahead of her when she did.

She stumbled back a step to avoid hitting him. The powerful stench of bourbon filled her nose as she stepped away from him, scrunching her nose at the stench of alcohol wafting off him.

The man startled when he noticed her, and if he didn't have a cane supporting most of his weight, he would have fallen over. He glanced in her direction, his cheeks red, and a thin coat of sweat glistened on his face, making his honey-colored curls stick to his forehead.

Margaid sucked in a breath, her heart quickening in her chest as she took him in.

"Sorry," the man said, giving her a sheepish smile that came to his lips a little too quickly. "I don't come in here much. Thought your voices sounded like they were comin' from 'round the corner." He laughed, his cheeks turning a deeper shade of red—he was clearly drunk.

Margaid shook her head, pushing away the thoughts of his laugh when she did. "It was my fault," she said. "I wasn't paying attention to where I was going."

The man offered her a crooked smile that rose higher on the right. "My fault for not noticing such a pretty face." He gave her a wink, and she felt her face flush before she turned her head away an inch.

She was here to marry the prince, not have some strange man flirt with her, no matter how attractive he was.

Her face turned redder at the thought.

Grian cleared her throat from behind where Margaid stood in the doorway.

The man glanced over her shoulder before his eyes settled back on Margaid. Something seemed to register in his mind because he offered her a half bow. "Very sorry again, Miss," he told her quickly, and without giving her enough time to form a proper response, he turned and walked away.

Margaid blinked as she watched him go.

Grian cleared her throat again from behind her, and her attention snapped to the woman giving her the tour before she stepped aside so she could exit the library.

"Who was that?" Margaid asked, her eyes trailing after the man.

Grian scrunched her nose in what looked like disgust. "Ronan Atkyn," she answered, her tone matching her expression. "The castle's Head of Security, though he drinks more than anything else. I don't think I've ever seen that man without catching a whiff of alcohol on him." She raised her hands and shrugged. "It's none of my business. The Prince likes him, and the King at least puts up with him. He seems to handle his job well enough, or Deovaria would've taken us by now."

Margaid glanced after the man again, but he had already disappeared around a corner.

"Well then," Grian said, shaking away the look of distaste. "Let's get you to your room and bathed before breakfast, shall we?"

Margaid nodded and followed her to the space she would call home during her stay in the castle.

Chapter 8

Caeden groaned as he rolled out of bed the next morning. Every inch of his body ached after his training the previous day, and a glance in the mirror hanging above the sink in the bathroom confirmed he was just as covered in bruises as his protesting limbs suggested.

A knock came on his bedroom door as he changed into a fresh pair of clothes.

"Hey, princy!" Ronan's voice called from outside before Caeden had enough time to respond to his knocking. "Ya gonna come get the door, or do I gotta break it down?"

Caeden frowned at the still-closed door. Ronan didn't come up to his room often, unless it was to hide from a court meeting he didn't feel like attending.

Caeden shook his head, an amused smile pulling at the corners of his lips. "I'd like to see you try," he called back.

The distinct sound of Ronan's cane hitting the door reached Caeden's ears. "Don't test me, princy!" Ronan warned. Humor was all Caeden heard in his friend's voice.

Caeden snorted a laugh. He almost wanted to see how long

he could make Ronan wait before he lost his mind and broke it down, but he did, in fact, know better than to test him. He walked to the opposite end of the room and pulled the door open. Ronan stood before him, an eyebrow raised impatiently as he tapped his foot against the floor. He was leaning against his cane again, and his face broke into a too-wide grin when his eyes landed on Caeden.

"Drinking already?" Caeden asked.

Ronan smirked at him as he shoved into the room.

"What do you need?" Caeden called as he shut the door.

There wasn't a court meeting to avoid this morning, only the arrival of the princesses, which Ronan wasn't required to attend since no proper welcoming ceremony was being held.

The court decided a couple of days ago that having their arrivals happen as quickly as possible was in everyone's best interest since no one wanted to attract any unwanted attention from Deovaria and the Dragon Lord. If they knew the princesses were coming to strengthen Aericora's army, there was no telling what lengths Deovaria would've gone to in order to ensure the arrangement fell through.

Ronan sat on the edge of Caeden's bed and ran his hands along the covers. "I always forget how soft these things are," he mused as he slumped back against the mattress. He dropped his cane, and it clattered noisily to the floor at his feet.

"You have your own downstairs," Caeden reminded him, amused.

Ronan waved at him without bothering to look up as if shooing away an annoying bug. "It ain't got all the embellishments. Takes all the fun outta it." He ran his hands along the sheets like a child making angels in the snow. "What is this? Silk? So soft." He sighed dramatically.

"If I have them send you down some of your own, will you

tell me what you're doing here? I have a busy morning."

A smile spread across Ronan's face again, and he sat up. "Deal."

Caeden waited for an answer, but instead of providing one, Ronan pulled a flask from where it sat on his belt and uncorked it. The powerful stench of bourbon filled Caeden's room, and Caeden wrinkled his nose in distaste while Ronan took a long swig.

After pulling the bottle away from his lips, Ronan coughed and gave the bottle a confused look. "Strong stuff," he mumbled, lifting the bottle and offering it to Caeden. "Want any?"

Caeden gave him a look, and Ronan replaced the bottle at his hip before lifting his hands in surrender. "I was only offerin'," he said, a grin hiding in the corners of his mouth again. "What did I come here for again? Oh yeah. How'd the trainin' with Eryn go?"

Ronan's sudden shift from playful to serious caught Caeden by surprise. Ronan often came prepared with a serious topic but would get drunk before giving himself enough time to have the conversation. The shift in his demeanor never failed to catch Caeden by surprise.

Caeden shrugged his shoulder. "It went well, I think," he told him. "I'm covered in bruises and bumps, and I will be enduring more later this afternoon. According to her, I'm incompetent in every category but sword fighting."

"Which we both already knew." Ronan laughed.

Caeden cracked a smile. "It worries me, since it's the only area I've had literal years to practice. But it was also the only thing I've practiced consistently, so we'll see." He shrugged again. "I'm not fond of how irritated she gets with me when I don't automatically do well, but I can understand where she's coming from. I hope she'll rein in her anger with me quickly. She seems to know what she's doing, but it makes it hard to focus on what she's trying to teach when she's snapping at me for being incompetent."

Ronan snorted a laugh. "She's like that. I told ya, she'll warm up eventually. You just gotta be patient. She'll be nice every once in a while, but it won't be till she gets to know you that she'll stop bein' mean like that. You've gotta give her time to realize you're actually tryin'."

"How long do you think that'll take? I'm worried she's going to start hitting me for fun if I keep frustrating her," Caeden joked, rubbing a large bruise on his upper forearm where Eryn had struck him with a sword the previous day.

Ronan laughed, clenching his side as if it were the funniest joke he'd ever heard. When he finally gained some composure, the smile that remained on his face was crooked with amusement. He nudged Caeden in the arm with a fist lightly, and Caeden winced from the small burst of pain that flared through him from the bruise Ronan bumped.

"Toughen up, princy. It's gonna take a while."

The dining hall was empty when Caeden arrived for breakfast after Ronan left his room. The smell of pastries drifted into the dining hall from the kitchen a short distance behind the servant's door. Caeden sat in his usual space beside his father's high-backed throne of a chair at the head of the table.

A time when both his father's seat and his mother's sat at the head of the table beside one another flashed through Caeden's memories. After she'd died, according to the court, the space was too open with only a single, smaller chair. At their suggestion, the king had had a larger chair made that practically swallowed him when he sat in it.

Caeden reached for the glass of wine set in front of him and cringed when he did, remembering his training session and the second time Eryn had knocked him to the ground during their sword fighting. Like the first time he'd fallen, he'd lost hold of his sword, which had gone flying into the air, and fell hilt first onto the tender part of his hand between his thumb and first finger. Eryn found it amusing, but even before it swelled up like a particularly nasty bee sting, he hadn't found the same level of joy in the experience.

He picked up the wine glass with his other hand. He'd save irritating the bruise further until his training later.

The large doors at the front of the hall opened, and the king emerged, wearing a grim expression. He kept his eyes downcast as he walked to his place at the table and took his seat. Worry was etched into his features.

"News from the field?" Caeden asked him.

His father nodded as he reached for the glass of wine in front of him and downed the whole thing. He set it down again before speaking, his eyes not leaving the space on the table in front of him. "Another camp was attacked two days ago. We lost a few hundred soldiers and weapons. They'll send you meeting notes soon, but that's the gist."

They were used to hearing similar news from the field, but the lack of good news only made the losses sting more. It made Caeden's stomach twist, and he could see it wearing away at his father.

A young servant peeked her head through the door that led to the kitchen. Her eyes roamed over the empty seats at the table, and she moved to shut the door behind herself again before Caeden's father spoke.

"Wine," the king said, his eyes still downcast. "I need more wine, please."

The girl nodded once before she bowed at the waist and disappeared again to carry out the king's request.

Finally, the king shook his head, knocking himself from whatever trance he'd been in.

His father had been getting noticeably worse over the past couple of weeks. Caeden stopped attending meetings a few days ago, but before he'd left, the amount of time between reports from the field had grown long enough to become concerning.

Caeden felt the same pain and frustration written into each inch of his father's expression, but it wasn't the same. His father felt it more deeply. He was the king. His people were dying each day, and he carried the weight of each death on his shoulders.

The effect it had on his father made Caeden's heart clench painfully.

What he wouldn't have given to have his mother and sister with them. Even with the war raging around them, it would've done his father good to have his mother simply lay a hand on his arm.

Lately, his father started taking a page out of Ronan's book and had been drinking far more often than he ever had before. It wasn't enough to impair his judgment, and he was nowhere near as reliant on it as the castle's Head of Security was, but Caeden worried for his father's health and sanity if he continued to go down the path he was on. Never mind the ways the kingdom would suffer if it went too far.

Caeden clenched his jaw as the anger inside him sparked up again.

This was the Dragon Lord's doing.

If Deovaria's insane king hadn't been so power-hungry and murderous, the war never would've started. Caeden's mother and sister would still be alive. His father wouldn't be killing himself by slaving over his work. His kingdom's people wouldn't be suffering. They wouldn't be *dying*.

Caeden balled his hands into tight fists beneath the table as the hall doors opened again, allowing three strikingly gorgeous women to enter the room. Caeden did his best to relax, even as his stomach twisted itself into knots as the full extent of what their visit meant.

He'd been so focused on the fact that he'd be training with Eryn that he hadn't taken any time since agreeing to the terms the court laid out to let himself fully absorb what their bargain would mean.

Marriage.

The word echoed through his mind.

He could taste the bile rising in the back of his throat before he swallowed, forcing himself to focus his attention on the three women standing in front of him rather than on his nerves.

The women stood in the doorway, looking uncomfortable as they took in the space around them and the two men seated ahead of them.

Caeden had hoped the lack of a welcoming ceremony would make the situation less awkward for all of them, but evidently, he'd been wrong.

The first of the three women wore a dark green dress that brushed the floor as she walked. Her blond hair was done up in a bun on top of her head. She stood with a sense of purpose, with her chin held high and her jaw set. Despite the confidence she emanated, her hands shook at her sides.

The second was a tall woman with dark skin and long hair that fell past her waist. She appeared as on edge as the first princess, but her posture was far more relaxed, as if she'd endured similar situations a hundred times before.

The last was a shorter woman with curly, bright red hair and a too-wide smile. She had laugh lines around the corners of her eyes. Her nervousness outdid the other two women combined, given how she fiddled with the ruby necklace hanging from her neck and how her eyes darted around the edges of the room. Despite her nervousness, something about her gave an intense air of determination that entirely outmatched the other two princesses.

The king rose, but his movement seemed to cost him. He wavered, but Caeden wasn't sure if it was due to the two glasses of wine he'd had, or the sleep deprivation apparent by the bags underneath his father's eyes that were as dark as Caeden's endless bruises.

"Welcome," the king said, spreading his arms out wide in a gesture that was too dramatic for the occasion. "Please, be seated, and we will begin our introductions." His words echoed throughout the room, despite only using a normal tone when he spoke.

The three princesses walked inside, and each sat at the table across from Caeden, their chairs scraping loudly against the tile floor.

Caeden's father cleared his throat, and Caeden avoided eye contact with any of the women for too long. Every bit of his body itched to run away from the scenario looming in front of him, but he'd already agreed to this, and the least he could do was ensure the three princesses couldn't see his discomfort as clearly in his expression as he felt it.

"As I'm sure you are well aware," the king began, "my son, Aericora's Prince and heir, is in dire need of a wife." He said the words lightly, like the prospect of Caeden picking one of them to marry was as simple as picking out a shirt to wear or a meal to eat.

The three women grinned uncomfortably.

Caeden clenched his jaw, his cheeks reddening at his father's words despite himself, but he stayed silent.

The king cleared his throat again and retook his seat. His father reached for his wine glass, which had been refilled for a second time, and Caeden used the opportunity to speak, ignoring the wave of nausea he felt when he opened his mouth to do so. "I'm sure you're all aware of the arrangements that have been made. I'm in need of a wife, but unfortunately, I will also be making this decision based on the military aid your kingdoms will be able to provide us once the marriage is official. I would like to have a good relationship with my future wife and partner, but it is not essential and will come second to the needs and safety of my kingdom."

The three women nodded in unison.

"The decision will be made in just over a month. At that time, we will host a celebration to announce the engagement. You are all welcome to attend the event, and your families have also been invited. However, due to Deovaria's recent attacks, this arrangement may change for your safety."

The women exchanged weary glances with one another, and the princess with the red hair bit her lip.

Caeden cleared his throat awkwardly. "As I'm sure you've all gathered, I'm Prince Caeden," he added.

"Smooth," a voice muttered behind him, and he glimpsed Eryn's bright blue eyes and dark hair as she sat at the table beside him.

He'd known her for only a day, but already he could picture the smirk on her face.

"I'll be ensuring your stay here is as comfortable as it would be in your own homes, and will be taking time each day to meet with you one on one so we can get to know each other," Caeden continued, ignoring Eryn's comment, despite the warmth in his cheeks having grown tenfold. "However, I will be doing this alongside receiving military training from Miss Gedding." He gestured to Eryn beside him. "I will do my best to avoid letting this affect our time together. However, it will mean I won't have the time to leave the castle to show any of you around the kingdom. If that is something you would still enjoy, I can see to it that you are escorted, barring that it is safe to do so. Not that this applies much to this arrangement, but I am twenty. I intend to serve beside my people on the battlefield once I've been married and have finished my training."

He could feel his father's gaze bore into the side of his face. They hadn't discussed Caeden being sent to the battlefield again since their last talk in his father's office, and it was a bold move to say the words aloud. But if his father had time to mull them over before they could speak privately, their conversation would be smoother.

"This is not a matter I will be swayed on, and I will need whoever I wed to accept this," Caeden finished.

The three women shared a glance before the princess with the long hair stood. She bowed her head before meeting Caeden's gaze, and though she didn't seem to know what to do with her hands, she seemed relatively relaxed. "Ceana Sobia, Princess of Nozac," she stated.

Her accent was heavy, and Caeden had to strain to understand her. He'd interacted with multiple ambassadors from Nozac, and they all had the same thick accent, but the ambassadors knew how to adjust their speech when meeting with rulers from other lands to ensure they could understand one another.

"I'm twenty years of age," Ceana continued. "I have had a seat on the council in Nozac since I was seventeen, and in that time, I have grown attuned to handling civil matters of law, as well as managing large events. My kingdom has an army of fifty thousand strong. They are well trained, but will require extra training before they can fight the dragons that Deovaria controls."

Caeden nodded. In his meetings with the advisors, they'd discussed the likely possibility of the soldiers who came from this marriage needing training in dragon slaying. Both Drura and Crevia trained their soldiers in the basics of dragon slaying, but Nozac would need more training to fight effectively alongside Aericora's soldiers.

Caeden gestured for the next woman to speak. It was important, and it would benefit his kingdom for him to choose from either Drura or Crevia, but that fact didn't outright remove Nozac from the running.

The woman in the green dress stood next, bowing her head as she did. She attempted to seem as relaxed as Ceana, but the knuckles of her clasped hands were stark white and suggested otherwise.

"Princess Kylana of Drura," the woman said. "I'm nineteen years old. I have specialized skills in hunting and weaponry and have overseen three military units in the past year. My men are strong and well-trained. I have trained quite a few of them myself. They will be more than capable of jumping straight into a fight, though they could use some mild training in dragon slaying. I trust they will serve you well regardless, should you have me as your wife."

Eryn made an approving sound beside him, and Caeden nearly jumped. He'd forgotten she was there. "If you don't marry her, I might," she mused, barely loud enough for him to hear.

He glanced at her. She had a half grin that matched the one

Ronan wore when he was trying to get under Caeden's skin.

No one else would've been able to hear her, but that didn't stop him from worrying.

The final woman stood as Caeden turned away from the Dragon Hunter. She brushed off the front of her dress before she spoke, her eyes not moving up past Caeden's chest when she did.

"I am Margaid, Princess of Crevia. I am twenty-two years old. I enjoy reading, and have learned to handle most political matters in my home kingdom, along with the help of the court and advisors. I am a fast learner and can quickly adapt to new situations and responsibilities. I am not well aware of the state of my military, but I can assure you the soldiers we have are strong and will serve you well."

From what Caeden recalled from a meeting he'd had with Muire, Crevia's military training covered basics of dragon's physical capabilities. It wasn't anywhere near as much as Drura, who covered more of their history and basic defenses against them, but they would still need less training than Nozac.

"Very good," the king said.

His words knocked Caeden from his thoughts. He glanced at his father, and his eyes lingered for a beat too long on the now-empty glass of wine in front of him.

"As you all know, the prince will be splitting his time between his training and ensuring each of you are comfortable during your stay here," the king continued, reiterating what Caeden had already explained. "We will all be spending our meals together, and Caeden will be devoting time each morning with you to discuss the logistics of what a union might look like."

"And to get to know each of you as well as possible in the upcoming weeks," Caeden added, though he had already said as much moments before. The thought of them thinking he was only meeting with them to discuss possible marriage plans made Caeden feel uneasy, even though that was the exact reason they were here.

Eryn snorted beside him.

Caeden faced her and took her in for the first time that day. She was sitting too straight in her chair, and her breath seemed almost shallow. She was dressed in a formal, light blue dress that hugged her slim waist and was likely the cause of her discomfort, though she looked like she was doing her best to hide it.

"And so that you can get to know one another, yes," the king confirmed after Caeden said nothing else.

The kitchen door opened then, and the servants emerged, each holding a silver platter of food. They placed the platters in front of each of the table's occupants before they left the room again.

The rest of the meal passed slowly. The king and the princesses exchanged small talk, and though Caeden knew he should attempt to join the conversation, he couldn't bring himself to. Instead, he wondered what they would do during his training session later that day.

Caeden still ached from their previous session, but every part of him craved more of the brutal training. He'd wanted to be trained for years, and something about getting it made it impossible to care that his muscles burned with every movement, or that his bones ached. Training was what he needed if he was going to see the Dragon Lord slaughtered for his cruelty.

And, despite the nausea he endured each time he thought of marrying any of the women seated across from him, he'd do whatever was required to be right there when Deovaria's ruler was killed.

Chapter 9

Once their meal ended, Caeden's father and Eryn excused themselves and left the room. Two servants entered as soon as they were gone to remove the discarded dishes on the table. Caeden explained to the princesses how he would only have a few hours to spend with them each day but that they would have servants assigned to them throughout the rest of the day. They were allowed throughout the castle and would be brought whatever they requested to keep them busy and content during their stay.

Ceana and Kylana left after Caeden explained he would find them later that day.

The large wooden doors closed behind them when they left, and an uncomfortable silence filled the space in their wake once the doors shut. Margaid wrung her hands in her lap and her eyes remained glued on the table. A pale pink blush spread across her cheeks, making the freckles dotting her cheeks and nose stand out.

She was pretty in the way one noticed more each time they looked at her.

Caeden cleared his throat awkwardly. "How was your trip here?" he asked, his voice coming out higher than he intended. He fought the urge to clear his throat again.

This entire arrangement was odd. This was a political matter that could determine the fate of his kingdom, yet he was supposed to choose whether he wanted to marry the woman seated across from him. He needed to determine if she would be a good queen for his kingdom, and if her kingdom could provide him with as much aid as they needed.

Margaid glanced up, her bright green eyes meeting his for a split second before she looked away again. Her anxiety had grown since the other women left. "It was lovely, Your Highness."

"Caeden," he corrected her, giving her a smile he hoped would ease her discomfort at least a bit.

She smiled back at him. "Caeden," she remedied. "Your kingdom is very lovely. I enjoy the greenery here."

"I haven't traveled to Crevia before, but I've heard whispers in the halls after our ambassadors have returned. They say that Aericora's beauty can't even compare."

Margaid flushed a bright red at the compliment, and her eyes darted back down to her hands in her lap. "I'm sure that's an overstatement," she mumbled.

"You said you enjoy reading?" Caeden asked her, attempting to keep the silence from filling the room again.

The princess nodded. "Yes," she said so quietly he had to strain to hear her.

"What do you like to read?" he prompted. Maybe he could find some common ground with her on the topic and their conversations wouldn't feel so stilted. He didn't read enough to consider it a hobby, but he had read a considerable number of books on war strategies and books on Aericora and Deovaria's history. He had found little helpful information on the latter subjects, but the war strategies were interesting.

Margaid's eyes widened for a split second before she reached to fumble with her necklace. She'd stopped attempting to hide her fidgeting beneath the table. "I-I like reading about dragons," she answered. "And military strategies. We aren't involved in a war, but we are fearful of being."

Caeden raised a surprised eyebrow at her. He'd hoped to find some common ground but was surprised to hear she read the same things he did. Everything about her so far made the idea of her reading military tactics seem unfitting.

Margaid's words spilled out of her. "I learn what I can to assist my kingdom. We've been discussing recently what our strategy against an attack from Deovaria might look like. I learned a few months ago that the area of study is rather interesting." She swallowed hard but met his eyes for a brief moment before turning away again.

Caeden nodded. "I enjoy the subject, too," he told her. "I hope it will lend well to fieldwork once I finish with my training."

"Why are you so intent on learning to fight?" Margaid asked suddenly. Her nervousness was replaced with an intense curiosity, but it disappeared quickly, and she continued fidgeting with her necklace.

Caeden's face warmed at the question. He found himself answering honestly after seeing the earnestness in her gaze.

"I want to be the one to kill the Dragon Lord," he told her, shrugging a shoulder as if it were the simplest thing in the world.

Her eyes widened, and shock hid in the edges of her expression. "Oh."

Caeden ran a hand through his dark hair and turned away from her. "And to fight alongside my people," he finished, hoping maybe the rest of the truth would ease the surprise etched into her features. "I can't stand to watch them die while we're all sitting here, tucked away from the horrors they're facing out there every day."

Her expression softened. "I'm sure your people appreciate your compassion," she told him. A kind smile spread across her crimson lips.

They lapsed into the uncomfortable silence Caeden had wanted to avoid, and it only broke when two servants entered with their dessert.

He and Margaid spoke briefly between bites of their dessert. She talked more about her journey to Aericora: how one of the carriage wheels broke halfway here, how her guards had to rush to fix it before the sun set and they couldn't see anything, and how they'd seen the dragons swooping low in the distance as they'd neared the castle earlier that morning.

When they finished eating, Caeden led her to her room. He explained that her servants would arrive shortly to ensure she had everything she needed and to help her unpack her belongings if she hadn't already finished. They said polite goodbyes, and she closed the door behind herself, leaving him alone in the hallway.

Next came his meeting with Ceana, and he found her waiting for him in the library, a leather-bound book in her hands. She opened it to a page depicting a large painting of a festival with hundreds of people dancing in the town's center.

"May I sit with you?" he asked as he came up beside her.

Ceana glanced at him briefly before her eyes returned to her book. She nodded once, but avoided meeting his gaze.

Caeden sat beside her awkwardly and waited for her to flip to the next page. She finished the page she was on before she folded down the upper corner and closed the book. She set her book down on the coffee table and turned her attention to him.

"I'm going to be blunt with you," Ceana said, before Caeden had enough time to open his mouth to say a proper hello. "I have very little interest in being your queen. I am here because my kingdom could use the money, and my parents thought it would be a good opportunity to form an alliance while also paying off our debts. I'm not here for love, and I have expectations that must be met before I will accept any proposal."

Caeden stared at her while she spoke, doing his best to decide on a reasonable response. He appreciated her openness, but her bluntness surprised him enough that his mind couldn't form a coherent thought.

"Okay," he settled with.

She nodded. "I felt you should know before we proceed."

"What kind of expectations do you have?"

Ceana cracked a half smile and sat back further in her chair. She was more relaxed now than she'd been with everyone in the dining hall earlier that morning.

"I need to know that I will have equal say, as your queen," she told him. "I don't plan to ever sit as someone's trophy. I certainly will not agree to it without any real reason, and my kingdom has not given me reason enough to stay if I don't want to."

The corner of Caeden's mouth twitched upward. He liked her more than he'd expected to.

"Queens in Aericora, regardless of where you were born and raised, are given equal say to the King," Caeden assured her. "There are certain matters where the King's opinion will carry more weight, or the Queen's will, but that is based on their experience, not their title."

Ceana nodded, seeming to mull over his words. "How many

are on your council?" she asked, curiosity lighting her features.

Caeden's smile widened before he could stop it. "Ten. Three military veterans, four courtiers assigned to ensure our people's needs are met, and one international advisor, the King, and myself."

Ceana clucked her tongue. "And, I assume, the future Queen would also have a seat, based on what you have said?"

He nodded. "Yes. We have both men and women on our council, and our future Queen would be no exception. Meetings were never held without my mother present when she was alive."

She looked pleased with his answer. "Good."

Caeden shifted in his seat while Ceana drifted into her thoughts. He liked how interested she was in the court. A future queen should be, and he hoped his future wife would be as invested in political matters as he was required to be.

"When you are sent to the field, do you still intend to act as King?" Ceana asked. "Provided that the war is still in progress when you assume the throne, of course."

He frowned, more to himself than to her. He wasn't sure how to answer her question. If things lined up in the way she was implying, he would still be Aericora's King, regardless of where he was. Leaving to fight didn't change that fact.

"I'm not sure I understand," he told her, offering her an apologetic look. "I would still be King, regardless of where I am."

She made an almost impatient gesture with her hand. "Yes, but would you ask that the court's decisions be halted? Could the Queen's final decision pass without you present?"

Caeden's head spun as he thought over how to answer her question as truthfully as he could. He hadn't thought so far into his future to consider the possible scenario. He'd considered what his life would look like once he was king and what it would look like when he was out in the field, but he hadn't considered the two scenarios together. He avoided imagining what it would be like if his father died at all.

Caeden shook his head and turned back to Ceana. "I suppose so," he answered, still unsure what answer she sought. The exact scenario would make his answer vary, but all he knew for certain was he would not allow the court to operate without at least receiving a report if he happened to be stationed on the battlefield while ruling. But if he was king when the opportunity to travel to the field arose, he doubted he would opt to go at all.

He didn't yet have the same responsibilities as his father. He could opt out of court meetings, and nothing would fall apart. The king couldn't.

"Good," Ceana said again, a smile lighting her face. "I know you said the King and Queen are equal here, but in my kingdom, the same is said, yet it is also very common for the Queen to be oppressed. I won't stand for that."

It was a valid concern. In her situation, he would've asked her very similar questions.

Ceana clasped her hands in front of her. The gesture seemed far more relaxed than her calculating expression suggested. "How many children would you require of me?" she asked next, and Caeden was sure his eyes bulged out of his head.

That wasn't something he'd expected her to ask at all.

"I – um – I don't know," he stammered. "An heir would be necessary, but any more than that would be up to us to decide."

She nodded and clucked her tongue.

This definitely wasn't the conversation he'd been expecting. He'd expected questions, but things like this hadn't crossed his mind.

From what the court explained about her, she was third in

line for the throne of Nozac, and he wondered whether that led her to be more interested in the specifics of her role as Aericora's Queen. Margaid certainly hadn't asked these sorts of questions, but she was guaranteed a throne whether Caeden proposed to her or not since she was the firstborn and heir.

It worried him that she was so concerned with whether she would face oppression as queen the further they got into their conversation. The manner in which she spoke made him worry she was too power-hungry. She'd said she wasn't interested in being queen, yet each question she asked contradicted that statement.

Ceana continued to ask her questions, and Caeden's worry only intensified after their meeting was over.

He shook himself as he exited the library after saying his goodbyes. He liked how interested she was in court matters, but it was also the same thing that made him worried about picking her. But this was their first time speaking. Hopefully, she was getting her questions out of the way, and the power-hungry impression he'd gotten from her would go away.

His meeting with Kylana was last. He found her in the training field, pulling back the string of a bow and arrow aimed for a target ahead of her that already had multiple arrows embedded into its center.

She offered him a bow as he approached, and he politely declined. His arms were still sore from the day before, and he'd rather save practicing until his training later that day with Eryn.

"You're a very good shot," Caeden commented as he watched her loose an arrow. It landed in the center of the target along with the others.

Kylana glanced over her shoulder at him. "I've been doing this for most of my life," she told him with a proud smile. She refocused on the target and made another shot. The center mark was already so full of arrows that this shot split another in half.

"You run the military back in your kingdom, right?" he asked her, recalling some of the information he'd learned about her from the advisors. She'd touched on it during their meal, but hadn't talked about her rank or position.

"Since I was fifteen," she answered, not looking back at him as she knocked another arrow. "I made a lot of soldiers angry when I was first assigned, but they got used to it. They've come to respect me since, rather than just thinking of me as a bored princess who was handed an entire army to do with as she pleased."

"That must've been difficult." Caeden had only been attending court meetings when he was fifteen. He'd been doing so for longer than his kingdom typically allowed, but it had been a lot to take in, despite having done it for years by the time he was that age. He couldn't imagine overseeing that much at such a young age.

Kylana snorted a quiet laugh. "It was hell for the first few months. I set them straight quickly enough. I'm unsure how well I would've handled it if they'd kept it up much longer."

"Would you want to continue leading the military if you became Queen here?" he asked her, his mindset still considering all the logistics since his meeting with Ceana.

Kylana laughed again, this time loudly. "I couldn't live without this," she told him. "I could step down, since it would be required of me to do so, but I don't think I could live without being a military officer. I don't want to be stuck up in a castle. I'll act as Queen and do all that is required of me, but I would refuse to do so if I cannot be a military officer as well."

Caeden nodded as he listened. He'd expected her answer would be something along those lines, given her history in her kingdom and the reputation that preceded her. She was as highly ranked and admired in her kingdom as Eryn was in Aericora.

Their dynamic likely wouldn't work well if he chose her, though. He also wanted to fight, and the court wouldn't allow them to both take time away from their responsibilities at the castle, especially not at once. They already opposed Caeden going, and it would be a struggle to convince them to allow him to leave. If his future wife also wanted to leave, they would fight him even more.

At least, once he was married, there would be someone to claim the throne if something happened to him and his father.

Kylana cracked an amused smile. "You don't seem to like that answer very much."

Caeden felt his face grow hot and turned away from her. "No, it's not that," he explained. "I understand where you're coming from. I also want to fight alongside my people, but I can't see the court loving the idea of both of its future rulers risking their lives."

Kylana lowered her bow for the first time since he'd arrived and turned to him with a confused look. "Why do you want to fight so badly?" she asked him.

It was similar to Margaid's earlier question, but he didn't have the same urge to tell her the truth.

"I want my people to know we are just as involved in this war as they are. Right now, they can't see that. They see that we're shut up in the castle constantly. I'm sure they all know we are doing our part to help win this war from here, but I don't want them to lose that understanding. I think it could do our people good to see someone of higher status risking their lives like everyone else is."

Kylana nodded. "I understand that. But wouldn't Aericora's people understand just as well if their future Queen fought in the war instead of their future King? They may even respond better to it if it were me, since I'm not of Aericora blood and would still be risking my life for this kingdom."

Caeden couldn't argue with that. The people would love it if their future queen from another land risked her life for the people of her new kingdom. However, the possibility remained that they could see it the opposite light, and assume Aericora's born rulers were too scared to take the risk themselves.

He chose not to say that out loud because what he'd told her wasn't the only reason he wanted to fight, and he wasn't prepared to share the whole truth.

Kylana turned and knocked another arrow. "I'm sure we could figure something out, if it came to it," she told him. "If you should choose me as a wife, we could agree on something that would make us both happy."

"I'm sure we could," Caeden agreed, though he worried just how true those words were.

Chapter 10

Caeden felt defeated when he finally finished his meetings with each of the three princesses. A marriage with any of them would be more complicated than he'd anticipated. Given what his kingdom needed, Margaid seemed like his best option so far. Or so he assumed, since she hadn't made it her top priority to express how much she wanted to fight in the war like Kylana had, or already give him a glimpse into how power-hungry she could be like Ceana.

As he considered his time with each of them, nothing stood out personality-wise to him about any of them. His interactions with them were pleasant, but he hoped something would stick out about one of them to make his decision easier. It was too soon to hope for that, but it still left him uneasy about the situation. He reminded himself repeatedly that this was only his first day with them as he wound his way through the halls toward the training field to meet with Eryn.

Eryn waited for him when he emerged through the back door. The bright sunlight assaulted his eyes and sent a wave of warmth over his body that was almost uncomfortable as he exited the castle. She sat on the ground near the back door with her legs crossed beneath her. A delicate-looking dagger with intricate patterns engraved into the metal along the fuller rested in her hand. The tip was pressed into the wooden upper limb of a bow. At first glance, the bow looked identical to the ones in the armory, but upon closer inspection, he noticed this one had hundreds of carvings engraved in the wood.

Clearly, this wasn't the first time she'd waited for a student.

As Caeden shut the door, Eryn set the bow down in her lap and replaced the dagger into the holster strapped to her thigh on her right leg. In one swift motion, she slung the bow over her shoulder while simultaneously lifting herself to her feet.

"About time," she grumbled as Caeden took a step closer.

Caeden bit the inside of his cheek to keep himself from saying anything to stoke the flames of her ever-present annoyance. He reminded himself again that he'd only known her for a day, and Ronan warned him it would take time for her to warm up.

"Nice to see you, too," he told her evenly, despite the sarcasm that begged to slip into his tone. "I had to meet with the princesses."

He could almost feel the frustration rolling off her in waves when the princesses or his future marriage were brought up. She'd made it clear she had no interest in being here, and the fact that she could only spend part of her day training him because of his arrangement with the princesses likely didn't make her happier.

"Mhm," Eryn grumbled as she placed her hands on her hips and rolled her eyes.

Caeden noticed for the first time that she had a large satchel slung over her shoulder beneath her bow. A surge of excitement fluttered through him. The yellowed corners of multiple pieces of paper peeked out from beneath the leather flap that kept the bag closed, and he raised an eyebrow at it.

"Well, you're here now," Eryn huffed. She turned on her heel before giving him a chance to respond and started toward the forest behind the training field.

Caeden followed. They hadn't yet covered anything about dragons, and he assumed the hundreds of papers filling her bag were intended to change that.

Eryn led him into the forested area where a small gazebo sat, with a table in its center. Unlike the last time Caeden was here, it was covered in dirt and grime. Time had allowed vines to grow up along its sides, and moss and mold grew between the cracks in what used to be pristinely painted wood.

Caeden hadn't been this far into the forest since he was a child. He and Amelia came back here often when they were kids, but he didn't have the enthusiasm for it that she had, and he hadn't bothered to venture back this far since she'd died.

A distant part of him wondered how Eryn knew about this little spot, but he didn't dwell on it.

The gazebo was built before Caeden was born. It was a gift from his father to his mother before they were married. There wasn't much Caeden knew about his mother's life before she moved into the castle and married his father, but he knew that wherever she'd lived before, there was a tradition where couples were married at sunset inside similar structures.

Their wedding took place in the castle, since it was Aericora's tradition for royals to be married in the throne room, despite being far less romantic in every way imaginable. After their wedding, Caeden's father and mother held a private reception out here. Given the state of it now, it must have been another thing his father found too painful after they died.

Eryn plopped down on one side of the small, dirt-covered

table beneath the gazebo. She cleaned the tabletop with the side of her hand, attempting to rid it of the filth while Caeden sat opposite. Once it was as clean as she could manage, she pulled the satchel off her shoulder and set it on the table beside her. From it, she pulled a large stack of what could've been hundreds of sheets of paper.

All Caeden saw was a hand-drawn diagram of a dragon depicted on the top sheet.

His eyes widened as he took in the intricately drawn details of the image. "Did you draw all of these?" he asked before he could think better of it.

Eryn glanced up at him through thick eyelashes. "Most of them," she answered before she continued setting the pages out on the table between them. She stayed silent for multiple moments while she worked on getting a few specific drawings into place and the others organized in a stack she kept in her lap. Once she finished setting them all out, the only ones remaining on the table depicted a different portion of a standard Royal Talon dragon, one of the most common breeds.

Eryn had assumed his knowledge of dragons was scarce, and she had been right. Caeden had only learned a few things from whispered conversations he'd accidentally overheard in hallways or from an occasional fairytale book as a child. The only true thing he could recall hearing was that Royal Talons were one of the deadliest breeds of dragons.

"Royal Talons," Eryn started, pointing at the drawing Caeden stared at.

It was a complete picture of the dragon, showing each part of its large, muscular body, from its long snout to the tips of its tail and wings. This one was blue, but they ranged in color to anything imaginable. They had four long, muscular legs, with two wings that protruded from their body at the shoulders on either side. Two horns jutted from its head, each curling into a single ringlet. They glittered in the picture, or so he assumed, from the small stars drawn in white along each one.

"They're the most dangerous breed. They're also among the most common breeds used by the Dragon Lord and his men. They are the only breed large enough to ride, and their ability to use minimal amounts of magic to manipulate their appearances or to manifest deadly substances from thin air are some of the most useful tools to the Deovarian army. They stand between forty and fifty feet in height when standing straight, and about eighty to ninety feet long." She tapped her index finger against the drawing to indicate the dragon's straight neck.

Caeden nodded, mentally noting manipulation and manifestation magic, along with their approximate size.

Eryn hadn't told him whether she'd test him on anything he learned. His progress in physical categories and weapons would be easy enough to gauge, but she hadn't talked much about this portion of his training. He supposed the field would test him at some point, but hopefully she wouldn't let him get to that point without ensuring her training had taken hold.

"Drakes are different," Eryn continued, pulling his attention back. "They're vicious little bastards. They can't use magic, but they'll tear you to shreds in seconds if they get the opportunity. Don't give them the chance."

The grim look on her face sent a chill running up Caeden's spine. She must have witnessed it multiple times for that kind of darkness to shadow her features.

"Injuries don't have any effect on them. They either can't feel pain, or they don't care, we haven't figured out which one it is yet. If you come across a drake, you must kill it before it will stop trying to kill you."

Eryn reached into her lap and produced another hand-drawn

image; this was one of a much smaller dragon with rows of jagged teeth visible even when its mouth was closed. It had long, razor-sharp talons and spikes lining the joints of its four wings and four stout legs.

Caeden shuttered at the thought of those tearing into his skin.

"Wyverns are more," she pursed her lips and tilted her head from side to side, contemplating how to accurately describe the creature, "elegant," she settled with. "They are beautiful creatures. Their movements are graceful, and their scales shimmer in the sunlight. They aren't useful on the battlefield, though. They can create illusions with their magic, which is great for disguising spies and orchestrating sneakier attacks, but not much else. They aren't an aggressive breed, even when soldiers attempt to command violence from them. They rarely obey, and we've started to see fewer and fewer of them brought to the battlefield. Very few soldiers are afraid of them anymore."

She pulled out another drawing. This one showed a larger, thinner dragon with long, almost delicate wings. Its talons looked like they had evolved to make them inept in killing and tearing apart prey, but perfect for perching in the rocky terrain of the Rayfait Mountains. Unlike the other dragons, the wyvern only had two legs, and its wings were nearly three times the length of their body.

He'd heard very little about any dragons other than Royal Talons, and certainly nothing about their magic being used to disguise spies. He was present for multiple court meetings where spies had been discussed, but he couldn't recall any of them having been disguised.

He'd missed few meetings, and even fewer where the notes never made it to him. It was possible he'd missed hearing about it, but it seemed unlikely that would be the case.

"Spies?" he asked, his eyes still focused on the image in

Eryn's hand.

Eryn nodded solemnly. "We've come across a few in the past couple of years," she explained. "We found them near the posts closest to the border. They were never disguised well, and we always discovered them quickly. The Dragon Lord's army would snatch a couple of our soldiers in the field during a fight and replace them with their men disguised to look identical to the soldiers they'd taken." She shrugged as if this wasn't anywhere near as monumental as it truly was. "They didn't know the personalities of the soldiers they were swapping out, and a friend or military leader would pick up on the differences right away. We'd have them executed as soon as we found proof."

"I've never heard of that," Caeden told her, even as his stomach turned uncomfortably at the realization that this information must have never made its way back to the castle.

She shrugged again. "We've had more problems with non-disguised spies in the past. Your court probably focused on those rather than the swapped men. I only know of four in total, and that's over multiple years. It probably didn't seem important enough."

He doubted that would've been the case, but he didn't state that aloud. Something as monumental as swapped soldiers never would've been so carelessly overlooked. It was more likely that someone had intercepted the messenger. He hadn't known their communication issues had been happening for so long. The court only noticed the communication issue last year, and it hadn't seemed so severe. If they'd missed this message years ago, what could they have missed since then?

Messengers often went missing, but that had been easy to watch closely. It was hard to miss information if you knew a messenger had never returned. Less than half of the messengers they sent ever survived, which was a trend since the beginning of the war, but there hadn't been much missed information until recently, despite the messengers disappearing. Or so they had thought.

It was the primary reason the princesses' arrival had been held as quietly as they could manage.

But, in this case, it was probable that a soldier from the field was tasked with informing the court rather than waiting for a messenger to arrive to relay the information. If that were the case, it would've been much harder for anyone to notice since no one in the field watched for those sorts of disappearances.

Eryn refocused her attention on the sketches, and Caeden did his best to do the same.

She moved some drawings aside and centered a second picture showing the entire body of a Royal Talon. Arrows in the picture pointed to particular body parts, and a few of them had circles connected to the ends with magnified images of the given portion of the body.

"Dragons are tough," Eryn said bluntly, returning to the topic.

She reached for her bag and pulled out a small notebook and pen. She tossed them haphazardly to Caeden, who fumbled when he caught them since she'd offered him no forewarning.

"Thanks," he said, doing his best again to keep any irritation out of his voice.

"However," she continued, ignoring him, "they aren't completely resistant to our weaponry. There are twelve weak points every breed of dragon has. Some have more, but not many."

She paused, and Caeden took the opportunity to open the notebook and uncap the pen. Regardless of whether she tested him, he couldn't afford to forget this if he wanted to live through the war.

"First are the eyes," Eryn said, tapping the image on the table, her finger smudging the charcoal lines of the drawing. "Obviously. Then the nostrils, a small space right beneath their chin." She pointed to the tender area at the top of her throat with her finger for reference. "Behind the jaw bone on both sides of the face, the base of each wing—which is either two or four per dragon—a thin strip of skin along their chest and belly, and the last ones are the joints where their legs attach to their bodies—their armpits, I suppose you could call them—which, again, is either two or four per dragon."

Caeden jotted down notes on the pad of paper as fast as he could while she spoke. His handwriting was sloppy, but she was speaking too fast to allow him enough time to ensure his notes were legible. He could discern most of his writing and hoped it would be enough.

"Most of the areas are no more than six to ten inches wide, except for the strip on the belly of larger dragons," Eryn told him. "The coloring of their weak spots is almost always lighter since they don't have the thicker, protective scales in those areas. But dragons are fast when you're firing at them, so chances are you won't be able to make out the color difference, anyway. Most soldiers rely on their memory of diagrams rather than their ability to see their target."

Caeden couldn't hit his target when it was still. He would need much more practice before he'd be able to manage something that advanced.

He recalled stories he'd heard from servants in the castle hallways of soldiers who had killed dragons. Most exaggerated the details and focused primarily on how the soldier's hands shook while they made the shot. Most always ended the story with the soldier's arrow landing between the dragon's eyes and puncturing straight through to its brain, which Caeden had never believed, but now knew was outright impossible.

Very few people talked about dragons in the calm manner Eryn did. Likely because most had never seen a dragon before, much less up close. Eryn had seen hundreds of them by now and had dedicated years to studying them and teaching herself and others how to fight them and win.

Eryn explained in detail each of the dragon breeds and their separate capabilities. She listed how the Royal Talons could use their abilities to spray fire, ice crystals, acid, water, or direct sunlight at their enemies. She said that so far, they'd learned never to assume something was impossible for Royal Talons to create. She talked about the drakes and their never-ending bloodlust, and wyverns and the songs they sang to everyone fighting on the battlefield while they looked on.

It was hours past dark when they were done with their training for the day.

They headed back inside, and Eryn took him to the library. She picked out five separate books on dragons for him to read and finish within the next couple of days, which was far more than her earlier comment about assigning light reading suggested.

He didn't know when he would find the time to read them all, but voicing that wouldn't end well, so he kept his mouth shut.

Chapter 11

Ronan

A soft knock on the door of Ronan's shack made him jump. It wasn't Caeden. He would've heard him approaching long before he knocked with how loud his steps always were. And it certainly wasn't Eryn. She wasn't capable of being gentle with anything. Few others visited him, and never at such a late hour.

He raised a curious eyebrow at the door and climbed to his feet, using the edge of the couch to help support his weight. His leg ached when he put weight on it, and he downed the rest of the whiskey in his glass to help dull it.

Another knock came on the door as he reached for his cane.

"I'm comin'. Gimme two seconds," he called to whoever stood outside.

No answer. Strange.

Ronan pulled the door open to reveal the same redheaded girl he'd almost run into that morning. The princess he'd been stupid enough to flirt with before realizing who she was. Idiot.

The princess smiled, her cheeks reddening along with the bridge of her nose, highlighting her freckles. Damn, Caeden was lucky.

"Hi," she said nervously, glancing into the shack past him before her eyes settled on his face.

"Hi." He leaned his shoulder against the door to support his weight rather than his cane. "What can I do for ya?" He said the words evenly despite the confusion threatening to spill into his tone.

She should've been asleep with all the others in the castle. What was she doing here instead? Most importantly, why was she attempting to find him? Knocking on his door hadn't been a mistake, or she would've responded differently when he'd answered.

"I'm sorry for the intrusion," she said, which didn't answer his question. "I just…" she trailed off, her face darkening. "I heard from a maid that you know the prince?"

Well, that made more sense.

Ronan raised an eyebrow at her. "What's it to ya?"

Although his friendship with Caeden was well-known, he couldn't see how that related to her being on his doorstep.

The princess shrugged a single shoulder, her eyes finding the ground at her feet as one of her hands trailed to her chest. He could make out the indentation of a necklace beneath the thick black cloak she wore, but aside from that, the cloak hid everything but her face. Most of her curly red hair hid beneath the hood as well.

"I talked with him earlier, but he seems rather reserved," she explained, looking more comfortable as the words spilled out of her mouth. "I wanted to see if you'd tell me a bit about him. What's he like? Like as a person once he warms up to people?"

It was odd that she'd opted to ask him of all people, but then again, Caeden's whole situation was a mess.

Ronan cracked a smile and stepped aside so she could walk

past him. She did, but stood a few paces inside the doorway, and her uneasy expression suggested she didn't know what to do next.

He hobbled to the couch, the pain in his leg duller since the alcohol had taken effect but never as far gone as he wished. He threw himself down against the cushions, allowing his cane to fall aside, before he gestured to the princess to come further into the room.

She stepped closer but didn't take a seat. Only stood uncomfortably beside the couch.

"He's a lot," Ronan said, a light laugh leaving him as thoughts of his friend swirled in his head.

The princess tilted her head to one side. "How so?"

"Well, he's got his head set on what he's got his head set on, and there ain't nothin' you can do about that. Stubborn as hell, that man. Fights for what he wants. Loyal, though. If he cares for you, he'll be there no matter what ya need."

Since he'd known him, Caeden had taken care of him twice when he'd had a bit more to drink than he should've, but he didn't tell that to the princess. Only Caeden and Eryn had done that for him. No one else knew of the instances, and he planned to keep it that way.

The princess nodded. "He seems to care for his people if he is so intent on fighting in the war."

Ronan nodded, careful with his word choice, when he continued. If Caeden hadn't told her his true intentions behind wanting to fight, he wouldn't be the one to let it slip. "He loves his kingdom very much," he agreed with her. "He can be a bit too hyper-fixated. Still doesn't seem to realize the risk he poses to his kingdom if he gets his royal ass killed on the battlefield."

Her eyes flicked down to the cane resting against the couch, then to his hurt leg before meeting his gaze again. "Were you a soldier before coming here?"

The question didn't apply to Caeden, but his thoughts were blurring too much for him to care. "Yes," he answered, but didn't elaborate. She was indirectly asking about his leg and whether the war had been the cause of his injury, but he didn't know her well enough to touch that subject. He'd never known anyone well enough to touch that story.

The princess stepped further into the living space and sat on the couch opposite him.

Ronan picked up the bottle of whiskey on the coffee table and poured himself another glass. "Want any?" he asked her, and she shook her head, a few of her pretty curls falling free from her hood when she did. He downed the glass while the princess collected her thoughts and prepared her next question.

"Do you think he'll live through it if he goes?" she asked, her fingers finding the necklace at her throat again.

The question surprised him. He wasn't sure how he was supposed to know that, but he couldn't fault her for asking, either. He could guess the chances of Caeden's survival far better than most others.

Ronan poured himself another glass. If he was going to talk about his friend's chances of death, he needed a lot more alcohol. He swallowed it all in one large gulp before he cleared his throat. "I don't know," he told her. "He ain't well trained yet, and I don't know how far Eryn can get him 'fore they're gonna decide she needs to go back."

"Eryn?" the princess asked.

Ronan cracked a smile. "We fought together. We've been on a first-name basis for a long time."

The princess nodded. "Is she good enough to get him there quickly?"

Eryn was the best. But that fact didn't suddenly make the

impossible achievable. She could eventually get Caeden fully trained, but he had no way of knowing the exact timeframe she had to accomplish that goal.

"She's the best," he answered. "But I can't say I know whether or not she'll have any luck."

She nodded again, a solemn look coming to rest on her face. She placed one hand in her lap, and the other continued to fiddle with her necklace before she let out a deep breath and pulled back her hood. "Is the offer still open for a cup of that?" she asked, nodding toward the bottle of whiskey on the table.

Ronan laughed lightly, surprising himself when he did. "Of course, Your Highness," he said, a joking tone to his voice that he hadn't intended to be there. Maybe those extra drinks hadn't been a great idea, given that she'd come to talk about serious topics.

The princess smiled in return.

Ronan moved to climb up from the couch, but the princess shot to her feet first. "Don't," she blurted. "Just tell me where the glasses are. I can get it myself."

Ronan stared up at her. She'd seemed so uncomfortable only a moment ago. "They're in the cupboard over the sink in the kitchen. Right side."

The princess nodded and walked through the small hallway separating the couch he sat on from the kitchen. He watched her go; his eyes focused on the way her crimson curls bounced with each step she took. He shook himself as she pulled down a second glass and closed the cupboard again. She returned to the living room and sat on the opposite end of the couch. Ronan picked up the bottle of whiskey and poured another glass for himself, despite his better judgment, before filling hers.

"Thank you," she said, before lifting the glass to her lips and downing the whole cup just as fast as he had his last. She didn't even shutter after swallowing the last bit of it.

His jaw nearly dropped open before a half smile formed at the corners of his mouth. He chuckled. "Damn, princess. Where'd ya learn to do that? Thought all you royals only drank wine."

The princess laughed, her cheeks reddening again. Her laugh was warm and gentle, and somehow even more attractive than watching her drink the whole cupful of whiskey straight.

He swallowed hard, pushing the thoughts from his head.

"I drink my fair share of liquor," she said with a sheepish shrug.

"I do too, but that's still impressive."

She smiled, but a faraway look in her eyes replaced it quickly. She looked down at the glass in her hand. "I don't know what I got myself into," she said, a light laugh escaping her as she swirled the nonexistent whiskey in her glass.

He looked up at her face again, taking in the light blush beneath her freckles.

"He seems nice, but all of this is a lot," she told him. "I don't know why I agreed to this in the first place."

Ronan opened his mouth to respond, but his mind was blank. He didn't have a solution for her. Aericora needed this arrangement, and her kingdom would get something from it too, which was likely why she'd agreed to it to begin with, but restating that wasn't helpful.

She took a deep breath and let it out, sitting up straighter. "Well, I'm here now," she said, her eyes still on her glass. "All I can do is make the best of it."

Ronan picked up the whiskey bottle again. "I find this helps me make the best of any situation," he joked, offering the bottle to her.

She laughed, and he felt his face warm the slightest bit at the sound of it. "If I didn't know any better, I'd think you were trying to get me drunk."

He shrugged. He felt his face heat more, but ignored it. "Best way to be," he said. "Only if ya wanna be, though."

The princess smiled and took the bottle from him. "I'll drink to that."

She poured herself another glass and handed him back the bottle, which he took before downing half of it. She looked at him over the rim, a grin pulling at the edges of her mouth, the glass only an inch from her lips when she spoke. "I'm Margaid, by the way," she said. "Princess of Crevia and all that."

Ronan laughed. "Nice to meet you, Miss Princess of Crevia and all that. I'm Ronan."

Margaid's smile widened. "Nice to meet you, Ronan."

His heartbeat quickened at hearing his name on her lips.

Caeden was one lucky man.

Chapter 12

By the time Caeden finished his training, he'd missed dinner with his father and the three princesses. He should've felt bad, but part of him was relieved he could avoid attending. He hadn't outright disliked his time spent with each of the princesses, but the tense atmosphere they'd endured that morning for breakfast wasn't something he'd been excited to repeat. Not right after Eryn finished filling his head with more dragon facts than he could count.

He wouldn't miss a meal again out of respect for the princesses and their time, but the silence he'd enjoyed while he ate alone in his room made him almost wish he could get away with skipping meals altogether.

It was close to midnight by the time he'd finished eating and was making his way through the castle halls toward the training field.

A maid passed him as he walked, startling him in the darkness. He hadn't expected to pass anyone on his short walk outside at this hour. The maid was young, and her skittish air matched that of the girl who found him outside a few days prior.

She held a large pile of towels in her hands that brushed her chin, and she was struggling to balance the mountain of clean linens. Caeden moved to the side to allow her to pass, but she stumbled, and the laundered cloths fell to the floor in a heap at Caeden's feet.

"Oh no!" she yelped, her voice so squeaky and high it pierced his ears as it bounced off the stone walls around them.

The maid fell to her knees and began picking up the towels.

"I'm so sorry, Your Highness," she squeaked as she worked at an inhuman speed to pick up the laundry. "Please forgive me."

"Please, don't apologize," he told her as he bent beside her and helped her gather the cloths.

He glanced up, observing how she refolded them, and copied the action with the ones he'd collected before adding them to her small stack.

The girl's cheeks reddened in the darkness when she noticed that her stack of towels had doubled in size. "Th-thank you, Your Highness," she stammered, her cheeks darkening so much they matched her scarlet lips.

"Not a problem at all," he told her as they stood again. "May I ask a favor of you whenever you have a free moment?"

She glanced at him, surprise etched across her face. She nodded her head vigorously before her eyes found the floor again. "Of course, Your Highness."

"Please ask your superior to ensure an order is placed for a new pair of silk sheets. Ronan Atkyn, our Head of Security, has requested them."

The girl raised an eyebrow in what Caeden could only assume was confusion, but she nodded. "Of course, Your Highness," she repeated.

Caeden thanked her, and she disappeared down the dark hallway past him.

The cold air outside hit him like a brick wall as he exited the castle a moment later, goosebumps rising along the lengths of his arms and legs. It still wasn't cold out, but he was used to the warm summer air.

Dim candlelight flickered from Ronan's shack ahead of him, casting ghostly shadows out into the grass through the uncovered windows. Murmured voices from inside reached Caeden's ears as he made his way across the small patch of field. One belonged to Ronan, and the other to a woman whose voice sounded familiar. He couldn't place it with the way the breeze blew around him, distorting the sound.

He rolled his eyes, even as mild amusement made the corners of his lips turn upward. Of course, Ronan was still with someone, despite the late hour.

Caeden walked past the shack and closer to the forest behind the castle, so Ronan's guest wouldn't take notice of him whenever she left. He sat in the cool grass and crossed his legs beneath himself, a shiver running through his body as the cold settled into his bones.

The wind picked up around him, howling through the trees between the buildings as he waited. The noises of the night filled the scarce beats of silence between gusts of wind. Occasionally, he could make out the gentle rustling sounds of a small woodland creature as it dared to venture closer to the castle, or the quiet hoot of an owl warning nearby creatures of its claim to the territory.

He'd lost track of how long he'd waited when the door to Ronan's shack opened, and a woman cloaked from head to toe in black exited. She snuck through the grass back to the castle.

After she'd slipped back inside, Caeden realized there hadn't been the usual silver cuffs on her sleeves.

He pushed the confusion away and climbed to his feet. He

lightly rapped his knuckles against the wooden door, the soft thuds echoing throughout the shack before the sound of Ronan rustling with a few things inside followed. He could make out his friend's heavy footsteps on the floor as he hobbled over to answer the door.

"Did you forget somethin'?" Ronan asked, unlocking the door and turning the knob on the opposite end.

The flirtatious tone Caeden expected to hear when Ronan thought he was speaking to a woman wasn't there. No silver cuffs and no flirting. Odd. It wasn't the first time Ronan spent time with a woman he wasn't sleeping with, but that didn't happen often.

Caeden raised an eyebrow at his friend once the door was open, a silent question in the otherwise noisy night. Ronan only stared at him, as if he needed time to realize the woman he'd been with wasn't who stood in front of him now.

"Oh, hey, princy," Ronan said, opening the door wider and stepping aside, allowing Caeden to enter past him.

"At least you're fully clothed this time," Caeden joked, giving his friend a teasing grin as he stepped inside of the shack.

"Well, when ya come knockin' right after a woman I've just spent my evenin' with leaves, I don't assume it's you who's on the other side of the door." Ronan shrugged before walking to the kitchen, his steps awkward and slow.

"Well, at least I know for sure you'll get good use of those new sheets," Caeden said, a smirk pulling at the corners of his lips.

Ronan perked up. "Ya ordered 'em?" he asked. He reached for a bottle of whisky in the kitchen and poured himself a glassful. "Those are gonna be so nice. Plus, it'll give me another excuse to invite company in." He winked jokingly before he pushed the cork back into the bottle and set it aside.

Ronan grabbed his glass off the counter and entered the living area, plopping himself on the couch and tossing his cane to the side. Caeden followed his lead and perched himself on the arm of the sofa opposite his friend, allowing him space to spread out on the furniture.

"How'd it go with the princesses?" Ronan asked suddenly. He raised a curious eyebrow at Caeden over the rim of his glass before pulling it to his lips. His cheeks darkened a shade in the dim candlelight and his eyes flicked away from Caeden's, refusing to return while he waited for a response.

His lack of eye contact was unusual and probably had everything to do with Caeden arriving right after the woman left. Or perhaps he was drunk enough that the surrounding room was more interesting than the conversation he'd attempted to start.

Caeden shrugged, choosing to ignore his friend's odd behavior. "They seem nice," he responded, though he knew Ronan was looking for more of an answer than that. He didn't know them well enough to elaborate much further yet. "They all seem intelligent, and each of their kingdoms offers us a good number of soldiers if I marry them. Ceana seems a little power-hungry and Kylana wants to fight in the war. I don't know how I feel about either of those things, but this is also the first day."

Ronan nodded. "I talked with one of them today," he said, his gaze on the coffee table. "Very pretty woman. Kind and funny. She's the redhead. Margaid, I think she said her name was."

Caeden stared at him, his jaw falling slack. It was the most polite way he'd ever heard Ronan speak of a woman he found attractive, and he wondered how much of it was for his benefit, considering he would marry one of them in just over a month. Maybe that was what had spurred his sudden discomfort. The idea that he might be worried Caeden would be upset that he'd talked with her was almost laughable.

"Is that who you were with?" he asked.

Nothing accusing hid in his tone. He wasn't sure he cared what Ronan's answer was, but his friend's cheeks reddened even further at the question, and he looked away.

"Yeah," Ronan responded, his voice wavering. "We didn't do anythin' other than talk. She was mostly askin' 'bout you."

The words spilled out of him, and Caeden couldn't help but feel bad for asking. It didn't matter that Ronan had spent time with Margaid, but he certainly seemed afraid that there was.

Caeden only nodded in response to his words, unsure what he could say that wouldn't make Ronan feel even more uncomfortable than he already did.

He wouldn't have cared even if Ronan had slept with her, which was a rather odd thought. He would be married to one of them soon, but he had yet to wrap his head around that fact. With how he felt toward them, he wouldn't have cared if Ronan had slept with all three of them.

"Is it strange that I wouldn't care if you had?" Caeden asked. Guilt at the admission welled in the pit of his stomach as soon as the words left his lips. He wasn't sure what answer he hoped Ronan would give him. He wasn't even sure he wanted to hear one at all.

Ronan looked up at him for the first time since the princesses had been brought up, confusion etched into his face. Ronan thought about the question for a long moment, mulling it over until Caeden wondered if he would not respond at all.

"I don't see why it would be," Ronan told him with a slight shrug of a single shoulder. "You don't wanna get married, last I heard from ya. Ya said so only a couple days ago, anyway. I don't see why them bein' here would change that, unless ya managed to instantly fall in love with one of 'em, but I don't believe that kinda stuff is possible."

Caeden shrugged. Hearing his friend agree with him didn't help him feel any less guilty. If anything, it almost made him feel worse.

The entire situation felt wrong. Something about his situation with the princesses wasn't right, and he couldn't shake the feeling. It didn't feel like this would help them win the war. It felt like this would only make it worse.

Caeden shook his head, pushing away the irrational feelings of imminent doom before he refocused his attention on his friend. Ronan stared down at the cup in his hands, his finger thoughtfully tracing over the rim of the crystal glass. He had a faraway look in his eyes.

A smile tugged at Caeden's lips as he watched him. He'd seen that look come across his friend's face before. It didn't happen often, but it amused him every time even though he should've found it the farthest thing from amusing, given the circumstances this time.

"You like her?" Caeden asked him, something teasing making its way into his voice.

It made sense, considering how strange Ronan had been acting all evening.

He'd seen Ronan when he'd caught feelings for other women in the past, and he'd acted the same each time. That faraway look on his face, the jittery nervousness, as if he'd been caught doing something wrong, even in situations where it made no sense for him to feel that way.

Ronan swallowed hard. "I…" His face turned so red that it rivaled the maid Caeden passed in the hallway. "She's nice," he said, by way of answer, even though it wasn't an answer.

Caeden couldn't help it when he laughed.

His situation was strange on every level, and it suddenly seemed ridiculous.

He'd been so intent on receiving military training that he'd agreed to the court's proposal of something as monumental as marriage, and on top of all of that, his best friend had caught feelings for one of the women he would choose his future bride from.

Maybe it was pure denial, but it took Caeden far longer than it should've to get his laughter under control.

Ronan was still looking just as intently at the rim of his glass when he stopped laughing. This time, the worry on his face was so intense it pushed away the last of Caeden's amusement. The situation wasn't funny at all, but he didn't know how else to react.

"Would you hate me forever if I did?" Ronan asked. His voice was so soft Caeden had to strain to make out his words.

For a moment, Caeden contemplated making a joke to lighten the mood. After what Ronan said about not believing in falling in love with someone instantly, there were so many jokes to be made, but that wasn't what his friend needed right now, so he kept his mouth shut.

Ronan opened his mouth to speak again, but Caeden cut him off. "No," he told him. "I could never hate you for that. You can't help your feelings."

It was the truth. He couldn't help how he felt. Even if he had feelings for the most inconvenient woman possible, it didn't change the fact.

Caeden offered his friend a smile, and he could see Ronan relax at the sight of it.

"I meant what I said. I wouldn't even care if you… chose to spend your evenings with her," Caeden said carefully. It wasn't the sort of thing he should admit to anyone, but Ronan was his best friend, and even if he shouldn't have said it, that didn't make his words any less true.

He wanted to care, but he wasn't sure he could, especially not while knowing his friend had genuine feelings for her.

Ronan took another long sip from his glass before he finally spoke. "I enjoyed a conversation with her, but I don't think we're anywhere near somethin' like that," he said, his usual light tone coming back. "I kinda like her. I think she's pretty and funny, but I don't know that I wanna date her or anythin'. I just wanna talk to her again."

Caeden cracked a smile.

Despite Ronan's words, something in him knew his friend had, at the very least, thought about something more than just talking.

Chapter 13

Breakfast the following day was uncomfortably quiet, and Caeden was relieved when he could finally leave. He would have to meet with the three princesses, but after that, he'd return to his training with Eryn—where he really wanted to be spending his time.

The princesses were nice, but there was hardly any point in them staying so long in the castle. His father meant well, but it would've been simpler for the court to pick which kingdom would provide the most help and arrange the marriage without all the extra steps.

The sound of Ceana and Kylana's footsteps receding down the hallway reached him as he stepped through the doorway and out of the dining hall. Margaid waited for him with one hand clasped around the fabric of her dress as the other fidgeted with her ruby necklace. She glanced up at him and offered him a tight smile that made her eyes crinkle ever so slightly in the corners.

Caeden returned the smile, hoping it didn't appear as forced as it felt.

"Hey," he said lamely as he stood beside her, maintaining a

respectable distance.

"Hi," she replied, her voice higher pitched than he remembered. He wondered if it was from the discomfort he was also feeling, or if she was worried like Ronan had been that Caeden would be upset if he knew about the time they'd spent together.

Caeden cleared his throat. He hadn't had time the previous day to arrange activities for him and any of the three princesses to do together. Having things planned for them to do during their meetings would make the time pass more comfortably, at least until they got to know one another better.

But he'd finished with Eryn so late that everyone had been asleep already.

"Would you like to take a walk?" Caeden asked her, gesturing at the hall ahead of them as if she hadn't already been given a tour of the castle when she arrived.

Margaid smiled and nodded, dropping her hold on the necklace. "That sounds lovely," she said. "I haven't had a good look at the garden yet."

Caeden returned her smile, this time without having to force it. "The garden is one of my favorite places. I'll show you around," he offered before he led the way to the back of the castle.

"I've heard wonderful things about Eryn Gedding," Margaid said as they walked, clearly desperate for a topic of conversation. She'd begun fidgeting with her necklace again. "It's quite impressive that you managed to get someone of her status as a personal trainer. I hear she's one of the best in Aericora's army. I wouldn't think they'd be willing to spare her."

Caeden glanced at her and caught the hint of a blush spreading across her cheeks before she ducked her head to hide it.

She sounded like she knew much more about Eryn's achievements than she could have heard from whispers in the halls during the single day she'd been in the castle. He didn't know information like that could reach the ears of a princess from another kingdom. Especially one that wasn't involved in the war.

Margaid cleared her throat uncomfortably as Caeden did his best to form a decent response. "Well, I suppose since you're the prince and all..." Margaid trailed off, her face turning an even deeper shade of red.

Caeden offered her another small smile. "She's hard to pin down, from what I hear," he agreed. "I'm fortunate to receive my training from someone as skilled as she is."

Margaid nodded her agreement. "Are there many of you left?" She cleared her throat again. "Who want to fight in the war, I mean." She refused to look at him when she asked, her eyes staying glued to the tile floor as they walked.

Caeden had to mull the question over before he responded.

In reality, they had almost as many soldiers as they'd had at the beginning of the war, but they were losing soldiers faster than they could be replaced. Each year, more and more men and women joined the military, which kept their number of fighters roughly the same, but too many were too old, too young, or had too many people relying on them to survive to be able to join the fight now. They had only recently learned that less than half of the usual number of new soldiers had been trained within the past year, and that number was becoming smaller and smaller with every passing month. It had taken longer than most had predicted, but they were running out of willing, able-bodied people, which was what had started Aericora seeking external soldiers to begin with.

It seemed odd for her to ask, given that it was her entire

reason for being here. They would run out of people to fight soon enough, but if they could swell the military ranks before then, it might give them the final boost they needed to win against the Dragon Lord.

"For now," he answered. "It won't last much longer."

"Your father is offering a sizeable sum of money to whoever you choose to marry in exchange for soldiers," Margaid explained. "From my understanding, your kingdom is rather desperate already."

He shrugged in response. "Almost. We'd rather stay ahead of the Dragon Lord, if we can. If we can acquire more military personnel before we need them, we'll have a better chance of winning the war."

His words sounded so diplomatic he almost cringed. He hadn't been good at speaking in such a manner until recently, and it still sounded strange to him when he heard himself doing it. It was even stranger when he found himself able to do it automatically. It reminded him of how his mother had sounded in similar situations. The questions Margaid asked made him switch automatically to the same manner of speaking he reserved for the court. She wasn't just any other ambassador from Crevia, though, and he hoped he wasn't making her feel like one.

"Lucky for you, Crevia has a large population, and a rather low stockpile of wealth." She smiled almost teasingly, but something serious hidden in her eyes made him pause before he remembered that this was a political decision and negotiation on her side as well. She could opt out at any point, just as he could.

"Are you implying you would only marry me for the money involved and not my stunning good looks?" he joked, all diplomacy falling aside. He hoped it would lighten the mood at least a little.

This was the first conversation he'd had with any of the three princesses that didn't have an underlying awkwardness beneath every word. A small part of him hoped that maybe, if he took this opportunity to talk with her like he would with anyone else, it could stay that way.

Margaid laughed and it made a smile pull at the corners of Caeden's mouth. "Oh, yes. Strictly for the money," she replied, her eyes alight with amusement.

Caeden laughed.

They reached the back hallway and the door leading out to the garden. At this time of day, the hall was lit with candles to show off the tapestries along the walls. He pulled the wooden door open for Margaid and let her pass in front of him.

The garden outside was lit in a blanket of early morning sunlight, making the dewdrops that hadn't yet dried from the leaves and flower petals sparkle. There were multiple pathways leading around the garden so visitors could see the thousands of fresh flowers and bushes planted around the vast space. A large section in the middle of the garden had tables, chairs, and a short picket fence to close off the area. It had been used for countless dinner parties with castle advisors, military commanders, and other people of higher class when Caeden was younger, but the area remained mostly vacant now.

The garden was next to the training field, but a large fence separated the two spaces just behind Ronan's shack. The fence blended in with the foliage of the forest behind the castle. It was covered in vines, and trees and bushes were planted along it to hide it.

The sunlight was warm against Caeden's face, even despite the chill to the air he could feel piercing through his skin when the wind blew. It would warm up later in the day, but the sunlight hadn't yet had enough time to chase away the cold of the night.

He led Margaid further into the garden and watched as her eyes flicked around to the many plants. There was something like awe in her expression, and a small part of him found it strange, considering she had a garden like this back in Crevia. From everything he knew about the culture of Crevia, they had traditions and styles similar to those of Aericora.

"It's lovely in here," Margaid said as she sat on a marble bench alongside the path.

Caeden sat beside her. "It was one of my mother's favorite places before she passed," he explained. "My sister, too. She used to spend all her time in that corner." He pointed to his left, where a large plot of sunflowers was growing.

"Your sister had good taste. Sunflowers are my favorite."

"They were hers, too." He didn't bother to tell her that the sunflowers hadn't been there when Amelia had been alive, that they'd been purchased at his request to remember her and the little tea parties she would host in the corner for the two of them and their parents whenever she got the chance.

Margaid looked around the garden again. She stayed quiet as she took it in.

Caeden watched her. She did her best to look distracted by the garden, but her mind was flooded with thoughts.

"How long do you intend to fight in the military?" she asked, glancing back over at him and holding his gaze.

That same intense look was back in her eyes, mingling with the curiosity always present in her features.

Her question surprised him. "Until we win," he answered, as if it were the most obvious thing in the world.

"I see," was all she said in response.

The rest of their time together passed faster than Caeden expected it to. Margaid explained some of her favorite hobbies, including some of the things she'd listed when she first introduced herself. Caeden listened to her speak and nodded in response at the correct times. He paid attention and offered his comments, or occasional questions. After a while, his mind drifted to the stack of books sitting in his room, waiting for him to finish reading. He thought back to his training with Eryn the previous day and the things he'd learned, and it became harder and harder to listen to each of the words Margaid said.

After another hour in the garden, Caeden walked Margaid back to her room and said his goodbyes. She curtsied and disappeared into her quarters, shutting the door behind herself.

He could hear her sigh behind the closed door.

He had little time to wonder about the fact before Kylana exited her room.

"Good morning, Your Highness," she said, bowing down to a level that seemed uncomfortably low, her long dress pooling around her feet.

Caeden had to force himself to smile when he turned to face her. He nodded in acknowledgment, and she stood straight. It felt strange that she'd bowed at all. It was proper, but she was here as his equal.

"I trust you were well taken care of last night?" he asked, unsure what else he could say to start a conversation.

"Yes," she responded, her tone colder than he'd expected.

He could see the frustration playing across her face for a moment. He contemplated asking her about it, but opted to keep his mouth shut.

"Shall we continue our conversation in the training field?" Kylana asked, gesturing with a hand toward the back end of the castle.

"If you'd like," he responded.

He'd been the most uncomfortable the previous day while

watching her practice, but anything would be better than standing silently in a hallway with his hands clasped so stiffly behind his back that his muscles were twitching.

A smile that looked far more genuine than she'd worn before spread across her face, and she led the way out to the training field.

"You're training with Eryn Gedding, aren't you?" she asked as they walked, a glimmer so bright in her eyes it risked blinding him.

"Yes," he answered shortly, taken aback since he'd had a similar conversation with Margaid.

"I was watching her yesterday," Kylana continued, speaking so fast her words seemed to string together into one long one. "She's one of the most amazing knife throwers I've ever seen. And I've heard she's killed more dragons than most other living soldiers. It's incredible. She's so young, too."

Caeden nodded in agreement. "She's quite impressive," he agreed. "I haven't gotten a chance to see her knife-throwing skills yet, but I wouldn't doubt they're impeccable."

Kylana grinned with an almost awestruck look in her eyes. "I'm sure you've learned so much from her already."

"I've learned a lot about dragons from her already," he told her. "My skills haven't yet had time to improve, but that's to be expected since we've only been training for a few days. I hope they will come along quickly, once I learn her teaching methods and how to apply her training."

Kylana clucked her tongue. "Considering what I've heard, I'm sure it will be far quicker than you may expect."

"I hope so."

Silence filled the space between them as they left through the back door and went to the archery range. The targets were still set up, and Kylana's bow and quiver of arrows were set neatly beside one of them, waiting for her.

"What made you want to start training?" Kylana asked as she picked up her bow and quiver. She slung the quiver over her shoulder and held her bow as she reached behind herself and withdrew an arrow. "I apologize if this is blunt, but was it because of the deaths of your mother and sister?"

No one had ever asked him point blank, though he was sure it was why most assumed he wanted to fight. It was a reasonable assumption, mainly because it was correct.

"Mostly," he told her. "But I also don't feel that it's right to sit on the sidelines while my people are fighting a war they didn't ask for. They've lost loved ones, too, and it only seemed right to fight alongside them rather than remain here to oversee the carnage. I've wanted to receive training ever since I was young, and originally, it was only because I wanted to fight back against those who killed my family, but it's changed to more than that since then. It's taken the court a long time to see that, and my father only recently found me a proper trainer."

Kylana nodded as she knocked an arrow. "That's noble of you," she said as she released the arrow. It cut through the air and landed as perfectly as the many arrows Eryn had shot a couple of days before.

Caeden felt his face grow hot at her compliment. "What about you?" he asked. "What made you join the military in your kingdom? As far as I'm aware, you're not involved in any wars."

"We aren't," she answered as she knocked another arrow. "I grew up with three brothers." She laughed. "We used to fight each other a lot, and one day, my parents grew sick of us beating each other up with our fists. They sent us outside with wooden swords and told us we would need to fight properly, with rules, and whoever won the match would win whatever argument had gotten us there. We got quite good after a while.

"When I got older, my brothers married and moved on with their lives, but fighting and weaponry had become such a large part of my life by that point that it felt impossible to move on from it. It sounds terrible, but I was bored, so I joined the military. I found comradery in the other soldiers I trained with, and I was so passionate about it that it became my entire world from that point on."

She said her words with a kind of emotion that lodged itself into Caeden's chest. He already knew he would not give up his training or the chance to fight once he was married, but he wasn't so sure he could take that away from her, either.

But he wasn't ready to bring it up with her again. It hadn't gotten them very far the day before, and they would likely end in the same place if he brought forth the subject again.

They spent the rest of their time in the training field, and when it was time for Caeden to meet with Ceana, a guard made his way outside to interrupt them. He explained Ceana was waiting for him in the library.

He said a polite goodbye to Kylana, who gave him a smile before she turned back to the target and continued shooting arrows into the already crowded center.

Ceana was by far the quietest of the three today, which caught him by surprise, considering the near interrogation he'd undergone the day before.

When he arrived, she held a book in her hands again, and she stayed silent for a long time while he sat down. Then she finished reading what he could only assume was an entire chapter.

Caeden studied the library walls while he waited for her to finish, taking in the lacquered wooden shelves, the distinct smell of old books, and the thin layer of dust blanketing the entire room.

"What do you enjoy doing when you aren't training?" Ceana

asked, as she set her book on the tabletop beside her.

Caeden startled at the sudden sound of her voice. He took a long moment to come up with an answer to the question. He didn't do much aside from court meetings and spending his evenings with Ronan when he could spare the time. He'd practiced often enough, but he doubted she wanted to hear about any of those things.

He shrugged a shoulder, feeling sheepish. "This may sound strange, but I enjoy painting my late sister's room."

Ceana raised an eyebrow at him, confusion settling over her features and making a crease form between her delicate eyebrows. He was aware of how strange his words sounded, and he could feel his face heat when she looked at him.

Caeden cleared his throat. "She wanted it yellow, and when she left, they'd begun to paint it her favorite shade. After she died, they stopped since it pained my father to have them here, knowing she was never going to return to see it. I paint it for fun occasionally. I think she would've liked it to have been finished for her, even if she could never see it."

Ceana's features softened at his words, and a small smile rested on her face. It wasn't a look he expected from her. He'd gotten the impression from her the day before that she was colder than most, and that she would prefer to avoid these types of feelings or conversations.

"That sounds lovely," she told him, seeming to mean it.

Caeden cleared his throat again, feeling uncomfortable. "What about you?"

She glanced over at the book on the table again before her gaze resettled on his face, and she clasped her hands gingerly in her lap. "I enjoy some art as well," she answered. "I mostly like to read, though. I enjoy history. I like seeing what has worked for kingdoms in the past and what has failed. I think it will help me in my reign, if I ever get one."

Caeden said nothing in response, hoping she would continue to fill the silence.

"I think the Dragon Lord's reign could've been prevented if people had paid more attention," she explained. "He spent years of his life hiding away in the mountains before he came back to assume the throne near the end of his father's life." She shrugged. "Similar situations have happened before. When rulers spend too much time away from their kingdom before they assume the throne, they always bring too much change for a kingdom to handle all at once. Deovaria has fought so many useless wars since his reign began, and it seems it can only be attributed to madness."

Caeden had heard similar things said about the Dragon Lord plenty of times before, but hardly ever so bluntly. He watched as her eyes flicked back to her book again, clearly eager to get back to reading whatever was printed into its hundreds of pages. "Is that what you're reading about right now?"

She nodded, picking up the book again and handing it to him.

The cover was dustier than most other books in the room, and the pages were so yellowed and old he was scared to touch them for fear they'd turn to dust beneath his fingertips.

"It's fascinating. I found it buried behind another stack of books," she told him. "I didn't know he wasn't the oldest sibling."

Caeden glanced up at her and lowered the book in his hands. "He wasn't?"

He'd never heard of the Dragon Lord having a sibling at all. He'd heard very little about the royal family of Deovaria, aside from what had come up after the Dragon Lord's reign began. And, from the dust covering the book in his hands, very few others had bothered to unearth that information either.

Ceana shook her head, her eyes lighting up like she'd just overheard the juiciest gossip in the castle. "The oldest was a daughter. I knew she existed, but I didn't know she was the true heir to the throne. The book doesn't say much about her. She was described in a lot of old literature from the middle of their parent's reign, but once they became adults, she disappeared entirely. I assumed she wasn't the oldest since she disappeared from the stories so suddenly, but that book specifically gave their birth dates since it specifies many large events during their parent's reign."

"Did she die?" Caeden asked. It wasn't unusual for a child of a royal family to die, and be forgotten about in later writings. It had probably happened to his sister.

Ceana shrugged again. "I'm not sure. It's possible. Or she could've been married off. She was old enough at the time of her disappearance. But that doesn't seem likely since she was the heir to the throne."

Caeden handed her back the book, and she took it, flipping it open to a page and placing it into her lap. Her eyes focused on the page in front of her before she glanced back up and spoke again. "But anyway, all I meant was that he was never trained to be the ruler. And since he disappeared to the Rayfait Mountains shortly before his sister's disappearance, he wouldn't have been able to learn how to run a kingdom. All those factors together should've been red flags to everyone, and it should've been enough to prevent him from ever being able to assume the throne."

"The disappearance of his sister could also have been what drove him so mad," Caeden put in, his mind whirring with the new information.

There wasn't much he could do with it, but he enjoyed learning facts like this about his enemy. He enjoyed learning the inner workings of the madman who had murdered his family, and hoped eventually it would help lead to his death.

Ceana nodded in agreement, her eyes falling back to her book. "It wouldn't be unlikely."

She went silent again after that.

Caeden attempted to get her to engage in some small talk. He asked her about her family, if she had any other hobbies aside from the few things she'd listed, and so on, but nothing got him more than a two-word answer from her. It was as if she'd said all she'd intended to for the day.

After trying and failing multiple times to get her to engage in a conversation, he disappeared into the stacks of books and returned with one of the ones Eryn had assigned him. They spent the rest of their time together reading silently.

Chapter 14

By the time Caeden finished meeting with all three of the princesses, he was half an hour late to his training session with Eryn. He hadn't intended to stay late with Ceana, but he'd gotten through the first book during his time spent with her in the library and started on the second, and he'd lost track of time. But that wouldn't keep Eryn from being mad at him.

Eryn was waiting impatiently in the center of the training field, this time twirling her intricately detailed knife between her fingers in a manner that was far more intimidating than it should've been.

"Finally," she grumbled when her eyes landed on him. She grabbed her knife by the hilt and re-sheathed it at her hip, her movements fluid. "How were your dates?" she asked, drawing out the last word with apparent disdain. She pursed her lips as if the question left a foul taste in her mouth.

Caeden shrugged. "This whole thing is strange," he told her, but didn't explain why he felt the way he did.

He didn't want to see how she would respond if he told her how uncomfortable it was that he was handed three women to court however he pleased. She already seemed to think of him as spoiled, given the annoyance she seemed to harbor toward their entire situation. If he expressed his true feelings about his future engagement, it would only perpetuate her beliefs.

She raised a judgmental eyebrow at him before she rolled her eyes and turned away. "We're doing hand-to-hand training today," she told him, not bothering to look back when she spoke.

Caeden cringed. He'd known this was coming, but she'd already beaten him up during their initial training session, and he hadn't healed from the multiple bruises and bumps he'd sustained.

Still, he was excited to hear her words and felt like a giddy child at the thought of learning the new techniques.

Eryn led him to the dirt patch they'd trained on two days ago. She unclasped her belt from around her waist and removed her many sheathes and holsters from where they were strapped to her extremities. She set them into a neat pile on the ground just outside the dirt ring.

"Alright, princy boy," she mocked. "Let's get to it." Eryn widened her stance and lifted her arms to protect her face and chest from the brunt of Caeden's potential attacks.

Caeden ignored her mockery and stepped up in front of her. He attempted to mimic her stance, despite feeling somewhat unsteady in it. The placement of his arms and shoulders was awkward.

"You're going to fall standing like that," Eryn chided him.

Without giving him enough time to react, her palm connected with his chest, and he stumbled backward, tripping over his own feet in his effort to keep himself upright.

Caeden glared at her. Telling him would have sufficed, though he didn't know why he would assume she'd be nice about it.

"One foot forward, one foot back," Eryn instructed. "Keep your weight on your back foot. It allows for a stronger offensive stance, and for you to throw a more powerful blow."

She aimed a punch an inch away from Caeden's face. She rotated her body when she threw the blow, her hips turning with her as she shifted her weight from her back foot to her front. When she pulled it back, she undid the motion, leaving her in the same stance she'd been in before.

Caeden's heartbeat quickened, although he knew she had no intention of hitting him this time. He ducked away regardless, more on instinct than anything else.

Eryn already had her arms crossed in front of her and her hip cocked to one side in her usual impatient manner when he looked back at her. She made a motion with her hand, instructing him to repeat the movement she'd done.

He mimicked her stance. It felt similar to the stance Ronan had taught him when he'd first been learning to shoot a bow and arrow, aside from the difference in weight distribution. He lifted his hands in front of his face and attempted to throw a punch forward as Eryn had. The movement felt awkward, and he couldn't help the mild wave of frustration when he felt Eryn's disapproving gaze drift over his body. He wasn't ready for her to give up all her patience with him for the day just yet.

They'd gotten nowhere when she'd gotten frustrated with him a few days ago. The more impatient she got, the worse his technique seemed to be, and the more his own frustration grew with hers.

Caeden braced himself for a snide comment and an eye roll from her when he glanced her way, but instead, he was met with pursed lips and a calculating furrow of her eyebrows.

He hadn't expected that from her. Hopefully, it meant today

would go more smoothly.

She studied him so intently that he shifted beneath her stare.

"You're missing the twist," she told him. "You're shifting your weight right, but turn your back heel out when you throw the punch, and let your weight transfer from your heel to the ball of your foot before you shift to your leading leg."

She demonstrated the movement without bothering to throw a blow at his face this time.

Caeden studied her movements, but when he attempted to copy them again, it still felt strange and foreign to his muscles. The pleased expression that lit Eryn's face when he looked at her for further input told him he'd done it correctly.

"You'll get used to it," she assured him, noticing the stiffness of his movements. "It takes a lot of practice, but you've got the basics down."

Caeden frowned at her before he could think better of it. It wasn't a compliment, but it was by far the nicest tone she'd ever used with him, and it was one of the few times he'd seen her without a look of annoyance on her face.

"Alright. Now that you've got that, defensive is just opposite weight distribution. More weight on your front leg." Eryn said as she took up a fighting stance again. "Let's see if you can hold your own today."

They sparred together for multiple hours, before Eryn told him she was seeing some improvement in his skills compared to where he'd started.

A few hours later, when the surrounding sky was turning purple and pink as the sun set, she said they could move on to other training for the remainder of the day.

Caeden's arms, legs, abdomen, and back were all throbbing from the places where she'd punched, kicked, hit, slapped, or jabbed him with one of her blows, and his whole body relaxed when she said they were done. It didn't outweigh the pride he felt at hearing he'd improved in the few hours they'd been fighting.

"Have you started the reading I assigned you yet?" Eryn asked while she worked on gathering her knives from off the ground where she'd set them before they'd begun.

"I started," he told her, hoping she wouldn't press him about it.

He didn't want to lie to her and tell her he was close to done, but he also didn't want to tell her he'd only gotten through one book so far. None of the books were long, and he'd wanted to make a larger dent in his reading but hadn't had time during the day and had opted to spend his evening with Ronan rather than reading.

His face grew warm at the immatureness of his actions the previous night, and he hoped she didn't notice.

"I was planning on finishing as much as I can tonight."

Eryn tossed one of her knives into the air before she caught it by the blade with the tips of her fingers along the fuller. "Mhm," she mused, looking unconvinced.

She didn't outright say it, but he knew she didn't believe a single word he'd said.

Chapter 15

Moonlight flooded Caeden's room from the large window next to his bed, making a silvery sheen spread across the lacquered wooden floors. He sat with his legs crossed beneath him on the bed with one of the many books Eryn assigned open in his lap. He held a lit candle up to the pages and read the words in a rather useless attempt to make them make sense in his head.

Eryn's lavender scent clung to his clothes and skin from their sparring session earlier in the day. The smell was somehow more powerful than the sweat and grime coating his skin from the heat and the number of times she'd pinned him to the ground. Her scent reached his nose each time he breathed in, and he found it distracting in his otherwise peaceful room.

Along with the scent, images of her bright blue eyes and the occasional sparkle of amusement that twinkled in them filled his mind. The quirk of her mouth when he'd thought he'd bested her during their fights only to be swiftly knocked to the ground followed.

Those small things got under his skin when they were training, frustrating him and making him feel even more incompetent than he already knew he was, but alone in his room hours after it, they were funny little memories that made a smile pull at the corners of his mouth.

Caeden shook his head, pushing away the thoughts of her.

It was long past midnight, and he'd spent every moment since he'd gotten back from his training poring over the pages of the books. So far, he'd finished three of the five books she'd given him, but he'd skimmed through them.

The ones he'd finished had been the thinnest three of the bunch, though none could be considered large even by a long shot. He doubted he'd be able to focus long enough to get through another. Eryn wouldn't take well to him not having the books finished within the next day or two, given how she'd reacted earlier when she'd asked about his progress, and the eye roll that had followed when he'd told her he hadn't made much. So, despite his tiredness, he continued to push himself to read. Luckily, they were each filled with countless diagrams, or he never would've been able to finish them all.

He refocused his gaze on the words in front of him. The font swam before his eyes, the edges of the letters blurring together before he shook his head to get his eyes to focus again.

He'd read about dragons in the past, but only ever in children's books. Dragons were still a mystery to most, but these books covered what felt like endless possibilities about what gave them their abilities for magic, how it was possible for such enormous creatures to fly, and so on.

Some tried to attribute certain things, such as the Royal Talons' ability to manifest things like fire and ice from nothing, to science. They claimed that the dragons' high exposure to the cold at the top of the mountains could have caused them to evolve to have such abilities. Along the same lines, they claimed that fire burned inside them to keep them warm against the fridged air and that this breed of dragon could somehow tap into the reserves as a weapon.

Caeden had a hard time wrapping his mind around how something like that could be possible. The theories explained certain parts of each dragon but never covered everything. According to Eryn, Royal Talons could manifest about any substance imaginable, and most of the theories forgot to account for more than fire and ice.

It was called magic for a reason, wasn't it? If it could be attributed to science, the word never would've been invented to describe such a thing to begin with. He read on, ignoring the nitpicking mindset he'd found himself in, and tried to consider the theories laid out in front of him. It was a difficult task, but he forced himself to do it.

His largest reading struggle was when the authors began using lengthy scientific language to describe certain features of the dragons. The wording did nothing to keep his head from spinning or to help him focus.

Eventually, Caeden sighed and slumped back against his bed, letting the book fall open against his stomach. His body sank into the soft sheets of his bed, every limb heavy. He stared at the ceiling for a long time, blinking to keep himself from falling asleep, even as every inch of his body protested.

He needed to finish the reading, but the thought of pulling himself back up into a sitting position felt like the most agonizing thing he could do.

"Come on," he grumbled to himself, his voice rough, even to his own tired ears. "You've got to get up."

After a few more moments of trying to convince himself, he sat up and threw his legs over the side of his bed. He closed the book and set it down beside his bedside table along with the still lit candle, the small flame illuminating half of the tabletop in an orange glow.

Caeden left his room and made his way through the dark hallways. He stumbled over his feet in the near-total darkness before he regained some control over his heavy limbs. It was quiet around him as he walked. The only sound that reached him was from his footfalls against the tile floor. He'd had enough sense to put on a pair of shoes before he left, but now he wondered if it was such a good idea with the way the sound echoed off the surrounding walls.

Despite his aching limbs, he stumbled out into the training field and over to Ronan's shack. The lights were on inside, as they always were, and he could hear muffled voices drifting out through the ajar windows. Caeden couldn't help it when he rolled his eyes.

His mind drifted back to their conversation the night before, and he wondered if maybe Ronan had taken him seriously and if Margaid was the one who was with him inside of the shack.

It was impossible to distinguish the woman's voice over the breeze and noisy creatures of the night hiding in the forest nearby, though, and after only a brief pause, Caeden disregarded the thought.

He hadn't been lying the night before, and whether Ronan had taken him seriously and was with Margaid didn't matter.

The thought was more of a punch to the gut than he'd anticipated. Not because he suddenly realized he cared for her, but because he realized, yet again, just how much he truly didn't. At least, not in the way he should care about a woman he very well could be married to.

Caeden let out a breath and, before allowing himself enough time to consider whether it was a good idea, he reached for the door and rapped his knuckles gently against the solid wood.

"Fuck," he heard Ronan swear from somewhere inside. It

wasn't loud, but with the open windows and thin walls, it sounded like he'd been standing only a few feet away. "Whatcha need, princy?" he called.

Despite himself, a smile tugged at Caeden's lips. "Just the armory keys."

The distinct shuffle of bare feet followed Ronan's overly dramatic sigh of complaint against the wooden floors. "I'm comin', I'm comin'," Ronan grumbled from inside.

Caeden heard the jingle of keys a moment before the knob turned, and Ronan opened the door only wide enough to hand him the keys, but not enough for him to see anything inside of the shack.

"There ya go," he said, holding the ring of keys out to Caeden with a rather impatient look.

Ronan was shirtless and leaning against the doorknob with his free hand. His hair was a tousled mess on his head, and his gray pants were wrinkled. From where Caeden stood, he could smell the liquor on the man's breath.

Caeden smirked at him but said nothing when Ronan gave him a warning look. He bit back the remarks forming on the tip of his tongue and took the keys.

"Thanks," he told him, before turning around and walking away in the armory's direction.

"Bring 'em back when you're done!" Ronan called before he shut the door.

"I will!" Caeden yelled back over his shoulder, though he wasn't sure if Ronan was still listening from inside the shack or not.

Caeden made his way to the other end of the training field and to the armory's entrance. He fumbled with the keys in the darkness until he found the one that fit into the small keyhole beneath the doorknob. He turned the key, and the door unlocked with a quiet click. The hinges creaked when he pushed the door open, revealing the pitch-black inside.

He lit one of the small candles set right beside the doorway, and it provided enough light for him to make out vague ghosts of shapes inside the ample space. He held out the candle as he entered the room toward the rack where the throwing knives were stored. He and Eryn had practiced with them only on their first day of training, and he might as well get more practice in with them.

He ran his fingers along the hilts of the blades before he selected a particularly old-looking one from the assortment. The blade was rusted at the base, but the edges were pristine, as if it had been recently sharpened.

If he was going to lose a blade in the forest, it should be an old one no one would miss.

He eyed the blade as images of Eryn so flawlessly playing with her knife drifted into his mind.

As ridiculous as it was, in his hazy, sleep-deprived state, he didn't have time to give it a second thought before he picked the blade up and tossed it clumsily in his hand, attempting to catch it by the blade in the same way Eryn had done earlier in the day. He lacked the finesse she had copious amounts of, so he wasn't surprised when the blade slipped a hair too far between his fingers and slid against the palm of his hand.

He hissed out a pained breath between clenched teeth as the blade bit into his skin.

Caeden set the knife back down before he took the time to examine the wound. It throbbed, and sharp pain radiated through his palm with each pulse of his heartbeat. It was only a thin gash, small enough that it could've been mistaken for a paper cut, but even when he applied pressure to it with his uninjured hand, the bleeding refused to slow.

Someone snorted a laugh behind him, and he jumped in surprise at the sound.

"Brilliant," Eryn said sarcastically. Her voice sounded higher than usual.

Caeden turned to face her, startled, but his arm collided with the edge of the rack that the knives were neatly organized on when he did. A few clattered to the floor and disappeared into the darkness at his feet.

"Impressive." She clucked her tongue playfully and giggled.

Actually giggled.

Confusion registered in his mind when the sound of her laughter faded. His focus was less on what she was doing here and instead on the sound that had escaped her lips. Maybe he'd heard her laugh once, but he'd never heard her giggle like that.

In the dim light from the doorway behind her, he could make out the silhouette of her long black hair tied up in a ponytail, and her baggy cotton tunic and leggings.

Eryn ventured deeper into the armory. Her steps were unsteady, and he heard when she slipped against the floor or bumped her shoulder into a rack of swords. When she stopped in front of him, he could make out the flush that spread across her cheeks and nose in the flickering candlelight.

Before he could stop her, she reached forward and grabbed him by the wrist, pulling his injured hand up close to her face, and angled it to allow the light from the candle to flow over his cut palm. He flinched as the skin pulled farther apart. More blood seeped from the wound and drip down his fingers. Training with the wound on his hand for the next few days would not be fun.

Eryn blinked rapidly while taking in his injury, as if she was trying to see through a cloud of fog.

Heat seeped into Caeden's skin where her fingers gripped his wrist, and her lavender scent filled his senses, along with something that smelled distinctly like alcohol.

"Are you drunk?" he blurted before giving himself enough time to consider whether it was a good idea to ask.

A smile spread across Eryn's lips, and she ducked her head when she laughed, as if it would somehow keep him from hearing it. A moment later, she caught her breath. "Very," she responded before giggling again.

Caeden wasn't sure if her confession made him feel any better or worse about their current situation. He wasn't sure if he wanted a drunk woman tending to his injury, which seemed to be what she was trying to do. But it was only a slight scratch, so he couldn't see the harm in letting her.

Eryn released his wrist and took a step away from him before she bent forward and picked up one of the fallen knives from the floor.

Caeden didn't have time to register what she was doing before she tugged at the hem of her tunic and slashed through it with the knife, cutting a long, thin strip of fabric.

Caeden's eyes nearly bulged out of his head as he stared at her.

Eryn ripped the few remaining unsevered threads free, leaving her tunic about four inches shorter in the front than in the back but still long enough to fall below the waistband of her pants.

Once she had the strip of fabric free, she tucked the knife into the holster on the side of her leg, which had been made for a much larger dagger than the one she'd picked up.

"What are you doing?" Caeden stammered, the shock he felt making his words sound more like a squeak.

Eryn rolled her eyes like his question was ludicrous, but the slight smile still pulled at the corners of her lips. "All that wine you privileged royals drink is affecting your cognitive abilities of deduction," she said, her words slurring together around the edges. "Give me your hand, you dummy prince."

"You say, while drunk off your ass," Caeden mumbled.

Eryn grinned up at him, and the look in her eyes was so genuine it took him by surprise. There was no irritation or annoyance in her expression, only what looked like pure amusement, with a hint of something that could almost be described as fondness.

She took a step closer again and snatched his wrist away from him. She wound the scrap of cloth from her tunic around his injury before she tied it tight.

"That'll help with the bleeding," she told him, her eyes still fixed on his hand while she examined her work. She looked up at him, and her smile widened again. "But don't think this will get you out of your training, if that was what you were going for."

Caeden cracked a smile in response. "Trust me, it wasn't."

He pulled back his hand and flexed his fingers, testing his range of movement with the cloth tied around his palm. The cloth was rough against the tender skin and stung each time he moved, but it was better to have it covered than not.

"Speaking of which," Eryn said as she dropped her hand to her side and retrieved the knife she'd placed there a moment before. "How about we get in some knife-throwing practice? Since, evidently, you aren't bothering to take this time to finish the reading I assigned you."

Caeden's cheeks warmed, and he hoped the lighting was dim enough that she couldn't see it. "I…" He trailed off, unable to come up with a better excuse than the truth. "I've been busy," he told her.

Eryn nodded her head. "It's hard work, courting three

women at once," she said sarcastically, pursing her lips as though she was taking this far more seriously than Caeden was sure she could. Despite her current, cheery mood, the same disdain she always had when she spoke of the princesses and Caeden's agreement with the court hid beneath her words. There was something else there too, beneath all those things, but he couldn't quite place what it was.

"Harder than I thought it would be," he agreed, ignoring the sarcasm.

Eryn grinned, mischief glinting in her eyes. "Whore."

Caeden stared at her, wide-eyed. "I never said I intended to sleep with all of them, or that I have."

She shrugged, as if the fact was irrelevant.

Caeden opened his mouth to retort, but closed it almost immediately after. There was nothing good he could say. He didn't like his situation, but that didn't mean he hadn't put himself right into it in exchange for her training.

Eryn stooped to collect more of the fallen knives off the floor, her fingers fumbling with the hilt of one before she got a solid hold on the metal.

Caeden held his breath as he watched her, unsure if he should stop her from touching weapons while in the mindset she was currently in. He wasn't sure she wouldn't shove one of those knives through his chest if he tried to, though.

She stood. "Come on," she said, nodding toward the armory door. "Practice time."

Caeden stared at her. She couldn't be serious.

"You're drunk," he argued.

Eryn waved a dismissive hand, but otherwise ignored him before she approached the exit. "I can still throw things!" she called over her shoulder without sparing him a backward glance.

She swayed more on her feet now than she had when she'd

first arrived, and he would bet that the alcohol in her system was only beginning to take its full effect.

Caeden sighed before grabbing the candle from where he'd set it on the daggers' rack and jogging to catch up with her. He didn't want to train with her being in the state she was in, but he couldn't leave her alone with that many knives and the intent to throw them, either.

Somehow, by the time he blew out the candle, set it back down on the tiny table, and left the armory, she'd already made her way over to the targets a hundred yards away.

Eryn tossed one knife into the air and re-caught it in her palm with only a small fumble. She avoided injuring herself, but Caeden's heartbeat still quickened at the possibility.

"Have you done any practicing outside of our sessions?" Eryn inquired, tilting her head to one side.

Caeden shook his head. "I haven't had time between the princesses and the reading you assigned." He left out the fact that he'd spent the previous night drinking with Ronan instead of being responsible.

Eryn raised an eyebrow at him, the corner of her mouth quirking upward as though she was trying to suppress a laugh. "Don't lie, you dummy prince," she said, repeating the same insult she'd used only a moment earlier. "We both know you've been doing your best to get those women to swoon over you instead."

He caught the distinct sound of real annoyance in her tone for the first time that night, but when he glanced at her again, he could only make out amusement on her face.

Caeden ignored her comment this time and instead focused his attention on the knife still in her hand while he tried to figure out an excuse as to why she needed to go back inside that wouldn't piss her off. She didn't believe she was too drunk for this activity.

"Shouldn't you be heading in to get some sleep?" he asked her, his eyes still trained on the blade.

She paused momentarily, and despite himself, Caeden hoped she would take his suggestion seriously.

Instead, she laughed after a few seconds of tense silence, a loud joyous sound erupting past her lips.

Her laughter lasted a long moment until she put her hand to her face and her giggles calmed.

"If I don't take the time to train you, princy, who will? We only have a few weeks to get you at least competent enough with a weapon to survive through your first day in the field. Anything after that is out of my hands."

He frowned. He couldn't remember how long his father had planned for Eryn to train him, but he could've sworn it had been longer than a measly few weeks. He'd assumed she'd be in the castle for at least a few months. It wasn't possible to learn everything he needed to know to fight alongside the people of Aericora in only a few weeks.

But, then again, his father did not intend to send him to the field, and it wouldn't be surprising if his father shortened the time Eryn would be here. Earlier that night, he'd gotten another note from the court. Deovaria overtook another small town near the border. Five hundred more soldiers were killed. Twenty imprisoned. Another fifty were so severely injured that they were being brought back to the capital for proper treatment before being relieved of their positions and sent home to their loved ones.

"Now, if you don't mind," Eryn continued, pulling Caeden away from his thoughts, "I believe we were practicing knife-throwing."

She turned away from him and to the target across the field, a good twenty feet away from where they were. She widened her stance and rolled her shoulders before squaring them and planting her feet against the ground. "Keep your body in line with the target and—"

Instead of finishing the sentence, she lifted the hand holding the knife and loosed the blade at the target. It flew end over end through the air and struck the target less than half an inch away from the center of the middle mark. A loud thwack echoed through the night air around them.

Caeden stared after the knife, his jaw slack. She was drunk, and she'd still managed to do that.

The noises from the creatures in the forest behind the target ceased, as if they, too, were holding their breaths in amazement.

She did an abrupt about-face and handed him a dagger he hadn't noticed her pick up. "You're up, fancy pants."

He ignored her use of yet another insulting nickname and eyed the knife wearily before he shook his head and took it from her. He was dimly aware of the thoughts in the back of his mind, telling him that entertaining her want to train in her current state wasn't a good idea, but he chose to ignore them. She wasn't at risk of getting hurt if he was the one holding the knife.

"Eyes forward, feet apart, shoulders square with the target," Eryn said, her voice almost gentle.

Caeden stepped up beside her and angled his body to how she'd been standing when she hit the target. His eyes found the target across the grass and focused on the center circle.

The leather encircling the dagger's hilt was cool and smooth to the touch, and he could feel the weight of the steel on the other end. He moved his wrist back and forth, testing the weight of the blade before he held his breath and lifted his hand. He threw the knife at the target, flicking his wrist when he released it so it would soar end over end in the same manner Eryn's had.

It spun through the air, but it missed the target by a few inches. Hilt first, it flew past the wooden board.

Caeden cringed as he watched it.

Eryn pursed her lips. "Don't focus on it landing blade first just yet," she instructed. "Just think about getting the knife to hit the target, hilt or blade first. Or sideways, for all I care. It doesn't matter right now. Just focus on your aim."

She stooped and retrieved another dagger from her small collection on the ground.

"Try again," she told him.

He took the knife from her and turned back to the target. He gripped the hilt of the blade so tightly he could feel his pulse throbbing in his palm.

Eryn came up behind him and touched her fingers to his wrist, making him flinch as the warmth of her touch spread through his hand. His face warmed, though he wasn't sure why.

When she spoke, her voice was soft, and he could feel her breath against his shoulder through the thin fabric of his shirt. "Relax," she said, her voice quiet.

Caeden wasn't sure if it was her closeness and the way her fingers trailed along his skin when she removed her hand or the chill to the night air around them that caused a shiver to work its way through his body.

He loosened his grip on the dagger.

"Good," she said, her voice so low it was hardly a whisper on the breeze.

She was standing so close to him he could feel the warmth radiating off her body in waves from the alcohol she'd had to drink. Lavender and tequila mingled with one another to create a new, almost sweeter scent that blurred the edges of his thoughts until all he could focus on was the way she smelled, the warmth her fingers had left behind on his wrist, and the whisper of her voice in his ear when she spoke.

"Now, focus on the target and throw."

Caeden heard her light footsteps against the ground as she stepped away from him again.

He had to shake his head to clear away the fog her intoxicating scent had caused before he could shift his attention away from her and to the target in front of him. He focused on the black dot at the center, letting the world around him blur around the edges as he felt the weight of the dagger against his palm again. His heart raced, and a split second before he was ready, he lifted his arm and threw the dagger across the field.

The pommel of the hilt hit the wood, and a metallic ding echoed throughout the night air. Twenty feet to the left of the target, something rustled in the grass as it scurried deeper into the forest.

A smile pulled at the corners of his mouth when the dagger bounced off the bullseye and into the grass.

Eryn gave a whoop of satisfaction behind him.

Caeden turned back to face her, startled by her sudden outburst.

Her arms were raised over her head, and a wide grin spread across her features, making her bright blue eyes crinkle around the edges. Her cheeks were still rosy from the alcohol, likely lending to her exaggerated excitement.

His success didn't feel as monumental as her excitement suggested, but he felt the smile on his face widen at the sight of her.

It was the first time in a long while that he'd seen someone smile like that, radiating pure joy that was contagious to those around them. Ronan was the only one he saw smile anymore, but his grins were more mischievous and used as a tool to aid in his humor.

"You should get back inside," he said as he stooped to pick up the remaining knives on the ground.

Eryn's smile disappeared before she rolled her eyes. "There's no time for sleep," she told him, an edge to her tone that surprised him.

The soft sound of a door closing reached Caeden's ears, and he turned abruptly. His eyes landed on Ronan's shack across the field, and in the dim candlelight flowing from Ronan's windows, he could make out the figure of a woman hidden beneath a dark cloak.

The woman glanced behind herself as if checking to make sure no one was there before she hurried off toward the door that led back into the castle. In her haste, her hood fell away, revealing shining red hair. She pulled the hood back into place before she disappeared inside.

"Have your reading finished by tomorrow evening," Eryn said, pulling his attention back to her.

He'd intended to get through at least one more of the books tonight, and since reading was all Ceana seemed interested in doing during their time together, he doubted finishing it would be a problem.

"I will," he promised.

Chapter 16

Eryn

Eryn watched Caeden leave, her mind drifting back to her first day in the castle. She'd watched him from her bedroom window her first night as the maid had escorted him through the field and inside the castle.

He'd gone to put up the knives they'd been using for knife-throwing practice. She still had her usual dagger in her hand, and a second one Caeden had forgotten sat in the grass a few inches away from her right knee.

She tested the weight of the knife in her hand, allowing herself to lean into the dimness of her thoughts from the alcohol so she could ignore her better judgment. She tossed her knife in the air and caught it with the blade between her thumb and first finger. She'd practiced the trick so many times before that it felt natural, even with her dull senses.

Ronan would've cursed her out if he'd caught her. Reckless, he'd called her all the time when they'd been in the field together. He'd made it his job to scold her for such things for as long as she could remember, especially during the occasions they drank together and she performed similar tricks.

She didn't use to drink as much when she'd first started fighting in the war; neither had Ronan. Ronan had always enjoyed the occasional drink more than she had, always making excuses to stop at taverns in towns they passed when they traveled from one station to another. Back then, he only used to spend his evenings with very few women, but both of those had changed after his injury. He hadn't even been recovered when he'd started drinking. He'd been in the infirmary for less than two days when she stopped seeing him sober. She'd caught him multiple times with women too, when he thought no one would be in to check on him. Luckily, she'd only caught them in the middle of the act once; that was something she still wished she could burn from her memory.

After he'd been let out of the infirmary, he'd been housed in a nearby town for multiple weeks before the King had summoned him to the castle for the job as their Head of Security. The combination of not being able to protect the one person who meant the most to her, along with seeing him so miserable for those weeks, had spurred her drinking, even if she couldn't call it as much of an addiction as Ronan's. Seeing how much he still relied on it all these years later though, only made her wearier of it.

She flipped the knife into the air again. She tossed it high enough this time that she had enough time to watch as the moon's rays reflected off its smooth surface while it soared end over end above her head.

The door to the castle's armory closed shut.

Eryn jumped, her hand closing around the knife at her side as she spun around, half expecting an attacker to jump out in front of her before she remembered it was only Caeden leaving after putting away the knives they'd been using.

Pain tore through the outside of her upper thigh and she hissed out a breath.

Her dagger.

She'd forgotten about her dagger.

Eryn sighed before she turned back and examined the wound she'd given herself through her stupidity. It wasn't deep, given all the other wounds she'd suffered over the years. It wouldn't even leave a noticeable scar, but with the alcohol in her system, it bled more than she wanted it to.

At least the alcohol helped with the pain. She picked herself up, abandoning the two knives on the ground. She tested her weight on her leg, which stung, but she had no physical impairments other than that from the cut. It hadn't gone deep enough to cut through more than skin, fat, and maybe a bit of muscle, but she doubted it.

"You okay?" Caeden's voice called from somewhere ahead of her in the dark.

Her heart rate quickened.

She evened her weight out so she was standing normally before she cocked one hip to the side, angling her right leg away from him in the dark. She could make out his figure standing near the castle, but he wasn't close enough to make out any details on his face, which she hoped meant he couldn't see the blood stain spilling across her pants from where he was either.

"You should worry less about me and more about that reading I assigned you," Eryn quipped. She'd meant for it to sound lighthearted, but the nervousness she felt at him seeing her injury made it come out sounding impatient.

Caeden was silent for a second, and she worried she'd upset him, though she wasn't sure why she cared. He laughed, and a weight lifted off her chest at the sound of it. "Maybe if you stopped playing with knives in the dark while drunk, I could worry more about the reading."

Eryn cracked a smile. Her thigh burned even more at his words, taunting her. "Goodnight, you dummy prince," she teased, a laugh hiding beneath her words.

"Goodnight, Eryn Gedding," he responded before turning and leaving her alone in the darkness again.

♥ ♥ ♥

Eryn knocked on the door to Ronan's shack, despite the dim lights inside suggesting he'd already gone to bed. She wasn't about to trek all this blood through the castle hallways. The staff would think someone was killed, and she didn't need that kind of attention on the subject if she ever had to admit to anyone other than Ronan that she'd been stupidly playing with a dagger while drunk.

"What'd ya do?" Ronan snapped as soon as he opened the door.

Eryn smiled and turned to allow the light from inside the shack to fall over her injured thigh.

Ronan took it in, his eyes widening, before the realization dawned on him, and he glared at her.

"Throwing accident," she said. She shrugged to cover up when she shifted her weight from her right leg to her left.

"Ya know, that's my least favorite phrase I've ever heard you say," he grumbled as he stepped aside and allowed her into the small living room.

"Not the first, won't be the last."

Ronan glared back at her again. "Next time, go find someone else to mop up your blood. Thought you were done bein' this stupid."

Eryn laughed. "Love you, too," she said, plopping herself

down on the coffee table as Ronan disappeared into his bedroom. "And you act like this is the thousandth time or something."

"It's the third," Ronan called from the bedroom. She heard a cabinet slam shut and a water spicket turn on. "And the first time was too many times."

A moment later, he returned with a wet rag and a roll of bandaging. He tossed her the rag, which she caught in midair, sending water droplets flying straight into her face.

Ronan smirked at her before he tossed her the roll of bandages as Ronan sat on the couch before her.

"Ya doin' okay?" he asked. His earlier irritation was gone from his tone, replaced with concern.

Eryn didn't look up at him as she set the rag aside and worked to wrap the bandages around her wound. It wasn't a permanent solution, considering she would need to change out of her pants before bed, but she had more medical supplies up in her room. All she needed was for the bleeding to ease enough that she wouldn't make a mess in the castle hallways.

"I don't feel like answering that question," she told him.

Ronan snorted a laugh. "You never do."

Eryn shrugged.

"I'm allowed to worry 'bout ya, you know."

She sighed. "I know."

Memories of the multiple times she'd come to him in similar states over the past many years flashed through her mind, and sadness settled over her, though she was careful to keep it from showing on her face. She hadn't cared to make sure that she didn't hurt herself back then. He was always right when he'd called her reckless, but this time was different. It didn't mean she wanted to talk about her feelings about her current situation any more than she'd wanted to talk about them back then, though.

Ronan sighed and sat back against the couch. Eryn finished wrapping her wound and set the remaining bandages aside before she stood and tested her leg again. It felt better without her skin having as much room to tear with each movement she made.

"Thanks," she said as she picked up the things she'd used to take them back to his room.

Ronan rolled his eyes. "Of course, ya idiot." He looked her up and down, a smirk pulling at his mouth again. He crossed his arms over his chest smugly. "I still win in the leg injury category," he said, motioning toward his leg with a wave of his hand.

Despite her best attempt to keep a straight face at his joke, Eryn couldn't help it when she laughed.

Chapter 17

Caeden woke early a week and a half later to birds chirping outside as sunlight streamed in through his window. He sighed and stared at the ceiling, giving his eyes time to adjust to the harsh morning light.

Today was the eleventh anniversary of his mother and sister's deaths.

Tears pricked at the corners of his eyes as memories of them flooded through his mind, and he wiped them away with the back of his hand before he sat up in bed. He lifted his arms above his head, stretching the sleep from his stiff muscles before shifting his legs over the edge of his bed.

His bruises and constant soreness had eased since his first days with Eryn. His muscles had grown used to the stress of his training, and he'd grown more competent in his skills, too. Eryn ensured he never left without at least a few bumps and scrapes, but now she actually had to work for it.

Caeden climbed to his feet, the floorboards creaking beneath his weight. It was a beautiful day outside. The sky was bright blue with small, puffy white clouds dotting it. In the distance, he could make out the silhouette of a dragon flying hundreds of feet in the air somewhere near the border between his kingdom and Deovaria.

Caeden clenched his jaw and turned away from the sight.

He ignored everything seeing the dragon could mean and instead focused on what the day ahead of him would hold. He and his father would go to the gravesites today, just like they had done every year since the passing of their family. He would need to cut his time with the princesses short to go. He also needed time to pick some of the sunflowers from the garden to put on Amelia's grave.

Choosing to pick flowers rather than meet with the women who he would soon choose his future wife from was not a wise decision, but he wasn't willing to brush aside something so important to him.

A light knock came on Caeden's bedroom door. "May-may I enter, Your-Your Highness?" came a quiet voice from the other side of the door.

Caeden recognized the voice of the young maid. "Yes, you may," he said, doing his best to keep his voice even despite the lump that lodged itself into the back of his throat.

As quiet as a mouse, she opened the door and slipped inside the room. Only the sound of the door's hinges creaking reached Caeden's ears.

"Breakfast is-is in half an hour, Your-Your Highness," she told him. She shifted her weight from side to side, making the ends of her black hair sway back and forth.

Caeden nodded. "What time are we visiting the gravesite?" he asked.

The young maid frowned, though it took Caeden a moment to notice since she refused to meet his gaze and her head was still bowed. "I-I believe it was-was canceled, Your Highness.

Were–were you not already told?"

Her words felt like a knife through his chest, and a flash of white-hot anger flared through him.

The visit to the gravesite was the only thing they ever did to remember and honor the queen and princess, and his father had canceled it as if it was nothing more than a dinner party.

The maid shrank back, her eyes finding the floor as she bowed her head even further.

Caeden's anger faltered as he watched her. He cleared his throat. "I'm sorry," he said quickly, though his anger still hadn't disappeared. He sighed before he continued, making sure his tone was neutral. "Thank you for letting me know."

The maid nodded before turning and leaving the room as silently as she'd entered.

Caeden got dressed before he wound his way through the castle's many hallways until he reached the dining hall. His father was already inside, waiting at the head of the table with a large glass of red wine.

Caeden sat in his usual seat to his father's right.

It wasn't unusual for his father to be drunk on the anniversary of Amelia and his mother's deaths, but he'd started early this year. He'd been drinking much more than before, and Caeden noticed even more of a difference over the last couple of weeks. It could have been in anticipation of the anniversary, or the stress of the war getting to him, but Caeden wasn't sure how to bring up that he should slow down. He'd reacted negatively the last time Caeden had dared to mention his drinking.

Resentment settled itself next to the anger Caeden still felt, and he kept his eyes away from his father. Instead, he let his gaze flit around the room. His father had canceled their trip to the gravesite, but he'd had the servants decorate the dining hall.

Candles lined the windowsills, twinkling stars hung from the ceiling above, bright yellow flower arrangements covered the table, and expensive crystal sets of dishware had been set out. Amelia's tiara and the crown his mother had worn every day sat on separate pedestals in the very center of the table.

Decorating the hall didn't make up for canceling their visit to the graves, but at least his father had done something to honor their loved ones.

The doors to the dining hall opened, and the three princesses entered the room with Eryn following behind.

Surprise flashed over all four women's faces as they took in the decorations covering the room. The princesses' expressions continued to show only awe as they took their seats, but Eryn retook her signature look of pure irritation.

Caeden offered each of the princesses a tight smile as they sat across from him. Kylana and Ceana returned his smile, but Margaid looked at him with sympathy, making a crease form between her eyebrows.

Eryn plopped herself down beside Caeden with an exasperated sigh. She crossed her arms over her chest and refused to look at him, opting instead to stare ahead.

Their food was brought out, and unlike most meals, this one passed in near total silence, aside from his father saying a few words regarding the day and the murder of the queen and princess. Caeden noticed the glassy sheen to his eyes when he finished speaking, but after he blinked, it vanished. He reached for his glass of wine again.

Caeden bit his tongue to keep himself from saying anything he would later regret.

Instead, he stood, shoving his chair back with a loud scrape against the tile floor. He clenched his hands tightly at his sides, his nails biting into the flesh of his palms. Warm blood wet his fingertips from the unhealed knife wound on his hand he'd inadvertently reopened.

"In honor of the passing of my mother and sister," he said to the three women across from him, his voice carrying through the now silent space, "I'm afraid our meetings today will be cut short. My time with Miss Gedding is limited, so I cannot postpone my lessons. I will still have time to meet with each of you, but I will be visiting my mother and sister's gravesites today, so our time will need to be cut in half to allow for it."

His father's gaze bore into the side of Caeden's face, his anger and irritation radiating off him in waves. It would've shaken him, had he not prepared himself for that exact reaction from his father.

Caeden retook his seat and focused his attention on the three women in front of him.

Kylana looked surprised, with an undertone of the same irritation Eryn perpetually had hidden in her features. Ceana looked like she could've cared less, and Margaid appeared to be gathering her thoughts before choosing to speak. Margaid opened her mouth to say something, but before any words left her lips, the doors to the hall were pushed open, and Muire burst through.

Everyone's attention turned to the advisor. A thin layer of sweat coated her forehead and upper lip, and she was panting, but she looked as though she was trying to hide any other signs that something was wrong.

Muire bowed her head. "I apologize for the interruption," she said before she looked up, and her eyes landed on the king at the head of the table. "Your Majesty, there is an urgent matter that requires your immediate attention." She spoke so fast that her words ran together. Her gaze found Caeden next. "You too, Your Highness."

All of Caeden's irritation faded away when Muire's eyes met his. Pure, undeniable fear shone in her eyes. Whatever this was, it was big enough that she'd told him and his father they were needed. He'd never seen Muire like this before. Usually, she was the most put-together of the entire court.

Caeden and his father both climbed to their feet, and the eyes of the other four women in the room fell on them.

"Please forgive us for leaving you so abruptly," the king said to everyone at the table. "Please enjoy the rest of your meal." He turned to the three princesses. "Prince Caeden will come to find you once this matter has been dealt with."

The three women nodded, and Caeden and his father followed Muire out of the room.

As soon as the doors to the hall were closed, Muire turned around to face them. Her eyes were wide, no longer trying to hide the fear she felt. "A soldier was found," she told them, still speaking so fast that her words were hard to distinguish from one another. "He-he was dropped at the front gates by a dragon. He's in the infirmary in critical condition. We haven't been able to ID him yet, but we are certain he was one of the soldiers taken from Cylemel."

Caeden's heart stopped as he listened to her words. Cylemel was attacked two weeks ago. Very few soldiers had survived being held captive by Deovaria for that long.

Caeden beat his father to speaking. "What do you mean, he was dropped by a dragon?"

Muire opened her mouth to speak, closed it, licked her lips and swallowed hard before she opened her mouth again. "Exactly that, Your Highness," she squeaked. "I didn't see it, but one guard said that a dragon landed only a few hundred yards away from the castle gates with the soldier in its claws. The dragon dropped the soldier and flew off before anyone had a chance to kill it."

"They dropped him and left?" a voice came from behind Caeden.

The three spun around to find Eryn standing just outside the dining hall's large doors. Caeden—and apparently neither of the other two—had heard the doors open or her slip through them.

"Miss Gedding," Caeden's father started, but Eryn cut him off by holding up a hand and fixing him with a look that could kill.

The king fell silent.

Caeden stared wide-eyed at his father. He'd never seen anyone aside from his mother get away with that. She had high status in their kingdom, given that she was probably the best Dragon Hunter they had, but even so, her gesture was disrespectful.

"Is the soldier alive?" Eryn asked.

Muire looked between the king and Eryn, unsure which to speak to. Eventually, her eyes found the floor in front of her. "Yes."

"Take us to him, please," the king said.

Muire nodded vigorously before turning on her heel and walking off down the hall at a pace so brisk Caeden almost had to run to keep up with her.

She wound them through the castle's many hallways to the infirmary near the doors to the training field and garden. Four guards were standing outside the door, and the chatter of multiple voices from inside flooded into the hall, along with the sound of hurried footsteps.

"He's barely alive," a nurse inside the infirmary said as they passed the guards standing in the doorway and entered the large space. "He's too badly hurt. We can't do anything else."

Five nurses huddled around a single cot near the back of the infirmary. They held bandages and other tools in their hands, and Caeden couldn't make out the person lying on the cot until one of the nurses stepped out of the way and turned around to face them. Caeden had to fight to keep his face neutral when his eyes landed on the bloody man on the cot, even as his stomach clenched so painfully he was sure he was going to throw up.

The man was barely recognizable. Most of his flesh was burned away, leaving exposed bone visible beneath the few shreds of his military uniform that remained. The shreds were no longer blue, like every soldier Caeden had ever seen, but a sickish shade of purple-brown from the dry and fresh blood coating his whole body. His limbs were bent at odd angles, and his chest heaved with each breath, causing more and more blood to leak from the three huge gashes that ran across his entire chest and abdomen.

Caeden's limbs felt heavy as he stared at the man. Deovaria had tortured him before bringing him to the castle. They'd tortured him and left him as a warning on the kingdom's doorstep. The nurses couldn't save the man because they were never supposed to be able to.

The Dragon Lord had sentenced this soldier to a long, agonizing death for the crime of simply fighting for his kingdom.

Eryn ran forward, but Caeden and his father stayed rooted in place. She knelt down beside the cot and held the soldier's hand in hers, his blood soaking through her fingers.

"Do you know him?" the king asked Eryn.

His voice was so even, and he seemed so calm that Caeden wanted to scream. The Dragon Lord had tortured this man — as good as killed him — before leaving him on their doorstep. It was the most horrendous, disgusting thing Caeden had ever seen in his life, and his father was calm.

His father had to put on a face. Caeden was doing his best to put on his own, but he couldn't keep his hands from shaking at his sides or the sweat from brimming on his forehead.

His father had none of those things.

"Yes," Eryn said. "Not well. His name is Damhain Gafraid." She spoke so quietly that Caeden could barely make out her words. She didn't look back at any of them, her eyes staying fixed on the dying man in front of her as she rubbed her thumb against the still intact flesh of his hand. "You were very brave," she whispered to Damhain. "I know you were. You served your kingdom well, and you will be honored and remembered for it."

Her words grew so soft that Caeden could no longer understand what she was saying.

The man's breaths grew more ragged as the seconds passed until finally, he gave one final, shuttering exhale and stopped.

Eryn stood, her eyes still fixed on the dead soldier, her hands bunched into fists at her sides. She turned on her heel and walked past Caeden to the king. "He was a good soldier," she said. "He should be honored as such."

"He will be," the king responded, his tone still even, unbothered by the entire sight in front of him.

She lifted her right hand, the same one that had been holding the soldier's while he died. "And I assume this is for you." Eryn unclenched her fingers, revealing a blood-stained piece of parchment in her palm.

Caeden watched as his father took the parchment from her hand. Eryn stalked out of the room without so much as a glance over her shoulder. His father opened the folded paper, revealing whatever the note written inside was. His face stayed blank as he read the words. When he finished, he handed it to Caeden.

"This was meant for us," he said, still not revealing an ounce of emotion. "Don't let it affect you. It's not worth it."

The king said nothing else before he left the room, leaving

Caeden alone with Muire, the nurses, and the body of the dead soldier still lying on the cot.

He opened the piece of parchment and read:

I enjoy the memory of their deaths a little more every year.
Now I can add his to the list.
-The Dragon Lord

Chapter 18

"What was all of that about earlier?" Kylana asked. She wasn't facing him, her eyes locked on the target as she drew back the bowstring.

Caeden was beginning to wonder if she did anything else with her time other than train. He'd never even seen her pick up a different weapon.

His mind flashed back to the dead soldier lying on the cot, his blood turning the sheets red, then to the note tucked away in his pocket, folded in a piece of fabric to keep that same blood from leaking through the layers of his pants. He wasn't sure if he could tell her what had happened earlier that morning, and he wasn't sure he wanted to, even if he was allowed. He hadn't had time to process what he'd seen earlier, and all he'd been able to focus on were the words written on the scrap of parchment.

"Are you okay?" Kylana asked, pulling Caeden's attention out of his head. She'd turned around, her bow lowered to her side. She had a concerned look on her face as she eyed him up and down.

Caeden swallowed hard, then nodded in response. "Yes," he

answered, his voice even, as he pulled himself up to his full height and attempted to keep his feelings from playing across his face. "Sorry, I'm a little distracted."

She stepped closer to him and slung her bow over her shoulder, giving him her full attention. "By what?"

She asked so calmly, as if she was asking about the most innocent thing. To her, she probably was. But in that moment, her question was so loaded he almost wanted to laugh.

"It's nothing," he told her. Their time together was almost over, and they'd spent it in near total silence. He preferred it that way today. He didn't want to talk; he wanted a few more hours to mull over what the purpose of sending a bloody, dying soldier to Aericora's doorstep was.

"The look you have on your face right now says otherwise." She crossed her arms and fixed him with a look.

Caeden didn't respond.

Footsteps approached behind them, and Caeden glanced over his shoulder to see a guard coming toward them. Margaid was behind him, waiting a respectable distance away, so they still had some privacy.

Kylana sighed, rolling her eyes. "Look," she said, her mood suddenly far angrier than she'd been only seconds before. "I didn't ask to come here. I don't want to marry you, and I never want to be a queen. My kingdom could use a little extra money; that's why I'm here. You, however, will need a wife regardless, yet you refuse to even have a proper conversation with me.

"I'd say I hope you treat the others better than you treat me, but I've spoken with them enough to know I am not the only one who feels ignored in this castle. You're the one who is supposed to ensure we are welcomed and comfortable, yet you spend all of your time off training. You never bother to see to it that the women who are here intending to be your wife feel any more important than any other servant in this godforsaken place."

Her words felt like a slap to the face.

He hadn't intended to ignore her these past couple of weeks. He'd tried to talk with her during their time together, but it was difficult when she always wanted to shoot a bow and arrow. He'd still stood with her, still asked her about her life, still talked with her about her techniques, and asked how she was getting along in the castle. Until this point, she hadn't given him much reason to assume she felt so strongly about his training and that he couldn't be around all the time.

That didn't stop the guilt from welling inside of him, though.

"I'm sorry," he told her honestly. He opened his mouth to continue, to give her some promise that he would try to do better, but the words died on the tip of his tongue before he could force them out.

He didn't know how to do any better right now. The only free time he had most days was late at night, after everyone in the castle had already been asleep for hours. He couldn't put off his training, and he couldn't make more hours appear in the day.

So, instead of giving her false promises he couldn't uphold, he said nothing else.

Kylana shook her head as if to rid herself of the anger she felt before she turned on her heel and stomped off back toward the castle where the guard was waiting a few paces away.

Caeden sighed and watched her go.

His day flashed through his mind, broken images filling his head: blood, parchments, Muire's face, Kylana's anger, Eryn kneeling next to a dying man on a cot.

"Is everything okay?" Margaid asked, a look of concern crossing over her features as she stepped closer to him. She glanced over her shoulder in the direction Kylana had stomped off in before she turned back to him with an even more puzzled expression.

He couldn't think about the soldier right now. He couldn't think about the note in his pocket. He had to meet with the princesses, then he had to get through his training with Eryn. He would have time to think later. He would have time to let the bubble of anger grow larger inside of him every time he thought of the soldier or the blood or the parchment and do whatever it wanted to once he was done with his things for the day.

Caeden shrugged in response to Margaid's question, but neither confirmed nor denied her inquiry.

Was what Kylana said about them all feeling ignored true? She was the only one who had ever voiced such a thing to him. Margaid had given him no inclination whatsoever about feeling that way, and Ceana spent most of her time ignoring *him* during their time together.

Margaid raised an eyebrow but didn't comment about Kylana or anything else. Instead, she gestured toward the garden, a silent offer to go to their usual meeting place, and Caeden followed her as she led him back inside the castle and through the other door that led to the expansive space.

Margaid sat on their usual bench, and Caeden sat beside her.

"For what it's worth, I agree that honoring your family's deaths is more important than entertaining three women you have no interest in," Margaid said.

Caeden tensed at her words, his face growing hot. Her words sounded like a jab, but when he glanced at her, she was smiling at him with something that looked like a teasing glimmer in her green eyes.

An involuntary smile formed on his face, despite everything weighing on his mind.

He laughed at her attempt at a joke despite himself, but it only lasted a second before he pushed away the amusement and forced himself to be serious with her. "Please don't think I dislike any of you," he told her. "I've been busy, but I never intended for any of you to feel ignored or unliked."

Margaid smiled kindly before she glanced away. She fixed her gaze on the garden, a faraway look settling itself over her features. "My mother was killed too, you know," she said, her voice barely above a whisper.

Caeden stared at her.

His heartbeat was deafening as he took her in, the silence stretching out like a canyon between the two of them. He wasn't sure why those words struck him as hard as they did, but he clung to them in a way that made everything else on his mind fade away. She hadn't talked about her family since he'd met her. He'd assumed both of her parents were alive and well. Margaid kept her expression neutral as she stared into the distance, but he caught the distinct shimmer of tears in her eyes.

"I'm sorry," he told her, unsure what else to say. He hated hearing those words more than anything else when they were directed at him, but for the first time, he understood why everyone said them. There was nothing else to say. He didn't know what words would bring her comfort. This was all he could offer.

The corner of her lip twitched upward. "Thank you," she whispered.

They lapsed into a comfortable silence, Margaid seeming as lost in thought as he was, though he was sure her thoughts were of her dead mother, while his were filled with images of soldiers being slaughtered by dragons.

"I was there when it happened," Margaid said quietly. "When she died, I mean."

She wiped away her tears with the backs of her hands, continuing to speak, but the glassy sheen in her eyes never went away.

"An army with dragons attacked us. They demanded that my mother surrender, and they would spare me. I was only a child at the time, but I knew what would happen."

Caeden's heart ached for what she went through, the things she must have seen, the innocence she lost. But he said nothing, only watching her as she wrung her hands in her lap and kept her eyes glued to the ground just in front of the tips of her shoes.

Caeden hadn't known about any attacks on Crevia. The other kingdoms had felt the wrath of the Dragon Lord, much like his own, but he hadn't known of an attack that killed any other members of royal families.

It wasn't surprising. Crevia was one of the kingdoms Aericora corresponded with the least. Since they hadn't ended up in a war like Caeden's kingdom had, it made sense that Crevia would want to keep it as quiet as possible to avoid upsetting the Dragon Lord and his armies by looking for sympathy from other kingdoms—or alliances.

"One soldier grabbed me and pulled me away from her," Margaid continued, the tears streaking down her cheeks again. "Three others surrounded her. Each of them had a sword pointed at her heart. When they said they'd spare me, she dropped to her knees and cried. She agreed, and one of them drove a sword through her chest anyway."

Caeden thought of Amelia, and how she must have gone through something very similar when their mother had been killed.

"What happened after?" Caeden asked, past a lump of sorrow in his throat. He wasn't sure if he wanted to know the answer to his question, but the words were out of his mouth before he could decide.

Margaid shrugged. She looked torn between answering his question and remaining silent. After a tense beat of silence, she spoke, but something about her tone made it clear to him that it was reluctantly. "My kingdom's soldiers saved me. I don't remember who, or how it happened. It was all a blur after she was killed." She refused to meet his gaze and fidgeted with the bright ruby hanging around her neck.

In the morning light, the gem almost glowed, and Caeden found himself transfixed by the shimmering crimson stone.

Caeden's version of what it was like to lose his mother was hardly comparable to Margaid's, but he knew the feeling well. After learning how his mother and sister had met their end, he'd had a similar reaction. The days that followed were a blank space of emptiness and sorrow in his mind.

Margaid cleared her throat. "Would you be opposed to company this afternoon when you visit your mother and sister?" she asked. She gave a kind smile, but there was an eagerness to it that made it too wide.

After their interruption in the dining hall, Caeden had forgotten that he'd told the princesses his plan to visit the gravesites. He grew tense again. The last thing he wanted was anyone with him. Time alone at the graves meant he would have time to mourn his family. He could cry or scream and no one would be there to hear it. But it also meant he could have time to decipher his feelings over the note in his pocket.

His father had told him not to react, but that seemed impossible. He was angry. Even angrier than he'd been in a long time, and he didn't want to let Margaid, or anyone else, see that.

"I…" He trailed off before figuring out what he wanted to say to her. He intended to tell her no, but he didn't want to explain why. He didn't want to hurt her feelings, either.

Margaid smiled, but this time, it seemed far more forced. "No is a perfectly acceptable answer," she told him. Without another word, she stood and left the garden.

Chapter 19

Margaid

Margaid shoved the comforter off, leaving only the thin silk blanket to cover her body. She was naked, but with Ronan beside her, she didn't feel as exposed as she expected she would. She felt comfortable.

"What do you think happened this morning?" she asked, propping herself on an elbow to look at him.

The windows in his room were all covered, and only a few candles placed along the nightstand provided any light, but it was enough to make out his features. She grinned, taking in his disheveled hair and the thin sheen of sweat that made his honey curls stick to his forehead.

He glanced over at her. "Whatcha mean?" He tried to hide the fear that crossed over his features, but his mask didn't fall into place fast enough.

She frowned. "The king and the prince were called out of breakfast this morning. The woman who informed them looked scared."

Ronan swallowed hard. He glanced around the room, looking

for some form of escape from this conversation, but he found none. He sighed. "I don't know if I'm allowed to tell ya," he started before swallowing hard again, "but there was a soldier dropped at the front gate this mornin'. He was in bad shape and died less than an hour after they got him inside. The ing and the court seem to want to keep it secret to keep from scarin' you or the other princesses."

Margaid's eyes widened. "What do you mean he was dropped at the gate?"

Ronan shrugged. "A dragon swooped in and left him. It was some sort of sick message from the Dragon Lord."

Margaid nodded, her mind racing. What benefit could the Dragon Lord have for doing such a thing? It was the anniversary of the queen and princess's murders, but that seemed exceptionally cruel to taunt the enemy on a day they would spend grieving.

Then again, torture came in all forms.

"Are the prince and the king okay after that?" she asked.

Ronan shrugged again. "Can't say. I haven't seen much of either of 'em. The king holds it together in front of everyone, though, so I have no way of knowin' what's goin' on with him. I haven't seen Caeden yet. He's gonna take it hard."

"Today seemed to be hard enough on him already."

"Always is," Ronan said with a sigh. "Can't say I blame him. Think I'd react the same way if somethin' like that happened to people I love."

Margaid only nodded in response. She laid back down beside him, his arms around her as she pressed her body against his. She fit nicely in his arms, and the thought warmed her cheeks. She nestled her face against Ronan's neck, leaving gentle kisses along his jaw as she ran her fingers up along his bare chest, his heartbeat quick beneath his warm skin. Everything about what she was doing was wrong. She was here for the prince, not for the castle's Head of Security, but something about the warmth of his bare skin against hers was enough to drown out her concerns. At least momentarily.

Ronan shuddered against her as she placed another kiss to his pulse, right beneath his jaw, his hands tightening around her waist.

"You should be careful, princess," he said, his voice husky with desire.

"Or what?" Margaid challenged, trailing her fingers down lower over his stomach until his breath hitched. She smirked at him in the dim candlelight.

Ronan kissed her then, deep and longing as he rolled on top of her, pressing her body into the mattress and drawing a moan from her lips. He smiled against her mouth before breaking the kiss and moving to leave gentle kisses along her jaw and neck like she'd done to him. She shuddered beneath him, desire pushing away every other thought but of him.

"Or I might start to fall in love with you," Ronan whispered against her neck.

Chapter 20

After training that evening, Caeden sat in his room, reading over another set of books Eryn assigned him a few days ago. They, too, consisted of dragon facts and theories. He'd found himself enjoying the reading over the past week, but tonight he was losing focus and unable to make sense of the jumble of letters on the page. The soldier on the cot kept flashing through his mind, along with Eryn's bloody hands as she handed his father the note.

His eyes stung from crying earlier in the day when he'd visited the gravesites. His tears this year were meant for his loved ones, as they always were, but after seeing the soldier, he'd cried for all his kingdom's people who were lost to the war, too.

Eryn ignored how puffy and red his eyes were during training. He appreciated it more than she would ever know.

Before coming to bed, he'd visited Ceana and Kylana. He'd picked each of them a small bouquet, along with the ones he'd picked for Amelia. He'd intended to do the same thing for Margaid, but she hadn't answered when he'd knocked on her bedroom door.

It wasn't much, but it was the best way he could think of to offer an apology for how they were feeling.

It was long past midnight when Caeden gave up his attempt to finish the last half of the only remaining book Eryn assigned this time. Instead, he laid the book down open on the table beside his bed, the leather-bound spine protesting the treatment.

He sighed and slung his legs over the edge of his bed before he stood and left the room. He meandered through the halls toward the training field before he gave himself enough time to think over pushing back his responsibilities until the following day.

The halls were silent, aside from the light crackle of the flickering flames from the oil lamps lining the halls. The usual candles were still lit, but they were reaching their wicks-ends, and the staff set out the oil lamps earlier in the day to avoid any of the hallways being entirely dark.

As he rounded the last corner, his body collided with another, and he stumbled backward a step. It took him a moment to regain his footing before his eyes focused on Margaid in front of him, a stunned expression on her face. Her eyes went wide, and she pulled the hood of her dark cloak back to reveal her curly red hair. The scent of alcohol wafted off her, despite there being no indication that she'd had any, and her hair was frizzy, as if she'd combed through it with her fingers.

"Oh!" she squeaked. "I didn't realize anyone else was awake. I felt like a quiet walk would do me some good after hearing about what happened today." She gave a sad smile.

She was lying about where she'd come from, but Caeden cared less about that and more about how she'd heard of the soldier. As far as he was aware, that news wasn't public yet.

He shook his head, clearing the thought away. "Me too."

No good would come from telling her that he was going to

see the same man she'd just been with.

Margaid nodded, clearly uncomfortable at having been caught on her way back. "Well, um… enjoy your walk," she told him, her cheeks reddening, then hurried off down the hallway without waiting for Caeden to respond.

Caeden watched her leave until she rounded a corner and disappeared.

Maybe he'd misread the note from the court earlier that evening, and the princesses were being told of the soldier after all. Other than her being made aware of the situation she'd agreed to marry into, he wasn't sure why the information would've been revealed to her. The court wasn't willing to risk diplomatic matters like this by giving away information that wouldn't help to keep anyone safe and would only cause unease.

He pushed away the thought, and it was almost immediately replaced by the realization that Ronan had taken him seriously when Caeden told him he wouldn't care if he spent his time with Margaid.

It still didn't bother him, but if she and Ronan had taken their relationship as far as he assumed after seeing the messy state of her hair, he worried for the first time whether it would complicate things in the upcoming weeks when he would need to make his official decision for a wife. So far, Margaid was his favorite of the three women, but he wasn't sure he could do that to his best friend.

Ronan's lights were still on inside of his shack when Caeden exited the castle.

Before he had time to reach forward to knock on the door, Ronan pulled it open and poked his head out. "Whatcha needin', princy?" he asked, his words slurring together around the edges. His voice was rough, as if he'd been half asleep only a moment earlier.

"The usual," Caeden responded. He gave Ronan a forced smile, but he couldn't muster his usual light-hearted tone when speaking to his friend.

The left side of Ronan's mouth twisted upward into a lopsided grin, his cheeks reddening even more in the dim orange light. "Gimme two seconds," he said, and shut the door.

Ronan's bare feet padded against the wooden floors in rhythm with the thump of his cane. It was followed by the sound of him rustling with things inside, and it took Caeden longer than it should've to realize he was putting on clothes. He snorted a laugh despite himself. Ronan was severely drunk if he'd opted to open the door before bothering to put on a pair of pants.

Another few moments passed before Ronan returned. He opened the door with the same lopsided smile and a bottle of amber liquid in his left hand. He motioned with the bottle for Caeden to step inside, and he did.

"I've been drinkin' this all night," Ronan said, holding the bottle to show off the label. It was uncapped, and if he hadn't had so much of it to drink already, the liquid would've sloshed out with how lazily he slung it around.

The label on the front said the bottle contained some kind of brandy, but Ronan pulled it away and pressed it to his lips too quickly for Caeden to read the rest of it.

Caeden made a face, but took the bottle from Ronan when he was done and copied his friend's example. He tilted the bottle up and warm liquid filled his mouth. It burned his throat when he swallowed but left behind a far more pleasant, almost peach-flavored aftertaste. He wasn't a fan of brandy, but he could get used to whatever this concoction was.

"Good, ain't it?" Ronan asked as he took the bottle back and took another sip for himself.

Caeden coughed, a shudder running through him as the

bitterness of the brandy finished wearing off. "Very," he said, his voice strained as he held back another cough.

Ronan nodded, pleased with the answer, before he hobbled over to the couch. He dropped himself down with a thud and exhaled.

Caeden took in the room, the crooked couch cushions, the spilled drink on the coffee table, the loose clothing he was sure Ronan wore before his meeting with Margaid, and the two barrettes neatly placed on the otherwise empty bookshelf.

"You had a wild evening," Caeden commented, giving him a teasing smirk.

A glimmer of mischief flickered across Ronan's face, and his smile widened. "I did, indeed." Ronan's face changed, and something that looked like pity replaced the cheerful air he'd had before. He glanced up at Caeden with sadness in his hazel eyes. "How'd today go?" he asked, and for a moment, Caeden was thrown back into the events of that morning.

The note in his pocket. The blood. There was so much blood.

"I heard 'bout the trip bein' canceled. Can't believe he'd do that, even with the stuff with the war right now."

Ronan's words pulled him back into the real world. He'd almost forgotten his father had canceled the trip to the gravesites. It was a messy blur in his mind, the scene in the infirmary that morning overshadowing everything else.

Caeden chose not to answer. Instead, he went over to the couch and took the bottle from Ronan again before downing another few mouthfuls of brandy. Goosebumps broke out along his arms and legs as he chugged down the liquid.

Almost reluctantly, he pulled the bottle away again and set it on the coffee table before him. He wiped his mouth with the back of his hand, allowing himself enough time for his throat to stop burning before he spoke. "Did you hear about the soldier?"

Ronan swallowed hard and looked away so quickly Caeden almost missed the way his face paled by a few shades. "I did," he mumbled.

Caeden pulled the note from his pocket and handed it to him.

Ronan took it gingerly, confused, before he opened the note and read the words scrawled across the bloodstained parchment. His eyes widened. "The soldier had this?"

Caeden nodded. "Yeah. They dropped him off half dead, and Eryn found it on him."

Ronan handed the note back and grabbed the bottle of brandy again. He said nothing else, instead sipping on the brandy while staring at the wall on the other end of the living room, seeming lost in his thoughts.

"My father didn't even seem to care," Caeden whispered, his voice even despite the flash of white-hot rage burning inside of him. "I know he has to put on a face. He's been teaching me how to do it for as long as I can remember, so I did it in there too, but his was different today. I can tell when something upsets him and when he's trying to be brave for the court. Today, he seemed entirely indifferent."

Ronan shook his head, clearing away whatever thoughts had consumed him before. "It ain't the first time the Dragon Lord has sent a message like that," he told him. "He used to do it out in the field all the time. Never heard of one reachin' the castle before, but the king would've heard of all those in the field."

Caeden had heard of those too, but they'd stopped long ago. But there was something different about this one. The original warnings were dead soldiers dropped off, or similar horrors, but they weren't personal. The Dragon Lord designed them to scare the soldiers out of fighting for Aericora at the beginning of the war, but he stopped trying when they didn't work.

This was a personal note, no doubt directed at Caeden's

father. It would not scare them out of the war. If anything, it was a taunt to anger the king even more. There was no reason for the Dragon Lord to taunt them unless Aericora was doing far worse in the war than Caeden had been told.

It wouldn't be like the court to hide something like that from him. If things were that bad in the field, they would've demanded he resume attending court meetings, not keep him in the shadows.

Caeden shook his head, clearing away the thoughts.

"What about trainin'?" Ronan asked, attempting to lighten the mood. "Or the princesses? How've those been?"

Caeden shrugged. "The princesses are fine. I cut my time with them short today to visit the graves before training. Kylana feels ignored and says that the other two feel the same way, but I'm not sure what I can do to change that. It's already the middle of the night; on any normal day, this would be my first free time. Margaid is nice to talk to, and Ceana is as distant as ever, but I have no idea if either of them is feeling the same way, and I'm not sure I want to ask, since I don't have a solution."

Ronan nodded. "And trainin'?" he asked, seeming to ignore what Caeden told him.

Caeden snorted a laugh. "I think she's trying to ensure I'm too injured to ever want to go to the field."

Ronan laughed, a loud, cheerful sound in the otherwise quiet space around them.

Caeden's smile widened. "She gives me so much to read I half expect my eyes to pop out of my head, and she beats me with a sword or her fists every chance she gets. I'm starting to think she just likes to see how many more bruises I show up with every day."

It wasn't the entire truth, considering in the past few days, he'd gained minimal bruising or injuries from his training, but he enjoyed seeing the amused look on his friend's face, regardless. Eryn's training was brutal, but he'd improved significantly over the past week. He couldn't deny that her tactics were effective.

"Toughen up a bit then, why don't you?" a voice said from outside, and Caeden jumped so high in surprise he was sure his head touched the ceiling. Eryn gave a light knock on the door once, almost mockingly, before she turned the knob and pushed it open, poking her head around the edge with her signature irritated look on her face. "These walls are thin," she pointed out as she closed the door behind herself.

"Lemme guess," Ronan said without giving Caeden enough time to respond. "You needin' a drink, too?"

Eryn rolled her eyes at him, but the corners of her lips quirked upward before she strode through the hall and to the small kitchen. "Badly," she answered as she rummaged through Ronan's many liquor cabinets.

She made herself right at home in the kitchen. They knew each other well, Caeden had known that, but this was the first time he wondered if maybe they knew each other as well as Ronan and Margaid were beginning to know one another.

"What?" Eryn snapped when she caught him watching her.

She twisted the lid off a bottle of tequila and pressed it to her lips before Caeden had enough time to come up with a response that wouldn't anger her more. She wouldn't want to hear the truth from him.

"Nothing," he told her, almost defensively, though he wasn't sure why it came out that way.

"So, the trainin'?" Ronan prompted, a devious smile pulling at the corner of his mouth.

Caeden glared at him before glancing at Eryn in the kitchen, who was giving him a warning look.

Ronan was enjoying this far too much.

"I already heard you complaining," Eryn reminded him from the kitchen, rolling her eyes. "No need to stop just because I'm inside now."

Ronan laughed.

Caeden sighed and turned back to face Ronan on the couch. "It's been fine," he responded, steering clear of his earlier jokes about how much Eryn wanted to mutilate him. "She's brutal, but her training works."

"Learn faster, and I'll ease up," Eryn said with a shrug.

Caeden glimpsed Ronan's surprised expression, but he chose to ignore it.

Annoyance burned inside him. He hadn't been frustrated with her or her attitude in what felt like a long time, but whatever was going on with her tonight was causing her to get under his skin for the first time since their first days together.

He opened his mouth to say something, though he wasn't sure what, but realized for the first time that her cheeks were already as red as the necklace Margaid wore. She was drunk, and he realized suddenly that he wasn't sober anymore either. He hadn't felt it when the alcohol began to have its effect, but he couldn't deny the fogginess that was blurring the edges of his mind, or the lack of control he felt in his fingertips.

He remembered again the soldier on the cot, and that Eryn had witnessed it, too. Part of the reason he'd come for a drink was to take his mind off those thoughts. Maybe the events of that morning were causing her sour mood. Maybe she'd come here with the same intentions as him, and hearing him make those jokes when she was standing just outside the door had had the opposite effect.

Caeden sighed, the fight he'd felt a moment ago leaving him, and he sank deeper into the couch. "I'm sorry," he told her, though he wasn't sure if she would know what he was apologizing for. He wasn't sure either, with the cloudy haze blanketing his thoughts.

Eryn raised an eyebrow at him, but she seemed to relax a bit herself.

"What are you doing here?" Caeden asked her.

"She's here to see me," Ronan answered, which seemed obvious enough to Caeden, even in his drunken haze. "I told ya we were friends."

"Siblings," Eryn corrected. She took another swig from the bottle still in her hand.

"Sort of," Ronan added.

Caeden raised an eyebrow as he looked between the two of them. Not only had Ronan never mentioned having any siblings, but when he'd first mentioned Eryn, he'd implied she was only a friend. He'd never assumed they could be siblings, considering that they looked almost nothing alike.

At least they weren't sleeping together, though he wasn't sure why it mattered.

"Sort of?" Caeden couldn't help but ask.

Eryn shrugged before she came out of the kitchen and into the living space. She still had the bottle of tequila in her hand, which she set down on the coffee table next to the bottle of brandy before she sat down on the couch between him and Ronan.

"I was unofficially adopted," Eryn explained. "My parents..." she paused for a beat before she cleared her throat and continued, "gave me up," she said carefully. "Ronan's dad took me in as a kid and trained me. It's how we ended up training in the same unit in the military."

"Until this happened," Ronan added, waving a hand at his injured leg. There was clear disdain in his voice, just like there always was when he mentioned his leg, but the bitterness Caeden heard caught him by surprise, given the good mood he seemed to be in.

"Until that," Eryn agreed, a faraway look in her eyes. Eryn shook her head, clearing away the look, and glared at Ronan. Caeden frowned in confusion, though he knew neither was paying enough attention to him to notice. "I told you not to go," Eryn said, anger and something that sounded like hurt seeping into her tone. In her drunken state, her mask had fallen away, and Caeden caught the same hurt he'd heard in her voice hiding behind her bright blue eyes.

Ronan shrugged, but not in his usual carefree manner. "I had to. You know just as well as the rest of 'em."

"What happened?" Caeden asked before he had enough time to think better of whether it was a good idea to do so.

Eryn turned her attention to him, but Ronan refused to look up from the bottle of brandy in his hand. Caeden hadn't even noticed when he'd picked it up.

"You don't know?" Eryn asked.

Caeden shook his head.

Eryn clenched her hands at her sides, but her tone was almost entirely even when she spoke. "He was offered a place in an elite group of soldiers who would be sent straight into the outskirts of Deovaria. The goal was to be stealthy—to collect any information they could and get out as fast as possible." She swallowed hard, clenching and unclenching her fists in her lap as if she needed a momentary distraction. "One member of the group turned out to be a spy in disguise. The ones they cloaked in magic that I told you about."

Caeden nodded, urging her to continue.

"They were caught because of him, and imprisoned and tortured for a month before we could send a rescue team. All but two of the original men died."

Caeden's stomach tightened. Images flooded his mind again of the bloody soldier, but this time, it was Ronan's face on the body. He'd heard snippets of information about that mission. It struck him that they had been tortured for so long, but the thoughts hadn't lasted for long before they were replaced with what seemed like more important matters. He wouldn't be able to forget anything like that again.

He couldn't recall any of those details mentioned when they'd discussed hiring Ronan for his position, but that had been years ago. It was possible he'd lost those memories to time.

"Ronan's leg was shot almost immediately after we got him out of the prison," Eryn finished.

Caeden swallowed hard, forcing down the lump in his throat. His eyes found Ronan on the other end of the couch, but Ronan refused to meet his gaze. Instead, he began picking at the peeling edge of the sticker on the bottle.

Eryn seemed so relaxed when she'd spoken about those spies during their training. It made him wonder now if she'd been hiding how severe certain situations involving them were to keep from worrying him, or if she was pretending for her own sake that nothing horrible had come from it.

It made no sense how no one at the castle had heard of this. His father and the court would have made a much bigger deal about something like this had they known about it.

"How did you get out with your leg hurt?" Caeden asked.

He couldn't imagine the amount of pain Ronan must have been in after enduring that kind of torture. The idea of him walking out in that condition seemed impossible.

Despite the question being directed at Ronan, Eryn responded when it became clear Ronan wasn't going to. "The leg hardly made a difference," she answered, more emotion seeping into her voice than Caeden had ever heard. "He was barely lucid from starvation and the injuries he'd sustained from the torture. They planned to carry him out from the very beginning."

Her eyes were glassy, and she blinked to clear them away.

This was what had caused her bad mood. Seeing the soldier that morning had undoubtedly brought back the emotions from when she'd seen Ronan after he'd received a similar torture.

"How do you know so much about it?" Caeden asked her. Clearly, the information hadn't spread far after the soldiers had returned. Very few people knew the details, and when they'd attempted to report back to the castle, the message must have been intercepted.

Eryn gave a half smile, but the sadness on her face never disappeared. "I was the one leading the mission, you dummy prince," she said, but the venom she usually had in her tone when she used an insult like that wasn't there this time.

Caeden stiffened at the realization.

That was how she'd worked her way so high in the ranks so quickly. Anyone who completed that mission would've been elevated at least one rank for coming back alive.

"I became an official Dragon Hunter only a few months before," Eryn explained. "No others were willing to go, but they needed at least one before anyone would volunteer for the rescue party, so I said I would do it."

Ronan, who had been sitting silently up until that point, looked up. "Don't lie," he told her, his usual mischievous grin pulling at the corners of his mouth. "We all know just how desperate ya were to save me so you could spend the rest of your days gloatin' 'bout it."

There was a loving glimmer in Ronan's eyes, and despite what Eryn had just explained about them being raised together, it still shocked him to see that kind of look on his friend's face.

Eryn waved a dismissive hand in Ronan's general direction, nearly smacking him in the face in the process, since she was only sitting a foot away from him. "The fact that I can gloat is just a bonus, you moron."

She leaned over the couch until her face was only a few inches away from Caeden's, and Caeden's heart raced in his chest. The smell of lavender wafted off her, making his thoughts even cloudier than the alcohol had. She had a small scar on the side of her left cheek, and the warm glow of the candles around them made the lighter skin almost glisten.

"The real reason I did it was because of the boost in rank I would get if I succeeded," she half whispered while making it clear that she was being loud enough for Ronan to overhear the joke.

Her words hardly registered in Caeden's mind, even as he watched her perfectly shaped lips form them. His face felt hot. Her closeness sent a nervousness through him that both made him want to back away from her and kept him paralyzed in place. He wondered what he could do to get her to stay right where she was.

"Ya did always wanna outrank me," Ronan mumbled in fake irritation.

Eryn laughed, and Caeden could smell the alcohol on her breath before she sat back up on the couch again.

A pang of disappointment spread through him when she moved away, even as a smile spread across his face at Ronan's words.

The more Caeden watched the two of them beside each other, the more similarities in their habits he noticed. They were subtle things, like the undertone of mischief they both had when they smiled or laughed, or the way they sat on the couch with one leg crossed beneath them.

The more Caeden thought about it, the longer the list became.

They weren't blood siblings, but having grown up together, they'd acquired so many small similarities they might as well have been.

Eryn picked up the tequila from the table again and pressed the bottle to her lips. She threw her head back and took a long swig. She swallowed four times before she pulled it away, and goosebumps broke out along her arms. She shook her head vigorously, and a shiver ran through her body.

"Booze hog," Ronan accused, reaching for the bottle and snatching it from Eryn's hands.

Caeden laughed, the sound surprising him.

Eryn and Ronan's surprised expressions matched the one he was sure he had on his own face, but after less than a second, Eryn joined in the laughter, and Ronan took a long drink from the bottle of tequila before doing the same.

Caeden took the bottle next and took a few sips.

The tequila was far more bitter on his tongue than anything else Ronan had, and the taste turned his stomach in a way he wasn't fond of. He couldn't even force himself to get down another small mouthful of the foul liquid without gagging.

Eryn watched him with an almost eager expression when he tried one last time to take a sip without gagging, and when he failed, her laughter rang out around them. She threw herself back against the couch while gripping her sides with her hands, her laughter making her cheeks turn even redder, to the point they nearly matched Ronan's.

Caeden felt his cheeks heat once again in mild embarrassment before he pushed the feeling away. He raised a questioning eyebrow at Ronan on the other end of the couch, who glanced again at Eryn before shrugging, as if to say that this kind of laughter was normal for her when she was drunk.

"So, Your Royal Highness," Eryn said, her words beginning to slur together. "Why've you been in such a sulky mood all day?" She swallowed hard, her face darkening as she seemed to remember what today was. She cleared her throat. "Aside from the obvious."

Caeden's amusement faded, and he cleared his throat before he answered her. "My father's reaction to the soldier this morning and the note have been on my mind," he told her, bitterness making its way into his voice. "Not to mention that I was already upset with him for canceling our events to honor my mother and sister."

His father would have reasons for all of it, but the foggy haze surrounding his thoughts made the anger easier to grasp onto and feed than the parts of him that knew his father had only been doing what the court and the people expected of him.

Eryn's face grew pale for a split second, her eyes darting to Ronan beside her as if to double check he was still there. It took a beat longer than usual for her to get her mask back into place, but the smile reformed on her mouth. She offered him a sad smile. "More alcohol?" she suggested, holding out the bottle of brandy to him. He hadn't realized she'd picked it up.

The smile returned to Caeden's face despite himself. "That's what I'm here for."

He and Eryn stayed in the shack with Ronan for multiple more hours, but each time Caeden inquired about their childhood, or why Eryn's parents had given her up, Eryn grew silent and Ronan changed the subject. It was odd, and only fueled his curiosity, but he did his best to avoid pressing the subject.

Instead, they laughed about him and Eryn's training sessions and when Margaid was mentioned, they laughed that Ronan was sharing his bed with one of the women who could very well be Caeden's wife in a few short weeks.

No one talked again about Ronan and Eryn's past, and no one brought up the events of earlier in the day. The tension still clung to the edges of the room for the first few hours, but eventually, it ebbed away until they were only three people, laughing at the ridiculous turns their lives had taken.

Eventually, the sun rose from behind the horizon, and Caeden and Eryn left before anyone would have time to realize they'd been up drinking the entire night.

The pale pinks in the sky were barely enough to see outside, but they were far more than either of them had with them the previous night when they'd found their way to the shack in the pitch darkness.

"Caeden," Eryn said quietly as he walked off toward the castle after saying his goodbyes to the two of them.

Caeden paused in his tracks.

It was the first time he'd ever heard her use his name, and something about the sound on her lips made heat rise to his cheeks and his heart skip a beat in his chest.

He turned back to face her, hoping beyond anything that the blush from the alcohol would be enough to cover up any redness that had risen to his face. "Yes?"

Her smile was gentle and kind. "Try not to be too upset with your father. I know you already know this, but he does have to put on a face. He loved both your mother and your sister, and I'm sure he felt something reading the note, just like you did. But he's also been overseeing this war for a long time, and as awful as it is, I'm sure he's seen things like that note before."

She gave an awkward shrug, but her eyes stayed locked on his. "I'm not trying to downplay or invalidate your feelings, and I know it's none of my business. I know you're upset and hurt, but I don't want to watch you grow an irrational bitterness toward someone you love over something that he is required to do. He has a kingdom to protect, and part of that is putting on a show of being unemotional when things like that happen so people don't get too scared."

Caeden sighed, the last of his anger receding. He already knew all the things she was saying, but something about hearing those words out loud made them wedge their way through his anger, breaking it apart until all he was left with was sadness.

He tucked his hands into his pockets and gave her the same sad smile she'd given him. "Thank you," he told her, truly meaning it.

Eryn smiled, her cheeks flushing a bright red. She said nothing else before she disappeared toward the castle.

Chapter 21

The warm sunlight shone down on the garden, its rays burning the exposed skin of Caeden's arms and face. Margaid sat beside him silently, swinging her legs back and forth in the warm afternoon breeze. They'd lapsed into an uncomfortable silence after he'd asked about the bruise marking the exposed skin between her neck and shoulder. He'd been trying to start a conversation with her, only to realize far too late that he knew precisely where that bruise had come from. She'd turned bright red and rushed to say she didn't know, which he knew was a lie, but nothing could have made him point that fact out.

He swallowed hard and turned away, the reminder of Ronan making his mind drift to the week before when he'd spent the entire night drinking with both him and Eryn. He relived the night in his mind, choosing to focus on those thoughts instead. His thoughts lingered on the memory of Eryn's closeness when she'd joked about her elevation in rank or when she'd spoken his name for the first and only time when they'd been leaving.

Those moments made his heart race like he'd never felt before. It was the most paralyzing fear he'd ever felt, yet it was laced with something that left him craving more.

A guard appeared through the castle's back door and made his way over to where Caeden and Margaid were sitting. He was early, considering he and Margaid had only been outside together for a little over half an hour.

"I apologize for the interruption, Your Highnesses," the guard said. He knelt in the dirt a few feet away from them, flinching as his knees touched the uneven ground beneath the weight of his body. "Your father has requested a meeting with you later tonight, my prince. After your evening meal."

Caeden stared at the guard, doing his best to let a look of confusion cloud his features, rather than the sense of dread he felt at hearing those words.

It was about the soldier who had been delivered the week before. There was no question about it, not with the look of fear hiding in the guard's eyes.

A bitter taste formed in his mouth at the thought of the conversations that awaited him.

After everything happened, he was sure he would be asked if he'd decided on a wife yet, and he would inevitably have to tell his father he was nowhere near that point.

Caeden shook his head and forced a smile. "Please tell him I look forward to it," he told the guard, despite the growing unease in the pit of his stomach.

The guard climbed to his feet and nodded once before he headed back inside.

Caeden watched him leave, his eyes focused on the glinting silver plates that made up the guard's armor.

Caeden and Eryn practiced hand-to-hand skills until the sun set below the horizon. Even as his body became more sore and bruised, their matches lasted longer as their training wore on. He still lost to her every time, but it took her longer and longer to win.

He arrived at the dining hall after their training session was done. To his surprise the three princesses were the only other people seated at the oversized dining table. He'd heard their quiet chatter before he had entered the room, but the second he stepped inside, their talk ceased.

His father was likely hidden away in his office, either conversing with strategists regarding the war, or meeting with event planners to organize Caeden's upcoming betrothal ceremony and eventual wedding.

Eryn was a different story. She'd made it clear she neither enjoyed nor took these meals seriously. Caeden wasn't surprised that she wasn't in attendance, especially since the king was not here either and couldn't take offense to her absence. He didn't understand why the pang of disappointment at not seeing her was so noticeable, though.

The three princesses watched him as he took his seat across from them.

Meals were his least favorite part of every day, and they'd become worse the longer the three women remained in the castle.

The meal was silent, apart from some occasional polite chatter between the four of them and the sounds of silverware scraping against ceramic dishes.

Once they finished eating, Caeden stood abruptly, his chair sliding across the floor and echoing against the stone walls around them. "Please excuse me," he told them. "I'm afraid the king has summoned me for a meeting, and I shouldn't keep him waiting."

He was met with curious looks from the three across from him, but they only bowed their heads and offered polite farewells before he made his way out into the hallway.

"Everything's always more important than spending time with us, we know," Kylana's murmured words reached his ears as the large wooden doors closed behind him. They were faint and sounded like they had been spoken into the rim of a wine glass, but they still left him stunned.

The surprise dulled to a mild irritation. He hadn't just avoided her the entire time she was here. He'd spent the same amount of time with her that he had with each of the other women. And, as much as he disliked the bitterness of the thought, it wasn't his fault that all she wanted to do when they had time together was shoot her bow and arrow. She hadn't yelled at him again, but she'd been cold this past week and had seemed to ignore his attempts to reconcile with her.

Caeden walked through the halls toward his father's office, pushing the thoughts away along with his irritation.

Raised voices reached him when he rounded the last corner leading to the short hallway where his father's office sat.

Caeden could make out a woman's voice along with his father's but couldn't discern who the voice belonged to with how muffled they sounded through the thick walls and closed door. None of the advisors would have dared to yell at his father the way the woman he was currently with was. He tried to decipher what they were arguing about, but it proved as hard, if not harder, than trying to determine who the woman in the room was.

The shouting ceased as Caeden turned the final corner, and the door to his father's office was thrown open.

Eryn emerged, and slammed the door shut behind herself, the paintings on the wall nearby rattling against the stone.

Caeden stopped dead in his tracks.

There was no way she could've been the one arguing with his father.

The thought seemed ludicrous. His father hardly let his advisors argue with him when they spoke calmly.

Eryn's hands were balled into tight fists at her sides that turned her knuckles the color of freshly fallen snow, and her body was ridged with frustration. Her eyes remained downcast, but Caeden caught the angry flush across her cheeks. She took a few steps down the hallway in Caeden's direction before her eyes landed on him. Then, she stopped, surprise flashing across her pretty features.

The mask of anger she'd been wearing when she'd exited the room faltered for a split second, revealing a deep sadness that made his heart clench. She tried to hide it again, leaning into the surprise she was still feeling at noticing him in the hallway, but now that he'd seen it, even when her mask fell back into its place, he could see right through it.

He had no clue what made her so upset that it led to that sort of argument, but the sadness he saw in her eyes left him feeling debilitated. They stood there in silence, neither saying a word to the other as they took each other in. Caeden opened his mouth to speak, but before he could get a word out, Eryn held up a hand to silence him.

She shook her head, the sadness disappearing beneath the frustration, and without another word, she walked past him and vanished around the corner.

Caeden had half a mind to follow her, but thought better of it and continued to his father's office.

She'd made it clear she didn't want to talk about it, and he didn't want to anger her any more than she already was. If she'd yelled at his father like that, there was no telling what she would do to him if he upset her, too.

Caeden frowned as he rapped his knuckles on his father's closed door. There were a thousand things they could've been discussing, but none of them should've led to an argument like that. Caeden waited a split second for a response, but when none came, he pushed open the door and walked inside.

His father was sitting behind his desk, his hands clasped in front of him. He rested his elbows on the desk, and his chin was pressed against his knuckles. His face was flushed with the same irritation that had been on Eryn's, but something about his father's demeanor suggested he was more perplexed by whatever they'd been arguing about than he was angry.

Curiosity nagged at the edges of Caeden's thoughts, but he didn't comment on what he'd witnessed.

The king cleared his throat. He removed his elbows from the desk and set his arms in his lap. "You're early," he remarked, sounding almost surprised. "How was dinner?"

Caeden shrugged in response. "They said you needed to speak with me?" he asked, evading the question.

There had been nothing interesting at dinner to note, and he didn't feel like having a conversation with his father about the princesses.

"Yes," the king responded. He leaned back in his chair. Whatever he'd been puzzling through from his earlier meeting was gone from his mind. "The matter of your betrothal has been brought back to my attention."

Caeden noted the formal way his father spoke and knew without his father saying anything else where this conversation was going. He'd been waiting for it since the soldier had bled out in front of him.

"What about it?" Caeden prompted when it became clear his father had no intention to speak before he acknowledged that he'd heard him.

"The event has been moved up," his father explained. "The ceremony will be in five days. You have three to make your official decision so we can have adequate time to have the remaining princess sent home to ensure her safety."

Bile rose in the back of Caeden's throat, and his stomach flopped in a way that made him sure he was a few seconds away from throwing up. He stared at his father, the realization still not sinking in, despite his growing nerves.

"Princess?" he asked. The full extent of what his father had said still hadn't registered.

The king nodded somberly. "It's come to my attention that Princess Ceana of Nozac would like to be sent home. She spoke with me this afternoon and said she would be leaving at first light tomorrow."

Caeden stared at him. Ceana had opted to be sent home?

It made sense, given her lack of interest the entire time she'd been in the castle, but it only made the realization of what was happening sink in further.

He'd expected this.

He'd been waiting for this.

He knew he'd have to decide quickly, but only three days? He had three days to decide which of the princesses he would spend the rest of his life with. And his only options were one who hated him and one who was in love with his best friend.

And only five days until the ceremony? Five days until he would be reintroduced to his kingdom with his future bride and their future queen by his side.

His head spun. He would be married soon. If the ceremony happened within the next few days, a wedding would follow shortly after. It was the first time he truly realized the gravity of what he'd agreed to.

It made his head spin even more to think about.

"Three days?" Caeden stammered.

His father nodded. He didn't look like he wanted to have this conversation any more than Caeden did. "Or sooner, would be preferred."

Caeden shook his head. "No. I need three days." He took a deep breath and held it for a long moment before letting it out. It didn't work to calm him, but it helped to take the edge off. "I think I have a decision, but I must be sure."

The king nodded in response.

Caeden swallowed hard before he broached the subject that lingered in the back of his mind, only momentarily repressed by the sudden realization of what awaited him in only a few short days. "What about my training? Will that be moved up as well? Will I be sent to the field early?"

The ceremony worried him, but a deep part of him had known what he'd been getting himself into. But his training being cut short—that wasn't an option. He'd agreed to this marriage with the intention of receiving full military training and being field-ready by the time Eryn returned to her post.

His father gave him a curious look, and Caeden realized he'd slipped up. He hadn't broached the subject of being sent to the field with his father again. He'd hoped he would've had enough time to consider the idea and reconsider his stance, but Caeden hadn't intended to test that hope just yet.

The king swallowed hard, his Adam's apple bobbing in his throat, all signs of confusion gone from his expression. "We will discuss the matter of your training at a later date," he said firmly, attempting to leave no room for Caeden to argue.

It wouldn't bode well for his objectives if his father avoided this conversation. A flare of anger he hadn't expected to feel burned bright in his chest. "Why?" he demanded.

The king narrowed his eyes—a dare to continue that Caeden had never shied away from, and had no intention of doing now.

"Why?" he repeated, clenching his fists at his sides until his nails were biting so hard into his flesh that he was sure he would find droplets of blood wetting his palms when he released the pressure.

He would not budge on this matter. He'd wanted this for years, and his father and the court had agreed to trade something as monumental as his marriage for it.

"The war is getting worse," his father stated. "Aside from what happened last week, we are losing soldiers left and right. We need a larger army and our army heads somewhere where they aren't wasting their time training a prince who will never be able to see the battlefield."

Caeden took a step back. The remark felt like a slap across the face.

He knew what his father thought about him wanting to be trained to fight, and he knew his training was progressing slowly. Aside from him being the heir to the throne, his moving so slowly in his training likely only added to his father's concerns about him being sent.

No king in their right mind would agree to what Caeden wanted, but his father had at the very least agreed to have him trained. It seemed that time was up, and he was now planning to have his teacher sent back to the field.

Even if it was the wisest decision for the kingdom, it still angered him.

He was left feeling more hurt by the implications than anything else. Aside from his responsibilities as the prince, his father, one of the few people who he still loved in this world, didn't think he would ever be capable of fighting alongside his kingdom's soldiers, even with the training Eryn was giving him.

The prince in him, the part that knew his father was right, battled with the son and brother in him, the parts that had vowed to be a part of putting an end to the Dragon Lord's reign by doing more than sitting safely inside the walls of the castle and giving orders.

Caeden shook his head. "So, you're ending it early then?"

He did his best to keep his tone even but couldn't prevent the anger from seeping into it.

"Miss Gedding will remain here to train you until after you are married but will be returning to her post not a moment after," the king said, his tone making it clear he was done with this conversation.

Caeden clenched his jaw. "Then what was the point in this arrangement? To coerce me into marrying a woman I don't love all for military aid that we could've gotten with enough money and a simple arrangement to have a member of a neighboring kingdom sitting in on our court meetings? I know the marriage makes it easier, but to promise me training only to take it away because of the war worsening—which we knew was bound to happen—is cruel. I will be bound to one of those women for the rest of my life, and I thought I would leave this arrangement with at least a chance to fight for my kingdom!"

The king rolled his eyes.

The bags under his eyes had gotten even worse, and for the first time since Caeden had entered his father's office, he noticed how much thinner he'd gotten and how hollow his cheeks had become. He was thin now, and his fingers looked as though Caeden could snap them in half between his own. It didn't help to ebb away any of Caeden's anger, but part of him knew that arguing with his father when he was in this state of mind wouldn't get him anywhere. It never had in the past.

"You're not being sent to the field, Caeden!" his father

shouted. "You are the heir! You need to be here, learning to take care of your kingdom! Yes, you will be married, but that is also for the good of your kingdom! You shouldn't be out there risking death when your marriage could bring us an army that is much more competent than you will be, even after years of training!"

Caeden dug his nails deeper into his palms, this time hard enough that he could feel the blood as it seeped beneath his nails.

He would not yell. It would be pointless. He would need to bring this up again later. His father was far too stubborn when he was tired.

"Fine," Caeden said.

He turned on his heel and strode from the room. When he reached for the doorknob, his father cleared his throat loud enough to catch his attention.

"Caeden," he said, his voice rough, though Caeden wasn't sure if it was due to his lack of sleep or if it was emotion he was hearing in his father's tone. It wasn't the anger he'd expected to hear from him, though, and it was enough to make him pause.

He turned around, and for the first time in a long while, the man standing before him wasn't just the king. This man was his father. The man who had first taught him and his sister how to hold a sword, who had played with them in the garden until long past dark despite his mother's protests, who had crawled around on his hands and knees with Caeden on his back because Caeden had been too young to ride one of the real horses in the stable.

"Are you ready for this?" his father asked, worry etched into his features.

Part of him wanted to scoff at the question, considering this arrangement had been his father and the court's idea, not his. But his father was only trying to do what was best for everyone by arranging it in the first place. He was trying to create a kingdom that was safe for everyone, including his only son, even if that meant having him marry a princess to help them secure a larger army of soldiers to fight against Deovaria.

Whatever barrier he'd put up between himself and his father over the years cracked.

He was only a child again, and the only person who would help him up off the ground when he'd first fallen off the horse that he was still too small to ride was his father.

But that wasn't the reality he was living anymore. His father had put it into motion, and Caeden was the only way to ensure his kingdom stayed safe. It didn't matter if his father or Caeden had second thoughts about the arrangement. This was what needed to happen, and it was what was going to happen, regardless of how he or his father felt.

Caeden shook his head, knocking himself from his thoughts and focusing again on his father in front of him. "I'm ready," he lied, but the relief he saw flash across his father's face at hearing those words was worth it.

Chapter 22

"Watch yourself," Eryn snapped. She was far more irritated than usual when Caeden missed deflecting her attack. He shouldn't have missed such an easy dodge. It had cost him, and she nearly grazed the skin on his upper arm. He wasn't out of the fight yet, though, but she wouldn't take it well if he told her his head wasn't on his shoulders today. Especially not if he told her it was due to his betrothal in a couple of days.

Eryn knocked her sword against his hard, and Caeden lost his balance. He only lost it for less than a split second, but it was enough time for her to press the tip of her dulled blade to the center of his chest, winning the fight.

Caeden cursed beneath his breath as she pulled the cool metal away from his sternum.

"Again," Eryn instructed.

They fought again.

This time, Caeden held her off long enough for the fight to last a few minutes, but that was it.

He grazed her lower leg, but as she enjoyed reminding him every time he landed similar blows, something as insignificant as a slight cut on the leg wouldn't protect him from a trained soldier in an actual battle. He wasn't the winner of a fight until his opponent was dead or so severely injured they could no longer move to fight him.

She won that fight, too.

And the twelve after that.

Throughout their fights, she was going harder on him than usual. She hadn't been initially, but the farther they got in their training that day, the tougher she was on him. He was keeping up with her well enough. He still lost to her every time, but that was to be expected with how she was going about it today.

"You have to get better!" Eryn shouted at him.

Caeden looked at her, surprised. His heart was racing in his chest from the effort he'd put into those fights. Sweat dripped down his forehead, burning when it reached his eyes, and his clothes stuck to his skin.

"We don't have time for you to be this incompetent still," she continued.

She spoke more to herself than to him, but her words stung. He wanted to argue that he was doing his best and that he'd kept up with her throughout their training after the first few fights, but instead, he kept his lips pressed together and concealed the irritation he felt.

"It's all going to be for nothing if you can't figure out how to apply even the simplest defensive skills in a fight with the most basic weapon in all creation!"

"I'm trying!" Caeden shouted, surprising himself with his sudden outburst. "I've gotten better. You can't deny that, but you can't expect me to suddenly be perfect overnight. We haven't even trained with swords more than a handful of times."

Eryn fixed him with a look that could've killed every soldier on the battlefield. "It's been three weeks!" she yelled, her cheeks flushing red. "You've barely improved. You've learned the basics, but can't seem to apply them consistently in a fight. Sometimes you do, and sometimes you don't! And I have, what? Another three, if I'm lucky, to teach you how to apply your skills well enough to fight in a war that's been raging for eleven years? You'll die within the first hour you spend in the field!"

Something flashed in her eyes, and her voice wavered when she said the last words, but Caeden was too frustrated to give it a second thought.

"It takes years to train soldiers! Literal years! You've been learning to fight since you were a child! I hardly learned half of the basics until you showed up!" Caeden ran a frustrated hand through his damp hair. "I know I'm not good enough yet. I'm trying to learn as fast as I can so this isn't a complete waste of either of our time."

Eryn stared at him for a long moment, and something in her eyes softened. She said nothing else, just held up her sword and swung at his ankle.

They continued to practice, only taking a handful of brief breaks in their training hours.

He won some fights, but his muscles were beginning to give out.

"I'm not going easy on you this time," Eryn warned as she readied herself for another round.

Her words were almost laughable, considering he'd barely been able to hold his own against her most of the day. Caeden was out of breath, and sweat dripped down his face. He wiped his face with the sleeve of his shirt, but it did little to help.

Eryn still wasn't so much as panting.

He nodded, but was too out of breath to respond.

She swung at his left side, but when he dodged out of her way and aimed his own strike, she pulled hers away and landed a blow to his lower leg. She danced close to him, and while deflecting another one of his attacks, landed a blow on his ribs with her fist.

"Hey!" Caeden said, wheezing from the effort and from the new bruise he could already feel blossoming across his ribcage. "That's an unfair strike."

Eryn snorted a laugh and gave him a look that suggested he was the most adorable thing she'd ever seen. She lifted her sword above her head and brought it close to his shoulder. He held his perpendicular to hers and shoved her away. She stumbled back a step, but caught her balance before he had time to register that she'd even lost it.

"Fights against your enemies are never going to be fair," she reminded him. "They won't consider your lack of training, or your lack of ability to think to use anything other than your sword in a fight."

He aimed for her side, but she stepped away again, hooking her foot around his ankle when she did. He tripped over her and stumbled forward but grabbed hold of her arm and pulled her down with him when he fell. Eryn grunted as she landed on top of him, their swords clattering against each other a few feet away.

"Good," she said.

She was still on top of him, her legs straddling his waist and pinning him to the ground.

A smile tugged at his lips as he moved to begin a hand-to-hand fight with her, but disappointment hit him less than a second later as she pulled her dagger from the holster on her hip and pressed it to his throat before he realized what she was doing.

"But not good enough," she finished. She tucked her weapon into the belt at her waist and climbed off him.

There was no sarcasm in her tone. No hint she was joking around at all. Her words were serious, and even though she was right, it still struck him.

"Prince Caeden," a female voice said from behind him as he climbed back up to his feet.

Eryn raised an eyebrow at him, and he turned around to face the owner of the voice.

Kylana stood before him with an irritated expression that could've rivaled Eryn's.

"May I speak with you?" she asked, but her tone made it clear she wasn't giving him a choice.

Caeden glanced back at Eryn, who rolled her eyes before waving a dismissive hand in his direction.

He cleared his throat and turned back to the princess. "Of course. What is it you'd like to discuss?" he asked, though he was certain he could guess what this was about.

He'd attempted to try harder to meet her needs over the past few weeks, and to make her feel as important as he could, but he could tell she still felt he wasn't trying hard enough. Even if he'd been given multiple more months, he didn't think he would've been able to make her see just how many things he was trying to fit into his schedule. But he also knew her feelings on the matter were valid, even if he wasn't sure how to express to her that he understood.

Kylana waited until Eryn left before she spoke. "You'll be marrying one of us in a few weeks," she hissed. She kept her voice low enough that no one else who may be standing nearby could hear. "And you'll be announcing your betrothal in five days!"

Caeden stared at her. "I'm more than aware," he responded. "I'm trying to make my decision official. I still have a few days left to—"

Kylana threw her hands up in annoyance. "That's not the point!"

She hadn't brought this topic up in weeks, and though he had fixed nothing between them, he'd hoped that the little things he had done to make it up to her would've done more to ease how she was feeling. They weren't much, but it was hard to do much more than try harder to converse with her properly when he stood by and watched her practice every time they were together.

"You'll be marrying one of us in a few weeks, yet you still can't be bothered to prioritize us."

She was seething, and Caeden swallowed hard. He wasn't sure what he could say to her. He didn't want to anger her more, especially since she wasn't in the wrong either. He was prioritizing his training, which he couldn't argue with, but he didn't feel he was putting it as far above them as she continued to imply. His time with Eryn would be coming to an abrupt end, too.

"I apologize," he said. "I've been rather busy with my training, as I won't have much time left with my teacher."

"Yes," she huffed. "We're all very well aware of your 'training'." She crossed her arms over her chest and cocked a hip to the side.

His mind raced with ways to help, but he couldn't think of anything to calm the situation as much as he needed. The whole point of this marriage was to gain an ally and win the war, but with how Kylana looked at him, he worried he'd just made a new enemy.

"I was planning to take the next few afternoons off from training," he lied, the words rolling off his tongue. "I hadn't realized until yesterday that I had so little time left, and I was making arrangements today to compensate as best I can for the lost time. I hope you will forgive me."

Kylana's expression softened, but there was still a distinct hardness to the set of her jaw. "This is more for your sake than mine," she told him. "I have a one in two chance of being your wife, but you will marry one of us. Personally, I would like a chance to get to know the man who may very well be my future husband, and I suggest you do the same with us." Kylana didn't give him a chance to respond before she pivoted on her heel and stormed off.

Caeden sighed, and the full weight of the situation came crashing down on him once again. It wasn't just about the marriage. It was about the alliance. It was about his kingdom. But it was also about these women as well. If they didn't feel they were being treated fairly, then maybe they hadn't been.

"You should take that advice," Eryn said, appearing from behind a nearby tree.

He hadn't heard her come back, but it only took a second for him to realize that maybe she'd never left in the first place. She twirled her dagger between her fingers, the same one she'd held to his throat earlier, and leaned her shoulder against the tree. It would've been an intimidating stance had he not gotten to know her well enough to know she meant nothing by it.

"I don't know what I'm doing," he confessed. Saying the words out loud helped lift some of the weight of the situation off his chest. He hadn't realized just how hard he'd been trying to convince himself—and everyone else—that he had all of this under control.

Eryn's eyebrows knit together before her usual, almost entirely unreadable expression returned to her face. "Well, that's obvious," she deadpanned.

Caeden glared at her. "Thanks for the vote of confidence," he murmured, rolling his eyes.

The corner of Eryn's mouth quirked upward in a half smile that, for some strange reason, made Caeden's heart skip a beat in his chest.

"I wouldn't want to be in your position," she told him. "Being a prince sounds miserable. All the riches in the world couldn't make me agree to it."

Nothing was comforting about the sentence, but something about her words made him relax ever so slightly.

"Me either."

Eryn laughed.

Chapter 23

Eryn

"Ronan!" Eryn called into the depths of the armory. It wasn't well-lit, but the door was ajar, and the stench of cleaning solution reached her nose, so he was in there somewhere. She had tried his shack first, but the door was locked, and since Margaid was at dinner with Caeden and the other princess, it meant he was off somewhere doing the things he had been brought to the castle for.

"Whatcha want?" Ronan answered from somewhere to her right inside the armory. She lit the small candle on the table by the door and entered the space. Once she was inside and darkness surrounded her, she could just make out the flickering flame of the candles Ronan was using to light his small workspace.

He had a sword on the table in front of him, and he was bent over as he inspected the rust stains with a cloth in his hand.

"I wanted a drink, but now seems like a bad time." Eryn shrugged. She was still angry about her meeting with the king the previous night, and that anger was hard to ignore. She shouldn't have yelled at him like she had, it was unprofessional and uncalled for given he was the literal king and she was nothing more than a soldier in their army of thousands, but that realization had only come to her after she'd left his office. In the moment, he was just another person—just someone making a decision that wasted her time and put lives in danger. It was nothing she wasn't used to, but she certainly wasn't used to handling situations like that calmly. She was a high-ranking officer when she was in the field, which was where she'd been for years. If anyone else said something like that to her, she would've reacted the same way.

Ronan glanced up from his work to look at her. He took her in, and she stood there, her hands twitching near the hilts of the daggers strapped to her legs as he gauged just how angry she was with nothing more than a look. It left her feeling vulnerable when people were able to do that, even if that person was him.

"You okay?" he asked, setting his cloth aside and giving her his full attention.

Eryn rolled her eyes and cocked her hip to the side. "Do I look okay?" she snapped, even though he didn't deserve the tone she gave him.

Ronan fixed her with a look, one eyebrow raised in a silent challenge. "What happened?"

Eryn sighed and leaned back against a rack of swords, her left shoulder blade connecting hard with the corner of the structure. "I met with the king last night," she told him through gritted teeth.

Ronan's other eyebrow shot up, his challenging look turning to surprise. "Oh?"

"The dates got moved up," Eryn explained. "They brought me here for nothing. Caeden's getting married in a couple weeks at most, and I'm getting sent back right after." She rubbed her temples with her free hand, her head throbbing as her anger coursed through her. "He's not even close to finished yet. I've wasted all this time trying to get him trained, and he's finally getting somewhere, but they're just going to send me back?

"I asked him to send me back now instead, before Caeden gets too full of himself and thinks he could actually win a fight. At least right now, he still knows he'll die if he fights out there, but if I train him for a few more weeks, at the rate he's going, his head is gonna get too big. He's going to get himself killed. Not to mention all the other soldiers I could be training, whose lives could be saved because of that training."

Ronan grinned, as if everything she'd just told him was unimportant. "You're worried 'bout him?" He looked like he was on the verge of laughing.

Eryn glared at him. "He's going to get himself killed," she said, not answering his question. "He's stupid, and reckless, and—"

Ronan's laugh interrupted her. "I know someone equally stupid and reckless." He gave her a pointed look, a smirk still clinging to the edges of his mouth, the right side higher than the left.

She glanced down at her still-healing leg before she rolled her eyes. "Last I checked, my recklessness saved your life," she snapped.

Ronan's grin widened. "And lost me my leg, but who's countin' that?"

Eryn glared at him again, and he laughed.

It took Ronan multiple moments to recover from his laughing fit, and Eryn tapped her foot impatiently against the ground. He may have been doing his job for once, but he was still drunk while he was doing it. And after he'd given her so much hell about handling weapons after drinking alcohol for all these years, too.

"But back to my point," he said once his laughter ceased. "You're worried 'bout the princy?"

Eryn took a long breath, attempting to calm herself before she snapped at him again. "He's the heir to the throne," she said through gritted teeth. "My training could mean the difference between that man dying or living when he's sent to the front lines. They're putting that sort of responsibility on my shoulders while not bothering to ensure I have enough time to do my job. It's the stupidest, most insane thing I've ever heard."

Her cheeks reddened in the dark room as memories of her argument with the king flashed back through her mind. She'd been calm until he'd denied her return to the field. That was when things took a turn.

"I may have gotten into a fight with the king," she mumbled, almost hoping he wouldn't hear her.

Ronan's jaw nearly fell open. "What kind of fight, Reckless?" he asked, using her old nickname for the first time in what felt like forever. She hadn't heard that nickname on his lips since right after she'd saved him from the Dragon Lord.

"I may have yelled at him," she answered with a shrug, as if the fact was irrelevant.

"You what?"

"Yelled at the king."

Ronan hit his forehead with the palm of his hand. "You're insane."

"I tried to explain to him what I just told you, but he wouldn't listen," Eryn said. "How Caeden's going to be just confident enough in his skills to get himself in trouble if I stay. He said I couldn't go back because they 'made an arrangement.' I tried to argue that their arrangement wasn't more important than the life of the heir to the throne, but he wouldn't listen."

Ronan sighed. "Ya know, I'm gonna pretend you didn't say any of that. You didn't argue with the king, you didn't try to tell him how to navigate his political arrangements, and you're worried about Caeden." The last bit was said with a smirk that matched his earlier expression.

Eryn rolled her eyes. "Whatever," she snapped. "Omit what you want, but I already told you why I'm worried about him, and it has nothing to do with what that smirk of yours suggests."

Ronan shrugged casually and wiped at a spot on the sword until the rust was almost entirely removed. "Whatever ya say." He set the rag down again and removed his keys from his pocket before tossing them to her. "Go get a drink, Reckless. Ya look like you're about to break your fists over there."

She caught the keys in one hand and relaxed her other around the candle as she spun the keyring around on her pointer finger. "Don't count on having any tequila left in that little barn of yours when I'm done," she told him, only half joking with the irritation still flaring through her.

He smiled up from his work again, but the smile was genuine this time. "I only bought it for you, ya idiot."

Eryn's shoulders relaxed. She'd missed him a lot, and the gesture suggested he'd missed her, too. It was ridiculous, considering they were siblings, but that he still cared enough to miss her left her feeling warm inside.

She didn't show any of that to him before she turned on her heel and left.

Chapter 24

Caeden knocked an arrow and sent it flying through the darkness toward the target ahead of him. He and Eryn had finished training together hours ago, but after he'd attended dinner with the princesses and his father, he'd come back outside to continue on his own.

She'd been right earlier in the day. He wasn't making enough progress, especially since she was going back to the field far sooner than he needed.

The shot hit the target, but as usual, it missed the center dot.

Caeden sighed.

"Wanna drink?" Ronan asked from behind him, and Caeden practically jumped out of his skin. "Looks like you could use one after that."

Caeden turned to face him, more startled than annoyed.

In the darkness, it was hard to make out Ronan's features, considering his back was to the castle and his face was hidden in shadow. The smell of vodka and whiskey wafted off him in waves that would've sent anyone who wasn't used to the smell stumbling away.

Caeden shouldered his bow alongside the quiver of arrows he wore. "That's far from the worst of them," he said.

Ronan nodded, but the quirk to the corner of his mouth hinted at his amusement. "Whiskey might help to ease your suffering," he joked, holding out a bottle by its stout neck.

Caeden snorted before taking the bottle and downing a mouthful that left his throat burning. He could feel the warmth of the alcohol as it pooled in his stomach and chased away the cold of the night that was seeping into his bones.

"What would that father of yours say if he knew what a terrible influence I've had on ya?" Ronan cackled and braced himself against his cane to keep from falling over into the grass.

Caeden grinned. Ronan clearly had a good night if he was in such a good mood.

"He'd throw you out before you even knew he'd found out."

Ronan nodded thoughtfully, but the playful glint in his eyes never faltered. "Very true." He winked. "He better not find out, then."

"That a threat, old man?" Caeden laughed. His cheeks felt hot suddenly, and his thoughts were slower and foggy.

The alcohol hit much quicker than he'd expected, and much harder, too.

He glanced up and took in the moon's height in the sky. It was after midnight by now, and though part of him wanted to continue with his practice, another part knew staying up too late into the night again wouldn't help him get any farther in his training, either. Maybe it was good the alcohol hit as hard as it did. He had a fine line to walk to avoid overdoing his training.

Ronan smiled, but it turned to laughter a moment later. "Nah. They'd have my head 'fore I could even get my revenge on ya for tellin' anyway."

Caeden cracked a grin. "Probably."

Ronan eyed him up and down, taking in the bow and arrows slung over his shoulder, then the target a hundred feet behind him. "Whatcha doin' out here so late?" he asked, reaching to take the bottle of whiskey back.

Caeden shrugged. "I need more practice. Eryn's already mad that my training is progressing as slowly as it is, and now she might be getting sent back early."

Ronan nodded. "She said the date got moved up for the betrothal, too."

Caeden raised an eyebrow. Eryn and his father had spoken about his training being cut short, but he hadn't expected her to be given the entire story, since the matter of the princesses didn't apply to her.

"Yeah. I only have a few more days to decide."

Ronan grunted. His fingers found the label taped to the empty bottle in his hands. He ran his fingernail along the top edge of the sticker absentmindedly as a look of concern crossed over his features.

Ronan cleared his throat before he spoke, suddenly refusing to meet Caeden's gaze. "Have you decided?"

Caeden thought back to the multiple times he'd watched Margaid leave Ronan's shack in the middle of the night and the times he'd caught her sneaking around when she thought no one was watching.

He didn't want to have this conversation with his friend, but he knew it was inevitable. There was no point in avoiding the topic, not with his father needing a choice from him so soon.

Caeden nodded. "I think I have."

Ronan swallowed hard. "Who?"

He stayed quiet, and Ronan became increasingly anxious in just a few seconds.

Caeden cleared his throat. "Do you really like her?" he asked, ignoring the question.

Ronan flushed so red that Caeden could make it out even in the shadows. His eyes shifted to the bottle in his hands as he continued to pick at the label. He'd gotten it halfway off already.

Caeden had never seen him blush so hard before, not even when the few other women he'd caught feelings for had been mentioned. Ronan had already been red from the alcohol, which only made it more noticeable.

That was all the confirmation Caeden needed, though.

"I do," Ronan answered, his voice as quiet as a mouse.

Caeden flinched at his response, even though his blush had already told him everything. He hadn't realized how much he'd hoped something had changed between Ronan and Margaid in the past few days. As much as he knew Margaid was his best option for a wife, he couldn't do something like that to his friend.

Ronan smiled, but it wasn't his usual playful grin that spread across his lips this time. This smile was far sadder than anything Caeden had ever seen on the man's face.

"You can have her, ya know," Ronan said quietly. "You were always gonna choose one of 'em. It wouldn't be fair to say ya couldn't have the woman who came here to be with you in the first place."

"I don't feel that way about her," Caeden said, though he knew the words were pointless. They wouldn't help ease any of his friend's emotions, but they felt necessary to say, regardless. "She's a friend to me, and that's more than I can say for Kylana." He let out a breath. "She's the best choice for a future queen. She would be a much better partner to rule with, and if something were to happen to me, she would be a far better queen for Aericora than Kylana. She has a good heart, which I know you know, and I think she would care for our people like they were her own."

Ronan shifted, but didn't respond. Instead, he sat in the grass with his legs crossed beneath him and focused on peeling off the remaining quarter of the sticker on the whiskey bottle. Caeden sat across from him, the sounds of the cicadas chirping from the forest to his back deafening in his ears.

A loud crash echoed around them, and Caeden startled.

"Fuck," Eryn shouted from Ronan's shack across the field.

Caeden hadn't heard her come outside at any point. She must have been in there since before he came back outside after dinner, or she'd snuck past when he and Ronan were talking.

Ronan flinched at the sound, but made no move to get up.

Caeden thought back to their earlier argument during their training session. He was angry about their situation too, but something about her level of anger was over the top. He was sure that whatever was happening in the shack across the field was likely related to it. No doubt some of her anger was due to the stress she was feeling from the war, the same way that his father's was. He couldn't shake the nagging feeling that something else was going on that she hadn't told him about.

"The king denied her return to the field," Ronan said, as if he'd gained the ability to read people's minds in the time it took him to peel off the label on the bottle. "When she learned she'd only have a few weeks left to train ya, she asked to be sent back instead of waitin' around, since she wouldn't be able to finish trainin' ya, anyway. The king told her she'd have to stay, since the trainin' was part of the deal to get ya to marry one of the princesses."

"Oh," Caeden responded, unsure of what else to say.

Ronan shrugged before he set the bottle down in the grass beside him and pulled a flask from his belt. "She didn't want to come here to begin with, ya know," he said, meeting Caeden's eyes for the first time since their awkward conversation about him choosing Margaid had been brought up. "She always thought it was a waste of time, but who's gonna argue with the king? Even when he demands somethin' as seemin'ly ridiculous as a few months trainin' for his only son."

It was meant to be lighthearted, which Ronan's goofy grin returning to his face had confirmed, but the joke didn't make him laugh.

Caeden hadn't realized Eryn was forced to come here and train him. She wasn't getting anything out of it like he was. She was doing what was demanded of her, and he knew her well enough to know that she would've stayed out there if she'd had a choice.

She viewed her time here as pointless, even before their time was shortened to less than half of the original plan. But now, her anger and animosity toward him clicked into place. How had he been so blind?

Of course, she was mad that she was told to come here. He would've felt the same way if he'd been in her position. He would've thought this whole situation was ridiculous, and he would've felt the same resentment toward himself that she was feeling if their positions were reversed.

Ronan chuckled lightly, more to himself than anything else. "She's always wanted to fight in the war. Could never convince her to try anythin' else. Nothin' else was ever an option in that single-minded head of hers."

Caeden glanced back at the shack, where the sound of something else breaking and Eryn's cursing flowed toward them again. "Why?" he asked. They'd danced around the topic of Eryn and her feelings about the war so many times that night a few weeks ago. She'd avoided talking about anything that dared to reveal any weaknesses about her past, including everything about her birth family.

He was beginning to feel like he knew her as a person, but nearly all her past was a mystery to him. She was an amazing fighter, a brilliant Dragon Hunter, hot-tempered as hell, and stubborn as an ox. He knew minor details from her childhood spent with Ronan and about her military career that made her so impressive as a soldier, but that was it.

He'd grown to like the person she'd turned into, but he wanted to know more about her. He wanted to know the intimate details of her life. He wanted to know where she'd grown up, why her family had given her up, or how she'd come to live with Ronan and his father as a child. He wanted to know why she'd decided to be a Dragon Hunter, or where she'd learned to draw so well that she could create such detailed diagrams.

Ronan shrugged again as he made his way to his feet. "You gotta ask her if ya want the answer to that one, princy."

Caeden frowned. Ronan knew the reason for Eryn's steadfastness in her choice to be a Dragon Hunter and to fight in the war, but he chose not to press him for an answer.

Ronan offered him the flask in his hand, and Caeden took a sip before handing it back. "Good luck with your archery," Ronan said, a smirk pulling at the edges of his lips. "I'm gonna make sure she hasn't destroyed the whole shack yet." He nodded toward the opposite end of the field, which had gone silent since the last time Eryn had cursed.

Chapter 25

Caeden stumbled over his feet as he walked through the quiet hallways. Despite his earlier decision to get to bed at a reasonable hour, he'd made the mistake of going to the kitchen and finding a bottle of wine before bed. He'd gone to bed an hour ago, but instead of falling asleep, he'd stared at the ceiling and contemplated everything Ronan had told him earlier about Eryn being forced to come here.

He felt worse for her the more he thought about her situation. Knowing she hadn't wanted to be here wouldn't have made him change his mind about receiving her training, but he still felt he owed her an apology.

Eryn's room was near the dining hall, a five-minute walk away from his room. He could make out a sliver of light coming from beneath her door as he rounded the corner and it came into view. The hallway was dark aside from a small lit candle on the wall and the light flooding out from beneath her door.

His heartbeat was quick in his chest, and his palms were damp as he reached to knock.

Confusion hit him when he realized he was nervous about

seeing her. He was too drunk to give the fact much thought. It was likely due to her cursing and probably breaking things in Ronan's shack earlier in the night, which he also didn't allow himself much time to mull over before he reached forward and knocked.

His knuckles rapped lightly against the door and he waited for an answer. Part of him hoped Eryn wouldn't hear it and he would have no choice but to turn around and leave. Another part of him worried she would, as little sense as it made, given he'd come here for no other reason than to see her.

He shook his head and wiped his hands on his thighs. Eryn was one of the most intense women he'd ever met, but he wasn't afraid of her. Still, the odd nervous feeling was unbearably persistent.

"Come in!" Eryn called from inside less than a second later.

His heart skipped a beat, then continued to race on even faster than before. He reached for the knob and pushed the door open, the smell of lavender flooding his senses as the door's hinges squeaked.

The room was small, maybe a third of the size of his own, but the few things Eryn had brought with her didn't fill the space. Her bed was pushed to one corner, and the door to the bathroom was near the opposite end. A set of drawers sat beside her bed, with only a sheathed dagger, a lit candle, and a small portrait of a young boy and girl whose faces he couldn't make out from this distance resting atop it. A table near the entrance to the room held two more candles and a travel bag that appeared to have several of her items in it.

Eryn wasn't anywhere in sight.

Caeden glanced around the space again, wondering dimly if his state of intoxication had caused his eyes to miss seeing her, but a second scan of the space revealed the same results.

Just as his confusion settled in, Eryn appeared through the bathroom door. She had a towel wrapped around her body and was running her fingers through her dripping wet hair.

She stopped in the doorway, her eyes growing wide as her hand fell away from her hair. She wrapped her arms around her body, attempting to hide anything the towel might not have covered.

Caeden's face felt hot as he took her in.

"Oh," she said, her surprise etched into her features. "I thought you were Kirsten."

Caeden frowned. He'd heard that name before, but his thoughts were hazy and he couldn't place it. "Kirsten?"

The name sounded so familiar on his tongue that it surprised him.

Eryn rolled her eyes in response. "The maid?" she said, as though it was the dumbest question in the world.

He raised an eyebrow at her. There were hundreds of maids throughout the castle, and though only a select few tended to guests and the royal family, there were still at least fifty or so that they cycled through, never mind any new staff members who were hired throughout the year. The name was familiar to him, but it wasn't familiar enough that he could put a face to it when her description of this woman was so broad.

Eryn waved a hand at him and disappeared into the bathroom, closing the door behind herself. Her still-wet feet left a trail of footprints on the floor behind her, the moonlight reflecting off the beads of water.

"The young maid with the dark hair? She has a bit of a stutter," she called from behind the closed door.

An image of a girl formed in his mind. She was the same maid who had found him in the armory a few weeks ago, the one who was scared of the dark.

"Oh," he responded, though he knew it wasn't loud enough for her to hear through the thick stone walls and the closed door separating them.

He glanced around the room again while waiting for her to return. A book was placed face down on her bed and a pen had been tossed onto the covers beside it that he hadn't noticed before. It took him a moment to recognize the style of the cover as very similar to the journal his sister had kept years ago.

He raised an eyebrow at it. He didn't think she'd be the kind of person to keep a journal, much less one while she was here training him rather than fighting in the war. Given the diagrams she had shown him, he could only imagine that the book's pages were filled with similar things.

He sat on the floor on the opposite end of the room from where her bed sat and leaned his back against the wall behind him, the alcohol running through his veins making his body feel heavy and his muscles weak.

Light spilled across the floor in front of him when Eryn opened the bathroom door again and returned to the bedroom. She blew out a candle near the door before she came over to where he sat. She tilted her head as she looked him over, a calculating expression on her face. It didn't take a genius to figure out what he'd spent his night doing.

She'd changed in the time she'd been in the other room into a loose-fitting night dress that hung down her mid-thighs, showing off her thin yet well-toned legs. The hint of a smile formed on her face as she took in the sight of him, giving Caeden pause. Something glinted in her eyes he couldn't quite place.

"You're going to feel that in the morning," she said, amusement hiding in the edges of her tone. "I probably will, too." Her smile widened for a second, and he realized that she, too, was likely intoxicated after her time spent in Ronan's shack earlier.

She crossed the room and sat on the edge of her bed, pushing the journal and pen to the side.

A pang of disappointment ran through Caeden's chest when he saw her smile had faded in the time it took her to cross the room.

"What are you doing here, you drunk prince?" she asked.

Memories of his earlier conversation with Ronan flooded back to him. His thoughts were hazier now, and only a few moments stuck out. It took him a long time to recall why he'd come to her room to begin with.

Caeden sat up straighter, crossing his legs beneath himself to make himself more comfortable on the hard tile floor. "I wanted to apologize," he told her honestly. "I didn't know they made you come here, and I'm sorry you have to stay and train me longer when you won't be able to stay long enough to finish it. I should've realized sooner how frustrating the situation I put you in must be."

Eryn stared at him; her expression was unreadable.

He cleared his throat half-heartedly to coax her to speak, but she stayed silent. He swallowed hard and wrung his hands in his lap. Part of him expected her to demand he leave, but after an eternity, she shrugged a single shoulder and let out a long sigh.

"I suppose it's not entirely your fault," she said, her eyes lingering on the tile floor.

It was, but Caeden wasn't sure he wanted to argue with her. Regardless of how badly he felt, he didn't want to anger her and make her decide to leave even despite the king's demand that she stay. He still needed her expertise if he was ever going to see the field.

It was selfish, and part of him hated himself for it, but he would not lose this chance to prepare to fight in the field, even if she could not stay long enough to get him there. This was the only chance he would ever get to have a trainer as well versed in their skills as she was.

"I always wanted to fight, too," Eryn said, catching him by surprise.

"Because you grew up with Ronan and a highly-ranked military officer?" he asked. He hadn't intended for the words to come out as bluntly as they did, but Eryn fixed him with a warning look before he could backpedal. He felt his face warm beneath her gaze.

She rolled her eyes at him. "No, you dummy prince. Because Deovaria brainwashes their people into believing that because dragons can wield magic, that makes them the most sacred creatures in the world. They believe that being in the favor of a dragon, especially a Royal Talon, is equal to being granted favor by the gods. It's why the kingdom follows the Dragon Lord so devoutly. They see him as a divine being with immeasurable power since he can control the dragons, which is only partly true."

Anger rolled off her in a way Caeden had never seen from her before. He'd seen her angry plenty of times, but this was different. This was a deep-rooted, burning hatred that she felt for their enemy kingdom.

He'd only ever seen that kind of anger in himself.

Caeden never considered why Deovaria's people might follow such a twisted man before. The Dragon Lord waged wars on countless towns and people, all for the sake of widening the borders of his kingdom. It didn't help his people. It put them in harm's way to constantly be fighting against other kingdoms. Those who lived near the borders were always at risk of being caught in the center of a fight.

Maybe he'd assumed it was because they feared him that they chose to risk their lives in such useless wars.

"What does Deovaria brainwashing their people have to do with you?" Caeden asked. He supposed it was a valid reason to want to fight—to free people from their tyrannical leader's indoctrination. But her anger toward the situation seemed far more personal than her explanation suggested.

Her anger reminded him too much of his own to be directed at the Dragon Lord for lying to his people to control them.

Eryn shrugged a shoulder. Though she was trying to downplay whatever reasons she had for feeling as strongly as she did toward the situation, it was a pointless attempt. In the time he'd known her, he'd learned a lot about how she acted. He didn't know about her past, but he knew when she was hiding something, or when she was attempting to act like something didn't bother her as much as it truly did.

Caeden stayed quiet for what felt like much longer than the few minutes it was. If Eryn didn't want to talk about it, she wouldn't, but a selfish part of him hoped she would, despite her obvious discomfort.

Eventually, she sighed. Her eyes flicked to the window to Caeden's right as if she were looking for some form of escape from this conversation. She glanced back down at her feet when she couldn't find one.

"I was a sacrifice," she whispered, her words so quiet he had to strain to hear her.

In his hazy state, the words took a long time to sink in. "A sacrifice?" he asked, partly to keep her talking, and partly because he wasn't sure what she meant.

Eryn nodded, a strand of her hair falling across her forehead. She brushed it away. The mask of indifference she tried to hide her feelings beneath vanished. Now, she stared at the floor in front of her with a faraway look in her pretty blue eyes.

"My family was from a small town in Deovaria, near Aericora's border," she explained. "I was six. The war hadn't started between the kingdoms yet, but my town was still in shambles after the war with Soborg. We were sick and starving, and none of the resources Deovaria gained from the war with Soborg were enough to help us."

She paused, breathing in heavily as if she needed to process her thoughts before she could continue.

Caeden stayed silent. He wanted to hear what she had to say, and he feared saying anything would scare her out of talking about what had happened.

Eryn let out a shaky breath.

"My parents and most of the other towns' people believed our only hope of salvation was the dragons and their magic. Our town was so poor we had nothing to offer them." Her voice cracked, and she cleared her throat. "So, my parents offered me."

Caeden's chest tightened at her words and he swallowed hard, the gravity of what she'd said still not sinking in.

"They didn't tell me where we were going, but we trekked through what was left of Soborg and through the Rayfait Mountains. It took us four days to get high enough into the mountains that we could hear the dragons inside and they decided that was as close as we needed to get. We made camp that night and my mother made a soup that was purple and bitter. It wasn't poison, but whatever it was knocked me out for long enough that they had time to pack up and leave me alone on the side of the mountain. I didn't even hear them leave."

Images flashed through Caeden's mind of a younger version of Eryn waking up in the snow with nothing but the small bedroll she'd spent the night sleeping on. Her cheeks were bright pink from the cold in his mind, and she shivered as the wind howled over the side of the mountains, loud enough to drown out the sounds of the dragons inside.

"They just… left you there?" he asked. The question had an obvious answer, and he expected her to give him another warning look in response, but instead, she only shrugged.

"I don't think they were cruel for what they did, and I don't think they meant to hurt me. They were trying to do what they thought was right, that's—"

"Bullshit," Caeden snapped, before she had time to finish her sentence or he had enough time to think better of his words. Either the alcohol was clouding his judgment or the pure hatred he felt for those people he didn't even know caused him to blurt the word out. "They left you there? A six-year-old girl, alone on the side of the mountain to be eaten by dragons, and you think they weren't cruel?"

Eryn sighed again, and her shoulders sagged as if he'd just placed the weight of the world onto them.

His heart broke as he watched her.

"They were brainwashed to think doing something like that would save the lives of everyone else in the town."

Was she serious? She couldn't possibly believe any real, loving parents would abandon their child, even if it meant saving the lives of everyone else. If they had loved her, they would have come up with another way to offer the dragons a gift in exchange for salvation. Hell, he was sure if it had been one of his parents, they would've sacrificed themselves before even entertaining the idea of leaving one of their children in the mountains like that.

He didn't say any of that to Eryn. He couldn't bring himself to. Not with the glassy sheen in her eyes and the almost pleading look that told him she was doing everything she could to make herself believe the lies passing through her lips. He couldn't bring himself to destroy the illusion she'd crafted for herself and shatter her heart like that.

Caeden shifted his eyes and leveled his gaze on her face.

For the first time, he didn't see his irritable, angry teacher when he looked at her. He saw a young girl abandoned by the people who should've done everything in their power to protect her.

Suddenly, all her aggression and anger made sense. It was her form of defense. She pushed everyone else away because she couldn't be hurt like that again.

"What happened after that?" Caeden asked her, his eyes still locked on hers.

She was crying now, silent tears rolling down her cheeks, but she hadn't looked away from him.

"Ronan's dad found me," Eryn said, her voice raw with emotion. "The dragons never came to collect me, and I was smart enough to follow the footprints my parents left behind. I only made it halfway down the mountain when he found me. He wrapped me in his jacket and carried me the rest of the way. Ronan told me a few years ago that his dad had seen me and my parents go up the mountain from his post near the border, and came to look for me when he only saw my parents come back down the next day."

She looked so fragile. A gust of wind could have been enough to crush the last of her strength and break her into a thousand pieces. It wasn't how he was used to seeing her, and part of him wished he could heal the hurt and pain she was feeling.

"I'm sorry."

It was the only thing he could say, even if it changed nothing.

Eryn only shrugged again.

"I want to destroy that kingdom," she whispered. Caeden

wasn't sure she'd intended for him to hear her until she continued. "They're all being lied to every day of their lives, and because of it, they believe that doing something as insane as abandoning their children in the mountains might save them."

Her anger had returned, and the hatred burning in her teary eyes could've scared off an entire army. Her hands were clenched into fists on top of her thighs. The muscles in her arms were flexed from the effort, and her knuckles were as white as the snow up in the mountains must have been.

Without thinking, Caeden climbed to his feet and crossed the room.

He sat on the bed beside her.

He expected her to shove him away or tell him to leave, but it was as if she hadn't noticed him at all.

"I want to burn that kingdom to the ground," she said through clenched teeth. "The Dragon Lord, his army, and every last one of his disciples who have helped to indoctrinate all of those innocent people and cause so much pain."

She hit her fist against her thigh hard enough that Caeden was sure she'd have a bruise there in the morning.

Before he could think better of it, he laid a hand on top of hers, squeezing it gently.

Eryn flinched at his touch, but she didn't pull away. She glanced up at him, and the anger in her eyes seemed to recede. With her free hand, she wiped the tears from her eyes. She offered him a sad smile before she looked away again, her shoulders sagging even more. She opened her mouth to speak, but whatever words she'd intended to say died on the tip of her tongue.

"Are you okay?" Caeden asked, mentally slapping himself for asking such a ridiculous question.

Of course, she wasn't okay. She'd been abandoned by her

parents in the mountains when she was a child and spent her whole life determined to kill the Dragon Lord and free Deovaria's people from his insanity.

And he'd been the one to take her away from all of that. He was the reason she was brought here, all so he could be trained to fight so he could take his revenge for the deaths of only two people.

Eryn laughed, a bitter sound escaping past her lips.

"I think we both know I'm not exactly okay, you dummy prince," she said, wiping her eyes once again with her free hand. "I've still got a little of that Deovarian insanity myself."

Her smile was soft this time, and a hint of amusement made her blue eyes sparkle.

Caeden's heart rate sped up, and heat rose to his cheeks. Was she always so pretty?

His eyes flicked down to their touching hands.

He pulled his hand away, every bit of him protesting the movement.

"I'd say there's a little more than only a bit of insanity in you," he teased.

Caeden's eyes flicked down to her hands in her lap again. She'd unclenched her fists, and they sat palms down on her thighs. What would she do if he took hold of her hand again? Would she swat him away, or would she let him?

Part of him wanted to take her in his arms and hold her until every piece of her broken heart was put back together again. He wanted to find her parents and make them pay for what they'd done to her.

He couldn't do either of those things.

Instead, he promised himself that no matter what he did, he would make sure he never hurt her like they had. He'd grown fond of her in their weeks together and never wanted to see her hurt again. So long as she would let him, he would be there for her in whatever way she needed.

Eryn punched him lightly on the arm and laughed. "Just because I said it first doesn't mean you're allowed to agree with it," she joked, her eyes alight with a happiness he'd never seen on her face before.

Caeden laughed. "I can agree with it because it's the truth. You are the best kind of crazy there is, Eryn Gedding."

Chapter 26

The next three days passed agonizingly slowly.

As promised, Caeden spent almost his entire day meeting with the princesses. He only sneaked in a few hours of training with Eryn every night after dinner, and though it was more than he'd anticipated, it wasn't enough. His skills improved in the few hours they had together each day, but she would leave soon, and he wanted to use more of his days to practice with her rather than focus all of his attention on the decision looming ahead of him.

He'd spent the past days considering his options. He liked Margaid as a friend, and he felt she was a kind person at heart who would do well as a queen for his people. He'd asked her more specifically about her experience in court, and she'd explained that she'd spent as much of her life as he had attending meetings with her father. Even if she hadn't cared to be in those meetings, she would've learned quite a bit by being there for so long. But she seemed to care, and she expressed enjoyment of the inner workings of the kingdom and decision-making with the help of her kingdom's court. If he chose her, he was confident that, even though they wouldn't have a romantic relationship, he would have a good queen by his side.

Kylana had ignored him for the past three days. She wanted to be a soldier in the military, that much he knew. She wouldn't want to give it up, and she didn't want to be tied down with court matters at the castle. But he wanted to be out on the battlefield, too. He would need to give up his ambitions to go to the field at all, and she would not be around at all until after the war was won—if she didn't die first.

His father told him to meet him in his study late that night, and Caeden's heart raced with anticipation the moment he woke up that morning. He didn't like what he was about to do when he knocked on the princess's bedroom door, but he had no other choice.

The door creaked open, and Kylana poked her head out, her expression neutral despite the anger he felt radiating off her. She'd had the same air to her every day since he'd been told he would have to decide so quickly.

"Good morning," Caeden said. They hadn't had breakfast yet, and he knew she hadn't been expecting him, but he needed to get this over with.

She nodded in return. "Good morning. What are you doing here so early?"

"I…" Caeden trailed off, his heart pounding in his chest.

He had to do this. He had to make his decision. But her possible reactions to his words made it nearly impossible to push them out past the lump that had formed in his throat.

She raised an eyebrow at him.

"I have to ask you something," he told her, his voice coming out higher than he'd anticipated.

"Okay." She looked annoyed now, and it only made him dread the words he was about to say even more.

"Will you marry me?" he asked, every bit of him protesting. At least if it had been Margaid, he wouldn't have hated the idea of spending his life with her. But Margaid was in love with his best friend, and his friend was in love with her. He couldn't do that to either of them. It might have meant he would need to spend his life with a woman who couldn't seem to stand him and give up his fight for revenge against the Dragon Lord, but Eryn was being sent back to the field early, anyway. He would not get the training needed to go out there and survive. But, if it meant Ronan's happiness, he would make that sacrifice.

Ronan was the only friend he'd had since his sister died, and he wasn't willing to give that up over his petty want for revenge.

Kylana's eyes widened as she stared at him. She said nothing for so long Caeden fidgeted beneath her gaze.

A smile formed at the corners of her lips, and Caeden felt relief wash over him at the sight of it. She was going to say yes.

Kylana laughed, and it was so sudden Caeden flinched.

"You think I'd marry you?" she said, through her continued laughter.

Caeden swallowed hard.

Kylana shook her head and her laughter quieted before she took on a more serious expression. "No," she said firmly. "I will not marry you. I'm free to walk away any time, just like Ceana did, and I'm doing that right now. You ignored us until a couple of days ago when the decision was shoved into your face, and I don't intend to spend the rest of my life feeling indispensable. Don't get me wrong, I didn't come here to find love, but I did expect to be treated with something more than complete indifference. And on top of that, our wants don't line up. I should've left after our first conversation, but I stupidly thought you were mature enough to come to an arrangement with me or to at least discuss it, but clearly, you're not, and quite frankly, I don't want that in a husband, either."

Caeden stared at her, his hope shattering into a million pieces. Her words didn't sting this time. She was right about everything she said. He had ignored them, he had treated them with indifference, and he had acted immature. But that didn't change that he was now only left with one princess, and that one princess was his best friend's lover.

Chapter 27

"You must be excited to be so close to done with your training," Margaid said beside him, knocking him from his thoughts about that morning and Kylana's rejection. She'd already packed her bags to leave the following morning.

They were in the garden again. The air was warm today, and the birds sang in the trees, the melody washing over them along with the gentle breeze. It had become their usual meeting place. Even when the weather wasn't as pleasant, they spent their time among the flowers and foliage.

Caeden fidgeted. He hadn't told Margaid that even though his training was ending, it wasn't yet finished.

"Very much so," he answered, though he wasn't sure why he lied.

"Will they send you to the field after the wedding?" she asked.

His father would do whatever he could to keep Caeden away from the field for as long as he could, and without being trained, he wouldn't have a hard time. Caeden could get himself, and plenty of others, killed with his lack of capabilities, and it wasn't worth the risk. But he could still go, now that Kylana had rejected him.

It was possible he could get someone out in the field to train him the rest of the way. He was the prince, after all. He could convince someone. Or maybe even continue his training with Ronan secretly, if Ronan didn't hate him after today.

"I hope so. No plans have been made yet."

"I see," she responded.

Her gaze shifted to the space ahead of her, where multiple small bees drank from one of the many sunflowers that were beginning to die off as the seasons shifted.

Caeden shifted in his seat. It was rare that he found himself on edge with Margaid, but something about her expression in that moment was calculating, like she was trying her best to get some kind of information out of him.

It made sense, given what was taking place later that night, but it still unsettled him.

Caeden cleared his throat, and Margaid jumped beside him at the sudden sound.

His face grew hot. "When I make my decision later," he started, and he could see the mix of confusion and earnest curiosity in her eyes. "Would you be opposed to marrying me if I chose you?" He didn't want to tell her about Kylana if she didn't already know. If she wanted to opt out like the other two princesses had, she still had every right to do so without feeling pressured.

A small smile pulled at the corners of her lips, and she ducked her head and looked away from him. "You're my friend," she answered. "I would much prefer to spend my life with a friend than a stranger."

It wasn't a yes, but it also wasn't a no. It was a good enough answer to his question, though.

After Caeden finished with Margaid and left from dinner with her, Kylana, and his father, he made his way out to the training field as stealthily as possible. Everyone likely knew he was still meeting with Eryn each day, but he didn't want to draw attention to it, especially after his promise to Kylana, even if she was leaving in the morning.

It was already dark outside, and an owl hooted in the woods behind the patch of dirt where Eryn waited for him. She leaned against a tree and had a cloth in her hand that she rubbed over the shining metal surfaces of a sharp-looking sword.

"I hate training after dark," she grumbled as she shoved the cloth into her pocket and stood straight.

She'd said very similar things the last two nights, only with much more irritation in her voice the first time.

"Sorry," Caeden responded, with a single shoulder shrug. It couldn't be helped, even if he agreed with her that only training at night wasn't pleasant.

His eyes lingered on the sharp-edged blade in her hand as she shoved it into the sheath strapped to the waistband of her pants. A mischievous smile, not unlike the one he was used to seeing on Ronan's face, pulled at her lips when she noticed his stare.

"What's that for?" he asked, already dreading the answer to his question.

She patted the hilt of the sword gingerly, as if mocking his question. "You've improved a lot over the past couple of days," she told him. "I think it's time we start with actual swords if we're going to get you anywhere near field ready by the time I leave."

Caeden's heart skipped a beat. Real swords? Was she trying to kill him? He certainly wouldn't put it past her to enjoy his torment.

Eryn reached behind the tree and produced a second

sheathed sword embellished with sapphire gems and gold patterns on the hilt. She pulled the sword from its sheath, revealing a pristinely shined blade that looked untouched by time.

She handed it to him, hilt first.

"Where'd it come from?" he asked. He'd seen intricate blades like this before, of course, but they didn't keep many like this in the castle. Certainly not in the armory.

Eryn's lip quirked upward again. "I had it made for you a few weeks ago," she said. "You were getting good fast, and I placed the order with your father. He added a few embellishments that are a little over the top, but it'll do the trick."

Caeden eyed the blade, taking in the gems and the gold, and the silver sheen of the moonlight and stars as they reflected off the sharp-edged blade.

"Thank you," he told her, his cheeks warming.

"You haven't fully earned it yet," she said, but a teasing glint in her eyes made him question whether or not she meant it.

Eryn went much easier on him during their training session than usual, which was likely because, with real swords, she could do much more damage than she ever could have with the dulled ones from the armory.

Despite her going easy on him, he wasn't yet good enough with the weapon to leave their session with no injuries. She nicked him a few times with her blade across his arms and legs. None of them were severe, but the blow that had split his cheek had stung, and blood dripped onto his shirt, staining the white cotton with bright crimson splotches.

He only got a single nick on her upper arm, which he hadn't been trying to do. After that, she'd been extra careful to evade every one of his attacks.

Their matches were longer today than they had been during

any other training session. During one of their matches, Eryn told him that, even though he'd only been training for a few weeks, he'd gained the skills of a soldier a year or two his senior. It was perhaps the biggest compliment she'd ever given him.

Eryn re-sheathed her sword at her hip. She stood there, watching him as he examined the many scrapes covering his body, and he wasn't oblivious to her stares. He could feel her gaze roving over him, but he couldn't tell whether she was assessing the damage she'd done, or just him.

"Sorry," she said sheepishly, confirming she'd been taking in his scrapes and bruises. He was sure that in better lighting, he would've seen a light blush across her cheeks. "They'll heal quickly enough."

"Not quickly enough for me to make it to my betrothal ceremony without looking like a raccoon attacked me," he joked.

Eryn laughed, a high-pitched, loud sound echoing off the trees and the side of the castle to Caeden's right.

The more he heard her laugh, the more sure he became that it was one of the most amazing sounds he'd ever heard. Something about it never failed to make his heart skip a beat.

"They'll have to throw me in a vat of makeup to cover up this mess," he said, gesturing at himself, his voice coming out strained from the laugh he held back.

Eryn gasped for breath, her laughter subsiding. "I'm sure you'll look beautiful," she teased, a smirk pulling at her lips.

Caeden smiled.

Her expression turned serious, and a pang of disappointment shot through him.

"Have you made your decision yet?"

Her voice sounded tight, as though she was still trying to calm her laughter while forcing the words out. There was no laughter in her tone this time, only a faint sadness that stretched in her voice, so far beneath her words that Caeden wasn't sure if he was only imagining it.

He shrugged, the amusement he'd felt before gone. "Kylana is leaving," he answered. "And I have to talk to Ronan again before I make my final choice."

Eryn raised an eyebrow.

He hadn't explained anything to her regarding his betrothal. She'd probably noticed by now Ronan was spending most of his time with Margaid, but she'd likely only assumed he was sleeping with her like every other woman he spent his nights with.

"Ronan cares for Margaid," he explained. "I told him it was fine, but I didn't think she would be my only option. I want to know I won't destroy him if I choose her. I'll ask her to say she wants to leave if it will."

"Oh," she responded. She was silent for a long moment, and Caeden waited for her to say something else. Instead, she quietly bid him goodnight and disappeared into the thick darkness toward the castle.

♥ ♥ ♥

The lights in Ronan's shack were duller than usual when he finished up his training with Eryn and made his way across the field. The main room was usually lit with candles, giving Caeden pause and making him question whether Ronan would be awake.

Caeden shook his head, pushing away the guilt at the possibility of waking him. This couldn't wait until morning. There wasn't enough time.

He knocked on the door, and despite being sure it wouldn't have been enough to wake a normal person, he could hear the loud creaking of Ronan's bedframe from inside as he got up to answer the door.

"Gimme two seconds, princy!" he called, his voice ragged and rough, like he'd either just been asleep or crying.

There was a shuffling sound as his bare feet hit the floor, and a few candles glowed inside. Caeden waited anxiously on the porch for multiple more moments before Ronan pulled the door open and gestured for Caeden to enter.

"It ain't polite to wake your elders," Ronan mumbled as he plopped himself on the couch and lazily tossed his cane to one side.

Caeden raised an eyebrow at him. "Elders, huh? Two years gives you the ability to call yourself an elder now?"

Ronan waved a hand at him. "Technicalities."

Caeden sat on the couch opposite his friend, the thick cushions sagging beneath his weight. He wasn't ready to have this conversation after how sad Ronan was a few days ago when Margaid and the prospect of Caeden choosing her was brought up. But he didn't have much of a choice. Not if he wanted to be a decent friend, at least.

He hated himself for it, but he swallowed down the lump of guilt in the back of his throat.

"Whatcha need, princy?" Ronan asked, but by the sadness in his tone, Caeden was sure he already knew what he'd come to ask.

He had to force the words out when he spoke. "Would you hate me if I chose her?"

It was the worst sentence he'd ever said in his life. He hated himself for every word as they passed through his lips.

She was his only option. If he didn't choose her, his kingdom wouldn't get the soldiers they needed. They would lose the war. It didn't help the bubble of self-loathing that sat heavy in the pit of his stomach, growing larger every second as he watched his friend.

Ronan swallowed hard. He stayed silent, his eyes unwavering from the bookshelf where Margaid's small pile of barrettes sat, despite the feelings of grief that washed over his features. "No," he said finally. "She was always gonna be an option from the beginning, wasn't she?" He laughed lightly, but there wasn't any humor in it. "I didn't think I'd get so attached, but that's on me, not you."

It wasn't the answer Caeden hoped for, but then again, he wasn't sure what he'd been wanting to hear either. At least Ronan was being honest with him.

"I don't love her, you know," Caeden clarified, though he wasn't sure why he was restating the fact. It didn't matter in the grand scheme of things. He would still marry the one woman Ronan had caught true feelings for. "I like her as a person, but she could still be your..." Caeden trailed off, unsure what word would fit best, before clearing his throat and pushing on. "If that's what you both want, I wouldn't stop you, nor would I want to."

It would be far more difficult than any of them would want, but it wasn't impossible.

Ronan shrugged in response. "Technicalities, princy. It don't matter much what ya think of it. If anyone ever figured it out..." He trailed off before shaking his head. "It wouldn't end well for any of us."

He wasn't wrong, but it only made it all feel worse. Caeden had already thought about it. He'd already run through the scenarios in his head, but he still hoped that he was just overthinking it. Maybe he was worrying too much and there was still a way this could work out that wouldn't leave his best friend with a crushed heart.

Before coming to see him, Caeden accepted that regardless of the risks, he would go with whatever decision Ronan made. But Ronan was right. There weren't many options that could keep everyone involved happy without risking a scandal that could end up making both Caeden and Margaid's lives as rulers miserable, and put Ronan out of a job, never mind that his reputation would be ruined for the rest of his life.

Ronan cleared his throat. "It ain't that bad," he said. "You've been needin' a wife, after all. She'll be a good one." His smile was genuine, but a deep-seated pain was hidden beneath his hazel eyes.

As much as Caeden wished he could ignore what everyone else thought of the inner workings of the royal family and the court, he couldn't. It wasn't something Ronan or Margaid could do either. Not with the positions any of them held.

Caeden sighed and climbed back to his feet, attempting to swallow down the nauseating guilt inside him. "Thank you," he told his friend. "And I'm sorry."

It was the most diplomatic way he'd ever spoken to Ronan, and he hated himself for it.

Ronan shrugged again. "It is what it is, princy. It ain't no one's fault."

Caeden did his best not to flinch at the words. It was his fault. He'd ignored the others. He'd told Ronan that having a relationship with Margaid was fine. But stating any of those things would not help.

Ronan walked him to the door and bid him goodnight before closing it behind him with a quiet sigh that Ronan likely hadn't intended for him to hear.

Caeden hadn't wanted to leave things that way, but he didn't have time to linger and ease the tension since he'd agreed to meet his father to make the final arrangements as soon as he was done with Eryn. His father had no way of knowing he'd made a separate stop, but he had to avoid anyone finding anything surrounding his engagement suspicious. He wasn't yet married to the Princess of Crevia, but, once he told his father his official decision, the fact that she and Ronan had spent even one night together couldn't be found out.

He wasn't sure what more his father would need from him other than his choice of a bride, and his stomach tied itself into knots thinking of what all would be required of him for the ceremony as he walked through the halls toward his father's study.

He knocked on the door, but walked in before giving the king enough time to respond.

"You're late," his father stated. The venom he'd expected to hear in his father's voice wasn't there. He sounded tired, and for yet another time, Caeden's heart broke for him.

"I know," Caeden responded, but didn't offer an explanation.

His father fixed him with a look. He gestured for Caeden to sit in one of the two chairs on the opposite side of his desk, and Caeden did.

"Have you decided?" the king asked. He sounded worried, like he thought maybe Caeden hadn't taken the deadline seriously and ignored the responsibility.

The realization that Kylana hadn't said anything about leaving to his father struck him. His father still thought he had a choice, but he didn't feel up for correcting him.

Caeden's throat felt tight, as if even his body protested the words he needed to say. "Margaid of Crevia," he answered.

It felt like a weight was lifted off his shoulders as soon as the words were out of his mouth. He didn't like the decision. It ate away at his soul in a way nothing had before, but his people needed him to do this. They needed more soldiers to win against the Dragon Lord.

Now that he'd said those words, this was over. Or as close to over as he would get for the next few weeks.

The betrothal ceremony, even the wedding, didn't feel as overwhelming as this moment had.

The king nodded and jotted down what Caeden assumed to be Margaid's name on a pad of paper in front of him. "Very good." He removed his glasses from his face and folded them before setting them down on the desk beside the pad of paper. "The ceremony is in three days," his father explained. "You'll need to be fitted for your proper attire tomorrow so the seamstress will have adequate time to prepare it."

Caeden sighed. After saying Margaid's name and making his decision final, it felt like all his energy had drained in that single breath. The betrothal ceremony would be the same as all the other large events held in the kingdom. The only difference was that he and Margaid would be presented together, and he would have to make a show of giving her an official engagement ring in front of the masses.

"How much longer until my training ends?" Caeden blurted before he could convince himself not to.

He hadn't even acknowledged his father's previous statement before asking what he truly wanted to know. It would irritate his father, but he couldn't have cared less. His end of the bargain was done, and he wanted to know how much of their end the court would hold up when everything was said and done.

His father watched him intently, and Caeden couldn't tell if he saw anger or curiosity in his expression.

When Caeden only stared back at him, his father's shoulders sagged and he spoke.

"Within the next ten to fifteen days," the king answered. "Miss Gedding has requested to be sent back, and another member of our military who is stationed near the border has also requested for her return as soon as possible. They took Sarean yesterday morning. We need every able-bodied person on that battlefield."

Caeden's breath hitched and his jaw nearly dropped open. They'd taken Sarean? Why was this the first he was hearing of it? He'd asked to be left out of court meetings, but he still should've received word from the advisors.

Sarean was nowhere near the first town Deovaria had overtaken since Silran at the beginning of the war, but it was the closest to Aericora's capital, where the castle was, than any other of their successful attacks. Sarean was within a few days' walk of where Caeden stood with his father.

"I understand," Caeden said.

He wasn't sure what else he could say. He would not start the same argument with his father and argue that if he continued to train, he could be out there helping their people in the war. Besides, they needed Eryn far more than they would ever need someone as unfinished as he was. Even if Eryn were training ten new soldiers in addition to him, it wouldn't be worth her absence.

The king cleared his throat. "I will send a notification to Crevia's rulers tonight about your choice. They should be able to travel here before the ceremony, and we will begin discussing payment for soldiers after the proceedings have finished."

Caeden nodded.

After that, he and his father discussed the logistics of the ceremony: how many guests would be in attendance, who would be invited, the schedule for the evening, and a general list of what foods they would serve. The rest, including decorations and completing the menu, would be handled the following morning with Margaid present. None of it interested Caeden, but he was required to be present for at least part of the discussion surrounding preparations. It was his betrothal ceremony, after all.

When they were done, Caeden's head spun with all the information.

"I have something for you," his father said as he worked to put away the many papers he'd been writing on while they'd discussed the ceremony.

Caeden raised an eyebrow at him, but stayed quiet.

His father reached into a small drawer on the side of his desk. From it, he pulled a small wooden box no larger than the palm of Caeden's hand. The king pried open the box, revealing a small ring designed in the same style his mother's had been before it was melted in the flames of the first attack. A blue gem sat at its center, lacking the hypnotic glow his mother's emanated.

"For your future wife," his father told him, handing the still-open box to Caeden across the desk. "Your mother always wanted to give you her wedding ring for whoever you would marry. She loved the idea of it being passed down through the generations, but since hers is in the state it is, I had a new one made to honor her wish, and for you to do with as you please. You are in no way required to give this to her, and she doesn't have to accept it, but I wanted to ensure I did my part to honor my wife's wishes."

The look in his father's eyes was so earnest that it gave Caeden pause. His father loved his mother, and wouldn't stop loving her even now that she was gone, but something about his father's gesture was so entirely pure it made Caeden's heart ache.

"Thank you." He took the box from his father and closed it gently before slipping it into the pocket of his pants.

His father gave him a small smile filled with more love than Caeden had seen from him in longer than he could remember.

It was long past midnight when Caeden finally left his father's office. His body ached from his training, and the multiple cuts and bruises covering his body stung when he moved, but even as he lay in bed and stared up at the ceiling, he couldn't fall asleep.

The box with the ring sat only a few feet away from him on the table beside his bed. It was a kind gesture from his father, and he loved his mother and wanted to give the ring to the woman he would spend the rest of his life with, but a nagging part of him felt the act of giving the ring to Margaid would somehow dishonor his mother.

He didn't love Margaid. He was going to be married to her soon, but his mother wouldn't have wanted him to marry a woman he didn't love. That he would give Margaid a ring that his mother would've wanted to be on the hand of a woman who held his heart made his stomach twist into knots.

His mind wandered to an imaginary world where he could've married for love, where there was no war between his kingdom and Deovaria. He wouldn't have met her yet, but someday. He would've seen her across the room at a ball or other celebration. They would've danced and talked and soon after, fallen in love. He'd have married her. They would've had children who he'd show the same love his parents had shown him. They'd take them into town and have picnics in the park, and he'd teach them the few fighting skills he'd learned from his father when he was a child, knowing they'd never have to use them.

Caeden tried to picture her in his mind, but rather than coming up with an image of a finely dressed woman in a silk gown and sparkling jewelry, Eryn was the woman whose face materialized in his thoughts. She was smiling at him with that rare smile he always enjoyed glimpsing, her blue eyes twinkling as they sat beneath the small gazebo behind the castle.

For a moment, Caeden was transfixed by the images flooding his mind, but just as quickly, he shook his head and pushed them away. He couldn't be thinking things like that about Eryn. She was his trainer and maybe even his friend, and he would be married to Margaid in a few weeks.

It was a nice fantasy, though.

Despite how much he wished something like his fantasies were real, there was a war, there were evil people who had brainwashed and manipulated innocents into killing for their cause, and he was marrying Margaid, a woman he knew he could never love.

Chapter 28

During the three days before the ceremony, Caeden continued spending his mornings with the woman who would soon be his wife. Now that it was just her, he was able to spend most of his time training each day.

He'd gained skills from Eryn in the time she'd been in the castle, but over those few days, he improved majorly. After the first day, she'd proclaimed he was good enough with a sword for them to move on to another portion of his training. After that, they'd spent the following day and a half working on his knife-throwing, and despite having tried to learn for so long and being unsuccessful, something clicked after their first day and he'd picked up the skill. He wasn't anywhere near as good as she was, but he was good enough to make the shot if he was close enough to the target. They'd practiced archery after that, but once it became clear he wasn't getting anywhere with it and Eryn tired of watching him, they'd switched over to hand-to-hand fighting, then back to using a sword since Eryn worried he would forget the new skills if he went too long without practicing.

Caeden wanted to learn more about how to craft bombs or

poisons, but Eryn had only argued, saying it was pointless to start something that would take weeks of work. She wouldn't be able to stay long enough to help him get the basic concepts down. Reluctantly, he'd agreed.

Now that he had made his decision and Margaid was the only remaining princess in the castle, he felt like a weight had been lifted off his shoulders. He could focus solely on his training, and not just because he had more time to spend in the field with Eryn and a sword in his hands. His mind felt clearer, and he hadn't realized how much their presence in the castle and the decision looming over him had affected his every waking moment. The guilt still hadn't subsided, and he wondered whether it ever would.

Since he'd left his father's office that night, his training had been easier. It was easier for him to put the pieces together and understand what Eryn was teaching him on a deeper level. He was able to make himself perform the motions she explained, understand that taking so much as a tiny step forward when knife-throwing was the difference between him hitting the target or not without getting frustrated, and, most of all, he was suddenly improving at a rate ten times faster than he had been before.

Eryn stumbled backward after Caeden landed a fist to her gut. She was wheezing, her hand pressed to the spot he'd hit her, but she was smiling in a way that made it clear she was happy to see the improvement in him as well.

"Again," she said after catching her breath. She took a defensive stance, her hands held in loose semi-circles and her elbows bent to protect her ribs.

Caeden mirrored her after wiping away the sweat from his forehead with the back of his hand. They circled one another in the dirt for a few seconds before Eryn ducked and swung her leg out, attempting to swipe his feet from under him.

He jumped out of her reach.

"I'm not falling for that again," he told her, amusement lacing his words.

Eryn snorted, her eyes twinkling with amusement. "About time you learned your lesson."

He aimed a punch at the side of her arm, but she deflected with her forearm. Her wrist slid down his arm in the process of deflecting him, and she clamped her hand around his wrist. She yanked him forward, her other hand grabbing hold of his shirt by his shoulder when he lost his balance and slammed her right knee into his midsection.

It was a light hit, likely because she wasn't trying to hurt him, but it still sent a gust of air whooshing from his lungs and left him breathing heavily from the pain as it radiated through his torso.

He hooked his arm around her left leg and applied pressure to the back of her knee. She fell to her knees, but lost her grip on him. Caeden rolled out of her range again and jumped back up to his feet. Eryn was back on hers when he refocused his attention on her.

"Good," she told him, lowering her arms to her sides and letting a smile form at the corners of her mouth.

Her smile was prettier every time he saw it.

Caeden sat on the hard ground near the edge of the dirt patch, still out of breath from when she'd kneed him, and Eryn sat a few feet away from him. He pushed the thoughts of her smile away as he focused his gaze on her.

A sense of pride washed over him when he noticed she was breathing as heavily as he was. It was replaced with a momentary wave of concern when he saw how she favored her right leg over her left. He hadn't meant to hurt her, though he knew doing so was fairly inevitable.

"Will you be at the ceremony tonight?" he asked, his fingers finding the small box holding the ring he'd kept in his pocket since his father gave it to him. It was an odd, absentminded habit that he'd begun over the past couple of days to flick the small latch open and closed inside his pocket when he was anxious. He was doing it now, but he wasn't sure what about the situation made him feel that way.

His question was random, but it had been on his mind all afternoon. She'd surely been invited. She was a guest in the castle, after all. She hadn't been discussed when he'd talked with his father, but no one would ever exclude a high-ranking military officer like her from any events while she was visiting. But he wasn't sure why he cared so much about whether she was planning to attend.

Eryn refused to meet his gaze when she spoke. "Maybe," she answered. She glanced at him then, a teasing twinkle in her eyes. "Depends on whether or not I feel like putting up with you royal snobs all night."

Caeden's lip quirked upward. "We can be rather irritating," he agreed.

"Can be?" she joked.

She nudged him with her shoulder, and his face warmed at the gesture. "You don't seem to understand how annoying you are, you dummy prince."

"Says the most difficult person in all of the kingdom."

Eryn laughed, and Caeden couldn't help it when he smiled in return.

They stayed silent for a while, and Caeden's thoughts drifted to the events of the evening ahead. He'd be betrothed to Margaid by the end of that night and married to her in a few weeks. The thought made his stomach clench, and bile rose in the back of his throat before he swallowed it down again.

He'd grown used to the idea by now, but it still loomed in front of him like the mouth of a dark cave. His day-to-day life wouldn't be much different, yet every bit would. He would be married. That alone came with so many subtle changes.

None of what was happening tonight felt right. It wasn't supposed to; it was a marriage of convenience. It didn't matter that they didn't love each other, and it didn't matter that he was stealing her away from a man who did care for her. But even if this was how it was always supposed to turn out, it still clung to the edges of his mind, pulling at his thoughts in a way that demanded his attention every second, even as he tried his best to ignore it.

Everything about this was wrong.

"You should get going soon," Eryn said, pulling him from his thoughts.

There was a sadness in her eyes he hadn't expected to see, but as quickly as he'd noticed it, it was gone.

He glanced up at the sky. The sun was setting behind the trees ahead of them, and the world around them was tinting with an orangish hue.

"Those cuts and bruises aren't going to cover themselves," Eryn teased, reaching over and tracing a finger along a cut running the length of his cheek. It was a few days old, but the skin around the scab was bright pink, and he still flinched when her finger grazed over it.

The warmth that had left his face only a moment before returned tenfold, and her hand felt cool against his burning skin. Suddenly, he was aware of just how close to her he was. Their thighs were nearly touching, and only a few inches separated the rest of his body from hers.

Eryn must have realized it too, because her face turned

scarlet and she pulled her hand back as if the touch of his skin had burned her. She moved over in the grass. "I should probably get going, too," she told him as she climbed to her feet, refusing to meet his gaze when she did.

She didn't look at him as she said a polite goodbye before she headed back inside, not giving him enough time to respond before her back was turned.

Caeden stayed where he was on the ground until she'd disappeared from his sight, his cheeks still warm from the touch of her hand.

A light knock came on Caeden's door as he changed into the new suit the seamstress had spent the past couple of days making for him. The fabric was soft to the touch, but it felt odd compared to the simple cotton shirts and pants he'd been wearing for his training sessions.

"Come in!" he called.

The door creaked open and Ronan hobbled inside. "You look real fancy," he noted, before making his way across the room and plopping himself down on the edge of Caeden's bed.

Caeden's chest tightened at the sight of his friend. He had seen little of Ronan since he'd spoken with him about marrying Margaid. He'd seen him around the armory and had seen him the day before when he came to speak with the king, but Caeden hadn't been close enough to strike up a conversation with him without going out of his way. Plus, the part of him that felt guilty about his decision was making him avoid his friend.

"I always have to look fancy," Caeden told him, a half-smile coming to rest on his face as he worked the last of the gold buttons through the fabric on his chest.

"Oh, the toils of royalty," Ronan joked, sighing dramatically for maximum sarcasm. His usual mischievous smile was back on his face, and even though it had only been a few days since Caeden had last seen him, he hadn't realized how much he'd missed his friend.

Caeden snorted a laugh. "What are you doing here?" he asked, as he finished getting dressed.

The corners of Ronan's lips quirked upward. "I'm your self-appointed escort, Your Highness." He bowed while still sitting on the bed, which made Caeden laugh.

"So, you don't want to go in by yourself?"

"Not even kinda, princy."

It had taken him years to learn that Roann only took the job at the castle because he'd been offered it, and because it was one of the very few things he could still do with his injury that were within his field of knowledge. Had he been able to do anything else that didn't require him to attend large gatherings and court meetings, he would've taken it in a heartbeat.

They left the room and made their way to the Grand Hall, where the event was being held. Most of the guests had already arrived, and the chatter from hundreds of conversations inside echoed through the hallways.

Two guards who were posted outside the Grand Hall bowed to the two of them as they approached.

A sense of dread washed over him as Caeden listened to his father's arrival being announced to the guests inside the room and the polite round of applause that followed.

"His Highness, Prince Caeden of Aericora, and Ronan Atkyn, Aericora's castle's Head of Security," an announcer said to the room, and the applause went up again.

Margaid was introduced to the room, and Caeden was surprised to hear she was alone. The King and Queen of Crevia would've barely had time to meet them for the ceremony, but everyone had assumed they would want to attend their daughter's betrothal. Perhaps they'd been mistaken.

The room was lavishly decorated. The usual chandeliers were replaced with larger, more ornate ones, each holding hundreds of lit candles to bathe the room in a warm glow. The tables were well set, each draped in flowing golden tablecloths, and large displays of flowers were dyed blue to match the kingdom's colors.

Caeden sat at the head table to his father's right, and Ronan sat on his father's left. A moment later, Margaid took her seat beside Caeden, her hands fidgeting nervously with the ruby gem hanging from the golden chain necklace at the base of her throat. She looked as anxious as Caeden felt.

Caeden glanced around the room, telling himself it was a good distraction from his feelings. His eyes scanned the faces of each of the guests, hoping to find Eryn's among the sizeable crowd. She'd made it clear she didn't want to attend, but he still felt a pang of disappointment sink deep into his chest when he didn't see her long black hair or bright blue eyes anywhere in the crowd.

More of the higher-ranking guests were introduced to the room as Caeden's eyes drifted over the crowd. Caeden recognized a few of the names, specifically the advisors and other court members, along with a few strategists who attended occasional court meetings. The others blurred together until they were an indiscernible mass of syllables in his head. All the guests who were announced joined them at the head table, each as lavishly dressed as the last. High-heeled shoes and boots clicked against the stone floor as the guests moved about the room to take their seats.

Plates of food were already placed at each of the room's seats, and a band began playing a quiet song with long notes and a soft rhythm. The melody was slow and peaceful, designed only to be background noise until the floor opened up later in the evening for dancing.

Once everyone was seated, the king stood. "Welcome, everyone!" he announced, his voice loud. It had an edge to it that Caeden could only assume was supposed to sound like excitement.

Cheers rang out through the room, and though Caeden could hear the difference in his father's tone when he was excited versus when he was faking it for the benefit of his people, not everyone in the room had that luxury.

"We are here today to announce the engagement of Prince Caeden of Aericora and Princess Margaid of Crevia!"

The cheers were deafening.

When the people quieted, Caeden's father spoke again, this time announcing the events of the evening. They would have their meal, then the dance floor would open, beginning with Caeden and Margaid's first dance and a small show where he would give her the ring, which would then be followed by dessert.

The king returned to his seat. Chatter rose in the room again as the people fell into conversations with those around them, and everyone ate.

"It's been a while since you've been around, Your Highness," a man across from Caeden said. He was a military officer who Caeden only recognized by his snake-like green eyes. He'd been in the most recent court meetings, but Caeden still hadn't learned the man's name.

Caeden tensed at the comment. He knew just as well as the other advisors and courtiers did that Caeden had requested time away from the meetings to prioritize his training and the princesses, and that he would be returning to the meetings as soon as he was wed, if not sooner. But Kylana's unhappiness had likely spread to the court during her stay. Even if she was gone now, Caeden would eventually hear about it.

"I've been busy," Caeden responded, an edge to his voice he hoped the man couldn't hear.

He didn't like the look the man was giving him. This man probably hadn't agreed with Caeden's choice to avoid meetings, and now that he'd heard about Kylana, he felt he had been right all along. Rather than outright saying so, the man's tone and stare were both laced with his true feelings toward the situation.

Caeden glanced down at the food in front of him, avoiding the man's gaze. A beautifully cooked piece of lamb with a side of honey-glazed vegetables sat on his plate. He stabbed his fork into the food and brought it to his mouth. As much as he wished he could escape this conversation, nothing could keep him out of it for long, even if he filled his mouth with food. The best-case scenario was that the man would take the hint and save his feelings for the next court meeting.

The man's eyes flicked to Margaid, who smiled at him before averting her gaze and staring forward at her plate. She was already nervous, but his presence seemed to increase it.

"I see that," the man said, his voice so quiet Caeden was sure only the people sitting next to both of them could hear him. He looked back at Caeden. "Tell me, is courting women more important to you than the fate of your kingdom?"

Caeden's jaw nearly dropped open at the accusation. He'd known what he was getting at, but he hadn't expected him to have the nerve to be so blunt about it. He was crossing a line speaking that way to the man who would one day be his king, and very few people ever dared to.

Caeden's grip on his fork tightened until his knuckles were a bright shade of white, but he kept his expression placid. It wasn't worth the argument, as much as it angered him to hear what this man was saying.

"Last I heard, this arrangement was perfectly acceptable," Caeden said, unable to keep the bite out of his words.

"Yet you seem to focus all your attention on the Dragon Hunter?"

He clenched his jaw. He hadn't expected that.

What was this man getting at? Caeden knew what the court thought of him wanting to be trained, but he'd thought they'd moved past being angry about it by now. Besides, it was their idea to make the exchange in the first place. Was this all because he'd spent so much time training with her instead of attending war meetings?

"I was offered Miss Gedding's training in exchange for this marriage," Caeden stated, reiterating the words the man already knew. There was a warning in his tone that he hoped the man wouldn't ignore this time. "The court and the king approved the arrangement before it ever got to me. I care for my kingdom, and my people, that is why I am training to fight alongside them and why I agreed to marry a princess from a neighboring kingdom. I will continue to carry out my duties as the heir to the throne once my marriage is finalized, as we agreed upon when I accepted the terms of this arrangement."

"And while you're off playing with swords and dragons?" the man asked.

He was baiting him, and Caeden hated that it was working. This didn't feel like an argument any other courtier would dare have with him, especially not in the middle of his betrothal ceremony where anyone could overhear the conversation. He was trying too hard to get Caeden to say something he shouldn't; trying too hard to get him riled up over something that had already been agreed upon weeks ago.

"I will return to the castle to attend meetings," he stated. He didn't owe this man an explanation. They weren't in a court meeting and his loyalty to his kingdom wasn't being questioned by anyone but the man sitting across from him. But he didn't want to go the entire meal with this man demanding an answer. "Spending time in the field will give me a better understanding of what is going on and what our soldiers are up against. It will provide me with more knowledge, and make me a more competent voice in meetings when I provide input. That's more than I can say for some."

The king nudged Caeden's leg hard beneath the table, startling him.

His leg throbbed where his father had hit him, and he glanced at him out of the corner of his eye. He hadn't noticed that while his father was having a conversation, he'd also been listening in on Caeden's. There was a warning look in his father's eyes, as if it hadn't been made clear enough by the kick to his leg.

It didn't make Caeden regret his words.

Most people in the room had already finished their meals and had moved to stand around the dance floor, their voices blending as they spoke to one another. He and Margaid would dance soon, but those at the head table still had plenty of their food left to eat and conversations to finish.

Anger was already coursing through him, and he doubted he could keep himself from exploding at this man if he had to listen to him anymore.

Caeden cleared his throat and stood up. "Please excuse me," he said but didn't wait for a response before he left to join the crowd.

Chapter 29

A few hundred people were gathered in the Grand Hall, and although it had been made to hold many more guests, Caeden couldn't make it through the room without bumping into multiple shoulders as he worked his way to the opposite end.

Multiple guests greeted him with polite hellos and smiles or did their best to strike up a quick conversation, but after his talk with the strategist, he couldn't bring himself to say anything more than a couple words to any of them before excusing himself to leave.

He was the prince, but he'd never enjoyed these gatherings. They stressed him out far more than he felt they should with the title he held. He'd had to attend so many by now that he'd grown used to the overstimulation of the chattering people around him, the swooshing of gowns, and the clicking of shoes, but if he could, he would never set foot in another ballroom in his life.

Caeden found an empty chair at a table on the other end of the extensive space. He watched the couples dance together at the edges of the dance floor, still waiting to move into the large open area until he and Margaid opened it.

His mind replayed the exchange with the man over and over in his head as he stared into the space. It wasn't the first time he'd been accused of prioritizing unimportant things over the well-being of his kingdom, but something about this time left him questioning his motives.

He was doing all this for his kingdom and his people, wasn't he? He was trying to prevent what had happened to his mother and his sister from happening to anyone else's family... right?

Even as he thought it through, a nagging part of him questioned it.

As much as he wanted to help his people, the hatred he'd felt for years sat beneath all of it. He wanted revenge more than he wanted anything else. He wanted to protect his people, yes, but he would've made the decision he had whether it had helped them or not.

He'd only recently shifted to the idea of doing these things for his people. After hearing what Ronan had suffered and what Eryn had survived at the hands of the Deovarian's, he'd finally understood how cruel this war was to those who were more involved than he was. After that, he'd stopped thinking about wanting revenge and had wanted to protect those who were suffering like his friends had and those who had lost loved ones like he had.

Originally, he hadn't had pure intentions at all. Especially not when he prioritized his training over everything when the princesses arrived.

Was that what the courtier was noticing? Was that what they'd all seen from the beginning, when he'd first started putting his energy into his training with Eryn rather than the three princesses?

Caeden sighed and shook his head, pushing away the wave of guilt for all the things he knew he should've done better.

If he'd seen these things before, maybe he wouldn't have upset Kylana; maybe he wouldn't be about to kneel in front of the woman his friend cared for and proclaim his nonexistent love for her to a crowd of people while slipping a ring onto her finger that was meant for a woman who held his heart.

"You look pissed off," a voice said from somewhere over his left shoulder.

Caeden jumped and turned to find Eryn studying him with a critical eye. She was dressed in a blue gown that matched her eyes with silver gems sewn into the skirt that twinkled like stars. Her hair was pulled back into a simple braid that hung loose with silver strings of tinsel woven through it, and her eyes and lips were painted with faint color. Her jaw was set, and she stood stiffly, her muscles tense in the areas where her dress clung to the curves of her body. His eyes lingered a moment longer than they should've on the curves of her hips before he settled his gaze on her face.

"So do you," he retorted, but the challenging tone he'd intended to have wasn't there.

Eryn grunted her disapproval in response.

She sat at the table beside him, but stayed quiet as she eyed the people in the crowd who he'd been watching since he sat down.

There was a sudden sadness about her that she hadn't had a moment before. Her expression remained unchanged and just as unreadable, but the rustle of fabric as she wrung her hands in her lap reached his ears, and there was a slight slump to her shoulders he'd never known her to have.

Part of him wanted to reach over and take her hand in his, like he'd done all those nights ago when they'd talked in her room. He wanted to say something that would make her laugh or, at the very least, not seem so depressed and defeated.

Instead, he kept his hands to himself and cleared his throat awkwardly. As much as he wanted to do either of those things, he couldn't give anyone any reason to question his loyalty to the Princess of Crevia.

"Are you enjoying the party?" he asked. His voice came out an octave higher than normal.

Eryn laughed loud enough to catch the attention of a few guests standing nearby. It was a genuine laugh, but it was likely only because she'd taken the question sarcastically.

"I couldn't have fun at a party like this even if I tried to," she said, lowering her voice when she spoke so the people turned in their direction wouldn't be able to hear her.

Caeden opened his mouth to respond, but his father caught his eye from across the room and waved a hand discreetly to tell him he was needed back at the head table.

He needed to open the dance floor and give Margaid the ring. He'd known it was coming, but the thought still caused his stomach to twist into knots.

He sighed and moved to stand. "Sorry," he told Eryn as he pushed his chair beneath the table. "I have to go."

Eryn offered him a sympathetic smile, but it didn't quite reach her eyes. "Don't have too much fun without me." It was a joke, but the sadness in her eyes made it impossible to laugh.

For a moment, he contemplated telling her that the few moments he'd spent with her were the best he'd had that night, but he thought better of it.

"I wouldn't dream of it," he told her instead.

Caeden weaved his way through the crowd again before he sat down beside his father. He could feel the gaze of the same strategist who had interrogated him earlier boring into the side of his face, but he paid him no attention.

He glanced over to where Ronan sat on the king's other side, but noticed for the first time that he was no longer there.

Caeden's stomach clenched even tighter. He wanted his friend to be with him through this, as selfish as it was. But he couldn't expect the man in love with the woman Caeden would marry to stick around for the event celebrating their engagement.

Caeden sat at the table silently while his father finished conversing with one of the other men on the opposite end of the table. Once they were finished speaking, the king stood. "May I have everyone's attention, please?" the king called out to the room.

The room quieted almost immediately, and the music ceased. Everyone's attention turned to their kingdom's ruler.

"I'd like to present Prince Caeden of Aericora and Princess Margaid of Crevia."

Margaid stood, and it took Caeden a moment longer than it should've to realize he needed to do the same. He climbed shakily to his feet and took in the crowd before him.

His eyes lingered on Eryn, who stood in the corner of the room. Her eyes stayed trained on his as she stood up and clasped her hands in front of herself, matching the composure of the rest of the crowd. She looked small, standing there alone in such a large space.

The sadness in her eyes had hardened into resolve, but it looked as though even a light breeze would be capable of shattering the walls she'd built up in the time since he'd left her side. He'd seen her upset, but only ever like this when she'd been crying over her parents abandoning her. Even then, she hadn't looked quite this fragile.

A hand wrapped around Caeden's and their fingers intertwined with his.

Caeden flinched at the sudden contact, but hid his surprised reaction when he turned to face Margaid. Whatever he felt for Eryn was a problem for later.

Margaid tugged on his hand, and he followed her toward the dance floor, only dimly aware of what was going on. The crowd parted around them, giving them a wide path to the center of the dance floor.

"Are you okay?" Margaid asked as she released his hand and turned to face him.

He wasn't okay. Everything in his life was changing, and none of it felt right.

He couldn't tell her that, though.

Instead, he offered her the most reassuring smile he could manage and pulled the small box from his pocket. He knelt on the ground in front of her, the stone floor cold against his knee, even through his thick pants. Every bit of his body protested the movement, as if even his nerves and muscles knew this was wrong.

"Margaid of Crevia," he stated, reciting the same speech he'd rehearsed over and over the night before. His voice rang out throughout the room. "You are a beautiful, wonderful woman. I was required to marry at the beginning of this arrangement, but I never intended to find the woman of my dreams in the group when you entered the castle a few short weeks ago."

The words were heavy on his tongue, but he knew he was saying the right words by the sound of the crowd's quiet gasps and sighs around him. Or at least, the words everyone expected to hear from him.

"Margaid, my dearest love, would you do me the honor of becoming my wife and, one day, the queen who will stand by my side?"

Margaid swallowed hard in front of him. A faint tinge of red hid in her cheeks. It took her a moment to smile. She cared for

Ronan too, and he was sure that the fact was running through her mind as she stared at him.

"I would be honored to," she told him, the lie in her words so faint no one else in the room would've been able to hear it.

The crowd cheered as Caeden climbed to his feet and slipped the small sapphire ring onto her finger.

A song flowed over the crowd then, and Caeden took one of Margaid's hands in his and slipped the other around her waist, pulling her into a dance.

He felt close to throwing up as he swayed with her to the music.

It was wrong. All of it was wrong.

But it wasn't.

This was how it was supposed to be. Yet he couldn't shake the feeling of impending doom deep inside as he looked at the woman standing in front of him: his fiancé.

The doors to the Grand Hall flung open, and a man in a guard's uniform rushed in. His hair was a disheveled mess on his head, and beads of sweat dripped down his face, wetting the front of his uniform.

The music died, and everyone's attention snapped to the man in the doorway.

Caeden used the interruption as an excuse to take a tentative step away from Margaid, adding a few extra feet of space between them for his own comfort.

The guard glanced around the room, a panicked expression on his face before he seemed to remember the reason for his untimely entrance. He walked through the room with his head bowed like a wounded dog, and made a beeline for the king.

The guard whispered something into Caeden's father's ear, and the king's expression changed from curiosity to fear within a matter of a second.

The guard stepped back, and the king rose again to address the room.

He cleared his throat. "Ladies and gentlemen, please remain calm, but it appears we are under attack."

Chapter 30

The entire crowd was panicking. The king was yelling at the few guards scattered around the room, while the men and women in the audience did their best to shove past one another to get out of the Grand Hall through the front doors or the servants' entrance near the back of the room. Some people were crying, but most were screaming in fear or at one another.

In the crowd's haste to leave the hall, Caeden was shoved and pushed toward the tables lining the edge of the dance floor and knocked to the floor. He found his footing as the doors to the Grand Hall were slammed shut.

"Quiet!" the king bellowed, his voice echoing off the stone walls above the sounds of the people's fear. His hands were raised above his head, as if it would somehow help will the people of Aericora to listen.

The room quieted, but terror played across the faces of every single heavily breathing member of the crowd, and even though they were momentarily stunned by his father's yell, the need for an escape was pulling at each of their thoughts.

"We must remain together," the king continued. "We have

hundreds of guards stationed throughout the castle. They are trained to the same level as our military, and they will keep us safe from this threat!"

He sounded so sure of his words, but his still raised hands trembled, giving away his fear.

Caeden's eyes scanned the room as his father continued to shout out to the crowd.

She'd been near the corner of the room when the guard first entered. She'd been closer to the door than anyone else. She could've left with the people who had fled.

Panic coursed through his veins, pulling his thoughts in directions that wouldn't help him or anyone else remain safe.

He shook his head to clear his mind, but it did nothing to ease his worry.

Eryn would be fine. Even if she were out there now, she'd be fighting alongside the guards to fend off the intruders. She was one of the best-trained soldiers in the kingdom. She was more than capable of taking care of herself.

But that didn't ease his fear. What if she was caught? What if she ended up surrounded by enemy attackers and killed? What if she was blown to bits by rubble shot from a Royal Talon's mouth?

He couldn't lose her to the Dragon Lord, too.

"We must remain in the hall until the threat has been eliminated!" the king shouted to the crowd.

It was enough to snap Caeden from his thoughts.

They'd be safe if they stayed together. The guards could protect the two entrances into the Grand Hall far easier than they could protect the entire castle if people left the room and ran off in every direction. There wasn't an easy way to get everyone into enough saferooms to hold them. They would need far more trained guards than they had in the castle to keep everyone in the fifteen to twenty groups they would need to separate into to get them there.

A loud bang echoed through the room, and everyone turned to the two enormous wooden doors that had just been sealed shut. The doors were shoved in again, another bang reverberating through Caeden's body and knocking him off balance.

The doors strained against the barricade that was dropped in front of them. It wouldn't hold for long. Whatever they were using to knock down the doors was too strong.

Screams rose in the room again, and the crowd ran toward the opposite end of the Grand Hall, tripping over their gowns, expensive shoes, and each other. It wouldn't do anything to protect them. They were sitting ducks if that door came down.

The guards were pulling at the barricade placed over the servants' door, but they weren't having any luck removing it, not that it would be possible to get everyone out before the main doors were broken down.

They were trapped inside. They had no weapons, aside from the decorative swords and daggers worn by some of the nobles. Some had drawn them out in the time since the door had first been shoved, but they would be useless in a fight. Their only option was to wait and hope there were enough guards close by to protect them when the doors came down.

A hand gripped Caeden's upper arm, and he spun around to find Eryn standing behind him.

Relief flooded through him at the sight of her pretty face, though she was no safer here with him than she would be out there with the guards.

Her jaw was set, and there was a hardness in her eyes that he'd never seen before.

She knew something.

Before he could register what she was doing, she yanked him down beside her, hard enough to make him stumble. Despite the fear rushing through his body, his heart raced from her closeness.

"We need to get near the door," she whispered, her lips brushing against his ear when she spoke.

She didn't give him enough time to process her words before she pulled him toward the front of the room. She stayed close to the right edge, crouched down low enough that they were out of sight as she weaved them through the tables lining the edge of the hall.

"What's going on?" Caeden asked, keeping his voice low. It wasn't hard with the screaming of the guests echoing around them.

A sudden gust of heat rushed at them as they neared the front of the room, and beads of sweat pricked Caeden's forehead. An inhuman roar filled the room, making Caeden's ears ring and his head spin. It was followed by the distinct crackling sound of wood going up in flames.

Caeden's heart pounded as the realization of what was happening sunk in.

Eryn swallowed hard. "They have dragons, you dummy prince," she hissed at him through gritted teeth.

The door burst inward, sending shards of flaming wooden debris flying into the room. A tablecloth on the opposite side of the room caught flame as a spray of fiery embers engulfed it. A fifty-foot-tall dragon barged into the room, its nostrils flaring as tendrils of smoke snaked around its mouth and nose.

Caeden barely had time to make out its face and the shimmering blue of its scales before he was shoved to the ground behind a table. Eryn climbed beneath the table in front of him, pulling him along behind her with the hand still wrapped firmly around his upper arm.

They were hidden by the shimmering gold cloth draped over the table, but the ringing was still loud in his ears as fear coursed through him. They wouldn't be hidden for long. It was only a matter of time before more soldiers or dragons rushed in and began searching for any guests who had hidden or escaped, if they didn't bother to light the room on fire and burn everyone to death first.

And he was the prince. If Deovarian soldiers were here for any reason, it was to kill him and his father.

Caeden's mouth went dry at the thought.

The king, his father, still stood with the crowd of guests. He was right in the line of sight of whoever was riding on the back of that dragon.

He'd be killed in a few minutes, if he wasn't already.

Caeden heaved at the thought of his father lying on the floor in a puddle of his blood, his eyes glazed over and lifeless.

"Stop it," Eryn warned, her voice barely above a whisper. She released his arm and placed her hands on either side of his face, pulling his attention to her. "He's fine, and he's going to stay that way," she said, her eyes locked on his.

He could see the terror etched into her features. She didn't believe her words more than he did, but she needed him to stay calm. He needed to act rationally, or they would both die along with his father and everyone else. They were the only ones who were hidden in the room. They were the only ones who could escape and find more guards.

"He's flanked by guards. They'll protect him," Eryn told him in a rushed whisper. Her voice wavered when she continued. "You only have me. It's just us over here. I need you to stay calm, and I need you to help me keep you safe. I need you to stay alive. Caeden, promise me you'll help me keep you alive."

Caeden nodded, unable to make his mouth form a response.

Her gaze was so intense, but there was emotion hiding in the depths of her beautiful blue eyes that Caeden didn't have time to discern before she released her hold on his face and took hold of his hand instead. She squeezed his fingers.

The dragon roared again.

The sound of leather boots hitting the floor followed as the dragon rider dismounted.

Caeden reached forward and lifted the hem of the tablecloth half an inch off the ground. It was barely enough for him to see what was happening, but he hoped it wasn't enough for the attackers to notice him and Eryn beneath the table.

"Well, well," the man said, his voice gruff. He was well-dressed, which was odd for a soldier in most kingdoms. Caeden had never seen one so finely dressed before, but then again, he'd never seen a Deovarian soldier. "This is a fun event you are having, Aillin." The man's tone sounded playful. Amused even. "I'm sorry for this very rude interruption, but it appears you have something that belongs to me."

Caeden's heart thudded in his chest in sync with his father's footsteps against the marble floor as he neared the dragon rider. His father had never been one to back down from a challenge, and certainly not in front of so many who relied on him to keep them safe, even if it meant putting himself in harm's way.

"It's been a long time, Colm," the king said.

Caeden wracked his brain, trying to remember if he'd ever heard that name.

He came up with nothing.

They were under attack from Deovaria. That much was certain given the dragon, but he'd never heard his father speak of anyone from Deovaria by name before, much less a soldier.

His heart sped up again, realizing that this could be the

Dragon Lord standing only twenty feet away from his father. But, if that were true, it was odd that his father was speaking to him as if he knew him personally. His father had only ever met a few ambassadors from Deovaria before the war started.

"Not as long as I wish it had been. Tell me, how is Anna?" the man asked. He had a snide smile on his face. He was trying to get a rise out of Caeden's father by bringing up his mother.

"She's dead," the king deadpanned. "I thought you knew, given your kind note a few weeks ago and that her death was by your hands."

The dragon rider clucked his tongue before chuckling. "Such a pity. She was a great queen, or so I've heard."

"What do you want, Colm?" Caeden's father snapped. His hatred laced every word coming out of his mouth, but Caeden heard the distinct sound of fear making his father's voice waver.

"I already told you," the man said, as though this was as simple as a trivial misunderstanding. His tone shifted to something dangerous when he continued. "You have something of mine, and I intend to see it returned to my hand."

Something of his?

This man was the Dragon Lord. There was no doubt left in Caeden's mind.

That realization alone was enough to make Caeden's stomach feel like it dropped right through his bones and straight to the floor at his feet.

"I have no clue what you are talking about," Caeden's father said through clenched teeth, his hands balled into tight fists at his sides.

"The stone, Aillin," the Dragon Lord snapped. "Give me the stone, and we will let you live another day."

"I'm afraid I can't help you," the king responded, but Caeden caught the subtle shift in his expression, the way his eyes darted from the Dragon Lord to the Royal Talon standing behind him, smoke leaking from the corners of its mouth and nostrils. "Whatever this stone is you're seeking, it isn't here. Leave, Colm."

Eryn tugged Caeden's hand and he dropped the hem of the table cloth before turning his attention back to her.

"We need to go," she said so quietly Caeden wasn't even sure she'd said the words aloud.

She didn't look scared anymore. The fear she'd had in her eyes had hardened again.

He wasn't looking at the woman who had gotten drunk with him and Ronan in the middle of the night and told stories. She wasn't the one who told him about her parents abandoning her up in the mountains as a sacrifice, and she certainly wasn't the nervous woman he'd seen earlier today who wouldn't look at him.

This was the woman who had trained him. The woman who had survived on her own on a fridged mountain as a child, who had fought on the front lines of this war for years, who had led a rescue mission into Deovaria to save his best friend from their enemies and had come out victorious when no one thought it was possible.

This was the woman whose want for revenge was as strong as his own.

Caeden nodded, fear hardening into a stone wall to keep all of his emotions, fears, and worries sealed up.

They couldn't do anything from here. He couldn't protect his father from the Dragon Lord standing in front of him.

But he could get out and find more guards. He could get out and fight some of them off if he got hold of a weapon. He could do something, anything, so long as he made it out of this room alive.

Eryn snuck out from beneath the table, and he followed behind, careful to stay low enough that the Dragon Lord wouldn't catch sight of them as they made their way to the exit.

"Well, that is rather disappointing," the Dragon Lord said with a click of his tongue.

Without missing a beat, thirty soldiers rushed into the room, their swords already drawn.

The guards positioned around the guests and unsheathed their weapons, beginning an attempt to hold off the enemy soldiers. There were only twenty guards, though, and more soldiers flooded the room with each passing second.

"You can't do anything," Eryn hissed as she pulled him closer to the door.

The words were true, and given any other circumstances, he would've been insulted by her comment. Then came the sound of blades hitting blades, cutting into flesh, and people screaming.

"There are too many of them, and you don't have a weapon."

No one would've been able to hear her words over the sound of the fight, but Caeden flinched at the thought of a soldier coming up behind them and embedding a sword into one of them.

Eryn dragged him to the door and out into the hall during a minor break in the flood of soldiers entering the room. As they rounded a corner outside, two soldiers in full armor with the Deovaria crest stitched in purple and red coloring on the fronts of their breastplates raised their swords.

Without giving him enough time to process what she was doing, Eryn released Caeden's hand and pushed the fabric of her dress to the side, revealing a slit cut into the material and a dagger she'd strapped to her upper thigh.

She pulled the dagger from its holster and ran at the two men. She dodged one of them while swinging her knife to the side and embedding her blade into the other man's leg. He cried out in pain and dropped his sword to the ground as Eryn ripped her blade free from his flesh.

Caeden stood frozen as her dagger met the other soldier's sword, her movements fluid.

"I didn't train you for no reason!" Eryn shouted. Her voice was strained from the effort of keeping the man's blade away from her face.

Caeden shook his head and snapped into action. The second guard, who had fallen to the floor while clenching his wounded leg, was reaching for his fallen sword, but Caeden got to it first.

He faced the soldier still squaring off against Eryn. She'd pushed him off her, but she was in a deadly position against a man with a sword when she only had a dagger for protection.

Caeden rushed the man, whose attention snapped to him a split second too late. The soldier hit his sword against Caeden's, but it slipped, and Caeden's blade cut a large chunk of skin and muscle out of the man's arm.

The dismembered bits of the man's arm hit the floor with a sickening plop, and the soldier screamed in pain while Caeden's eyes widened at the sight of the flesh on the floor and the blood pouring from the man's arm.

Eryn came up behind him, and ran her dagger along the man's throat, silencing him.

The man gurgled on his blood, his eyes wide before the life in them disappeared and his limp form dropped to the castle floor with a soft thud.

Caeden's heartbeat pounded, and a ringing filled his ears. He felt dizzy, like he might throw up.

The man was dead.

He'd been alive not even a second ago, and now he was gone.

He glanced at the man's arm again, where he'd taken out a

chunk of his flesh with his sword. Blood dripped down his arm to his hand, but it flowed much slower now that the man's heart was no longer beating. Through the blood, Caeden's eyes landed on a ring on the man's finger. It had a shining blue crystal in the middle that emanated light in a hypnotic glow. He stared at it for a long time, his thoughts hazy still.

He'd seen a crystal like that before.

"Caeden!" Eryn was screaming his name, tugging on his arm while he stared at the dead form of the man.

They were looking for his mother's ring.

That was the stone the Dragon Lord wanted.

Caeden snapped back into the real world and took in the twenty soldiers running toward them. He glanced at their hands, each holding a raised weapon. None of them wore rings like the other soldier.

He gripped Eryn's other hand and pulled her down the hallway opposite from the guards.

His father's study was on the other side of the castle.

His father had only said the castle was under attack, but not how much of it they'd overtaken before the guard had gotten to the Grand Hall. It was possible they were already over there, but they couldn't risk not going. There was still a chance they could keep the Dragon Lord from finding the ring.

His engagement ceremony wasn't an event that was happening out of nowhere. Chances were, the Dragon Lord planned to come on this specific date, knowing the royal family would be in the Grand Hall and that most of the castle's residents would be in the same area.

Part of him questioned how the Dragon Lord could've learned of the changed date.

What if he was wrong? What if they hadn't planned to corner them all in the Grand Hall? What if their end goal was to overtake the castle and not just get their hands on the queen's ring?

Why would they want it, anyway?

It was only a ring.

Yet that soldier had been wearing an identical one.

That couldn't be a coincidence.

If they were planning to take the castle, he and Eryn would be trapped if they went to his father's office. There were only two of them. They wouldn't survive long if their attackers were already waiting for them. They wouldn't survive long if they stayed where they were, though. If overtaking the castle was their plan from the beginning, it wasn't likely that the Dragon Lord would've said anything about a stone.

Either way, if the Dragon Lord was here for the stone, they couldn't risk him getting his hands on it. Whatever that stone was, if they were so intent on getting it that they would come to the castle like this, they had to ensure it never fell into the Dragon Lord's hands.

"We have to get to my father's study," Caeden said, his voice breathy.

Three of the twenty soldiers were still chasing them. The others had joined the Dragon Lord and the rest of the soldiers in the Grand Hall. They could handle three of them. They couldn't allow any of them to live if they overheard what Caeden was about to say.

"What?" Eryn shouted. She sounded angry. "We need to get you somewhere safe. That's the first place they'll look if they're looking for something important!"

"I know, I know."

But it wasn't the first place they would assume. There was a hall dedicated to expensive trinkets Caeden's family had collected over the years. His father's office would be high on the list of places to search, but it wouldn't be the first. They would search that hall before venturing anywhere else.

"They're after my mother's ring. We have to get it, then we can hide."

Eryn yanked back on his hand hard, pulling him to a stop. She pulled again, trying to get her hand out of his, but he held her tight. She glowered at him. "I need to keep you safe!" she yelled. "I can't have you getting killed!"

Something like worry flashed in her eyes, but it was gone as quickly as it appeared.

She reached for her dagger as the attackers drew closer. They'd gained some ground, but the men were catching up now that they'd stopped.

They couldn't risk being followed if Caeden was right.

Caeden lifted his sword and widened his stance like Eryn had taught him. He was lucky he had time to prepare himself for this fight. He would be dead in no time if he had to figure out how to avoid tripping over his own feet while a sword was coming at his head.

He ducked out of the way as one attacker swung near his face, all his thoughts disappearing. His first reaction was to step back and ready his sword to launch his attack, but instinct took over and he aimed a punch right at the man's gut before dancing out of his reach.

The man doubled over and coughed while Caeden rightened himself again. The soldier was prepared for his attack when Caeden tried to strike him again. He dodged, and struck Caeden's sword from the side, forcing the tip of his blade to the ground. It clanged against the marble floor, and Caeden's hands shook on the other end of the sword.

The soldier kicked him in the back of the knee, and Caeden tumbled to the ground.

Panic gripped him as his face connected with the stone floor. This was it.

After one simple mistake, this was how he was going to die.

Metal struck metal above Caeden's head, and he climbed to his feet as Eryn forced his attacker back with her dagger against his sword. "If you want to kill him, you're going to have to go through me," she snarled at the soldier.

Eryn shoved him backward, and the man stumbled. She took the opening and ducked beneath his flailing sword as he tried to righten himself and stabbed him in the stomach. She pulled her dagger through his side and out of his body near his hip, droplets of scarlet flying from the tip of her blade and onto the floor as it flew free from his flesh.

The man fell to the ground, instantly dead.

Caeden's heart stopped as he stared at Eryn. The other two soldiers were already dead on the ground a few paces to Caeden's right. Her hands were smeared in blood from the four men she'd killed, and Caeden's eyes lingered on the crimson dripping from the tips of her fingers for longer than they should've.

"We need to hide!" Eryn yelled; their earlier start of an argument was not forgotten.

She wanted to keep him safe. It was her job. It was what she'd trained her whole life for; to protect Aericora's people, him included. But they couldn't hide when he knew what the Dragon Lord was after. He couldn't let him get what he wanted.

"Not yet!"

They were almost there. Another few hallways and turns and they'd be at the door.

His heart pounded in his chest as fear worked its way through every inch of his body. They were going to run straight into another mess of soldiers. There would be a trap waiting for them. He was sending both himself and Eryn to their deaths, and his heart wrenched at the thought.

He wanted to make her stay behind, make her hide like she wanted him to, but she wouldn't listen, and if they spent any more time arguing, the Dragon Lord might find the ring. He braced himself to run into a fray of soldiers when they rounded the corner, but it was silent as they reached the main hallways leading toward the bedrooms and to the king's study and library.

It felt too easy, but there was no one else around.

Caeden walked toward the door to his father's office, and pushed it open a fraction of an inch, half expecting another dragon to burst forth.

The sound of footsteps inside gave him pause. He let go of Eryn's hand, his heart rate quickening, and she gripped her dagger.

He pushed the door the rest of the way open, his sword and Eryn's dagger ready.

A yelp reached his ears a moment before his mind recognized the face of the man in front of him. It was the advisor from dinner, the one who had questioned his loyalty to his people and kingdom.

Confusion settled over him as he stared at the advisor.

The man's eyes flicked from Caeden to Eryn and then back again, terror etched into his features.

He was holding the queen's ring in his hand.

Rage erupted in Caeden's chest. His anger was uncontrollable, and he wasn't sure where it was directed, but the adrenaline working through his veins made it impossible to care.

"What are you doing with that?" he yelled.

"The Dragon Lord," the man squeaked. "He'll-he'll kill us all if we don't give him what he wants."

The man was a coward, and it only stoked Caeden's rage.

This man was going to sacrifice the one thing they had over the Dragon Lord, so he might let them live.

They wouldn't have risked coming here like this if that ring wasn't important. It was a large event, and given how few soldiers had been in the halls after Caeden and Eryn had left the Grand Hall, this wasn't a large-scale invasion. They were after the ring. But they wouldn't have risked that if the ring couldn't…

The realization dawned on him.

It made so much sense.

"The king doesn't know he wants the ring!" the man continued, rambling on uninterrupted as Caeden let the truth sink in. "You saw how he reacted when the Dragon Lord asked for it! All we have to do is give it to him, and they'll leave!"

He had a manic look on his face, and he couldn't seem to sit still, every muscle in his body twitching as if it was all he could do not to shove past them and bolt from the room.

If Caeden was right, giving up the ring could be the equivalent to signing Aericora's death warrant.

That ring could be the one thing he needed for his people to finally win this war.

Caeden stepped forward, reaching out to snatch the ring back from the man, but Eryn gripped his arm and held him in place.

"He's lying," she said, her eyes still trained on the man with a deadly glint hidden beneath them. "He's a spy."

Chapter 31

The man scoffed, but Caeden noticed the sudden shift in his air at Eryn's conviction.

"Lying?" the man asked. "A spy? I am no such thing! We are all going to die if we don't give the Dragon Lord what he wants. You're wasting precious time by standing here and accusing me of being a traitor to the crown. They may already be dead because of you!"

The lack of meeting notes he'd received from the court sprang to the forefront of his mind. That was why he had heard nothing about the attack on Sarean. What other information had he prevented Caeden or any of the others from getting?

The advisor moved to step past them, but Eryn blocked his path, her hand gripping her dagger so tightly her knuckles had turned a stark shade of white. "You work for him," she said, her voice even, unphased by his words. "You were planted here a few months ago to gather information about that ring, weren't you?"

The man stiffened, then seemed to force himself to relax before he scoffed again. "I was being vetted for the position as an advisor. How would I have managed to do that?"

Eryn shrugged, unconvinced. "Magic," she responded. "I wonder what your actual face looks like."

The man clenched his hands into fists and set his jaw, giving up his façade. "Well, aren't you smart?" he sneered. He grabbed Eryn by the arm and yanked her out of the way so forcefully she stumbled.

She rightened herself almost immediately.

Caeden grabbed the man by the wrist and wrenched his arm backward when he tried to pass him. He would not get away that easily.

The man cried out before he turned and met Caeden's eyes, a slow smirk pulling at his lips. "You think you have it all figured out," he whispered, his words barely loud enough for Caeden to hear. "But watch yourself, prince. We have far more weapons to use against you than magic and dragons, and trust me when I say they will do a lot more damage."

He was trying to get under Caeden's skin. Trying to distract him. He hated how well it worked.

Deovaria had never housed more weapons than the dragons. They'd never fought with anything other than swords, arrows, and the magical beasts they controlled.

He froze for a split second too long as the thoughts circled in his mind, and a blazing pain surged through his leg. He dropped the man's wrist and stumbled back against the wall, the pain working its way through his thigh, down to his knee and up to his hip. The movement caused the pain to sear even deeper. His leg felt useless.

Caeden steadied himself with a hand braced against the edge of the doorway, but his leg wavered beneath him, unable to withstand the weight of his body. A small knife, no bigger than the palm of his hand, protruded from the front of his thigh.

Tears stung Caeden's eyes as the realization that he'd been stabbed settled itself over him.

Eryn came up behind the man and pressed her dagger to his throat. The movement was so quick Caeden would've missed it had he so much as blinked.

"Give me the ring," Eryn growled. She pressed the dagger just deep enough into his flesh that beads of blood pooled against the sharp edge. "Comply, and I might decide to let you live."

Her knuckles were white on the other end of the blade, and the murderous look in her eyes told Caeden she was doing everything in her power to keep from slitting the man's throat right there and now.

The spy's eyes were wide and his body was stiff and ridged. He knew he'd been caught, and was too much of a coward not to take Eryn's proposed offer of life.

The man unclenched his hand and lifted it; his palm opened wide enough for Caeden to see the faint glow of his mother's ring against his shaking hand.

Caeden hobbled forward, another burst of pain shooting through him as warm blood spilled down his leg, and snatched the ring from the spy's hand.

"Good," Eryn said, her voice a deadly whisper near the man's ear. "Now, run off to your pathetic king and tell him the stone has gone missing. Tell him you can't fathom where it could've disappeared to, or I will end you before you have time to consider uttering a single word of the truth. Do we have an agreement?"

The man swallowed hard, his Adam's apple bobbing against the blade of the dagger at his throat. More droplets of blood flowed down the tip of Eryn's blade and dripped onto the front of his shirt. He nodded once.

Eryn released him and shoved him forward through the doorway and out into the hall. He stumbled hard and fell face-first against the stone floor. He scrambled to his feet and ran off.

Caeden fell back against the wall as Eryn tested the weight of her dagger in her hand. She had a deadly glint in her eyes as she lifted the dagger and sent it flying through the open doorway, straight toward the man's turned back. Caeden waited for the thud of the dagger hitting its mark, but his ears were only met with the sound of the metal blade pinging against the stone floor.

He was dimly aware that he'd never seen Eryn miss a target, but he couldn't focus on the thought over the pain radiating through every inch of his leg.

"Come on," Eryn said as she ran toward him. She slung one of his arms over her shoulders and positioned her arm around his waist. "We need to get you hidden and taken care of. I know there are safe rooms around here somewhere. Which way?"

Caeden tucked the ring into the same pocket where he'd kept the small box with the ring for Margaid before he pointed to Eryn's left. Eryn followed his direction down the hallway and around multiple corners before coming to the safe room hidden behind a large painting just outside Caeden's bedroom.

His fingers roved over the smooth surface of the wall until they landed on the correct brick. He pushed it inward, and it popped out of place. He pulled the stone free and reached into the wall, feeling around for the lever inside. Once his fingers found it, he pulled it upward, and the picture slid out of the way, revealing a small room with only a single cot and a small sack of food that was replaced by only the most trusted servants in the castle, and a single candle and match to light the space.

Eryn helped him hobble into the room and grabbed hold of

the candle before he pulled a similar lever on the right side of the wall. The picture slid back into place, sealing them into the room.

For an agonizingly long moment, they sat in absolute darkness.

Eryn struck the match, and a warm, orange glow filled the small space, illuminating her face and shaking hands in its light.

Caeden sat near the edge of the cot, gripping his injured leg with his hands as crimson flowed from the stab wound. His pants would be stained, not that it mattered.

Eryn glanced over at him. Her eyes lingered on his leg before she squatted down beside the bag of supplies and riffled through it. She pulled out a small piece of cloth and a bottle of cleaning alcohol before she stood again, placing the cloth and bottle beside him on the cot.

"What are you doing?" he asked, though he already knew the answer.

The look she gave him confirmed it.

"What do you think I'm doing, you dummy prince?" Eryn knelt on the ground a foot away from him. Her eyes met his briefly, and she offered him a sympathetic smile. "This is going to hurt." Her eyes flicked down to his wounded leg again.

Caeden clenched his jaw and nodded.

He knew it would, but that didn't make him want to endure it any more than he'd wanted the stab wound in the first place. He'd felt the sting of alcohol on his wounds before, but never something like this. The most he'd ever suffered was a scraped knee or a broken bone, and somehow, even the broken bone hadn't amounted to the level of pain coursing through him from the small blade that stuck out of his flesh.

Eryn placed a hand on the back of his injured leg, moving it slowly so his leg was outstretched.

Caeden sucked in a breath through clenched teeth. Tears pricked the corners of his eyes, and he pressed his lips together to keep from crying out. He couldn't afford to be loud. Not with the attackers still outside. A quiet whimper escaped past his lips, despite the effort.

She poured a small stream of alcohol over the wound before she wrapped the cloth around the knife protruding from his leg, securing it in place so it could be tended to once they were out of the safe room.

If they made it out of the safe room.

His mind drifted back to his father, still in the Grand Hall, facing off against the Dragon Lord and his men, if he wasn't already dead.

"Sorry," Eryn said as she let go of his leg and took a seat on the cot beside him. "That will have to do for now."

"Don't be," he told her, his voice strained. It didn't hurt as badly now that the endorphins were working their way through his body, but it still throbbed terribly. He breathed in a shaky breath and let it out, attempting to block the pain from his mind. "Thank you," he whispered, the words barely audible.

"Of course," Eryn responded.

He glanced over at her. Her eyes were downcast, and a thin layer of sweat coated her face that hadn't been there before.

She wiped her face with the back of her hand. When she lowered it, she placed it over her side.

That was when he noticed the blood seeping through her dress along her ribcage.

Caeden had thought little of the blood covering her until then. She'd killed four men and her hands were covered in it. Plenty of it had splattered onto her dress, and only now did he notice that the spot of red on her side was much larger than any of the other splotches. Beneath her hand, he could make out a rip in the fabric of her dress, so thin it would've been impossible to notice had he not been looking for it.

"You're hurt." He reached over and moved her hand away from her ribs.

She flinched when he touched her and sucked in a breath through gritted teeth. "It's nothing," she told him, waving a hand to swat him away despite the look of pain that twisted her features when she did. "I've had much worse plenty of times. It's just a scratch."

That was putting it lightly. Despite the thin line cut into the fabric being as small as it was, blood poured from the wound, and it looked like the blade she'd been cut with had gone much deeper into her skin than the small gash in the dress suggested.

Caeden ripped the hole in her dress open wider, revealing the severed strap of her bra underneath and allowing him to see the cut more clearly.

It was, in fact, deeper than she was implying, and the gash ran from her lower ribs to the edge of her breast. It wasn't the worst injury he'd seen, especially not after laying eyes on the soldier the Dragon Lord had dropped at their front gates, but it was deep enough to be concerning.

"That's not just a scratch."

She rolled her eyes at him. "It'll be fine." There was a warning in her voice that he chose to ignore. "There's nothing else to wrap it with anyway, and I don't even know how I would, so leave it alone."

Caeden sighed and released her hand, which she placed back over her side. She flinched when she did, but continued to apply pressure to it.

"Lay down and leave your side where I can see it."

She made a frustrated grumbling sound in her throat, but did as he told her and laid down on the cot.

Caeden unbuttoned the front of his vest and tossed it onto the floor a few inches from his feet. He unbuttoned the long-sleeved, silk shirt he had on beneath the vest next, and shrugged it off his shoulders, careful to keep his movements to a minimum to avoid shifting his leg too much and undoing Eryn's work.

This was the first and only time he'd been grateful for having to wear so many layers when dressing for castle events.

He set the shirt aside and grabbed the bottle of alcohol.

"Don't you dare," Eryn warned when she noticed what he was doing.

"I'm sorry," he said, then poured a small stream of the liquid onto her wounded side before she could protest any further.

She whimpered and put her forearm into her mouth to keep from crying out.

Caeden used his vest to blot at the extra blood and clean up the mess to the best of his ability with her dress still on. Once he finished, he twisted the silk shirt so the length of it was wrapped around itself, creating a thick bunch of fabric to press over the wound while leaving the sleeves free so he could tie it around her.

He pressed the wrapped part of the shirt to her side and instructed her to sit up, which she did, before he tied the shirt's sleeves around her waist to secure it in place. It wasn't a permanent solution, and it didn't fully cover her wounded side, but it was better than leaving it uncovered with only her hand to apply pressure.

She'd told him she needed him to stay alive earlier, but she didn't seem to realize that he needed her to live too, and he certainly would not let her bleed out if he could help it.

Eryn laid back down almost immediately after he was finished and refused to look at him. "Thank you," she said irritably.

He wasn't sure if her anger was directed at whoever had stabbed her earlier or if it was directed at him for helping her despite her telling him not to. It didn't matter. She could be mad at him for eternity if she wanted to, so long as she was alive and safe.

Caeden's mind drifted back to the Grand Hall. He thought of his father, standing in front of the Dragon Lord and welcoming death by doing so. He hadn't allowed himself much time to think it over, but now his heart ached. His father could very well be dead. The Dragon Lord likely ended him when Caeden and Eryn fled from the room.

He should have stayed. He should have helped the guards fight off the Dragon Lord and his men somehow. He should have taken Eryn's dagger and turned around and embedded it into the Dragon Lord's back before anyone had time to stop him.

But that wasn't realistic.

They were outnumbered in that small room. The Dragon Lord hadn't brought many soldiers, given how empty this half of the castle was. His goal was a heist. He planned to get what he wanted and flee as quickly as possible once all the guests were secured in the Grand Hall.

At least Caeden and Eryn had gotten the ring. At least, regardless of what happened, the Dragon Lord hadn't gotten his hands on it.

His fear left him feeling paralyzed, though. Hiding the ring and leaving the Grand Hall could've been the equivalent to signing his father's death warrant.

Caeden pushed the thoughts away again. He couldn't do anything before and certainly couldn't do anything now that he was locked in a safe room on the opposite end of the castle, never mind the state his leg was in. He'd hardly be able to walk over there if he tried.

A glance at Eryn confirmed she was in a similar state. And even if she wanted to go back, he wouldn't have it in him to let her. She was an amazing fighter, but her side was bleeding out fast, and most of it was likely because she hadn't stopped to tend to it sooner.

He and Eryn couldn't go back to help, but the Dragon Lord wanted the stone, and Caeden had it safely tucked away in his pocket.

Would the small ring be worth his father's life?

"I'm sorry for the scene in the hallway," Eryn said, pulling him from the thoughts he'd spiraled into and startling him simultaneously.

"What do you mean?"

He replayed the time they'd spent in the hall. She'd killed four men without a sign of hesitation. She'd killed hundreds, if not thousands, of people in the time she'd been fighting in the war, but seeing her do it in the halls had caused his stomach to tighten in on itself.

It was one thing to watch the soldier die from the hands of people he knew were evil, but it was different to watch people die at the hands of a truly good person.

"I saw the look on your face," she said. She sat up slowly, but didn't meet his gaze. Instead, she focused on the exposed area of her leg where the slit had fallen away. "I'm not heartless, if that's what you were thinking. I'm just..." She paused for so long that he wondered if she would even continue. Sadness came over her as she sat there. "I've killed a lot of people. I'm used to it now, as awful as that is."

Without thinking, Caeden took her hand in his. It was still sticky from the blood coating her cool hands, but he hardly noticed. He gave it a light squeeze, and even with only the dim lighting from the candle, he could've sworn he saw a blush tint her cheeks in pale pink.

"I don't think you're capable of being heartless.".

She wanted revenge as much as he did, and it was a dark longing that had led her to where she was and led her to kill so many people. But it wasn't her fault the Dragon Lord had waged a war against Aericora and sent so many like her down such a dark path to end so many lives, or be killed themselves.

"I've only ever seen death like that when the soldier showed up, and it was different when I only saw the aftermath. Watching that was different than watching someone drop dead in a split second." He took a deep breath. "As weird as it is, after seeing what you are really capable of, I only admire you more."

Eryn breathed out a laugh, but her expression was grim. "I'm not a great person to admire, princy," she said. There was something playful about her tone, but her words came out forced. The look of sadness hadn't left her face, and there was a sheen to her beautiful blue eyes.

Caeden laughed lightly. "Take the compliment," he told her, gently squeezing her hand.

She rolled her eyes, but her mood seemed to lift. "Fine. But only because I don't feel like arguing with you."

He shrugged. "A win is a win, I guess."

She went silent before letting go of his hand again and laying back against the cot.

Caeden watched her as she stared at the wall above their heads. His eyes roved over her face, taking in the paleness of her skin from her blood loss. His eyes drifted to other things after that, though: the coat of red on her pretty lips, the arch of her eyebrows, the cool blue of her eyes, and the way the candlelight glistened off her glossy black hair. He glanced at his shirt that he'd tied around her chest and waist to ease the bleeding, but after, his gaze traveled to the curves of her body beneath the dress and then to the fair skin of her exposed thigh.

His breath caught in the back of his throat. She was one of the most beautiful women he'd ever seen.

Caeden shook himself and looked away from her, his cheeks reddening.

They'd just been attacked and were both injured. He should be focusing on what was going on in the moment, not on his ridiculously confusing feelings for a woman who both scared the hell out of him but was also one of the most amazing and, in her own strange way, kind, people he'd ever met.

"Can I ask you something?" Eryn whispered.

He glanced at her. She was staring at the ceiling with a faraway look in her eyes. She still seemed sad, but it was more distant now.

"What is it?"

She sat back up and met his gaze. "Do you really love Margaid?" she asked. "Or did you only choose her because she was the best choice for the kingdom?"

Genuine curiosity lit her eyes, and something about her question sent Caeden's heart racing in his chest.

He swallowed hard. He wanted to turn away from those deep blue eyes of hers, but he couldn't bring himself to. Something about her gaze pulled him in and held him tight in its grasp.

"She's my friend," he answered honestly, though the words weren't an answer at all. "I chose her because she was the only one who hadn't left. I could have refused, but Aericora needs an army, and I think she will be a good queen to my people. And as much as I hate the situation, I'll at least enjoy having her by my side as a friend. I don't..." He trailed off before he cleared his throat and continued, "I don't love her."

Eryn nodded and fell back against the cot again, hiding any reaction she felt to his answer beneath the distant look in her eyes. "Okay," was all she said.

They stayed silent for a long while. Caeden mulled over the question in his mind, trying to figure out what could've prompted her to ask such a thing, but he came up with no good conclusion. She'd never cared about his time with the princesses before. She was always so frustrated by it that he'd assumed she hadn't paid enough attention to know the name of the woman he'd chosen.

Caeden opened his mouth to ask her why she'd asked, or why it even mattered to begin with, but thought better of it when he saw her half-closed eyes. Unprompted, a smile tugged at the corners of his lips as she yawned and closed her eyes the rest of the way. He climbed up from the cot and stumbled to the floor.

Eryn's eyes snapped open like she'd heard the dragon roar again, and she sat up. She glanced down at him and raised an eyebrow. "What are you doing down there?"

Caeden sat back up, the rough stone floor biting into the palms of his hands as he propped himself up. "I wanted to give you some space to sleep."

The corner of her mouth twitched up into what was almost a smile. She turned on the cot and adjusted her legs so she was fully on the small mattress before she patted the empty foot of space beside her.

"You're not going to get any rest on the floor," she told him. "It isn't much space, but it's better than sleeping on literal stones."

Caeden glanced at the ground beneath him. He hadn't been planning on getting much rest, but he couldn't think of a good reason not to get a little. It was unlikely anyone would come looking for them for quite a while. They had to win the fight before anyone would begin searching.

What if they didn't win?

Even if they didn't win, he and Eryn would be found. They could try to sneak out of the castle, but their chances of succeeding were unlikely if the castle was overtaken, never mind the disadvantages their injuries would cause.

Caeden sighed and climbed to his feet. He sat down on the cot's edge beside her before turning and lying down.

The right side of his body was pressed against hers, and he could feel her warmth seeping into him. Her lavender scent filled his senses as he lay beside her, making his thoughts blur around the edges like only Ronan's strongest bottles of alcohol could do. She smelled nice, he realized for what was likely the hundredth time since he'd met her.

Eryn shifted beside him, her dress rustling in the otherwise silent space. He wasn't comfortable either, but he did his best to shift himself as close to the edge of the mattress as he could to allow her some extra space.

After a moment, she grabbed his wrist and tugged on his arm.

"Can we do this instead?" she asked before moving his arm beneath her head and nestling herself against his side.

Caeden's heart raced at her closeness, and he could feel his face heat to an unnatural degree. Her hair and skin were soft against him, and he liked how well her body fit against his.

"Is this okay?" she asked, and he realized he hadn't answered her previous question.

He nodded, though she couldn't see it. "Yes," he managed. His throat felt tight, and he was grateful his response hadn't come out as an indiscernible squeak.

The dragon roared from the other end of the castle, and Caeden flinched. It was faint from where they were, the sound so distant it could've come from miles away.

As much as he tried to relax, his thoughts drifted back to the fight outside their small safe room, and how he couldn't do anything to help.

His breathing quickened as a rush of panic settled over him again.

He pictured his father dead on the floor like the soldiers Eryn had killed in the hallway. He imagined the guards fighting against hundreds of Deovarian soldiers pouring into the castle. He watched the walls go up in flames as the dragon spewed fire at every flammable surface it could find. He smelled the smoke from where he lay.

And he was powerless to do anything to stop it.

Eryn rested a hand on his chest and shifted so she could look up at him. "The only chance we have is to stay hidden," she whispered. "I know it's hard, but we'll die if we go out there."

She was right, but her words did little to ease his mind.

Chapter 32

A laugh woke Caeden early the following morning. Eryn startled awake beside him and lifted her head to glance around. Dim morning sunlight flowed into the small safe room through the open doorway.

Ronan stood with his shoulder against the doorframe, a broad smile on his face that was both amusement and a bit of his usual mischief. He had a cut running the length of his cheek that almost matched Caeden's still-healing one, and a bruise spread out across his temple.

"Looks like y'all had a comfortable night," he teased, wiggling his eyebrows suggestively at the two of them. His gaze shifted to the shirt around Eryn's waist, and the cloth wrapped around the knife embedded into Caeden's leg. He frowned. "Or not."

Eryn sat up, and Caeden removed his arm from behind her before doing the same. He moved over on the cot to give her some space, but nearly fell off the edge.

Ronan eyed him, a smirk still pulling at the corners of his mouth, but said nothing.

Caeden's thoughts filled with the previous night's events: the

Dragon Lord breaking into the Grand Hall, Eryn shoving him beneath the table, the men attacking them in the hallway, the advisor who turned out to be a spy, and his mother's ring tucked away in his pocket.

His hand fell to his side, and he felt the edges of the ring through the thick fabric of his pants. It was an odd comfort to feel it was still there.

"We gotta get the two of ya checked out," Ronan said.

Eryn opened her mouth to say something, but Ronan held up a hand to silence her. Whatever she'd been about to say, it hadn't been in agreement with Ronan's statement.

"No arguments. You're still bleedin'." He gestured to her side and to Caeden's bare chest, where her blood had smeared onto him in the night, leaving behind a large splotch of red on his side. There wasn't a concerning amount, but that she was still bleeding wasn't a good sign. "And he's got a knife stickin' outta him."

Caeden glanced down at his leg. Ronan wasn't wrong about either, but he was far less worried about his injury than he was about Eryn. She'd probably shifted in her sleep and caused the wound at her side to reopen past the clots that formed, but her face was paler than it had been the night before, and it sent a wave of worry flooding through him.

He glanced at Ronan, who had entered the safe room and was now kneeling on the ground in front of Eryn, examining her side despite her displeased expression.

There were more cuts on Ronan than he'd originally seen. They lined the man's hands, legs, and his back. He had a thick layer of cloth wrapped around his upper calf on his already injured leg.

Ronan noticed Caeden's staring when he moved to check the knife wound on his leg. "It's not as bad as it looks, princy," he told him. "Quite a few find scars rather attractive, and I've been in the market for some new ones." He winked, but Caeden could see the truth of his feelings in his eyes.

He was limping far more than usual, and despite the easy expression he kept on his face and the playful tone to his voice, Ronan had gotten a second injury to the same leg that could leave him with more permanent damage and make it even more difficult for him to get around.

Caeden cracked a smile. "Whore," he joked. Ronan didn't like to talk about it, and he wasn't going to make him when he so clearly wanted an excuse to avoid the subject of his injuries.

Eryn snorted a laugh, but nodded in agreement.

Caeden cleared his throat, his amusement disappearing as his mind drifted back to last night. "How's my father?"

He braced himself to hear the worst, but Ronan only shrugged in a manner that was so relaxed it lifted the weight off Caeden's chest.

"He's fine. He's banged up pretty bad, but nothin' too severe. He'll be back to normal in no time."

Caeden nodded. "Good."

He had to keep it together, no matter the flood of emotions that ran through him at hearing those words. He was still in mild shock from the events of the night before, but he was the crown prince. He would be the king one day, and he had to ensure that a strong, able-minded man was the only thing his father, the advisors, the court, and the kingdom's people saw of him. Ronan was one thing, and he was beginning to know Eryn well enough now that maybe she would be a safe person to let his guard down entirely with, but someone else could walk by this room at any moment.

Ronan helped the two of them through the halls and to the infirmary. Only ten to fifteen cots were set up inside, but after the attack, they had filled the room to the brim with fifty more.

Soldiers who were too wounded to stand on their own lay in the beds, moaning and gripping their injuries. Those who could stand or who no longer needed around-the-clock attention had been seated outside in the hallway in chairs or had been sent back to their homes with orders to see a physician in the town as soon as they were able.

Caeden's heart sank at the sight of it all.

His conversation with the spy from the night before rang through his mind again. He'd only been attempting to get under Caeden's skin, but his words still wedged themselves at the edges of his thoughts. There had been truth laced into the man's words.

Guilt weighed heavily on his shoulders as his eyes scanned the room of injured castle guards again.

A nurse tugged him by the arm and led him to one of only three empty cots at the back of the room. Another woman brought Eryn over and told her to sit on the cot beside him. The two women left them there while they disappeared to gather the necessary supplies to tend to their wounds.

"Don't scream, or whimper, or anything when they pull that out," Eryn whispered to him, her tone far more serious than he'd expected to hear. She was even quieter when she continued, "They'll see it as weakness." She nodded toward the guards in the room. "Most of them have gone through that or much worse, even when they were just in training."

Caeden nodded as the women came back toward them.

It was similar enough to what he was already doing, keeping his expression neutral to put on the show of a leader who didn't let his emotions cloud his judgment no matter how severe the circumstances. If he could pretend to be as unfeeling as a block of stone, he could keep himself quiet. He could ignore the pain if it meant his people would respect him for it.

The nurse helping Caeden cut the leg of his pants off before she removed the cloth securing the knife in place, and the one taking care of Eryn removed the blood-soaked shirt that Caeden had wrapped around her midsection. They gave her a warm blanket that she gripped tightly up to her waist, beneath the line of the cut. She shivered beneath it as the warmth seeped into her.

"This is going to hurt," the nurse told him as she examined the knife in his leg, bringing his attention back to his situation. She had a sympathetic look that she'd likely become good at after tending to all the people around him. She placed a hand just above his knee and wrapped her fingers around the exposed part of the knife. "Ready?"

Caeden bit the inside of his cheek and gripped the thin linens of his cot.

A hand brushed against his knuckles, and he glanced over to see Eryn giving him a small smile. She rested her hand on top of his, and Caeden loosened his grip on the sheets enough for her to lace her fingers through his. It wasn't the best way to put on a brave face in front of his people, but with the way her cool fingers felt against his, he had a hard time caring.

He nodded to the nurse and squeezed Eryn's hand so hard he was scared he might break her. She only squeezed his in return.

Pain ripped through him as the nurse pulled the knife free from his flesh. Warm blood spilled out of the wound before she pressed a thick cloth to it to slow the bleeding.

After an agonizing half an hour, the bleeding had slowed enough to allow them to stitch his leg up properly. Now, his leg was wrapped in thick cloths and a pair of crutches was waiting for him beside his bed. The nurse told him that he would need them to get around for the next few days. If he didn't use them, his leg would take much longer to heal.

Eryn's cut had also been stitched up, and they'd wrapped a new bandage around her side that was far less bulky than his shirt had been.

Ronan returned after the nurses finished caring for the two of them.

"They're holdin' a meetin' in the king's office," he told them. "They want both of ya there for it, if you're done."

Caeden groaned at the thought of hobbling to his father's office, but shifted off the cot and grabbed hold of the crutches before using them to pull himself to his feet, regardless.

They needed to hold a meeting quickly, and putting it off wouldn't be wise, but a small, selfish part of him wished they could've given them one more hour to recover.

The three of them made their way to the king's study in near total silence, aside from their shoes against the floor and the thumping sounds of Ronan's cane and Caeden's crutches echoing off the walls and the tile floor. The door to the king's study was already propped open when they arrived, and the chatter of multiple voices washed over them before they made it halfway down the small hallway. When they entered the room, all eyes turned to the three of them, and their talking ceased.

All the king's usual advisors and military strategists were crammed into the small room, minus the snake-eyed man who had turned out to fit the description Caeden had given him far better than he ever could've expected. Only a few of them had space to sit, leaving the others no choice but to stand around the edges of the room.

"Finally," a man Caeden recognized as Cormac, a military veteran who was now one of the king's most trusted military strategists after retiring a few years ago, said. He wasn't present at most court meetings, but Caeden's father called on him often regarding military planning for the upcoming months of the war.

Caeden ignored the comment and turned to his father. The king had a distinct patch of burned skin on his shoulder and upper arm and multiple bruises from where he'd taken a beating from enemy soldiers.

He was alive, though. That was what mattered.

"After the attack," the king said, forgoing introductions as usual, "it's come to our attention that we had multiple spies in our ranks. Most were killed during the fight, but we're sure there are still others around. They are looking for some sort of stone, but no one has been able to determine what this stone is or why they want it. The best we can assume is that it is some form of magical artifact that will aid them in the fight. However, to our knowledge, they were looking in the wrong place.

"One thing is very clear after this attack: we need to strengthen our armies and push Deovaria back further. This war has gotten us nowhere in the past eleven years, and they have made it clear that they are much stronger than us. They only have to overtake a few more towns before they will be marching straight up to our front gate with the full force of their army. We must push them back before they have another chance to attack us like this."

"Crevia's armies are on their way," Margaid whispered from somewhere near the back of the room.

The crowd of advisors parted so Caeden and the others could see her.

She flushed bright red, but continued despite her obvious embarrassment. "The dowry has been paid to the king and queen, and my marriage to Prince Caeden is still underway. Crevia is aware it will be postponed until the matter of the attack has been dealt with, as you've already stated, Your Majesty.

Aericora has held up its end of the bargain, and Crevia intends to do the same. The soldiers will be sent within the next few days and should arrive at the Deovarian border within a week of their departure."

The king nodded. "Very good," he said to her before turning to address the room. "What of the attack? We can't allow this to happen again."

"We'll interrogate the few prisoners we took," Fionn stated.

"Hopefully, we will gain some valuable insight from them into what Deovaria is planning," Muire said. She didn't sound convinced, but she sounded hopeful.

It was unlikely they would gather any useful information from the interrogations. They rarely had in the past. The Dragon Lord trained his men too well to withstand the torture they would be put through if they were ever held hostage, and though it turned Caeden's stomach to think about the kinds of torture, they must have sustained to learn how to keep quiet, he couldn't deny it worked well.

Aericora trained in that field mildly, but Deovaria stopped attempting to take prisoners a little over a year ago. It was probably around the same time they'd figured out how to place disguised spies.

Ronan cleared his throat. "Our guards were spread too thin, Your Majesty."

It was an obvious statement, and in his still shaken mind, Caeden almost wanted to laugh. Ronan had brought that point up plenty of times, but no one else seemed to believe that an attack of such a magnitude could happen on the castle when they hadn't even taken half of Aericora's land yet.

It seemed a strange thing to ignore, but there had been other things to focus on, and up until last night, Deovaria hadn't given them any reason to suspect an attack on the castle. They were still going after their land and working to kill off as many of their soldiers as possible.

"We've only got a few hundred right now," Ronan continued. "It was enough to fend them off last night, but they weren't intendin' on takin' the castle yet. And they ain't gonna make the same mistake when they come back. Once we've got some of Crevia's soldiers on the battlefield, it might be wise to send a couple hundred of our own back to the castle so we can be ready for another attack. Deovaria did bring dragons with 'em, but that's nothin' we can't handle with enough men."

Eryn stepped forward. "Dragons are quite literally my specialty, Your Majesty. If you allow me even an extra few days to train the soldiers who are brought back here the proper techniques to kill them and to protect themselves against them, I can have them more qualified to defend the castle against similar attacks."

The king nodded, his brow furrowed in concentration as he listened. "How long do you require to train the soldiers for field work?"

It wasn't a question Caeden was expecting to hear from his father. Eryn wanted to be sent back, and the soldiers in the field wanted her to be, too. But if it was the difference between keeping her here for a few days or a week, it made sense to keep her until the guards were fully trained.

Eryn shrugged. "Generally, only a couple weeks, so long as the soldiers cover the material fast enough." She waved a hand in Caeden's direction. "The prince can attest that a lot of reading is required, and that it takes quite a bit of time to get through all of it. The hardest part is the repetition and getting the soldiers to retain the information."

The king listened to her, his gaze trained on the table where his hands sat clasped together against the hardwood. "Very well," he said. "Plan to stay a few weeks extra, then. We need them as trained as possible to prevent future attacks. If it is not possible to train them within a month, then I will see that you are sent back, and I will send for a lower-ranking Dragon Hunter to finish their training."

Eryn looked like she wanted to scoff at the idea of anyone else doing the training that only a First or Second Rank Dragon Hunter ever should, but she kept her lips pressed together and nodded.

"And who will we be sending to retrieve these soldiers?" Muire asked.

Caeden ran his finger along the jagged edges of the ring in his pocket, feeling the smooth surface of the sapphire stone sitting at its center. He shifted as the pieces of a very basic, very dangerous plan took form.

The stone had to be related to the Dragon Lord's ability to control the dragons. It was the only thing that made sense. But he would not say that in front of the court. They'd already found one spy who had hidden so well no one had suspected him for months, and the fact that he had the stone sitting in his pocket at that moment wasn't something he could let any other possible spies figure out. He couldn't let his father know what he was planning to do, either.

"I'll go," he said before he had enough time to think better of it.

They would argue. But it was his best chance. They wouldn't opt to send anyone else for this sort of mission, not with the level of security breaches they'd just learned of.

All eyes turned to him, and he could feel his nerves stand on end at their stares, but he stood his ground.

"We have next to no idea what's going on in the field right now," he continued. He hadn't been to a meeting in weeks, but he'd heard enough and doubted much had changed in such a short time. It had gotten much worse, considering how stressed and tired his father looked over the past weeks. "We send messengers back and forth, but it's been ages since one hasn't been killed or the messages haven't been lost. I can go to the field, gather information about Deovaria's attacks and strategies from the military leaders stationed there, and bring it back with the soldiers we need. Plus, it will be near impossible for me to be replaced with a disguised spy." He gestured with a hand toward his father. "I'm the Crown Prince and my father would notice any changes in my behavior, and so would all of you. Most of you have known me since I was a child; you know my life, who I interact with, and what I do in my spare time. If something were to go wrong, you would easily figure it out. And no offense to any of you, but a court member has already been found out as a spy, and I don't think we can afford to take that kind of risk."

"You're untrained," an advisor from the group who was younger and new enough to the court that Caeden couldn't recall his name yet put in.

Caeden was almost glad he'd opted to point that out rather than the fact that if anything happened to him, Aericora wouldn't have its next ruler.

"He's trained in the basics," Eryn countered, an edge to her tone Caeden smiled at. "I've been training him myself, as I'm sure you're all aware. He isn't finished yet; he still needs more practice, but he knows the basics and can hold his own. I saw it myself during the attack."

Pride warmed Caeden's chest at her words. He'd nearly been killed and would've been if it weren't for her, but he knew her better than to think she would lie about something like this. She thought he was capable, and hearing that from her made him feel like he could do anything.

"That's not enough to ensure his safety," Cormac argued. "He's in line for the crown. We can't have him waltzing into a death trap."

"Agreed. It would be better to send someone else," Fionn agreed.

"Who else would we send?" the king asked. "He already made a very valid point about our options."

Caeden's attention snapped to him, confusion crashing into him like a title wave. Was his father arguing in favor of his suggestion? It was so out of character for him that Caeden was sure he'd misheard him.

"I'll go with the prince," Ronan volunteered. "I'm gonna need some help to travel, but I can keep him safe."

A laugh rang out in the room around them, and the combined rage radiating off both Ronan and Eryn made Caeden's intensify tenfold.

"You're a cripple!" Cormac said, not bothering to hide his preexisting dislike for the man. "How will you keep him safe? You're only use is to be a human shield."

Caeden could've strangled the man if it wouldn't have ended badly for all of them.

Ronan's face turned a dangerous shade of red, but his tone remained even. "I've fought plenty more than you have," he shot back. The man was at least double Ronan's age, but Caeden knew Ronan was stating a hard truth. "Even with my leg, I held my own alongside those guards last night. I can't say I saw you doin' the same. I'm more than capable of keepin' the heir safe."

His words gave the room pause, but only momentarily.

"I'd feel much better about someone else escorting the prince," Muire said. "We must be sure of the prince's safety, and as Niell said," she gestured to the young courtier, "he is still unfinished with his training."

"What if I went as well?" Eryn asked. The anger she felt seeped into her voice, but no one else seemed to notice. "I managed to keep him alive during the attack. I can manage to keep him alive while we walk down a trail."

She made it sound like the simplest thing in the world.

Caeden had to suppress a smile from forming on his face.

Hundreds had died walking down that same trail, but he did not doubt that he would make it through just fine with Ronan and Eryn by his side. He may not have been entirely trained yet, but the two of them had survived far worse than the Deovarians waiting along the trail would have for them.

"I'll go as well," Margaid said from the other side of the room before anyone could respond to Eryn. "The soldiers we are sending have orders, but I am still their princess. They will acclimate better to the changes in leadership if I am present."

Her voice was much stronger than Caeden had ever heard from her. The quiet, gentle woman he'd come to know was gone, replaced by a strong, determined woman who would not take no for an answer.

Ronan's eyes sparkled with something Caeden only recognized as delight as he watched Margaid, and he wondered if maybe he hadn't gotten to know the woman who was going to be his wife as well as he thought he had.

Caeden glanced around the room, waiting for an argument from any of them. But after a few moments of silence, his shoulders relaxed as the tension and worry subsided.

It wasn't a great plan, but they were out of options. The war had been going on for too long, and none of them held much hope that they would come out victorious. Deovaria was already multiple steps ahead of them.

"Very well," the king said, his voice gruff. He looked almost disappointed that no one had a good enough argument to keep this plan from playing out, but he also looked resigned to the idea. "You have a week to heal up, and then we will see to it that the four of you are sent to the front lines to acquire information about Deovaria's attacks, and to bring back more soldiers to guard our castle walls."

Chapter 33

Caeden's leg throbbed, and pain shot up to his hip as he maneuvered onto the hard ground outside of Ronan's shack to wait for Margaid to leave. He let out a breath between clenched teeth and listened to the sounds of the night around him while he waited. It was louder out tonight than usual.

They'd begun construction on the damaged parts of the castle, and the men yelled at one another as they worked. Their shouts were loud, but they were unmatched by the sounds of the thousands of tools cutting through stone and shaping metal to rebuild the walls.

Though the sounds were ear-piercing when close enough, they were far more peaceful than his mind had been when he'd attempted to fall asleep a little while ago. He spent the better part of the night lying in bed, staring up at the ceiling as thoughts of the attack circled through his mind. The injuries he'd sustained were nothing compared to what he'd seen on his father. Those burn marks would leave permanent scars, though he was thankful his father hadn't succumbed to any of those injuries.

Thoughts of his mother and sister followed. The Deovarians had orchestrated an equally surprising attack that had resulted in their deaths. He couldn't count the number of times he'd wished over the years that they'd also been fortunate enough to live through their injuries.

Tears pricked at the corners of his eyes as the memory of his mother's warm smile and Amelia's contagious adoration for life itself flooded back to him, despite his attempts to keep them at bay.

"Are you okay?" a gentle voice asked from not far off.

Eryn sat on the ground a few feet away from him, grunting from the wound at her side. He hadn't even known she'd been close by, much less close enough to take a few steps and be right by his side. If he didn't know better, he could've mistaken her for a trained spy.

Caeden wiped the tears from his eyes before he offered her a shrug.

They sat in silence, listening to the continued sounds of construction, and the occasional bursts of laughter coming from inside Ronan's shack.

"What are you up to?" Eryn asked suddenly, catching him off guard. There was an edge to her voice that made him sure she was on to him. Her breathing was labored next to him, suggesting her side was hurting her far worse than she'd let on to earlier in the day.

Had it not been for the darkness, she would've been able to see the redness he felt rise to his cheeks.

"What are you talking about?"

She wouldn't buy it, but he needed to try. His plan was dangerous and tremendously reckless. She wouldn't be happy if she knew what he would do once they got to the battlefield, and he wasn't sure he could go through with it if the same worry he'd seen on her face the night before during the attack returned after she figured it out.

His fingers trailed along the outside of his pocket, searching for the small ring inside. The odd, melted shape of the metal was somehow one of the most comforting things he'd ever had.

"You didn't mention the ring to the court," she said, eyeing him suspiciously. "And then you offered to go to the field. You're planning something, and it's not something the court would approve of." She turned to face him, her intense blue eyes meeting his in the darkness.

Caeden's heart skipped a beat, and his stomach tightened as he stared at her. His mind drifted to their night spent together in the safe room and how she'd nestled up against him, then to their short time in the infirmary and how she'd reached for his hand when they'd removed the blade from his leg.

She was one of the most intense, stubborn, and terrifyingly brave women he'd ever met, but she was also one of the kindest, loyalest, and most beautiful.

Eryn sat back when he said nothing. "You're going to try to use it, aren't you?"

Caeden swallowed hard.

So, she'd made the connection, too. He wasn't surprised she had, but part of him wished she hadn't.

As much as he wanted to hide the truth, lying wouldn't get him anywhere. She could read him too well, and he knew she would continue to press the subject until she got the truth from him.

He'd planned to keep the ring a secret even before they'd gone into the meeting earlier. They didn't know how many spies were in their midst, but when the chance to go to the field presented itself to him, everything fell into place.

Caeden's fingers found the edge of his pocket again, and he

reached in to feel the cool, jagged edges of the ring, then its smooth stone set into the top. He gripped it in his palm before he answered her, refusing to meet her gaze.

"Yes."

The door to Ronan's shack swung open, and Margaid, draped in her usual dark cloak, slipped outside and disappeared into the darkness toward the castle.

Eryn shook her head but waited to say anything until they heard the faint sound of the door closing as Margaid reentered the castle.

"You're going to get yourself killed," Eryn hissed. Rage flashed in her eyes, but something that looked like hurt also hid beneath it.

"What's he doin' now?" Ronan called from the still-open door of the shack before Caeden had time to answer or decide if he hadn't only imagined what he'd seen in her eyes.

Eryn turned away from him, but he caught when her disappointed expression softened at Ronan's words. She let out a light laugh.

A small smile of his own pulled at the corners of Caeden's lips.

They climbed to their feet and met Ronan at the door. He was shirtless with only a pair of loose-fitting pants on to cover up the rest of him. The hem on his leg was rolled up so his injury was left uncovered, and Caeden took in the multiple stitches that were woven through his torn skin.

Ronan shut the door behind them and hobbled over to the couch. He stumbled more than usual, but Caeden and Eryn pretended not to notice.

"Do you want to explain yourself, or should I?" Eryn grumbled, turning to face Caeden with her arms crossed over her chest.

The fierceness he was used to seeing in her eyes was back, and his face heated again before he looked away from her. He'd expected her anger, but he hadn't expected her to be this enraged. He also hadn't expected the hurt hidden deep in her gaze. Seeing that was worse than enduring her rage ever could be.

Caeden sighed and sat on the couch opposite Ronan, Eryn's gaze boring into the back of his head.

"They control the dragons with these," he explained to Ronan as he pulled the ring from his pocket and held it out for the man to see. "Or at least, that's the best assumption I have."

Ronan's eyes lingered on the blue gem at the center of the ring. He didn't look convinced.

"How?" Ronan asked, raising a suspicious eyebrow.

Caeden shrugged. "I have no idea," he told him.

And in truth, he didn't. He'd come to the conclusion after seeing the soldier wearing a ring with the same stone set into it. It wasn't proof, but when paired with the fact that the Dragon Lord had orchestrated a whole attack he likely knew they would lose to get the stone Caeden held in the palm of his hand, it didn't seem as ridiculous as it would've otherwise. If the secret to their control over the dragons was at risk of being found out, it would have been a good enough reason to risk such a reckless attack.

Another question nagged at the back of Caeden's mind: if he was right about the stone, how had his mother acquired it? He knew little about the ring, but it was his mother's before she married his father, and the only change made to it after their marriage was having their initials engraved into the metal.

Had she known about the magic?

Caeden shook his head, clearing the thoughts away until he had a better time to think them over.

"This is what they were looking for," he explained to Ronan. "We found the spy holding it, which proves this is it. And I saw a soldier wearing a gem like this when they attacked us."

Ronan sat back against the couch, crossing his arms over his chest in a way that was identical to the stance Eryn still held. "How much have ya had to drink, princy?" he asked, his tone turning to amusement despite his skeptical expression.

"He hasn't," Eryn said. She was still just as angry as when they'd first entered the shack. "Hear him out."

Caeden cleared his throat. "The first thing they did when Deovaria started attacking other kingdoms was expand through Soborg. They wanted to have access to the Rayfait Mountains, and the only logical explanation for that is because they wanted to gain a larger army of dragons. After that, they started attacking us. It made sense because we also border the mountains, but the very first time they attacked, they attacked a town where my mother and sister were attending a festival. This is my mother's ring. That can't be a coincidence. I don't know how they left without it then, but we know they had plenty of spies placed in the castle. One had to have told the Dragon Lord that my father kept this stone in his study.

"What other reason would they have for wanting so badly to get their hands on this? Even during a gathering like yesterday, and while we were low on soldiers, we could still fight them off. It was a losing battle, and they had to have known that. But if this stone has the power to do something like control their dragons, then they would have been able to justify taking that kind of risk if it meant we didn't have time to figure out just how powerful it is."

Ronan reached for a half-empty bottle of brandy, sitting open on the coffee table before pressing it to his lips and taking a long swig. He glanced over at Eryn, who stood beside the couch with her arms crossed. He gestured toward her with the bottle of brandy in his hand. "You got all that too from seein' a spy try and steal a ring?" he asked her.

Eryn gave him a warning look, and Ronan raised his hands in surrender.

"Aight, aight," he said before downing half of the bottle. He eyed the remaining brown liquid. "I'm gonna need more of this after listenin' to the two of ya, I hope ya know that."

Caeden did his best to stifle a laugh.

"You two sound half insane," Ronan continued, relaxing back into the couch again. "But unfortunately for me and my sanity, I guess I can see where you're comin' from." He turned back to Eryn. "So, he's gonna get himself killed tryin' to tame a dragon, huh?"

"Yes," Eryn grumbled. She was visibly frustrated, but her shoulders slumped when she said the word, and the same hurt Caeden kept seeing in her eyes showed in her expression again.

It was enough to make him question whether he was willing to go through with it. But this was the only way to know if the ring worked as they suspected, and as much as it pained him to see that look on Eryn's face, he didn't have any better ideas. And given that neither of them had offered any suggestions, they didn't either.

"Thought you were the reckless one," Ronan said to Eryn, before turning back to face Caeden again. He eyed him up and down, and Caeden knew he was thinking over the chances of his survival if he went through with his plan. "Why do you wanna try to use it so bad?" Ronan asked. "We already know how to weaken their dragons, and if that ring does control them, they've likely got thousands and we've got one. Don't even know where we'd begin to find more of 'em."

Caeden shrugged. It was a good point, but he couldn't see

how confirming what they were using to gain control of the dragons couldn't help his kingdom. "We can weaken the dragons, but we're still losing," he said. "Even if we can control one dragon with this, it could help. Even if there's something more in play, if these rings are linked to their control over them and we confirm that, then taking away the rings from all the soldiers we can would help. If we can weaken their hold on the dragons, we even the field, or even turn it in our favor. We have more soldiers than them, especially with Crevia. The only advantage they have over us is the dragons. If we have a chance at doing any of those things with this," he pulled the ring from his pocket and held it up to show Ronan for emphasis, "then we have to try."

Ronan nodded, a smirk pulling at the corners of his mouth. "Aight. Just had to check one more time that ya hadn't entirely lost it."

Eryn rolled her eyes. She looked ready to smack Ronan upside the head. "I thought you already decided we weren't insane?"

Ronan shrugged, but he was holding back a laugh when he answered. "Can never be too sure with the two of ya."

Caeden cracked a smile.

Eryn stomped off toward the kitchen to find some more of that tequila she seemed to enjoy. "Prick," she muttered.

Caeden couldn't help it when he laughed.

Chapter 34

"You're pulling your punches too much," Eryn said as she danced out of Caeden's reach for what felt like the hundredth time that afternoon.

"I'm trying not to hurt you," Caeden told her, his eyes flicking down to her side where the faint outline of her bandaging was visible through her thin shirt before he could think better of it.

She glared at him with a warning in her eyes. She'd been moodier than usual over the past couple of days, and it seemed entirely because of his plans once they were in the field. She'd tried to convince him the day before to give her the stone so he wouldn't do anything stupid, and when he refused, she'd nearly lost it.

"You're going to get yourself killed!" she'd snapped, and he hadn't been able to give her a good enough response to convince her that this was their best option to confirm their suspicions about the ring.

Eryn had left in a huff, and her anger hadn't subsided overnight.

Over the past few days, he'd worried he wouldn't get the opportunity to try the stone in the field at all. If Deovaria didn't attack them in the few days they might get away with being out there, he would lose his only chance to try, considering his father would never allow him to travel back again once they had extra soldiers from Crevia.

Caeden pushed the thoughts away.

"You're not going to hurt me, you dummy prince." Eryn rolled her eyes as if it was the most ridiculous thing she'd ever heard. "You're pulling them so much you're not even getting close. Try to actually land a hit. When you manage to do that, then you can worry about hurting me, but good luck."

She waved a hand at him, signaling him to try again.

They started up another round, but despite her telling him to try to hit her, he couldn't bring himself to do it. His thoughts drifted back to the night they'd been in the safe room. He remembered her waking up every half hour and shifting beside him. He'd pretended to be asleep when she would whimper from the pain, but he couldn't get the memory to leave his mind. Something about it hurt him nearly as much as the memories of his mother and sister.

He didn't want to hurt her. She wouldn't allow him to, given he was still considerably worse at hand-to-hand fighting than she was, but that didn't ease the worry.

Unprompted, the memory of how she'd snuggled up beside him when they'd been on the cot together filled his mind. He remembered her warmth against him, the softness of her skin, and the way her scent could wash away his thoughts. It was about the thousandth time that memory resurfaced since that night.

Heat rose to Caeden's cheeks, and he barely had enough time to step backward to avoid a blow to the face.

"Where's your head at, princy?" Eryn snapped. She'd begun using the same nickname as Ronan for him, and even though he'd only ever tolerated it from Ronan before, he didn't bother telling her to stop. "We're leaving in a few hours, and I need…" She trailed off, her cheeks turning scarlet as she pressed her lips together in a thin line. She shook her head and refused to look at him.

Caeden waited for her to continue, but she stayed silent.

"You need what?" he prompted, despite his better judgment. The possibility of agitating her was better than answering her original question.

She sighed impatiently, but the red on her face grew darker. "I just need you not to die, okay?"

A smile pulled at Caeden's lips, but he did his best to stifle it.

He wasn't sure why her worry surprised him, considering she'd been worried about him during the attack too, and that it was every soldier's job to protect the members of the royal family.

Her worry seemed different now, though. She hadn't cared that he was the prince when they first met. He liked that she cared enough to worry now that they knew each other.

"Okay," he said, the smile not quite leaving his lips.

They continued their training late into the evening, and didn't stop until after the sun had set.

They'd held a meeting the previous evening to decide the logistics of their travel to the field. The advisors suggested they travel at night to avoid being seen, and both Ronan and Eryn agreed without complaint.

Caeden worried about the ring drawing attention in the darkness, but he didn't dare bring that up and figured, if nothing else, he could wrap it in layers of cloth to ensure it stayed hidden.

Caeden and Eryn walked together to the stables after their

training session, where Ronan and Margaid, along with the king and a few of the advisors and other court members, waited for them.

Four horses were saddled. Large packs rested on the horses' sides with plenty of food and supplies for all four of them, and Eryn and Ronan had covered themselves from head to toe in various weapons.

Caeden had brought the sword Eryn had made for him, as well as a bow and quiver of arrows. The bow would be little to no use in his hands, but only having the sword left him feeling defenseless when he compared it to the ten to fifteen weapons Eryn had strapped to various parts of her body.

"How are you three feeling?" the king asked, examining Caeden, Eryn, and Ronan, each in turn.

He was doing his best to show them all equal attention when he asked the question, but his eyes lingered for a beat longer on Caeden's leg than on either of the other two.

Caeden's leg still throbbed with each step he took, especially after his training with Eryn had exhausted nearly all his strength, but he'd learned over the past week how to hide the pain when he walked. He would need another couple of weeks of rest before it would be fully healed, but he didn't have that kind of time to wait, and he would not miss this chance due to his leg being sore.

"Like new," Ronan said, testing his already bad leg in front of the advisors to prove his statement. He could barely take a full step, but it was, in fact, in the same shape it had been in before the attack.

Caeden had no doubt Ronan was putting on a bit of a show himself. There was no way the wound he'd seen on Ronan's leg was already healed. At best, the scabs were barely beginning to peel off around the edges.

Eryn shrugged. "Not entirely healed yet, but I've traveled and fought in much worse conditions than this. I'll manage."

Caeden hesitated before he answered. He could feel his father's eyes on him. He was waiting for any sign that Caeden wasn't fit to make the journey. He may have agreed with him during their meeting, but the last thing his father wanted to see was his only living child sent to the battlefield, regardless of Caeden being his only heir.

"I'm fine," he told them, rubbing a hand over the stab wound on his leg tenderly. He hoped it was enough to prove his injury wasn't as bad as it was. "It's still tender to the touch, but it's hardly noticeable anymore."

It was more of a lie than he wanted to tell, but he made it sound natural. All he needed was for his father to buy it long enough for them to leave.

His father fixed him with a look, and for a long moment, Caeden worried he'd underestimated his father's ability to see right through his lies. He'd always been good at it, and Caeden had rarely had reason to practice his ability to keep the truth from his father.

Instead of calling him out on it, though, his father nodded to the three of them. "Have a safe journey then," he told them. "We will expect to hear back from you within a week, and if we do not receive word from you by then, we will expect to see you back within two before sending someone after you."

His words were laced with a worry Caeden had never heard. He'd never known his father to let something that could be attributed to weakness slip into his tone when members of the court were around.

Eryn stepped up to one of the four horses and climbed into the saddle. She pulled two of the daggers strapped to her legs from their holsters and placed them into the saddlebags at her sides. "We should be back long before then."

They'd run over the risks plenty of times, but Caeden had ignored the fear of them until now. So many messengers had gone missing or been found dead. It wouldn't be surprising if they came across whoever was responsible for the fate of those messengers while they were on their way down the same trail.

The hard set of his father's jaw only added to Caeden's growing worry.

The remaining three stepped over to their horses and climbed into the saddles. Ronan struggled to lift his hurt leg over the horse's back, and Caeden hoped no one else in the room had noticed.

A hand rested on Caeden's knee, and he flinched at the unexpected touch as tendrils of pain shot through his leg and up to his hip. His father stood beside him, his expression softer now. The worry Caeden had heard in his voice was now displayed across his features, and thin worry lines were creased into his forehead in the dim lighting.

"Please be safe," the king said, his voice so low no one else could hear him.

Worrying about Caeden's safety when he'd been one of the people to back him wouldn't sit well with the court. Worrying too much about anyone, even if Caeden was his only son, wouldn't sit well with them either. In their opinion, he'd be too distracted to lead, which was one of the last things his father needed to deal with right now.

"I will," Caeden promised. A half smile pulled at the corners of his mouth, and he nodded in Eryn's direction. "She's kept me alive before, and I trust her to do it again."

A curious look came across the king's face as he glanced over Caeden's shoulder to see Eryn sitting atop her horse, still working to arrange her weapons before they took off into the forest.

Caeden felt his face warm.

The king's expression morphed into a smile as he looked back up at his son, but Ronan's shout echoed through the room before Caeden had a chance to ask what he was smiling at.

"We all ready?"

Ronan had chosen the horse beside the one Margaid was on, and when he looked at each of them for confirmation, his eyes lingered on her the longest.

When each of them nodded their response, Ronan flicked his reins and rode off into the night ahead of them.

Eryn and Margaid followed, and Caeden took a deep, steadying breath before doing the same, the ghost of his father's touch still lingering on his leg.

Chapter 35

Ronan

Ronan led their small group down the trail into the early hours of the morning. He hadn't been down any of the trails leading to the battlefield in so long, but it was still automatic when he veered left at a fork in the trail, then right at the next. They'd discussed where they would go with the court, but Eryn was the one to make the final suggestion that seemed to align with everyone's agendas. They would meet up with her unit a few miles from the castle. It was one of the closest camps to the castle, and Eryn knew all the officers already stationed there, so it would be easiest to fall in with them. The soldiers from Crevia would meet them there after arriving at the castle for specific directions.

Their group traveled in near total silence, with only a few words exchanged between them when they heard odd noises rustling in the forest or when someone suggested a quick break for the horses. Aside from that, the only sound that night was the gentle thuds of the horses' hooves against the ground and Ronan's own racing heart as memories he would rather not relive replayed over and over in his mind.

They stopped when the first rays of sun crested the horizon, as they'd planned to do at the advisors' suggestion. They got the horses settled, and Margaid passed around a large, freshly baked loaf of bread for them to split while they waited until the sun was high enough in the sky so they could see. They made camp a short distance north of the trail and spread their bedrolls in a small clearing only large enough for the four of them to fit with their horses.

Ronan's body ached terribly from the ride, but it was nothing compared to the pain that radiated through his leg. He and Margaid crawled into their bedrolls next to one another and he listened to her breathing slowly as she curled into a small ball and fell asleep.

Eryn's footsteps in the foliage littering the ground caught his attention, and he watched as she woke Caeden by poking him in the shoulder with the end of her bow. "Time to train," she whispered to him, and her footsteps disappeared into the woods.

Caeden groaned as he stood, and Ronan smirked, despite knowing his friend wasn't paying him any attention.

Once he was sure the other two were far enough away that they wouldn't see, he moved his bedroll closer to Margaid's and laid down behind her with an arm around her waist and his face buried in her soft red curls, the scent of her and the feel of her warmth against him the first comfort he'd felt that day. He took a deep breath, allowing her scent to wash away the memories of the blood, the pain, and the darkness that had tormented him for so long, even if only momentarily.

Margaid stirred against him, and he moved to allow her more space on her bedroll, but her hand seized him around the wrist and she pulled him closer. He relaxed into her again, pulling her body tighter against his now that he knew she was also awake.

Margaid's finger traced a circle along the top of his hand. "Are you okay?" she whispered, her voice broken.

The memories flashed through his mind again. He'd told her about many of them, but he'd never told her about the darkest ones; about his time spent in the Dragon Lord's dungeon as he and his blond-haired daughter's plaything.

Ronan pushed the thoughts away again. "Yeah," he lied, hugging her close again and burying his face against the crook of her neck.

She sighed, and he knew she'd caught the lie, but he was grateful she didn't point it out.

"Do you think you'll be okay being in the field again?" she asked, her voice cracking.

His chest hurt at hearing the worry in her tone.

The field itself had never been what scared him after returning home. It was the darkness. The blanket of black that surrounded him each night after the sun set, reminding him of a time when darkness was all he would see for days on end.

Maybe seeing the field again would bring back its own memories, but he hadn't given himself time to think too much about it. But just Margaid's presence at night had chased away his fears of the dark. He hadn't expected to fall asleep soundly the first night she'd been beside him, but he'd been grateful for it every night since. Grateful for her.

Maybe if those same fears presented themselves when they arrived to the field, she would be enough to chase them away this time as well.

"I'll be fine," he promised. He placed a kiss against her neck, right beneath her ear, and she shivered beneath his touch. He grinned. "I've got you to worry about while we're there. Makin' sure you're safe is gonna take up enough of my time. I won't have time to think 'bout all that."

Margaid turned to face him; her chest pressed against his as she wrapped her arms around his neck. "I can take care of myself, you know," she teased, kissing his lips gently.

"That's not gonna stop me from worryin' 'bout you," he told her.

She opened her mouth to retort, but he kissed her again, deep and longing, until whatever she was going to say died on her perfect lips.

Chapter 36

Caeden and Eryn returned from their quick training session a few hours before the sun set below the horizon.

They slept for the rest of the day, and Caeden woke later that night when someone nudged his shoulder. His eyes fluttered open to see Margaid standing over him, her gentle smile barely visible in the darkness. "Time to go," she whispered.

Caeden nodded and climbed to his feet.

After their previous night of travel, they were close to the battlefield and would be there within a few hours if they worked their horses hard enough. A messenger was sent ahead of them to prepare the military officers for their arrival, but they had no way of knowing whether the messenger had made it to their destination.

Caeden untied his horse from the tree where he'd secured it and climbed up into the large mare's saddle before the four of them set off again.

Eryn led them down the trail this time, and Caeden followed beside her. Margaid and Ronan rode alongside one another a short distance behind them, and he could hear their whispers back and forth and Margaid's occasional quiet giggles.

"Sounds like they're having fun," Eryn whispered, catching Caeden by surprise. He could hear the smirk in her voice, but something else was hidden in her tone he couldn't quite place.

A small smile touched his lips, but it didn't last long as his thoughts drifted to his and Margaid's engagement

He thought back to their engagement ceremony and how awkward it had been to dance with her in front of the enormous crowd of people, how he'd had to kneel before her and give her a ring like she was the only woman he would ever love, when in truth, he didn't love her at all.

He'd hated every moment, but he would have to continue faking affection toward her for the rest of his life.

The night he and Eryn spent in the safe room sprang to the forefront of his thoughts again, and his cheeks heated in the dark. He shouldn't have been so comfortable with her touch that night. He should've stayed on the floor, not joined her on the cot. If anyone other than Ronan had seen the two of them together, it could've ended much worse than it had. The worst part was that he'd liked when she was close, liked the feel of her touch, and even though he shouldn't, the fact felt impossible to ignore.

He didn't know what he felt toward her, but after that night, he couldn't deny that his feelings toward her were far more than just friendly.

"Where's your head at this time, princy?" Eryn asked beside him.

It was the second time she'd asked him that question at a time when he would've given anything to ignore it.

Caeden felt his cheeks turn an even deeper shade of red and was thankful for the thick darkness that surrounded them.

"You seem tense," she said before he had time to think of an answer to her question without giving her the entire truth.

How she could see he was tense in the darkness was beyond him, but he made a mental note to make sure it didn't happen again.

Caeden took a deep breath and let his muscles relax to the best of his ability, hoping it would cover up his discomfort. "The night of the attack," he explained. "The way the Dragon Lord spoke to my father was strange. They sounded like they knew each other."

It wasn't what had been on his mind just then, but it had been on his mind plenty of times since that night.

The light rustle of fabric reached his ears as Eryn shrugged beside him. "You know better than most how important international relationships are. The war started long ago, but both your father and the Dragon Lord were already seated on their thrones before then. They probably met each other multiple times before the war."

The same thought had crossed his mind each time the question popped into his head. It was a convincing argument, but it was still strange how the Dragon Lord had attempted to shake his father by bringing up Caeden's mother.

It hadn't worked on his father, but it had worked on him.

"He's an evil man, Caeden," Eryn said, as if she could read his thoughts. "He doesn't pull his punches. He never has. I know what he said hurt you too, but you have to remember that was his intention. His goal is to destroy Aericora's royal line and take their land. It's the same thing he did with Soborg, and he hopes to do it again."

Caeden opened his mouth to respond, but no words came out.

She was right, after all. It was his end goal, and he intended to hurt them. He would've said anything to shake them before the attack. Ripping open an emotional wound like that could've caused the king or Caeden to make a rash decision and a reckless attack against the Dragon Lord. It would've been easier for the Dragon Lord to win the fight had Caeden's father played into his hands.

"I'm sorry about your mother and sister," Eryn whispered. She rode close enough to him now that when she reached over to brush her fingers against his hand, he wasn't worried about anyone else noticing.

Her words made something shift inside of him. They didn't fix what happened all those years ago. His mother and sister were dead, and the rage he felt inside burned white hot, waiting for the day Caeden could douse it with the Dragon Lord's spilled blood. But her words calmed him, regardless.

Margaid screamed behind them, and Caeden and Eryn pulled their horses to an abrupt stop.

Eryn had her bow drawn, and an arrow knocked before Caeden had time to grab his off his back.

"I'm okay!" Margaid shouted to them, much louder than necessary, considering the four of them had all stayed so close together during their journey.

She was lying on her back in an awkward position on the ground, her ankle caught in the stirrup of her horse's saddle. It was hard to see in the darkness, but she looked unhurt aside from a few bruises that would likely mark her skin the following day.

"What happened?" Eryn asked, an edge to her tone Caeden now recognized as her being prepared for an attack.

Caeden started to dismount from his horse to help Margaid off the ground, but Ronan was already halfway out of his saddle by that point, so Caeden stopped.

"I'm just clumsy," Margaid said, laughing through her

obvious embarrassment. "I thought I saw something and slipped, and well…" She trailed off, not bothering to finish the sentence.

Ronan pulled her foot from the stirrup and helped her back to her feet.

Margaid thanked him, but made no move to get back on her horse. Instead, she walked to the edge of the tree line and ran her finger along the bark of a large tree sitting on the edge of the path.

Eryn climbed off her horse and examined whatever it was Margaid saw. Caeden thought about joining her, but instead pulled his bow off his back and held it at the ready, his nerves tense as he watched the two of them.

"Arrow marks," Eryn said quietly, no doubt more to herself than to any of them. She turned back to Margaid, a questioning look on her face. "How did you notice these?" She gestured with her hand as if to emphasize the darkness blanketing them.

Margaid stayed quiet for a moment, and Caeden could hear her shifting. "I was trained for the military as well," she said, sounding almost unsure of her answer. "Not to your level or Ronan's, and I don't advertise it like Kylana did because I'm not good at much, but I am very good at tracking and am very vigilant of my surroundings." She gave a sheepish laugh. "My skills with a sword are lacking, though."

"Good eye," Eryn said, ignoring Margaid's attempt at a joke. There was an edge to her tone and Caeden could make out the hard set of her jaw in the dark. "Stay quiet," she instructed the group, turning back and remounting her horse. "Let's get to the field quickly and hope we aren't ambushed."

Chapter 37

Somehow, they got to their destination with no surprise encounters. A knot was forming in Caeden's neck from being on such high alert for the entire ride, but the relief he felt once they neared the edge of the camp was enough to make his whole body relax.

It was still dark out when they arrived at the camp, but lit torches placed every ten yards away from one another lit the camp in an orange hue. Ghostly shadows were cast along the sides of the hundreds of tents that filled the large clearing from the dim light.

A woman with salt and pepper hair awaited them when they reached the camp. She was tall and had laugh lines around her eyes despite her somber expression. A pin poked out from beneath her loose hair on the collar of her shirt. It was gold and displayed a dragon's wing, identifying her as a Dragon Hunter.

"Isbeil," Eryn greeted the woman. She had a smile that suggested she and the woman knew each other well. "Good to see you again."

Isbeil smiled in return, and once Eryn was off her horse,

wrapped her arms around her in what looked like a rather crushing bear hug.

Eryn grunted in response, but the smile still pulled at the corners of her mouth.

"Gods, how I've missed having you around!" Isbeil told her as she released Eryn from the embrace and took a few steps away.

She turned to face the group as Caeden and the other two dismounted.

Caeden slipped on his way down and landed hard on his injured leg, sending a wave of agony up to his hip, but he did his best to hide it from the rest of them.

"Prince Caeden," Isbeil said as she offered him a slight bow of her head. "I apologize for the minimal welcome. We've been quite busy with the Deovarians, and the messenger only arrived earlier this afternoon."

Caeden was glad to hear that the messenger had arrived, but he didn't voice that to Isbeil. Instead, he only shrugged, unsure what to say in this situation. "You have much bigger concerns than me, and I will forever be indebted to all of you for your service."

It was so over the top that he had to suppress a grimace at his own words.

Isbeil gave him a curious look, but continued speaking as if whatever she'd found strange hadn't existed.

He was thankful to her for it.

"We were told you've come to gather information regarding the Deovarian attacks and collect some of our soldiers to guard the castle. Is that correct?"

Eryn nodded. "Yes. We know you need as many people as possible, but they're sending reinforcements as we speak, and they should be here very shortly." She gestured to Margaid, who nodded to confirm Eryn's statement, though Caeden had to wonder whether Isbeil even knew who the redheaded woman standing before her was.

"Well," Isbeil responded, "we'll certainly have use for them with how things are going. Please," she gestured to the camp behind her, "tack up your horses in the stable and meet me and the others once you've finished. We have a lot to go over and I'm sure you're anxious to return as soon as possible."

"That we are," Eryn agreed.

It wasn't how Caeden felt, but it was Eryn's preference to get him out of there as soon as they could so he wouldn't have time to do anything reckless. Despite having had plenty of time to accept how she felt about his intentions, it still stung that she didn't agree with him.

Isbeil turned and left, and Eryn led the three of them toward the stable near the opposite end of the camp. The space around them was quiet for the time being, but that could change at any moment. The camp was close to being awake now, though the sun hadn't yet crested the horizon. The likeliness of another attack wasn't off the table by any means, either.

The most recent news Caeden had learned over the past week was that the attacks were happening nearly every day, sometimes multiple times a day. They were spread out, usually one taking place in the morning at a base in the north while another would take place in the evening at a base farther south, but it said something that Deovaria was getting brave enough with their attacks to risk losing that many soldiers in a single day. It confirmed they were confident and that they weren't losing as many soldiers in the fights as Aericora was.

The stable was only a large canvas tent supported by nearby trees, and held up in its center by two large support beams secured deep into the ground. There were multiple other poles to tie the horses to, each with hooks to hang the horses' tack. There wasn't a proper place set up for them to store their saddles, but very few of the horses inside the stable weren't saddled as it was. Three saddles that weren't in use were set on top of large piles of hay in the center of the stable, but at least thirty horses were tied up inside.

Once the four horses were as comfortable as they could manage, they headed toward a second large tent, which was only half the size of the stable but still larger than every other tent in the camp.

Candlelight flickered from inside, and the shadows of multiple people were visible on the fabric walls. Their voices reached Caeden's ears long before they got near the tent, but he couldn't understand what they were saying with the way they spoke over one another.

The arguing quieted once they entered the tent.

There were six other people in the tent besides the four of them, including Isbeil. None of them looked much older than their mid-thirties or forties. A table sat in the center of the space, holding a large map with Deovaria's and Aericora's main camps marked in bold black pen marks. The territories they were fighting over had shifted since the last time Caeden had laid eyes on a similar map. Aericora's border was pushed back ten miles, taking three separate small towns with it.

Isbeil nodded to the four of them. "Prince Caeden and Princess Margaid," she said, introducing them to the group.

So, she knew who Margaid was. It made sense that her name would've been brought up in their conversation with the messenger earlier in the day, but it surprised him anyway.

"And all of you know Eryn and Ronan."

The other five in the room bowed their heads to the two royals before returning to their earlier conversation.

"We can't afford to give up that many soldiers," a stocky man standing to Isbeil's left said.

"It's the king's order," a woman with a jagged scar across the side of her neck countered. She crossed her arms. "What choice do we have?"

"We'll be left defenseless!" the stocky man shot back, which earned a few murmured agreements from the others in the small group.

"Reinforcements are on their way," Eryn spoke up, just before Caeden said the same thing.

It felt like an intrusion to put forth the information they had so freely, but it was what they were there for. They were talking about the soldiers Caeden and the others would be taking back to the castle with them.

"They should be here within the next day or two," Eryn continued, restating what she'd told Isbeil.

The military members glanced around at one another, seeming to weigh their options and share their opinions without saying so much as a word. Given how quickly their silent conversation ended, they must have all worked together for a long time.

"What if we are attacked between now and then?" a pencil-thin man who looked like he was barely strong enough to lift a sword challenged. His voice was high like a child's, rather than the thirty-something year old man he was.

He wore a flaming crown pin, ranking him as a general. He lacked any specialty pin, like the one Isbeil wore and that Eryn had pinned to the collar of her shirt shortly after they arrived, but regardless, he'd climbed as high as anyone without a specialty could.

"We were pushed back two days ago," the woman with the scar put in. "The chances of us being attacked to that degree again before reinforcements arrive is slim. We'll be able to handle a large attack just fine, even if we are a few hundred men short. Deovaria is also still recovering from the attack. On the off chance they decide to attack us here, we can put up enough of a fight to give us time to wait for the soldiers to arrive."

The stocky man scoffed. "With only a thousand of us left? They have dragons! Fifty dragons attacked us last time, and we barely had enough time to pack up and fall back. We lost hundreds last time, but we managed to kill off many of them. If they attack us with those numbers again, we'll be dead before we have time to raise our swords!"

"Even though it is a slim chance, he is right," another woman, this one dressed in full battle armor from head to toe and a calculating expression on her face, agreed. "It's a huge risk."

"We can stay until after the soldiers arrive," Caeden offered, the words slipping from his mouth before his mind had time to consider what his father or the court would think of such a decision. They had to return within a week, but they could still do that if they stayed an extra day or two.

The chances of the camp being attacked again with such voracity so soon were nearly impossible, but he didn't want to take the risk any more than the stocky soldier did. Plus, it might give him enough time to see whether the ring really work like he suspected, as selfish as that felt given the circumstances. If he could convince the others, they could extend their stay by an extra couple of days to allow the soldiers from Crevia time to get to the camp, and hopefully, the Deovarians enough time to reconvene and launch another attack.

It was terrible to wish upon his people, but another attack was inevitable, and he needed to know if the ring worked. If it worked to control their dragons, even at all, the ring could be the key to defeating Deovaria, or at least help his kingdom match their strength more evenly.

The room quieted as the soldiers took in his words.

From the corner of his eye, Caeden noticed Margaid and Ronan looking at him with questioning gazes. He couldn't see Eryn's face, but after how she'd reacted when he'd first talked with her about using the ring, he was sure she wasn't anything less than enraged by his suggestion. He could feel her stare boring into the side of his head.

"You'll have far more after they arrive than you do now," Eryn said, which, surprisingly, wasn't an attempt to convince the soldiers to ignore what he'd said. "If we stay, you'll have enough time to get the reinforcements situated as well, and Princess Margaid has already offered to help with that."

Murmured agreements flitted through the air from the soldiers around them, and eventually they were replaced with nods. Caeden hardly noticed any of that.

What he'd said had made logical sense given what his kingdom and his soldiers needed. Still, he hadn't expected her to agree with him out loud, though he wasn't sure why.

"Very well," Isbeil said. "It doesn't appear there are any who disagree with your suggestion."

Caeden doubted there would be any here who would, but he couldn't say for certain that his father or the advisors would feel the same way. It was what needed to be done, but if they stayed as long as they now planned, there was a small chance they would no longer return to the castle within the week his father had allotted them.

They wouldn't begin searching for them right away, and they would make it back long before they began such a thing, but he still worried his father might change his mind about waiting the two weeks if they took longer than he felt was necessary. They could send word to the castle easily, but he didn't want to risk another messenger being killed or kidnapped over such a simple message.

"Good," Caeden responded, pushing his worries aside to focus on the conversation. He could worry about what the advisors and his father would think of his decision later.

He stood a little straighter in what he hoped resembled the stance his father always took when trying to command the respect of everyone in the room. He earned a sideways glance from Eryn, and Ronan coughed to cover up a laugh, but no one else batted an eye.

"And what of the recent attacks? Are there any obvious patterns or strategies the Deovarians are putting into place?" Caeden asked, relieved when he finished the sentence without his voice wavering.

The stocky man waved him closer to the table and Caeden looked down at the map in front of them. The soldier pointed to a few locations on the map that were further into what was now Deovarian territory. They were marked with black Xs, and Caeden gathered that they had to have been Aericora's camps from earlier in the war.

"We're fairly sure their strategy has been to rely on spies," the man explained. "They've attacked our weakest camps within only hours of soldiers having left to defend other territories. We know there are a multitude of spies within our midst, and after seeing these numbers skyrocket in the past month, we're sure there are more. It's possible they've even managed to create a strategy to use the wyvern magic to disguise their soldiers amongst our ranks, but we have no hard evidence of disguised spies being in play yet, though we are treating the situation as if we already have found them to avoid any losses from doing otherwise."

"We are losing," the woman with the scar cut in, making Caeden flinch. "There is no simpler way of putting it. If we don't figure out a way to combat their tactics, whatever they may be, we will lose this war within a couple months to a year, if we're lucky. As of right now, we are only prolonging our inevitable defeat."

The words made Caeden's blood run cold and his mouth dry.

He'd hardly considered the possibility of them losing the war. It had been raging for more than half of his life and had become a constant that he'd never fully considered would end. Especially not in their loss.

White hot anger burned in his chest.

They'd murdered his family in cold blood, and they were going to get away with it. Deovaria was going to win the war if they didn't stop them.

"We implemented new protocols," Isbeil was saying.

Caeden shook his head and pushed down the anger just enough to allow him to think straight, even as every part of him itched to do something, anything, to turn the odds in their favor.

"What new protocols?"

"We're holding soldiers who survive after their camps are attacked. If they are injured, we tend to their wounds, but they aren't allowed near strategy meetings or any other soldiers aside from a select few. After a week of questioning, if nothing seems suspicious, they are free to go about life with the other soldiers, but if they cannot answer certain questions correctly, we will ensure they are transported to the castle for further interrogation and imprisonment."

Caeden hadn't heard about any of this before. It seemed like a smart plan, aside from running a huge risk of preventing perfectly capable soldiers from fighting if needed. The potential benefits seemed to outweigh the costs.

"Have you sent any yet?" Ronan asked, echoing the same question that was running through his mind.

Isbeil hadn't specified how long ago they'd implemented this strategy, but she made it sound long enough for them to have received some of those soldiers at the castle by now.

Everyone's attention turned to the castle's Head of Security.

"A few," Isbeil answered. "Only eighteen that we know of have been held, and of those, six were sent to the castle for further interrogation."

Caeden's heart stopped as her words sunk in. He swallowed hard, trying to hide the fear that washed over him. "We haven't received any."

That could be why their messengers were being killed. If they'd implemented this strategy long enough ago and those soldiers who were sent to the castle had been spies who had managed to overpower their escorts, they might have killed off the messengers and other soldiers traveling to and from the castle to compromise Aericora's correspondence. It didn't seem likely, given that they would be living off what was available in Aericora's forests, but it wasn't impossible.

But it couldn't just be them. They hadn't heard that these procedures would be implemented back at the castle, and they'd had trouble corresponding with the field for years. Nothing as bad as this, as far as they were aware, but it seemed this had been going on for far longer than they realized.

Isbeil nodded grimly, her lips pressed together in a tight line. "We'll have to take that into consideration for the future."

The woman with the scar nodded. "We'll send more escorts with the prisoners," she agreed. "Hopefully that will be enough to solve the problem."

It wasn't a good enough solution, and Caeden doubted sending a few extra guards with the prisoners would be enough to make any changes, given that not a single one of those six possible spies had made it to the castle. He didn't have any better ideas, though, so he kept his mouth shut.

"I doubt that'll be enough," Ronan said.

"A squad could be sent to search for the spies," Eryn suggested. "I'm sure you've also noticed that your messengers haven't returned. Those spies who have disappeared could have decided to pick off any lone or small groups of travelers to hinder our communication."

"With what people?" the stocky man challenged her. "We're already low on soldiers."

"Even with the reinforcements, we can't afford to send a task force to track them all down," the thin man agreed.

"The most we could afford to send would be twenty soldiers, and it wouldn't be enough to cover the entire forest to find all of those potential assassins," Isbeil said. "We have no idea how many could be out there, but we know there are more than just the six spies we sent."

They made a good point, but Caeden could feel the disappointment radiating from Ronan and Eryn. Eryn had a calculating look on her face, but she said nothing in response to either of the two soldiers, confirming she was just as clueless as the rest of them about how to help the situation.

"We'll have to risk it," the woman with the scar stated. She sighed as though the idea was one of the worst things she could've agreed with. She gestured halfheartedly at the map on the table. "We're losing this fight, and us not being able to communicate with those at the castle and other camps is what hurts us most. We can't afford not to take the risk."

"She's right," the woman in the armor agreed. "It may put us at risk, but we're already losing and it could only help us to be able to communicate with our fellow soldiers."

Isbeil sighed. "What would the prince have us do?" she asked, turning her attention to Caeden.

That was probably the last thing he expected her to say.

Caeden swallowed hard as he took in the faces of the soldiers staring at him. It was the kind of question his father would've been asked when the advisors couldn't reach an agreement. But Caeden had never been put on the spot like this before. He'd never had to be the one to make the final decision.

It caught him far more off guard than it should've, given he'd been learning to make these decisions for most of his life.

Eryn nudged him in the side, and he realized he hadn't yet provided an answer to Isbeil's question.

He cleared his throat. "Ready a task force," he told them. "Twenty to thirty soldiers at the most, but keep it quiet. If there are any spies still lingering around, we don't want them to know about it, or they'll have them picked off in the woods before the task force will have a chance to do us any good."

Isbeil's expression turned grim again, but she didn't argue with him. She turned to the woman with the scar on her neck. "Silis, I'll have you head that."

Silis nodded. "I'll have the force assembled by the week's end."

Chapter 38

Caeden and Eryn stayed in the tent with the stocky man, whose name Caeden learned was Samuel, for only another hour before heading to the empty tents that had been hastily set up for them earlier in the day.

They went into more detail about the Deovarian's most recent attacks. All the attacks had happened within a day of a large number of the camp's soldiers being reassigned. They happened fast, using Royal Talon dragons to burn all their supplies before bothering to kill off any of the soldiers in the camps. Once everything was up in flames, enemy soldiers were flown in on more dragons and killed off as many soldiers as they could who were still within the borders of the camp, attempting to salvage supplies or help any who had been wounded during the initial attack.

The attacks were brutal, and few survived them. Any who weren't killed from the flames were killed quickly after the enemy soldiers were flown in, or died due to too much smoke inhalation alone. Those who escaped hardly ever had enough supplies on them to make it to a new camp before dying of starvation, or being picked off in the woods, likely by whoever was responsible for the deaths of the messengers.

The soldiers who survived claimed the Deovarian soldiers could walk through the flames. Samuel and the others figured it was due to whatever magic Deovaria and the Dragon Lord had that was allowing them to control the dragons.

When they finished their meeting with Samuel, the sun was just beginning to rise over the edge of the horizon.

They walked quietly toward their tents, and Caeden did not try to break the silence. They were attacking the camps eerily similarly to the way they'd attacked the town his mother and sister had been in when they were killed. The only difference was that the events happened almost in reverse, or so they were fairly sure. No one survived the attack, so no one could be entirely sure what happened, but the carnage that was left of the town suggested that the Deovarians had come in and trapped everyone in the town's center before making a spectacle of killing Caeden's mother, given that her body was the only one on the small stage that had been set for the festival. After that, everyone had been burned to their deaths in a wave of flames from Royal Talon dragons.

Rage burned in his chest, and he clenched his fists so tightly at his sides that his nails bit into the palms of his hands.

The same questions he'd had since the beginning of the war still burned at the edges of his mind. Why was the Dragon Lord waging a war against his people? So Deovaria could expand its lands? Gain more riches? Neither seemed like a good enough reason for this to go on, but he didn't have any better ideas.

The camp was waking around them. Multiple soldiers, still in their sleepwear, emerged from their tents, making their way toward a tent past the one they'd been in with the camp's leaders. Steam wafted out from the open flaps of the doorway, but no smell from the food they were cooking inside reached them on the opposite end of the camp.

"Find something to eat," Eryn said, catching him by surprise.

The thoughtful look she'd had on her face since they'd been in the middle of their meeting had finally disappeared, and he wasn't sure what he saw in her eyes when he glanced at her. It resembled desperation, but so many emotions were laced throughout it.

"Okay," he responded, unsure how else to answer her.

"We're getting you as close to finished with your training as we can today," she told him, her tone steady and firm. She clenched her fists at her sides, and her knuckles turned as white as the clouds above their heads.

He remembered suddenly that she was still mad at him. He'd forgotten during their time with Samuel. After the anger he'd felt radiating off her in the tent when he suggested they stay until the soldiers from Crevia arrived, he'd gotten lost in the following conversation. He was in for all kinds of hell during his training.

She spoke through gritted teeth when she continued. "I'm not going to let you get yourself killed if I can help it."

For a moment, he wondered if she meant she would do everything in her power to prevent him from attempting to use the stone or if she meant all she could do was train him as much as she could before he got the chance to try.

"You can't stop me from doing this," he told her, keeping his voice as gentle as possible. He didn't want to anger her, as much as he was sure there was no way of avoiding it. But he wouldn't be swayed in his decision, either. He had to do this for his kingdom. They were out of options.

Eryn scoffed and rolled her eyes. "I'm not going to try to stop you, you dummy prince," she snapped. "Even if you're being an idiot." She shook her head and turned away from him.

"If me training you today can keep you alive for even a few seconds longer against the Deovarians, then I will do it. And even though this plan of yours is insane, I know it needs to be done, and I'll be there with you when you do it."

Caeden's jaw nearly dropped as he stared at her, and his cheeks warmed. Even though she disagreed with his plan, she was going to stand beside him, regardless.

Despite her anger, it was one of the kindest things she'd ever said to him. He was long past the point of thinking she hated him, but he still wasn't sure where he stood with her all the time. Sometimes, she seemed to genuinely like him, maybe even as much as he was starting to like her, but other times, she seemed frustrated by every other word that came out of his mouth and would rather run him through with a sword herself before any dragons would get the chance to kill him.

"Thank you," he said. Regardless of her tone, he appreciated hearing those words from her.

Eryn's face flushed red, and she turned her head further away to hide it. "Just don't die, okay?" she murmured, but the unwavering irritation was gone, replaced with something that sounded like fear.

Caeden cracked a smile. She was beautiful, but there was something about when a blush bloomed across her cheeks that set his heart to racing.

"Just for you, I'll do my best," he told her, and didn't wait to hear her response before he quickened his pace and ducked inside the tent that had been set up for him.

Ronan had taken Caeden's supplies to the tents with him when he and Margaid left the meeting earlier. They'd gotten their things situated for the four of them for the day. In exchange, Caeden had agreed to relay the information they learned from Samuel to him before they returned to the castle.

It wasn't necessary for both of them to be present for the conversation, but Ronan needed to have the same information Caeden and Eryn had to help them devise a strategy against Deovaria once they returned.

Caeden pulled out a fresh pair of clothes and a small pack of dried berries and nuts he'd snuck in with his things before they'd left. The castle staff had packed primarily breads and cheese for them, since they didn't intend to be gone for more than a handful of days. Caeden would've eaten the tasteless food if he'd been given no other option, but when he'd snuck down to the kitchen the day before they left and found that the nuts and berries were brought in only a few days earlier, he'd had a hard time passing up such an opportunity.

He tossed a handful of his snacks into his mouth before removing his weapons from where they sat on his body and setting them aside. He changed into a fresh pair of clothes he'd packed, strapped the dagger back to his thigh like Eryn wore hers, and slung his bow and quiver back over his shoulder before rehanging his sword at his hip.

Outside, Eryn rummaged around in her things in the tent next to his. Caeden used the remaining minutes to finish the last of his snack before leaving his tent.

Eryn was waiting for him with an impatient look on her face when he emerged.

Caeden stared at her for a long moment. She'd somehow fully changed and reequipped herself with almost every weapon she'd had on her in the same time it had taken him to finish the nuts and berries. He couldn't comprehend how it was even possible.

"Come on," she said, gesturing toward an empty patch of grass a few hundred yards away.

It would put them far enough away from the camp to stay out of everyone's way and to avoid waking Ronan and Margaid while remaining within the camp's borders.

Caeden followed her to the small clearing, his limbs heavy from exhaustion. He didn't want to train. He wanted to curl up into a ball on his thin bedroll and sleep for a thousand years if he could, but Eryn was willing to train him, and he would not miss the opportunity.

Trees boxed them in on three sides of the small clearing, and a row of now unoccupied tents fifteen yards away from the general area they would remain in made the fourth wall.

"What are we practicing?" Caeden asked as Eryn turned on her heel to face him.

It felt like a dumb question, but she'd said they were getting him as close to finished as possible, which wasn't informative. He needed a lot more work on everything, and he wasn't sure how getting him close was possible in a single day. If it were, she would've done it a long time ago.

"A little of everything," she answered. It didn't answer the question of how that would get him finished in a day, but he chose to ignore it.

She drew her sword from its scabbard and set it aside before reaching for her daggers and doing the same with them.

"I'm giving you a disadvantage in every area. Your leg will provide that well enough when we fight hand-to-hand, but while I wield a sword, you'll have a dagger. When we practice your knife-throwing abilities, you'll have to stand on one leg, and so on."

Despite the irritation he was bound to get from her for his reaction, he gave her a skeptical look.

Eryn ignored him and held her hands in front of her face, widening her stance. "Come on, princy."

Caeden pushed away his doubt and mimicked her stance.

They fought hand-to-hand for the next several hours. Caeden

beat her nearly half of the times they fought, which was better than his average, but still not good enough. Despite his leg burning in pain, he'd had the injury long enough and had practiced enough times with Eryn since getting it that he'd learned how to appropriately compensate for it. It was still a disadvantage, but he'd learned to work around it. And though he didn't want to point it out to her, her side was still just as injured as his leg was, and this fight wasn't as unequal as she had suggested it was.

She was trying to pretend her side wasn't bothering her, but he could see the way she leaned her weight toward the opposite side of her body and avoided using her arm on that side if she could get away with it.

"Swords," Eryn said, tossing him a dagger longer than the two Caeden had brought with him. She was panting, and her hand twitched up to her side as if she was going to place her palm over her injury. She pulled it away quickly and instead grabbed her sword.

Before Caeden had time to righten himself on his feet, Eryn swung her sword at his face. He jumped back in time to avoid a nasty blow to the temple that would've left him bleeding and lightheaded.

"I wasn't ready!" he shouted.

He expected her to smile, or at least to see that usual glimmer of amusement in her eyes she always had when she caught him off guard intentionally, but her face remained blank of emotion.

"You're not going to be ready when you're attacked in a battle," she reminded him.

Her voice struck him harder than her blade ever could've. She was speaking to him like she had when they first met again. She was frustrated with him, but her frustration had gotten them nowhere back then, and had only stoked his own, which had caused them more than enough arguments. They knew each other better than that and learned how to communicate far more effectively, even if she was frustrated with him.

Eryn swung at him again, and he took another step backward, barely deflecting her blade with his own. He stayed on the defensive as she pushed him back farther and farther toward the edge of their small clearing.

Her attacks were lightning quick, much quicker than she ever had been during their sessions, and with the impairment of his shorter blade, he couldn't turn the tables long enough to throw any of his attacks. She backed him up until he was only a few feet away from being backed into the trees lining the edge of the clearing.

Fear seized him in the same way he'd felt in the castle when the soldier had nearly killed him.

He glimpsed the line of trees behind him as Eryn's blade came down close to his right shoulder.

Instinct took over as he deflected her swing. He ducked beneath her arm and sword, and hooked his leg around her ankle just before he was pushed to the tree line. He stood up straight behind her as she stumbled forward.

Caeden watched as she used the momentum of her fall to her advantage and leaned into it. She spun around as she fell, her shoulder blade hitting hard against the trunk of the tree as she swung her sword toward his abdomen.

It was a smart attack, but he'd expected something like that from her.

He pivoted around the attack and closed in on her before she had time to pull her sword out of the swing. He lunged for her wrist and grasped it before pinning it firmly to her chest, her sword thumping to the ground at their feet. Caeden pressed his dagger to her throat with his other hand, but turned it at the last second so the sharp edges of the blade faced up toward her chin and down toward the ground, only allowing the cool metal of the fuller to touch her skin.

His breaths came in short, shallow gasps, and the pain in his leg radiated through his body at an intensity he hadn't felt since the day he'd been stabbed, but he let a smile touch his lips.

Eryn didn't have a smile on her face like she usually did when he beat her. Instead, she was looking at him so intensely it sent his heart racing.

"Good," Eryn said, her voice coming out as a winded breath.

He could feel her breath against his lips when she spoke, and he realized suddenly just how close his body was to hers. He was pressed almost entirely against her, the warmth of her seeping through the thin clothes he wore. His hand was still wrapped around her wrist and pressed to her chest between her breasts, and he could feel her heartbeat racing almost as quickly as his own was. Her lavender scent filled his lungs with each inhale he took, clouding his thoughts and filling his mind with only her.

Memories from their night in the safe room flooded back to him again. He hadn't been this close to her since that night, even with all the training they did, and he was all too aware that this time, she would be able to see the blush that crept across his cheeks.

"Why does it matter whether or not I love her?" he asked quietly. Their conversation from that night when she'd asked about his true feelings for Margaid replayed in his head for the thousandth time.

Eryn swallowed hard, and the dagger still in Caeden's hand bobbed when she did.

He pulled it away from her throat and took a step away from her, but his eyes stayed trained on her face as he waited for an answer.

She pulled herself off the tree and picked up her sword from where it had fallen to the ground. "It doesn't," she answered, not looking at him. Her voice was too forceful when she spoke.

She was lying, but despite how sure of it Caeden was, her words still sent a pang of hurt through him. He liked her, and for the first time since he'd had the fleeting thought that he might, he realized how much he wanted her to like him back.

"Then, why did you ask?"

Eryn gripped her sword so tightly her knuckles turned stark white. "I don't know, okay?" she snapped. Her face was red when she turned to face him, still not meeting his gaze, and he wasn't sure if it was from embarrassment or rage.

She re-sheathed her sword at her hip and extended a hand to him for the dagger. He was sure she was going to hand it back to him for another round of practice within the next few minutes, but he gave it back to her, regardless.

Her eyes met his briefly before she looked away again and tucked the dagger into the holster on her left leg.

That single glance was all the confirmation he needed, though.

"You're lying," he said, as he dared to step closer to her.

He wanted her to look at him. As much as she tried to hide her feelings from the world, those beautiful blue eyes of hers were like a window right into her heart. He could see what she was feeling behind those eyes, and he knew that was why she was avoiding his gaze.

Eryn rolled her eyes and jabbed her finger into his chest, frustration rolling off her in waves. "I'm not lying," she snapped again.

Caeden's cheeks still burned from their closeness a moment before, but something about seeing her so flustered made the corners of his mouth quirk upward, and an ounce of bravery rose in him. He caught her hand in his before she had time to pull it away, his fingers resting against hers, not holding hard enough that she couldn't pull hers out of his grasp if she wanted to. She sucked in a breath when he did, and his heartbeat quickened as he took another step toward her again.

"Why are you so flustered then?" he asked.

Eryn's eyes darted around as if she was looking for any way to avoid him, but after a second, she gave up and met his eyes. "I'm not flustered," she said, her voice coming out with a nervous waver.

Another lie.

A smile touched his lips. "I like you, Eryn Gedding," he told her, and despite him never daring to think too much about it when he was alone, he couldn't deny how true those words were.

As much as he liked his training and as much as he needed it so he could destroy the Dragon Lord and his armies, seeing her had also turned into a reason for him to show up every day. She was part of the reason he continued long after his muscles had given out and his body ached with each movement.

Eryn's cheeks turned crimson, and she stuttered over her words. "I—no. You-you can't say that!" she snapped, more frustration flashing in her eyes.

Gods, she was beautiful.

"Why not?"

"You're getting married!" she exclaimed, losing the mask she'd been trying to force into place and letting her emotions show across every one of her pretty features. "You-you're getting married," she whispered, her anger subsiding for a moment before coming back just as strong as it had before. "You dragged me away from the war to train you to fight, but you can barely hold your own. You seem to think me teaching you to fight is more important than me fighting alongside those who need me." Her eyes flicked down to his leg. "Not to mention you already managed to get yourself stabbed the first time you fought someone, as if all the training I've done with you meant nothing. You're a complete waste of my time and—"

Caeden lifted her chin gently with his free hand so he could see her face, and she froze. She was trying to avoid the subject, but he didn't think he'd ever get the nerve to ask her what he wanted to know if he didn't do it right then.

Everything she said was valid, even if not all of it was true, but his impending marriage didn't matter in that moment. He knew that beneath all of her complaints about his incapabilities, she still cared enough about him to worry.

"Do you like me, too?" His voice sounded quiet, but it didn't waver like he'd expected.

"I—why would I possibly like you after all of those things I just listed?" she challenged.

Caeden only shrugged in response.

Eryn glared at him, but she rolled her eyes when he said nothing else. Her expression softened before she let out a huff. "Fine. I…" she sighed, as if fighting with herself over whether she wanted to say whatever words were on the tip of her tongue. "I—maybe I like you, too."

Caeden's smile returned to his face. "Maybe?"

She fixed him with a warning look that made him want to laugh. "Maybe is as good as you're getting, you dummy prince," she told him sternly.

He couldn't help it when the laugh escaped him. "I suppose I'll take what I can get," he said, even as his heart leapt inside of his chest at hearing her say those words.

It didn't matter that she felt the same way. It couldn't matter, because nothing could ever come of it, but part of him didn't care as he took her in. A very small, very stupid part of him hoped maybe it could mean something.

Eryn smiled up at him, and his heart skipped another beat. He'd always thought she was beautiful, but something about the smile on her face and the flush across her cheeks in the early morning light made her absolutely stunning.

He'd barely opened his mouth to tell her so when shouts rang out from behind them.

Caeden's hand slipped out of hers, and they turned to face the camp.

A fire was ablaze near the center of the camp, and soldiers ran around frantically, doing their best to put out the flames.

The realization of what he was seeing barely had registered in his mind before a dragon swooped low over their heads, releasing another torrent of fire over the meeting tent they'd been in only a few hours earlier.

Chapter 39

Eryn was gone before Caeden registered what was happening in front of him.

His mind was a hazy blur as he took in the growing flames, and the smoke and ash billowing in the air. Soldiers ran to and from the fire with buckets of water from a stream close by, making every attempt to put out the raging flames. Some pulled other soldiers from tents as the inferno began to set them ablaze, or from beneath fallen debris the dragons knocked over in their low sweeps over the camp.

Caeden's feet were moving beneath him before he realized what he was doing. He drew his dagger from the sheath strapped to his leg for protection against the enemy soldiers who would arrive in minutes if they followed the same strategy they had for the last multiple attacks.

This was precisely the attack he needed. He needed to get to one of those dragons and use the ring.

He ran for Ronan's tent, pulling back the canvas flaps of the door before ducking inside. Ronan was inside, working frantically to get himself dressed and his weapons ready.

"When did they get here?" Ronan asked as Caeden tossed him one of the swords lying on the ground near the tent's entrance. Ronan tied the sword around his waist before reaching for the same shirt he'd worn the previous day and pulling it on over his head.

"A few minutes ago," Caeden responded, his voice ragged as he took in heavy breaths.

His heart raced after running the hundred yards from the small clearing to Ronan's tent. He wasn't sure if it was due to his exertion of energy, or if it was due to the fear and determination that were coursing through his veins.

"The soldiers will be dropped in soon," he continued, his eyes searching the small space in the tent as he spoke. "Where's Margaid?"

Ronan shook his head, his eyes wild. "She left to her tent 'fore y'all came back from the meetin'," he responded. He jumped to his feet and rushed out of the tent past Caeden.

Caeden glanced back just long enough to see that his friend had gone to check on Margaid before he bolted off toward the edge of the camp, his footfalls hard against the uneven grass.

Enemy soldiers were being swooped in on the backs of dragons along the edge of the camp, and his people had taken up swords and arms to defend the camp further, abandoning their attempts to put out the fires almost entirely.

A large blue Royal Talon dragon landed beyond the edge of the camp. Sparks and smoke flew from its mouth as half a dozen more Deovarian soldiers slipped off its back and ran into the camp. They were met with an equal number of Aericora's soldiers, the pinging of blades hitting one another nearly impossible to hear over the roaring of the flames.

"Caeden!"

Eryn's voice hardly reached his ears through the crackling of the blazing tents and his racing heartbeat pounded in his ears as he ran to meet the soldiers.

Caeden drew his sword and replaced the dagger in his holster as he ran, not glancing at Eryn as he did.

She would try to stop him if she got the chance. She said she would fight beside him, but if he gave her the chance to tell him to stop and he dared look back into those blue eyes of hers and saw the same fear he'd heard in her voice, he wasn't sure he could go through with any of it. He wasn't sure he could take the risk, knowing she didn't want him to.

The last thing he wanted was to make her feel the fear he'd heard in her tone, but he needed to do this. He needed to know if Aericora could possess the same ability to control the dragons and give them a fighting chance in this war. He needed to know if he could use the Dragon Lord's power against him and destroy him and his kingdom.

Caeden and a dozen of Aericora's soldiers ran into the fray of warriors. Metal struck metal around him, and shouts rang out loud in the air, deafening him.

His eyes landed on a burly man in full battle armor as he charged straight for him, his sword held high above his head, the metal gleaming in the early morning light.

Caeden dimly noticed the unnatural sheen to the man's clothing, a blueish hue that he recognized shouldn't be there. He didn't have enough time to decide if it was a trick of the light or the protection magic that Samuel had told him about that allowed them to enter the camp safely without feeling the heat of the flames.

His blade met the other soldier's and they clanged against one another. Unlike any time he'd ever fought against Eryn, the world around him dimmed until all he could see was the soldier in front of him and the blade the man wielded.

It was an oddly comforting trance, even as he fought against the man, knowing he had every intention of killing him if he got the chance.

Caeden jumped out of reach of the soldier's sword as he aimed a slash across his ribs. Their swords met in the air again, and Caeden used every ounce of his strength to force the soldier's blade away from him. He aimed a punch at the man's gut as the blades slid against one another with a sickening scrape that reverberated through his bones, and the tip of the soldier's blade collided with the ground.

The man grunted and stepped back, giving Caeden the opening he needed. He drove his sword forward, aiming for the man's chest.

An arrow ricocheted off Caeden's sword as he thrust it forward, and he lost his balance.

He glanced to the side to see where it had come from, but the smoke around them was too thick now to make out who had fired the arrow.

He turned his attention back to the soldier as the man aimed another blow for Caeden's right side. He ducked out of the way of the attack, but he was too late. The tip of the blade ran along Caeden's upper arm, tearing a thin line into his flesh and sending a wave of agony shooting through his extremity.

It was hardly a scratch, given the stab wound he'd suffered the last time he'd been involved in an attack, but Caeden still let out a hiss between clenched teeth as the pain eased.

He shouldn't have looked away.

He'd been lucky this time, but he wouldn't make that mistake again.

The man swung at Caeden again, but this time he ducked beneath the blow, the sword swinging harmlessly above his head.

Without thinking, Caeden grabbed the dagger he'd replaced in its holster on his leg. He slashed out at the man's stomach, and his blade tore through skin and muscle. He could hear a sickening crack when he hit the man's rib bone, and he yanked the dagger free. Blood poured from the man's side, and the warm liquid coated his hand and forearm. It seeped between his fingers as he gripped the blade and watched the man crumple to the ground in front of him. Bile rose in the back of Caeden's throat as he stared at the man he'd just killed through the thick haze of smoke in the air.

He'd done that.

He'd ended that soldier's life.

Thoughts of his mother and sister surfaced in his mind again.

Did this soldier have loved ones at home? Would they miss him like Caeden missed his family? Would they mourn his loss and plot out their revenge against Caeden for the hole he'd torn open in their hearts when he'd pulled his dagger through the soldier's stomach?

"Move!" Eryn's voice shouted.

Someone hit him from the side and he and the other person crashed to the ground.

His vision went black as the air whooshed from his lungs.

After what felt like an eternity, Eryn's face came into focus above him. She was shouting something to someone he couldn't see, but he couldn't make out her words over the ringing in his ears. Eryn looked down at him and met his gaze for a split second before she climbed back to her feet.

His hearing returned, and the sounds of the chaos around him filled his senses once again. A dragon roared in the distance, and the screams of multiple soldiers followed it.

Caeden pulled himself back to his feet, his blood-soaked dagger still in his hand, and looked at the scene ahead of him.

There were half as many soldiers from Deovaria as there were from his kingdom on the battlefield around him. Whoever had informed the Dragon Lord that they'd been coming to take several of the camp's soldiers back to the castle must have either failed to learn that they would be replaced by ten times the number of soldiers from Crevia, or they'd been unable to alert their Deovarian contact that even though the soldiers were leaving, they wouldn't be able to attack effectively since Caeden and the others had changed their plans and hadn't left yet to return to the castle.

They would win this fight.

Deovaria had been caught off guard by their sudden change in plans the night before, and there was no way for them to suddenly send enough soldiers to join the fight and tip the scale in the Dragon Lord's favor. The battle would be won by the time anyone would have time to inform them that more soldiers would be needed to guarantee a victory.

Deovaria had already lost.

The Royal Talon dragon standing near the edge of the camp slipped back into Caeden's line of sight. The weight of the ring in his pocket felt overwhelmingly heavy, and his fingers absentmindedly reached inside to pull it free.

"Caeden!" Eryn shouted again, drawing his attention away from the ring in his hand and the dragon standing less than two hundred yards away.

She was in the middle of a fight with another soldier. She had a large gash across her cheek that would leave a scar, and blood dripped down the side of her face and neck from it, mingling with the sheen of sweat coating her whole body.

Her eyes pleaded with him in the same way he'd hoped he wouldn't have to see.

He would've given anything to avoid seeing that fear in her

eyes. That hopelessness and dread.

If she was right about his plan, she was about to watch him run straight to his death, and he hated himself for making her fear that. He hated himself for taking the risk when he knew it would hurt her.

There was no way to know whether the ring would work without trying it, but what if the dragon engulfed him in flames before he could even get close? What if one of the archers who had already gotten so close to hitting him sank their arrow into his flesh once he was out in the open?

Those were her fears. He was scared of it, too.

But what if it worked?

If the ring in his hand was the key to controlling the dragons, then they could use that power to kill the Dragon Lord.

"I have to try!" he called to her, shaking away the image of her pretty face and terrified eyes as he turned away.

He hated himself for doing it, but he had no choice. He wouldn't let anyone else take this risk.

He didn't wait for her response before he ran toward the dragon.

His leg throbbed as he ran, and his mind raced with every possibility of what he could be throwing himself into as he balled his hand into a tight fist around the ring, the cool, jagged metal biting into his palm.

The dragon was a hundred yards away from him.

Fifty yards.

Twenty.

He wouldn't let himself think about the risks.

He couldn't let himself think about it or he might turn around and run straight back to Eryn.

A cry rang out through the air, and Caeden's heart stopped.

That was Eryn's voice.

That was Eryn's scream.

Fear seized him, and he tripped, falling to the ground as the ring flew from his hand. It bounced away from him and disappeared into the overgrown grass.

Caeden clambered to his feet and turned around, all thoughts of the dragon, the ring, and the possibility of the magic leaving his mind as his eyes landed on Eryn across the battlefield.

He could see her through the mess of soldiers. She was lying on the ground, her face twisted in agony. A sword protruded from her upper chest, just beneath her left collarbone.

The soldier who had stabbed her was dead beside her with an arrow shot clean through his skull.

Good. If he was already dead, he wouldn't have to kill the man himself.

Caeden ran for her.

The pain from his leg was gone, and the battle happening around him melted into the background as he knelt beside her in the grass, his heart pounding as adrenaline and fear coursed through him in a raging current.

Caeden reached for her, and she winced as he pulled her up and laid her back down against him, keeping her propped up to slow the blood flow to the wound.

"It's fine," she wheezed, barely getting the words out. "I'm fine."

Blood leaked from the stab wound and drenched her shirt in crimson. Tears were streaming down her face, and pain and rage like Caeden had never felt before rushed through him.

He ignored her words.

He pulled his shirt off and wrapped it around the sword in her shoulder to keep it steady. He did his best to avoid moving her, but she still flinched at his touch, though she didn't try to fight him.

Once the sword was as secure as he could manage, Caeden stood with her still in his arms.

Eryn whimpered in pain and dug her fingernails into his arms as she buried her face against his chest.

"NO!" someone screamed, so loud their voice could be heard throughout the battlefield. "RONAN DON'T!"

Caeden whipped his head around at the sound of Margaid's yell.

Margaid stood at the edge of the fight, her eyes locked on the same dragon Caeden had been running for only a moment before.

He shifted his attention to the dragon, and fear gripped him again.

Ronan stood a few feet in front of the giant beast with his hand outstretched, the blue stone of the ring gleaming in the sunlight from where it sat in the palm of his hand.

The dragon huffed one smoky breath near Ronan's face, tousling the man's hair and singeing the ends of his curls.

For a moment, the creature hesitated, only staring at the seemingly small man in front of it.

Then, it bent its head forward and pressed its scaly snout to Ronan's outstretched hand.

Chapter 40
The spy

The spy waited impatiently in the shadows of the forest. They tapped their foot against the ground and glanced over their shoulder at the camp, hoping no one would take notice of their sudden absence.

Sounds flooded out of the camp from the soldiers working to repair the damage from the attack the day before. More than half the tents had burned to the ground, but the other half, including the infirmary where that godforsaken Dragon Hunter woman was being cared for, along with a hundred other soldiers, was still standing.

More than half of the soldiers were in fine health and had spent a good portion of the day gathering the bodies of their dead compatriots into a pile in the center of the camp, where they would be holding a ceremony to honor them once night fell again in a few hours.

The soldiers from Crevia arrived late the previous day and had brought with them plenty of supplies. If they hadn't, the state of Aericora's camp would be far worse. They would've run out of supplies to tend to the wounded long ago, had the soldiers not brought carts full of first aid materials, considering everything in the supply tent had been burnt to the ground.

Maybe the Dragon Hunter woman would be dead by now, too. A fiery turret of hatred flooded through their veins at the thought.

A faint rustling sound in the woods alerted the spy to the Dragon Lord's presence only a split second before the hooded figure came into view. His dark green eyes gleamed in the late afternoon light beneath his hood, and the glint of his raven-colored crown caught the spy's eye. He never took that thing off except when he slept.

The spy bowed their head respectfully, though they knew by now that the Dragon Lord couldn't have cared less whether they showed him such a level of respect when the two of them were alone.

"They've learned of the stone's power, my lord," the spy told him, their voice quiet to avoid drawing the attention of anyone in the camp.

Everyone in the camp had busied themselves, and it was unlikely any of them could hear a faint whisper coming from the woods, but the spy had never dared to take such unnecessary risks. The Dragon Lord had trained them far too well for that.

"The prince brought it with him from the castle, and the castle's Head of Security, a prisoner we kept years ago, used it to tame one of our dragons."

The Dragon Lord stayed silent. The spy fidgeted with the hem of their shirt. His silence was never a good sign, and it never failed to put the spy on edge.

After an agonizingly long moment, the Dragon Lord let out a low chuckle. "He's smart, that prince," he said, his voice rough. "See to it that he is brought to me."

The spy wanted to cringe at the request. "That will be rather difficult," the spy said, though they hated to admit it out loud.

The Dragon Lord's mouth quirked up in a dark smile. "I'm trusting you to handle it," he stated. "I think it's about time I finally met my nephew."

About the Author

Mase Evans is a fantasy and romance author who enjoys a story that immerses readers in new worlds full of fun characters, adventure, and swoon worthy love stories. She primarily writes fantasy romance books, with occasional outliers, that are geared toward younger adults.

She grew up in Houston, Texas with her younger siblings and began writing at the age of 10, finishing her first full length novel when she was 14. She continues to live in Texas with her husband and her three fur babies.